A

Deadly

Bouquet

Also by Janis Harrison

A Deadly Bouquet

JANIS HARRISON

Mystery
Harrison

ST. MARTIN'S MINOTAUR ✷ NEW YORK

www.minotaurbooks.com

ISBN 0-312-28422-5

First Edition: December 2002

10   9   8   7   6   5   4   3   2   1

This book is dedicated to three ladies who
free up my time so that I may write. My thanks
to Cathy Bartels, Sugger Gauchat, and Melissa Roberts.

Acknowledgments

As I write this acknowledgment, the words of a John Cougar Mellencamp song run through my mind. I've always lived in a "Small Town." I most definitely daydream in this small town. I probably haven't seen it all in this small town, but I've seen enough. I won't forget where I came from, and I won't forget the people who care about me.

On that note, I'd like to express my appreciation to the following:

Librarian Phyllis Jones and her board of directors for the wonderful book signings they've held in my honor.

Attorney John Kopp for attempting to answer my strange questions.

To the citizens of Windsor, Missouri—population thirty-two hundred. Thank you for allowing me to be myself in this small town.

A
Deadly
Bouquet

Chapter One

🌸 "Death tapped me on the shoulder, so I figured my time was up." Oliver adjusted the strap on his overalls and looked at me. "Bretta, that heart attack nearly sent me to my grave." His eyes sparkled when he grinned. "But I'm still here. I've got holes to dig, only they aren't for my old body."

I touched the leaves of the golden spirea shrub Oliver was about to plant. "Old gardeners never die. They just *spade* away."

He chuckled. "Ain't it the truth. Fifty years ago, when I began my landscaping business, my only qualifications for a job were my love of plants and a new spade. This is that original tool." Oliver caressed the worn handle. "Whenever I touch this wood memories of bygone years flash into focus."

Oliver lowered his voice. "But I can't trust my memory like I used to. Since I came home from the hospital my old noggin goes out of kilter. I see things, remember things, but I don't always make the connection."

"Your body has been through a rough time."

"Yeah." Oliver nodded. "That's true." His grip tightened on the wooden handle. "One thing is for certain. I haven't forgotten how to plant a shrub. My father was a gardener pure and simple. 'Just as the twig is bent, the tree's inclined.' From an early age I knew what my course in life would be."

1

I watched Oliver ease the sharp tip of the spade into the soil. He was a nice man, and I enjoyed visiting with him, but I wondered if it was a good idea for him to be working. He appeared to be in fair health, but his heart attack had been just six months ago. His eyes were bright, his weathered cheeks flushed, but that could be from the warm sun shining on us.

River City Commemorative Park was a lovely place on this June morning. A gentle breeze stirred the oak and maple leaves and carried the sweet scent of petunia blossoms. Birds twittered with importance as they brought food to their newly hatched offspring. It was peaceful and should be an ideal spot for a wedding. Just how ideal would be proved a week from today when the Montgomery/Gentry nuptials put my flower shop's reputation on the line.

When Evelyn Montgomery first approached me with plans for her daughter Nikki's wedding, I'd seen the event as a way of stretching my artistic talents, as well as getting the word out that I was capable of more than sympathy and hospital bouquets. I'd visualized turning the park into a floral fantasy. My shop would get the kudos, and my River City floral competitors would choke on my creative dust.

If my husband, Carl, were alive, he'd have cautioned, "Bretta Solomon, when ego comes into play, the brain takes a holiday."

I hoped my little gray cells were stretched on some sandy beach soaking up sunshine, because the rest of this ego-ridden body had been trapped into making sure every floral detail of this wedding was perfectly executed. I would triumph if it killed me—and the way things were going, it very well might.

Since my initial contact with Evelyn, my doctor had

treated me for a severe case of hives. I also had a persistent burning in the pit of my stomach that disappeared only when I was sure Evelyn was otherwise occupied. Too many times, I'd been surprised by her popping into the flower shop to have "a brief confab" over a detail we'd settled an hour ago.

Today's appointment was for ten o'clock, but it was only nine thirty. I'd come to the park early so I could look over the lay of the land and perhaps zero in on something that would soothe my ragged nerves. It had been my good fortune to find Oliver Terrell and his son, Eddie, hard at work on the plantings Evelyn had donated to the park.

As Oliver lifted another scoop of dirt, Eddie said, "Dad, take a break. I still think it was a lousy idea for you to come on this job. I could've handled it."

Eddie was around my age—forty-five—and had fabulous blue eyes. I was sure he had hair, though I'd never seen it. A cap bearing his company's name—Terrell Landscaping—usually sat atop his handsome head.

Oliver took a red handkerchief from his pocket and wiped his brow. "I'm fine. I need this work to get in shape for when we tackle Bretta's garden next week."

I flexed my fingers. "I can hardly wait. I plan on being right alongside both of you, pulling weeds, chopping stumps, wheeling mulch—"

"—smoothing Ben-Gay on your aching muscles," finished Eddie.

I grinned. "Probably, but I'm looking forward to the challenge. Being a florist is more cerebral than physical. I don't get much exercise toting bouquets."

Eddie dumped a wheelbarrow load of shredded bark on a tarp he'd spread near the shrubs Oliver was planting. "Surely, toeing Mrs. Montgomery's line has kept you in tiptop shape?"

I reached into my pocket and flashed a roll of antacid tablets at him. "Does this answer your question?"

Eddie grunted. "I should buy stock in that company."

"When Evelyn asked me to design the flowers for her daughter's garden wedding, I listened to her general outline, then calmly replied, 'Sure, no problem.' And there's been problems galore."

Eddie muttered something under his breath. I didn't catch his comment, but Oliver did. "A job is a job, son. We're here to please the customer." Oliver turned to me. "I haven't met Mrs. Montgomery, but from what Eddie has told me, it sounds as if she has more money than common sense."

Wasn't that the truth? I left father and son to their work and meandered down the path that led to the area of the park known as Tranquility Garden—the site of the upcoming nuptials. For weeks, I'd reminded myself that Evelyn Montgomery had a right to be persnickety. As mother of the bride, she wanted everything perfect for her daughter's wedding.

Nikki and her fiancé were on a tour of the United States with a ballet company from France. When the troupe hit St. Louis, they'd be a hop, skip, and a pirouette from River City. There would be a two-day layover before the dance company continued on with the tour.

Two days to be fitted for gowns and tuxedos, the rehearsal, and the main event. Thank heavens, I only had to make sure the flowers were petal perfect.

Only?

I stuffed another antacid tablet into my mouth and heard voices off to my left. The tone of one stood out from the other: Sonya Norris, wedding coordinator, had arrived. Brides paid dearly for her services because if a job had to be done, and done right, Sonya would see to it. She wouldn't physically do the work herself, but her instructions would be carried out.

The women came into view. Sonya was tall and thin and favored "power" suits, tailored blouses, and plain gold-hoop earrings. Her hair was dark and cut in a no-nonsense style. Today she was dressed in a teal-blue straight skirt and matching jacket. Her blouse was a lighter shade.

The woman with Sonya was Dana Olson, a River City caterer. I liked Dana. She was as sweet as the cakes she baked. Soft and pudgy, her figure was a testimonial to her prowess in the kitchen. For children's parties she not only decorated the cakes but also dressed as a clown. This added bonus had made her popular with frazzled mothers.

As the two women walked toward me, I had a mental flash of Dana in total clown regalia cutting the Montgomery wedding cake. The image made me shudder. Why had Evelyn given Dana, whose forte was birthdays and anniversaries, total responsibility for the food for such a lavish party? Perhaps Sonya was thinking along those same lines. Now that they were closer, I could make out their conversation.

"—can't bring all that food across this path to the tent. There's to be a display of flowers, candles, and hurricane lamps. Think, Dana," Sonya ordered sharply. "You'll have to hire extra help to carry your supplies from the other side."

"I already have three girls on the payroll. I'd like to make a profit for all this worrying." Dana shook her head, and her brown curls bounced. "And to think I turned down four ordinary birthday cakes and a golden anniversary to cater this wedding."

"It will work," said Sonya. "My job is to spot a potential problem, but you have to follow my suggestions." She turned to me. "Bretta. It's good to see you here early. I hope everything is shipshape on your end of this gala?"

I only had time to nod before Dana started again.

"That's all well and good, Sonya, but where were you this morning when Mrs. Montgomery called to tell me to look at the sunrise?" Dana didn't wait for an answer. "Our mother of the bride wants me to match that particular rosy apricot color for the punch." A hot flush stained Dana's plump cheeks. "Who gives a flying fig about the punch when the cake has to tower six feet in the air?"

"Six feet?" repeated Sonya, frowning. "I thought the cake was to be spread over three tables with sugar bridges connecting the tiered layers. When was that changed?"

"Try eight o'clock last night. Mrs. Montgomery says Nikki has decided she wants a cake that will stand as tall as her six-foot fiancé."

"Oh my," said Sonya. "Not a good plan. The tent is to have a wooden floor, but as people walk about, the shifting of the boards might topple—"

"Don't even say it." Dana moaned. "I wish I'd never taken this job. I feel as if I'm being punished. Nikki will be in St. Louis. Why not have the wedding there?"

I added my two cents to the conversation. "I have to admit I'm surprised Evelyn would hold such an important event in a town she's called home for less than a year."

Sonya shrugged. "She's made more influential friends in the last eight months than I have all my life. You should see the guest list. The mayor is coming, as well as bankers, doctors, lawyers, councilmen, judges, and all of River City's elite. At last count there's to be five hundred people milling around this park."

"But why River City?" whined Dana. "Why us? Why—"

"Dana," said a woman coming down the path toward us, "will you stop that screeching? I could hear you clear out to the parking lot."

This new arrival looked like a sixties reject who had found her way back into style. She wore bell-bottom slacks and a tie-dyed shirt. A narrow band of cloth was fastened around her forehead and kept her stringy blond hair out of her eyes. She was as thin as a willow branch. Her arms were like twigs.

"You think you've got problems?" she said, pointing to a mammoth oak. "See that tree? Workmen are coming this week to build a platform so I can take aerial photos of this wedding." She tossed her head. "I've been ordered to dress as if I'm a guest so I won't be intrusive. Can you explain to me how I'm supposed to climb that tree in a skirt and panty hose while carrying a video camera and equipment?"

I shifted uncomfortably. All these last-minute changes bothered me. For the past twenty-four hours I hadn't heard a peep out of Evelyn. I turned to Sonya. "Exactly why were we asked to meet here this morning?"

Before Sonya could answer, another woman sprinted toward us. Her hair was a shrieking shade of green. Her eyes glittered like emeralds. She wore an orange uniform with a lemon-colored apron tied around her narrow waist. "Hi, guys. Am I late?"

"Would it matter?" asked Dana, staring at the green hair.

"Nope. I've got a business to run, and Claire's Hair Lair has to come first. I can't be away for more than an hour. I'm on the trail of a hot piece of gossip, and Mrs. Dearborne is coming in for a perm. If I phrase my questions just right, she'll never know what I'm after, and I'll—"

"Claire, what have you done to your hair?" demanded the

photographer. "All those chemicals aren't healthy."

Claire gave the woman's own limp hair a sharp study. "Cut, color, curl. The three C's will earn you a man."

"Like your track record makes me want one."

I laughed politely with the others, but had the feeling I was being left out of some private joke. While Sonya and I had a professional acquaintance, and I'd often sold Dana fresh flowers to decorate her cakes, the other two women were strangers.

I asked for an introduction, and Sonya quickly responded, "I'm sorry, Bretta. Since we know each other, I never thought you'd be left out of the loop. The woman with the broccoli-colored hair and contacts is Claire Alexander, beauty shop owner." Sonya turned to the other woman. "This is Kasey Vickers. She's a local celebrity. Her photo-essays have earned her national recognition in environmental circles."

I must have looked as confused as I felt. An environmentalist was shooting the photos for a wedding?

Sonya said, "I know what you're thinking. But regardless of the subject, Kasey's photo techniques will give Nikki a wonderful keepsake."

Impatiently, Claire said, "What are we waiting for? I have to get back to my shop." She lowered her voice. "After I talk to Mrs. Dearborne, I may have some news that will knock you all onto your fannies."

Sonya frowned. "You keep hinting at some great secret. Are you going to let us in on it?"

"Not till I get more information."

Sonya said, "It's no wonder you became a beautician. You thrive on gossip. What's going on?"

Claire shook her head. "I'm not saying another word."

"That'll be the day," muttered Kasey.

Dana turned to me. "Ignore their bickering. Our friendship goes back to high school."

I looked from one face to another. "You're all the same age? What year did you graduate?"

"Nineteen sixty-six," said Dana, fluffing her brown curls. "I'm the baby of the group."

While the others razzed her, I did some fast calculations. If they had graduated when they were eighteen that meant these women were fifty-four years old. Of the four, only Sonya looked her age. Dana's plump cheeks were wrinkle-free. I wouldn't have guessed the green-haired Claire to be past forty. As for Kasey, her skin was stretched so tightly over her bones my estimation of her age would've been way off the mark.

Claire thrust her hands into her apron pockets. "That's how we can get away with the insults. We've been friends too long to let a little criticism separate us. Besides, nothing any of us could say would be new." She studied her friends and softly chanted, "You can boil me in oil. You can burn me at the stake. But a River City Royal is always on the make."

Dana's mouth dropped open. Sonya stiffened. Kasey said, "No, Claire. You—" But then she stopped and bit her lip.

In the silence that followed, we heard Evelyn's voice. Her tone was sharp. "I want everything perfect, right down to the leaves on the shrubs."

Evelyn walked toward us with Eddie and Oliver trailing along behind her. When I met Eddie's gaze, my stomach muscles tightened. The man had fire in his eyes. Oliver's skin was mottled. His chest rose and fell with sharp, agitated breaths.

I looked back at Evelyn. She was a beautiful woman—

blue-black hair and deep brown eyes, her complexion as smooth as a magnolia blossom, her makeup flawless. She possessed a figure a teenager would have envied. Pointed breasts, a narrow waist, and nicely rounded hips were displayed in a bronze-colored dress.

"As I've told Mr. Terrell," Evelyn said, coming into our circle, "my goal for this wedding is a tribute to an exquisite woman." She dazzled us with a smile. "Thank you for coming this morning. I thought it best to be on-site for this discussion. If you have any questions, suggestions, or complaints say them now. You'll have my undivided attention. Oliver and Eddie have heard what I want." She nodded to them. "You may both go back to work."

It was a cool dismissal, but Eddie had something else to say. Oliver tugged on his son's arm, but Eddie wouldn't move.

Evelyn ignored him and said, "All right, ladies, who wants to go first?"

Claire stepped forward. "I have to get back to my shop—"

"That hot piece of gossip from Mrs. Dearborne won't wait, huh?" asked Dana.

Oliver stared at Claire. "Dearborne? Gossip? Who are you?"

Claire raised an eyebrow. "I'm Claire Alexander, owner of Claire's Hair Lair."

Oliver studied her face and shook his head. "I don't know you, but suddenly something is niggling at me." He gazed at the ground. "I wished I could remember."

Evelyn said, "Please, we have to discuss the fine points of Nikki's wedding."

Oliver closed his eyes and cocked his head as if listening to some distant sound. His hand moved up and down the handle of his spade. "So long ago," he murmured.

Eddie said to Evelyn, "Dad and I have done like you asked. We took out the euonymus shrubs, and we're planting the golden spirea. The look is natural. To spray the foliage with gold paint would be ridiculous."

"Spray the foliage?" I repeated.

Evelyn turned to me. "Yes, Bretta. The color of the shrubs is too yellow. I want Nikki to stroll down a gilded path."

"She also wants us to plant dead trees," groused Eddie. "Dead trees, mind you, so the bare branches can be draped with hoity-toity lights."

"I saw the idea in a magazine. The effect against the night sky was—"

"—not done by Terrell Landscaping," finished Eddie.

Oliver opened his eyes. "Where are the markers?"

Eddie shot his father a puzzled look, but said to Evelyn, "I've had it. Dad and I are done. Plant your own shrubs. Drape your own damned lights."

Evelyn's smile was cold. "Fine. Pack up your stuff and get out."

Eddie waved an arm. "It's a public park."

"Son?" said Oliver weakly. He stumbled forward. "Chest hurts. Heart."

Eddie whipped around. "Where's your pills?"

Oliver sunk to his knees. "Can't . . . get . . . breath." He gasped and fell forward.

Sonya used her cell phone to call 911. I knelt next to Oliver. "Help me turn him over," said Eddie.

Once we had Oliver on his back, he opened his eyes. Eddie found the pills, uncapped the brown bottle, and slipped a tablet under Oliver's tongue.

"Hang in there, Dad," he coached. "Give the medicine a chance to work."

Spittle drooled from the corner of Oliver's mouth. Eddie used his shirttail to wipe it gently away. Oliver gazed at his son. Love reflected beyond the pain he was enduring. He turned his head and stared directly into my eyes. Softly, he said, "Bretta . . . Spade."

Chapter Two

✿ My flower shop has always been a safe haven, a place I can go to regroup and put my thoughts in order. I headed for that calming piece of real estate when I left River City Commemorative Park.

As a florist, I've helped bereaved families choose a fitting memorial for their loved one's service. On a personal level, I've had my own share of dealing with an unexpected death. But never has my name been on a dying man's lips. Never have I stared into his eyes as he drew his last breath.

I pulled into the alley behind the flower shop and climbed wearily out of my car. It felt as if an eternity had passed since the morning. As I went up the steps to the back door, I checked my watch, but my wrist was bare. The timepiece had stopped a few days ago, and I hadn't bought a new one. I entered the workroom and glanced at the clock. It was only eleven thirty. The shop closed at noon on Saturdays. My employees, Lois and Lew, were finishing a couple of last-minute orders.

"Oh, boy," said Lois, eyeing my grim expression. "I take it the meeting didn't go well. What does that woman want now? White doves released from gold-plated cages?"

Lew said, "More like trained seals barking 'Ave Maria' from the reflection pool."

I moved a tall stool closer to the worktable and sat down. Lois Duncan is my floral designer, and while I value her work, I treasure her friendship. Over the years, I've tried to analyze why we get along so well when we have so many differences.

Lois is taller than I am, and has the metabolism of a hummingbird. Her weight never varies even though she sucks down candy like a vacuum cleaner in an M&M factory. My hips expand when I so much as smell chocolate. She has five children. I have none. Her bouquets are flamboyant. Mine are conservative. Sometimes she's bossy, especially when the subject concerns my lack of a social life.

Lew Mouffit is my deliveryman and perhaps the most annoying male in River City. He has the answer to everything and pontificates with such pomposity that I'm often tempted to fire him. However, he has a following of well-to-do women who patronize my shop, so I bite my tongue again and again.

Before I plunged into the story of my morning, I looked around me, drawing strength from what was near and dear to my heart. Years ago, when I had to name my business, a cutesy title didn't cut it. I'd settled on the Flower Shop, which suited my practical nature. I ran a tight ship. I believed that everything should have a place, that an object should be where I wanted it when I wanted it.

Bolts of satin ribbon were neatly lined on shelves. From where I sat I could see the front cooler, displaying fresh, colorful arrangements. Next to the cash register was a vase of white carnations, their spicy scent an open invitation for my customers to make a purchase.

I took a deep breath, then released it in a sigh. "You can't begin to imagine what happened." I filled them in on everything. My visit with Oliver and Eddie. Meeting the other women involved with the wedding. Eddie's and Evelyn's disagreement, and finally, the morning's distressing finale.

"The paramedics arrived, but it was too late. Oliver had already passed away. Eddie was devastated. He jumped in his truck and tore out of the park."

"Poor guy," said Lois.

I glanced up, saw the concern in her blue eyes, and knew what she was thinking. Carl had died from a heart attack, too. Lois was worried that my morning's experience might send me into a deep depression.

I summoned up a smile to ease her fears, then turned to Lew, who was muttering under his breath. Lew was thirty-five and rapidly going bald. I've never seen him dressed in anything but well-pressed slacks, a shirt, and a conservative tie.

Against my better judgment, I asked, "Are you talking to us?"

Lew checked to make sure he had our complete and undivided attention. "If Oliver used his dying breath to whisper 'Spade' to you, then it must have been important." He added piously, "I've figured it out."

Lois rolled her eyes. I had to control an urge to do likewise. This was so typical of Lew. I'd skimmed through the account of my conversation with Oliver. I'd briefly explained his brush with death six months ago. I'd ended my story by repeating Oliver's dying words. I'd been there, I'd seen everything that had happened, and yet, *Lew* had drawn a conclusion.

I said, "Let's have it. Why did Oliver say 'Spade' to me?"

"If I understood you correctly, Oliver actually said, 'Bretta . . . Spade.'" Lew's balding head shone in the fluorescent light. "He was asking for your help. It makes sense. Bretta Spade."

When I didn't shout "Eureka!" or do a cartwheel across the floor, he demanded, "Don't you get it? Oliver was drawing a parallel between you and Dashiell Hammett's fictional detective—Sam Spade."

Well, that was stupid, and I would have said so, but Lois beat me to it.

"Get real. The man was dying. He could've been confused. Disoriented. Bretta told us he cherished that gardening tool. Maybe he was asking her to keep it safe for Eddie."

Lew's chin rose several degrees. "As my great-grandmother would've said, 'Balderdash!' If Oliver wanted his son to have the spade, he'd have said 'Spade' to him. According to Bretta, Oliver actually turned his head toward *her*. He spoke *her* name. He knew who he was talking to, and he knew exactly what he was saying."

Lois said, "You won't convince me that a man on the brink of death was playing some convoluted mind game."

Lew straightened his tie. "All right, how about this? Spades are the highest suit in bridge. What if Oliver used the word *spade* to denote an event that was of supreme importance to—"

I didn't let him finish. "I doubt that Oliver ever played a hand of bridge. Let's drop it. I'm too tired to discuss it further."

Lew frowned. "Too tired? I'm amazed you aren't hot on the trail of this latest mystery. Or is it because these theories came from me?" When I didn't answer, he turned on the heel of his well-polished shoe and stomped to the back room. "I'm taking these last deliveries. See you Monday."

"Thanks for the warning," said Lois under her breath.

After the door had closed, I said, "He's in a foul mood. What's his problem?"

"My first thought is that he isn't getting any, except he never does. I don't know why things are different today. He's been a grouch all morning, and he's taken to critiquing my bouquets." She grabbed a broom and swept the littered floor. In a haughty tone, she mimicked, " 'Red, purple, and yellow are so gauche, Lois. Must you always pick that combination for a hospital order?' "

I chuckled. "So what's been going on here, besides Lew being a bigger pain than usual?"

Lois shrugged. "Not much. Business is slow for a Saturday." She swept the flower stems into a dustpan and dumped them into the trash bin under her table. "If you don't need me to close, I'm going home." But she didn't look happy about it.

Last month, Lois had agreed to let her sister's daughter, Kayla, come live with her. Lois had raised five children, but all were finally out on their own. I didn't think it was a good idea when Lois talked it over with me. In Cincinnati, Kayla had been in trouble. Her mother thought a change of scenery might change the girl. That hadn't happened. Kayla, a junior at River City High School, was in trouble again. Lois hadn't told me the problem, which was unusual. She and I had few secrets.

"Is there anything I can do?" I asked.

Lois's smile was pinched. "No thanks. I assume we'll be putting in overtime on this wedding?" After I'd nodded, she continued, "I have a ton of dirty laundry, and I need to go grocery shopping."

I waved her on. She hung the dustpan on its hook, then picked up her purse. Hesitating at the door, she asked, "You aren't going to let Oliver's death get to you, are you?"

"I'm fine. But I wish I knew what he tried to tell me. Not to agree with Lew, but it sure seemed like Oliver expected me to do something."

"Not necessarily true. His mind could've flipped back to your earlier conversation with him. He'd talked about the spade. He saw you leaning over him. Put it out of your mind. We have enough to deal with when it comes to this wedding."

I made a face, but Lois didn't see it. She'd already gone. I counted out the cash drawer, then glanced through the day's orders, but saw nothing interesting. I checked the walk-in cooler to jog my memory as to what fresh flowers were available for Oliver's upcoming funeral.

Would Eddie want red roses for the spray on the casket or something earthier, befitting a gardener? Bronze and yellow mums with an assortment of greens—ivy, variegated pittosporum, and some gold and orange croton leaves—would be appropriate for a man who'd made his living from loving plants.

I turned off the workroom lights and strolled up front, where I flipped the lock and put the CLOSED sign into place. I particularly like being in the shop when the doors are shut to the public and the lights are off. The pressure eases, and I can relax and let my mind drift. I stared across the street at Kelsey's Bar and Grill and felt a need for an order of their curly fries.

Two years ago, after my husband, Carl, had passed away, I'd lost one hundred pounds. My struggle to keep the weight off is an hour-to-hour battle. With the stress I'd been under, I yearned for a plate of comfort. But I summoned up some willpower and turned my back on Kelsey's, staring instead at the shop's shadows.

This month was the second anniversary of my husband's death. It had taken every one of those days to accept the fact that he was gone and my life was forever changed. For twenty-four years, Carl had been at my side. I'd been married to him longer than I'd been alone. We'd been friends before we became lovers. I could tell him anything, talk to him about everything under the moon and stars, and he'd listened, really listened to what I had to say.

I hadn't known the true extent of his faith in me until he became a deputy with the Spencer County Sheriff's Department. He'd trusted me with the facts of cases he worked on. Together we'd explored possibilities as to what might have happened. We'd made wild conjectures. I was a great one for taking that "shot in the dark." Carl had urged me to let my mind flow even if the picture seemed askew.

Carl's legacy had been a bountiful education, but the art of solving a mystery had been a fraction of his tutoring. From the first day I'd met him, he'd tried to teach me to trust and to forgive. I hadn't been a willing pupil. When your heart's been broken, it isn't easy to give those emotions another chance.

When I was eight years old, my father walked out of my life. For more years than I care to count, he was simply a name on a birthday card or a box of grapefruit at Christmas. This past December he'd come to River City for a visit, and I'd learned that you can't have trust without forgiveness.

I smiled sadly. It hurt that Carl wasn't here to see that I'd gone to the head of the class. The lines of communication with my father were open. In fact, last night I'd gotten a call from him. He'd said he had a fantastic surprise for me and that it would arrive this afternoon.

I wasn't particularly curious. He'd gotten into the habit of sending me trinkets. What I really wanted, he wasn't ready to give. I needed a detailed account of why he'd walked out. So far all I'd gotten was the old cliché—irreconcilable differences with my mother—which didn't tell me squat.

And neither did the words "Bretta . . . Spade."

What had Oliver meant? What was he trying to tell me? Lew had been right about one thing. If Oliver had used his dying breath to whisper those words to me, it must have been important to him. Of course, the man couldn't be sure he was dying. He'd fought death before and won. Only this time he'd lost the battle and had left me with a final plea.

Damn but I hated not knowing what was expected of me. By not doing anything, by not having an inkling of what I should do, I felt as if I was denying Oliver his last request.

Guilt was a great motivator. I grabbed my purse and started for the back door. I could go to the park, pack up Eddie's tools, and take them by his house. I wouldn't knock on his door. I'd simply leave everything in plain sight. It wasn't much, but it was better than—

The telephone rang. Irritated, I stopped and stared at it. Now that I had a plan, I was anxious to put it into action, but it's difficult to ignore a ringing phone. Two more jingles and I picked up the receiver.

"The Flower Shop. Bretta speaking."

"This is Claire. I met you this morning at the park."

"Yes, Claire. I remember." Green hair. Green eyes. How could I forget? "What can I do—"

"I've got to see you."

"If you have any questions about this wedding, go straight to Evelyn. I'm not about to second-guess what she wants."

"I can't discuss this on the phone. Can you come to my beauty shop? The address is 3201 Marietta Avenue. You have a reputation for getting to the bottom of suspicious doings. I can't make heads or tails of this information, but I'm not sitting on it."

"What information?"

"Just get here—" Claire's voice lost its excited tone. "Well, hi," she said calmly. "This is a pleasant surprise."

I frowned in confusion. Was the woman crazy? Perhaps all those chemicals she used on her hair had seeped into her brain. "What's going on?" I asked.

Instead of answering, Claire plunked down the receiver, but I could still hear her talking. "Just making an appointment. If you'll take a chair, I'll be right with you."

Oh. A customer had come in. Claire said, "Sure, I have time. Let me finish this call."

The receiver was picked up, and Claire asked, "You have the address, correct?"

"Yes. I'll be there in a few minutes."

"No hurry," she said quietly. "My pigeon just walked through the door." She hung up.

I replaced the receiver and went out to my car. Pigeon? That was a strange way to refer to a customer.

I made a left turn, headed for the park, but after a few blocks I detoured back the way I'd come. I was curious as to what Claire wanted.

Marietta Avenue was located in the old historic district, which sat on the limestone bluffs overlooking the Osage River. The area with its brick-paved streets was undergoing revitalization, which I was glad to see was progressing well. I had a fondness for this part of town, and had done a bit of research on its history.

In 1810 a man named James Horton and his wife, Hattie, had organized a group of people intent on finding a new land and new beginnings. On their trek west, these pioneers had gotten lost. Finding themselves on the bank of the Osage River, they had either lacked the will to travel forward or liked what they'd stumbled upon. For whatever reason, the settlers had put down roots in this soil, and River City, Missouri, had sprouted.

I traveled up Marietta Avenue, stopping often to let cement trucks go around me. The area was a beehive of activity. Scaffoldings were everywhere. Workmen called back and forth from rooftops.

The building that housed Claire's Hair Lair had already received its face-lift. The front was painted burgundy with gray shutters flanking the plate-glass window. Styrofoam heads topped with stylish wigs were on display, along with several bottles of enriching shampoo and cleansing rinses.

I leaned closer and read a sign: DON'T LET YOUR UNRULY HAIR MAKE YOU A SOURPUSS. CLAIRE WILL HAVE YOU PURRING WITH SATISFACTION IN NO TIME. For emphasis two stuffed lions had been added to the exhibit. One had matted fur, his mouth opened in a snarl. His companion sported a glossy, manageable mane.

Chuckling, I opened the door and stepped inside, where my nose was assaulted by the smell of fresh perm solution. Fanning the air with my hand, I called, "Claire? It's Bretta Solomon."

"Just a minute," was the muffled reply from a curtained doorway at the back of the building.

"I know I'm early," I said, "but I decided to come by before I did another errand."

My answer was the sound of a toilet flushing. I peered at my surroundings and forgot my burning nose. Blue, red, green, and yellow stripes raced up and down the walls. The floor was covered with a vinyl pattern that screamed kindergarten finger painting. But it was the ceiling that grabbed my attention. I tilted my head and marveled at the sight.

Painted directly on the tiles was a ten-foot picture of a lovely girl who might have been fifteen years old. My gaze skimmed over her face, noting the closed eyes and gentle smile. She was dressed in a robe and looked angelic surrounded by an aura of light achieved by the shading of brush strokes. Her hair was a crowning glory of flowers, painted in meticulous detail, sprouting from her head.

I squinted at the blossoms. These weren't flower shop varieties. The pinkish purple daisylike flower was echinacea. An evening primrose curled seductively around the girl's left ear. The brilliant orange blossom of the butterfly weed was an exact replica of the ones that lived on the farm where I'd grown up. Rose mallow, milkweed, and elderberry were all Missouri wildflowers.

Standing just above the other flowers was another blossom that was a cluster of eight blooms on one stem. Each was yellow-green, tinged with purple. The individual flowers had five tubular hood-shaped structures with a slender horn extending from each.

I didn't recognize this last flower, but I was impressed with the overall appearance of the painting. "How neat," I said aloud. My voice echoed in the silence.

The absolute stillness of the building finally penetrated my preoccupation with the ceiling. Impatiently, I called, "Claire, if you're busy, I can come back later."

This time I received no answer. As I made my way across the floor to the curtained doorway, the soles of my shoes made tiny *tick-tick* sounds like I'd stepped in something sticky. I checked but saw nothing except wild swirls of color underfoot.

"Claire?" I called again, pushing the curtain aside. A strong herbal odor rushed out. I moved farther into the supply room. Here there was a total absence of color. The walls were unfinished Sheetrock, the floor bare concrete. Metal shelves held bottles of shampoos and such. The bathroom was on my right. I rapped on the door, then pushed it open. The room was empty.

I turned to my left, and my breath caught in my throat. Claire lay on her back. With a cry of surprise, I hurried to her side and carefully felt for a pulse. There was none. A pale green froth oozed from her mouth and nostrils. Near her body was an aerosol can of herbal mousse. A bit of green foam clung to the nozzle.

At first I couldn't comprehend what I was seeing. If Claire was dead, then who'd answered me when I'd first entered the beauty shop? Who'd flushed the toilet? I looked from the can to the watery foam that filled Claire's mouth and nostrils and nearly fainted as I put my own interpretation on these details. Someone had knocked her unconscious, then squirted the thick foam into her air passages so she'd suffocate.

Slowly I dragged my gaze up to her wide-eyed stare. Since I'd met her in the park, she'd changed her emerald contacts for ones that resembled a cat's eyes, with lentil-shaped, hyacinth-colored pupils.

Because of the lack of natural moisture on her orbs, the thin pieces of plastic were losing their shape. Even as I watched, one of the lenses curled, popped off, and landed on her cheek.

Chapter Three

Two dead people in one day were more than this old girl could handle. My chest hurt from the thumping of my heart. I clamped my teeth tightly together to keep them from chattering and stumbled out of the storage room into Claire's beauty shop. I couldn't leave the salon unattended with Claire's body in back. A phone was on the desk by the door, but I knew better than to touch it. I stood in the middle of the floor like a dolt, wondering if I should step out into the street and scream for help.

"Bretta?"

I whirled around to find Evelyn peering at me from the doorway. "I was just by your flower shop." She came farther into the room. "I've been tracking everyone down so I can apologize for the way I've acted. Nikki's wedding is important, but when I saw Oliver die—" She shuddered. "I've been a real nag, and I'm sorry."

"You can't come in here."

Evelyn's shoulders stiffened. "Good heavens, I said I was sorry. Surely you aren't going to get on some righteous high horse and back out of—"

"Do you have a cell phone?"

"Yes, but I—"

"Pass it over. I need to make an emergency call."

"What's going on?" She peered around the empty beauty shop. "Where's Claire? I have to talk to her, too."

I held out my hand. "Please. I need to use your phone."

Evelyn frowned but reached into her purse. "Here," she said, thrusting the gadget at me. "But there's a phone right over there."

She nodded to the desk, but I ignored her, punching in 911. Evelyn drew a sharp breath when she saw what I was doing. Her head swiveled as she looked about the room. Seeing the curtained doorway, she took a step in that direction, but I grabbed her arm and shook my head.

"This is Bretta Solomon," I said into the receiver. "I'm at 3201 Marietta Avenue, Claire's Hair Lair. I've just found the owner, Ms. Alexander, dead in the storage room."

Evelyn gasped and looked ready to keel over. I tightened my grip on her arm, but she shrugged off my helping hand. "I'm fine," she said. "But what am I going to do now? The girls are expecting a beautician in residence at the park."

The helping hand I'd offered clenched into a knot at my side. I wanted to slap her. Did this woman think only in terms of the wedding?

"Yes," I said into the phone. "Yes. I know. Yes. Yes. Okay. Yes. I'll be right here." I disconnected and handed the phone back to Evelyn.

Absently, she tucked it into her handbag. "I'm leaving," she said. "I wasn't here when you found—uh—Claire. No need in me staying until help arrives."

"You have to stay. Your fingerprints will be on the doorknob. I used your phone to make the call. We have to stand right here and not touch anything."

Evelyn didn't like this, but whether it was my commanding tone or the command itself, I couldn't be sure. Her chin came up, and she glared at me. "My fingerprints will be here anyway. I've been in this shop before. I sat in that chair while Claire and I discussed the wedding. Besides, fingerprints are only important in a murder—"

I said nothing.

Her jaw dropped. Slowly, she closed it and turned to look at the curtained doorway again. "Oh, God. Murder? Is there blood? I can't stand the sight of blood. I think I'm going to be sick."

The wail of sirens overrode her need to upchuck. "I can't believe this is happening," she whispered. "What in the world will Nikki say? Her hairdresser murdered. Oh dear. Oh dear."

"Yeah, Claire's untimely death is a real inconvenience. If she were here, I'm sure she would express her regret."

"That isn't what I meant."

I took a steady bead on her. "I know *exactly* what you meant."

A River City patrol car arrived first. The officer took one look behind the curtain, then radioed for reinforcements. Paramedics soon arrived, followed by a Spencer County deputy and, finally, a Missouri Highway Patrol officer. It was a fashion show of uniforms. Khaki for the county. Blue for the MHP. Green and gold for our town's protectors. Jurisdiction fell to the city officials, but in the case of a suspicious death, it was all hands on deck.

I knew and was known to most of the men because of Carl's involvement with law enforcement. I was treated with respect, but nonetheless, Evelyn and I were hustled out of the beauty shop and were told to wait so our statements could be taken. I can only guess at what went on in that storage room, but I surmised plenty. The coroner was followed by Jean Kelley, River City's chief of police.

Jean is a willowy blonde who looks as if she ought to be on a runway, modeling chic clothes. She maintains a good relationship with her deputies, has earned every ounce of their admiration. Her mind is sharp, her need for thoroughness a mantra cited by her staff.

Jean nodded to me, then hurried into the shop. "Who was that?" asked Evelyn. The officer standing near us shook his head. "No talking, ladies."

Evelyn pursed her lips and glanced at her watch. "How much longer am I to wait? I have an appointment in half an hour."

"It'll keep," he murmured, watching a new arrival stride toward us.

I followed his line of vision and gulped. Sid Hancock, the sheriff of Spencer County, was on the scene. Sid and I had a tentative relationship, or perhaps it would be better called tenacious. Tentative in that our relationship tends to come and go depending on if I'm muddling in one of his cases. Tenacious because even though he disapproves of my amateur detecting, he's been Johnny-on-the-spot when I needed his help.

He was not very tall, about five foot eight or so, and slight of build. His hair was red, his complexion pale but freckled. A fiery temper and crotchety disposition summed up his personality. Seeing the glint in his eye, I knew I was in for a sampling of both.

"Holy crap," he said in greeting. "Why the hell am I not surprised? I heard that a body had been reported, and here you are."

He rolled his eyes and turned to Evelyn. His surly stare swept her in one fluid motion. Apparently, he liked what he saw. He squared his shoulders, and his mouth curved upward. "At least you're keeping better company, Solomon," he said to me, but held out his hand to Evelyn. "I'm Sheriff Hancock. And you are?"

Evelyn lowered her eyes, gazing up at Sid through thick, dark lashes. "What a pleasure, Sheriff. I'm Evelyn Montgomery. I moved to River City a few months ago, and I've heard nothing but wonderful things about your work in this county."

An enamored Sid was pretty tough to take. That the attraction was reciprocated was nauseating. Thank God Sid didn't shuffle his feet and stammer, "Aw, shucks, ma'am, 'tweren't nothing." But he might as well have. He thrust out his chest like a preening rooster. "I do my job," he said.

I cleared my throat. "Beauty shop. Body. Statements." I waved a hand at Evelyn. "She's in a hurry, and I—"

"Bretta, please," said Evelyn. "This man has important things to oversee. We'll have to wait our turn."

"But you said—"

"The dressmaker will understand when I explain that I've been unavoidably detained."

Sid's smile grew to a cheesy grin. "Damned fine attitude, Mrs. Montgomery. It's appreciated." He turned to me. "What the hell's been going on?"

"Are you taking my statement?"

"Not formally, but I want the facts."

"Fine. Claire called because she wanted to talk to me about some information."

"What information?"

"She was dead when I arrived, so I don't know."

"Didn't she tell you the nature of said information?"

"No. I'm not sure of her exact words, but she said something along the lines of 'Bretta, I've got to see you. You have a reputation for getting to the bottom of suspicious doings.' " I raised my voice to override Sid's nasty comment. " 'I can't make heads or tails of this information, but I'm not sitting on it.' About that time someone came into her beauty shop. I heard Claire greet this person, say something about it being 'a pleasant surprise' and that she had 'plenty of time.' I figured it was a customer. When Claire came back on the line to me she ended our conversation by saying, 'My pigeon just walked through the door.' "

"Pigeon?" said Sid.

"Yeah. I thought that was an odd way to refer to a patron."

Sid snorted. "Sounds to me like this Alexander woman was thinking along the slang version—someone easily deceived and gullible. Wrong assumption. Her meek little pigeon turned into a nasty bird of prey."

I shuddered. "When I arrived, I didn't sense a problem. I hollered that I was here. A muffled voice answered me."

Sid's attention sharpened. "You say someone answered you?"

"Yeah. The toilet was flushed, too. I think I was in the shop alone with Claire's killer."

"Have you told anyone this tale?"

"No one has asked—yet. We were hustled out here, and we've been waiting—"

Sid spun on his heel and stomped into the beauty shop. Evelyn eyed me. "That was really good. I'd have babbled like a fool. How did you know what to say and in what order?"

"My husband was one of Sid's deputies, and I've been involved in a few cases of my own. However, Sid doesn't like—"

The officer stepped closer. "Ladies, please. The sheriff doesn't like gabbing."

I sniffed. "That's exactly what I was going to say, Officer."

"Don't say it. Do it."

Evelyn smiled. "May Bretta and I have a conversation if the subject isn't the—uh—present situation?"

The officer lowered his eyebrows. "What?"

"My daughter is getting married a week from today, and Bretta is designing the fresh flowers, but I'm not sure if she has the manpower to plant and spray the shrubs."

Evelyn took a hurried breath and turned to me. "Spraying the leaves gold will take more time, but the effect in the candlelight will be just the look I'm after. I wanted to let you know that if you need help, I'm sure Sonya will have an extra person or two lined up."

The officer folded his arms across his chest. "I believe you've said all that's necessary. I don't want to hear another word out of you." He looked at me. "Either of you. Have I made myself clear?"

"Absolutely," said Evelyn, with a swift glance at me. "I think we've covered the territory."

This woman had more nerve than a cliff diver and possessed an annoying one-track mind. Claire lay dead—murdered—just inside the building, and Evelyn was worried about gold-sprayed foliage. Jeez!

I turned my back to her, looked up and down the street, and then wished I hadn't. The sidewalk across the way was lined with rubberneckers. The sirens were a calling card to a free show. Boldly, I met the gaping stares. I had nothing to hide, and yet their attention made me feel like a bug stuck on a pin under a microscope.

As I swept the crowd, I saw a tall figure in the shadow

of an old drugstore. The front was covered with scaffolding. The bricks, weathered and worn by time's ruthless fingers, were scheduled for a fresh coat of paint. I scrunched up my eyes, trying to make out the man. Something about the way he held his head seemed familiar.

Before I could decide if I knew him, he turned on his heel and disappeared up the alley. It was the ambling walk that cinched it.

"Bailey!" I shouted. "Bailey! Wait!"

The man didn't pause. He didn't even turn his head. Was I mistaken? My heart had fluttered with hope, but now it fluttered with disappointment.

Back in April I'd made the acquaintance of Bailey Monroe, a DEA agent. Bailey had jump-started my engine, making my heart race. A floral convention was the last place I thought I'd find romance. And while the only kiss Bailey and I'd shared had been fleeting, his smile, his eyes, and his irritating manner had left a lasting impression.

When we parted ways, I was sure I'd hear from him, but it had been eight long weeks without a word. So I'd written him off as hopeless, and I was helpless to contact him since I didn't have a phone number or an address.

"Old fool," I muttered.

"Couldn't have put it better myself," said Sid, coming up behind me. "Who the hell were you yelling at? Let's get your statement so you can scram. We have enough of a mob without you inciting a riot. Judas Priest. I should've known better than to leave you in plain sight on the sidewalk. You could stir up trouble in a funeral parlor."

Since that was exactly what had happened last fall, Sid's face turned carnation red at the memory. He jerked his head at me. "Get going."

Evelyn and I were taken to separate patrol cars. It didn't escape my notice that I drew Police Chief Kelley as my inquisitor, while Sid escorted Evelyn into his car for a private tête-à-tête.

Chief Kelley settled herself in the backseat and pulled a notepad from her purse. "You know how to push all of Sid's buttons, don't you?"

"It's usually not intentional," I admitted, "but he can be the most infuriating man on earth."

Kelley studied me thoughtfully. "With so much emotion involved, some people would say there's an attraction between you."

I stared at her in openmouthed wonder, then gave over to a good belly laugh. "You're right. Hate is supposed to be close kin to love, but in this case the answer is no. I don't hate Sid, and I might like him if he wasn't so . . . so . . . Sid. I admire him. Sometimes, I even respect him. Carl classed him as a friend, but the idea of there being something more between us is as ludicrous as—uh—Claire getting up off the floor and walking out that door."

My words put a deep frown between the chief's eyes. "There isn't much chance of that happening."

"I know," I said soberly. "She was hit over the head, dragged to the back room, and her mouth and nose were filled with that green mousse."

"You've got it all figured out, huh?"

"I checked to see if she was still alive. She wasn't. I saw the can. The foam was losing its substance, becoming all watery and yucky, but there was enough of it left that I could draw a conclusion." I shivered. "Did Sid tell you I must have walked into the shop not long after she was killed? I think the murderer actually spoke to me."

"He told me, but I want to hear it from you. Start where you think it's the most relevant, then we'll tie up loose ends."

"If that's the case, I'll need to go back to about ten o'clock this morning, when I met Claire in the park."

The chief twisted on the seat to stare at me. "Ten o'clock? I thought you came here—Nope. Never mind. Tell me."

And I did. I covered everything. I tried to repeat verbatim all the conversations I'd been privy to up and until I arrived at Claire's beauty shop. When I was finished, forty minutes had passed. Evelyn had been allowed to leave. Claire's body had been taken away.

Once I was out of the squad car and in my own vehicle, I switched on the engine. I should've gone home, but while events were fresh in my mind, I decided to go back to the park.

Chapter Four

꙰❋ I'd only gone eight blocks when I came to the conclusion that every one of River City's thirty thousand residents must be on the streets. Hoping to make better time, I caught the outer-loop highway that circled the metropolis. I bypassed traffic lights but got hung up in a snarl of slow-moving vehicles driven by people looking for entertainment on a Saturday afternoon. The entrance to the Westgate Mall was off the loop, as were three cinemas and the newly constructed Menninger Civic Center, which featured a weekend puppet show for kiddies.

I zinged in and out of traffic until I spied the exit sign for the park, then switched lanes once again, taking the off ramp into a quiet wooded area. After the roar of gas engines, the silence was welcome. I took my foot off the accelerator and coasted around the first of several lazy bends in the road. Filigreed tree branches laced overhead created a tunnel of shade. I rolled down my window and breathed deeply.

My shoulders ached with tension. I tried to relax, but images of Claire's body kept my muscles taut. To take my mind off that vivid picture, I thought about events leading up to her death. We'd been in the park. Oliver had died. A short time later, Claire was murdered.

Was there a connection between Oliver's heart attack and

Claire's murder? He had said he didn't know Claire. Had his heart attack been brought on by the tension in the air? The situation between Eddie and Evelyn had been volatile, but Oliver hadn't seemed concerned about the landscaping for the wedding.

I frowned. But he had asked, "Where are the markers?" Had he been thinking about another job? Tree markers? Plant markers?

Oliver's heart condition was a fact. That he'd died at that point in time was a fact. I wanted to assume his death was from natural causes, but where murder is concerned, it would be foolhardy to assume anything. Maybe I should make a discreet inquiry.

My mind flip-flopped back to Claire. In the park she'd been fired up about some gossip. Beauty shops had a reputation for being the center of spicy gossip. But so did local taverns, church choirs, or any place where more than two people congregated. Should I make the assumption that Claire's tidbit of news had something to do with one of her clients? There was Mrs. Dearborne. But if I understood Claire's earlier reference, she was using Mrs. Dearborne to confirm something she'd already heard or suspected.

My eyes narrowed. Hmm? Oliver *had* been interested in Claire's reference to the Dearborne name.

I caught up to a line of cars making their way between the stone pillars that marked the entrance into the park. The fifty-acre tract of land contained tennis courts, a swimming pool, bike and jogging trails, a three-acre fishing lake, and numerous shelter houses and playground equipment. The smell of roasting hot dogs and burgers overpowered the scent of flowers. The peace and quiet I'd noticed this morning was shattered by the shrill screams of children hard at play.

Tranquility Garden was secluded from the rest of the park by a line of cedar trees. The garden couldn't be seen until you passed that screen of vegetation and took the path Eddie and Oliver had been landscaping. I squeezed my car into a slot, locked the doors, and headed for that path.

An elder gentleman sat on a bench soaking up the sun. We traded polite nods. He commented that it was a lovely day. Weatherwise it was perfect—warm, sunny, blue skies, and clouds sculptured like giant heads of cauliflower.

I hadn't eaten in hours, and the aroma of grilled food had made even the clouds take on the shape of sustenance. I would gather up Eddie's tools, deliver them to his house, and then head for home.

But all the tools were gone. The shrubs were planted, mulch layered at their bases. Amazed, I walked down the path, touching a leaf, raking the toe of my sneaker against some wayward wood chips on the bricks.

Spinning on my heel, I headed back the way I'd come. I wondered who was responsible for finishing the work, and stopped near the gentleman on the bench. "Did you see anyone over there?" I asked, indicating the area where I'd been.

"Just Eddie Terrell. Always knew he was a hard worker, but the man acted possessed, heaving tools into the back of his truck."

"Did he plant the shrubs and spread the mulch?"

"Sure did. Dust fogged the air as he worked."

I thanked him and went back to the path, taking it to the gazebo that would serve as the altar. The latticed structure was six-sided with a dual set of steps—one for the bride and her attendants, the other for the groom and his. Wood shingles covered the peaked roof.

Squinting, I envisioned the results of my hard work. Brass

baskets filled with masses of white flowers were to be hung in the gazebo's arched openings. Extensive use of ivy, Boston ferns, brass and copper containers, helium-filled balloons, and yards of gold-shot white tulle were to dazzle the immediate surroundings. Highlighting the altar would be twelve large hurricane lanterns. The reflection pool in front of the gazebo was to have floating wreaths made of flowers.

Plans called for five hundred candles, under protective globes, to be placed in designated areas and lit at a strategic moment before the wedding ceremony. Thank heavens this chore fell under the heading of wedding coordinator. At last count, I'd heard Sonya had hired twelve people just to light wicks.

I went up the steps to the gazebo and stood at one of the arched openings. Staring down at the reflection pool, I should've been mentally concocting the wreaths, thinking about the mechanics that I'd need to make them float. Instead my mind skipped back to Oliver's death and Claire's murder.

I waited for some revelation, but after twenty minutes nothing came to me except an overwhelming desire to eat.

Last October I moved from the house Carl and I'd shared to a mansion that we'd dreamed of someday owning. His life insurance had provided the down payment, which was a bittersweet turn of events. In those early days of ownership, I cared for my new home with all the maternal instincts of a proud mother. I saw my child's flaws—peeling paint, cracked plaster, and cluttered attic—but knew it would mature into a fine specimen if I gave it the loving attention it deserved.

That was the rub. When I first moved into the house, I'd

worked myself into a frenzy renovating the downstairs. At that time I'd had a goal. I'd scheduled my flower shop's annual Christmas open house to be held in the stately mansion, and I'd wanted everything impeccable. I grimaced. What I'd gotten was murder and an inheritance that wiped my debt for the house clean.

I owned it. I lived in it. But I didn't love it. My original plan had been to turn it into a boardinghouse. I'd wanted people around me. I'd wanted to come home from work to lights and conversation, not darkness and my own spiritless company. But those holiday catastrophes had squelched my enthusiasm for the restorations that needed to be made before I could rent the first room.

The lane up to the mansion was a quarter mile long. Majestic pine trees lined the drive and would have embraced me with a warm fuzzy feeling that I was home if I'd let them. I couldn't. It had been months since I'd discovered the history of this land, and I still hadn't come to terms with my findings.

Hoping to bolster my waning interest in the house, I'd put painting and plumbing on hold and had plunged into a rejuvenation of the overgrown garden. It had taken less than a week to see I needed professional help. There were so many different species of plants that I couldn't tell a weed from a flower. Brush needed to be hauled off, trees had to be trimmed or removed. That's when I'd called on Eddie and Oliver to discuss what I wanted done.

I'd supplied them with pictures from gardening magazines of fancy stepping-stone paths, lattice arbors, arched bridges, statues, and a tire swing like the one I'd played on as a child. I wanted a secret garden where I could go to wile away a few spare minutes. I wanted beds of bright annuals that I could tend. I wanted well-kept trees and rosebushes bursting with color.

To my left, past the furthermost edge of my property, was a cottage. At one time it had been part of this estate, but when I'd bought the mansion and land, that piece of property had been excluded from the sale. The structure was empty. I'd made numerous offers to buy it, but so far my bids had been ignored.

I wanted that cottage because it would square out my holdings. But most of all, the cottage—with its vaulted ceilings, hardwood floors, and fireplace—would make an ideal chapel. By coupling the chapel with my garden plans, I hoped to replace the wickedness this land had once seen by holding weddings on my property.

I pulled my car into the garage and climbed from behind the steering wheel. Before I'd taken two steps, the door leading into the house opened, and DeeDee stuck out her head.

For the first time in what felt like hours, my lips spread into a genuine smile. Twenty-three years old, DeeDee was my housekeeper. Today she wore her dark hair straight to her shoulders. Her prominent eyes were brown. Her cheeks were rosy. I'd never had a child, but this young woman filled that void in my life. Overprotective, overindulgent parents had home-schooled her. By rights she should've been an obnoxious brat. She was caring, loyal, and when I'd needed her the most, she had always been there for me.

"W-what's w-wrong?" she stammered.

DeeDee's stuttering was the reason her parents had kept her out of public schools. They'd sheltered her to the point she'd almost stopped speaking when we first met. Elocution lessons and the responsibility of an entire household had built up her confidence. Her faltering speech was evident when she didn't concentrate on what she wanted to say or when she was excited or worried.

I had no intention of going over the events of my day before I'd stepped foot in the house, but her sharp brown-eyed stare had ripped away any attempt I'd made to appear composed.

I forced a cheerful note into my voice. "Nothing's wrong," I said. "I'm just tired."

"Nope. Won't f-fly."

I rolled my eyes as I brushed past her and into the house. She trailed me like a curious kitten, batting at my arm, imploring me to dump my worrisome load on her slender shoulders.

I hung my purse on the doorknob to the back staircase, then headed for the kitchen. With my head in the open refrigerator, I said, "Is there any more of that gazpacho left? Cold vegetable soup isn't my first choice, but I'm starved."

"I have f-fixed a v-very nice s-s-supper, B-B-retta."

DeeDee had discovered that she loved to cook. She watched the food channel on television, took note of the fabulous recipes, and turned them into low-cal treats that kept my weight stable.

DeeDee tugged on my sleeve. "Look."

I turned and followed the direction of her finger. Through the kitchen doorway I saw the dining room table set with my best china, crystal, and flatware. Sprigs of English ivy cascaded from a vase and twined over the burgundy linen tablecloth.

"Pretty fancy for us," I commented before counting the place settings. There were five. I closed the refrigerator door. "I'm not in the mood for company, DeeDee. I've had one helluva day. All I want is food, a hot bath, and a good book. Maybe then I can forget my—"

The doorbell rang.

DeeDee galloped away.

"Damn it. Damn it. Damn it!" I would've stomped my foot in frustration, but I recognized the voice coming from the foyer and mellowed out.

Avery Wheeler and I had met during the Christmas open house fiasco. A florist and a lawyer make a dubious team, but we'd pooled resources, escaped a harrowing experience, and carried between us a secret we'd sworn never to reveal.

I crossed the polished oak parquet floor and listened to him tease DeeDee. His tone was melodious. Once I was closer, I saw his eyes twinkle with humor. As his lips moved, the salt-and-pepper mustache under his bulbous nose twitched.

"—your cooking is only surpassed by your delightful company," he was saying to a blushing DeeDee. "My evening meal usually consists of lukewarm soup and a dry contract. I've anticipated this repast all afternoon." He touched DeeDee's hand, then turned to me. His bristly eyebrows shot up. "Oh," he said. "Been one of those days, has it?"

I grimaced. For those who know me well, there seems to be no area of privacy. The eyes are the mirror to the soul—or, as in my case, an invitation to invade my solitude. I waved a hand. "I'm fine. You're the first guest to arrive, but from the places set in the dining room it looks as if we have more to come."

DeeDee mumbled something that sounded like julienne and sauté. I watched her disappear through the kitchen doorway. "She's a real treat, Avery. The best thing to happen in my life in a long, long time." I turned to him. "So how have you been? When I left this morning there was no mention of a dinner party. What developed in the last few hours?"

Avery leaned heavily on his cane. "Might we have a seat? My old legs aren't as forgiving as they used to be."

"I'm sorry. Let's go into the library." I started to lead the way, then stopped when the doorbell chimed again. "This must be the second member of our dinner party."

Avery glanced at his watch and frowned. "Shouldn't be. I was to have at least thirty minutes alone with you."

"Why? What?"

The bell pealed again.

Sighing, I swiveled on my toe and headed for the door. Before I could reach for the knob, the oak panel swung open. My father stood on the veranda.

When he saw me, he threw out his arms and yelled, "Surprise!"

I looked past him and saw a cab parked at the end of the sidewalk. My heart sank. The driver was unloading what looked like a mountain of luggage.

Trying to keep my expression composed, I focused on my father. He was a handsome man in his seventies. His hair was thick and gray, his eyes blue. In his younger days he'd been lean and wiry. Age had added pounds, particularly around his middle. His joints were stiff, and sometimes he carried a walking stick, which wasn't evident at the moment.

"Gotcha, didn't I?" he said. "Bet you thought I'd mailed you another dust collector to set on a whatnot shelf." He awkwardly patted my shoulder. "Bretta, we can't rebuild our relationship with all those miles separating us. I've burned my bridges in Texas. I've come back to Missouri for good." He leaned close and whispered, "I've got plans. Big plans, and I'm fired up to put them into motion."

He directed the cabbie to set the suitcases in the foyer, then ignoring Avery, who was standing not more than five feet from us, took my hand and towed me toward the library.

I mouthed "Sorry" as we passed the old lawyer, then made an attempt to curtail my father's barrage. "Dad, please," I said, applying the brakes. "You're going too fast—both physically and mentally. Besides, I have another guest. When you were here at Christmas, you met Avery Wheeler. Avery, you remember my father, Albert McGinness?"

My father scarcely acknowledged the introduction. "I've kept my plans bottled up for the last two months." He dropped my hand and did a clumsy two-step jig. "We'll make a great team, Bretta. You have a way of attracting trouble, and I have a problem-solving mind. Look at all the money I made with that cattle-branding tool I invented. It's one of a kind, just like us. We'll sweep this town of its crime."

I shook my head. "What are you talking about?"

"You still don't get it?"

"Get what?"

"A detective agency." He frowned. "We have to get in sync if we're going to be a team. I'm having the sign painted." He swirled his hand in the air. "Can't you see it? McGinness and Solomon Detective Agency."

When he leaned closer, I sniffed to see if he'd had one too many on the flight from Texas. I wrinkled my nose. Garlic. Whew! I turned my head, but I didn't miss what he said.

"Fact is, I have our first case. You know that cottage at the edge of your property? Well, someone is there. When I talked to DeeDee earlier, she said it was empty. I thought I'd set up shop close by until I find an office downtown. Before I came to your house, I had the cabbie drive past the cottage, and there was a truck parked under the trees. It wasn't out in plain sight, but back where some bushes camouflaged it."

He paused for a breath, but he was far from finished. "It looked damned suspicious, Bretta. It's up to us to find out who it is and report him to the local authorities. It could be drugs. What better place to make a drop? It's out of the way. No close neighbors. And you're at work all day."

In his younger days my father had been a painter, a poet, and a freethinker. He was artistic and creative, and I'd attributed my design talents to him. As I watched him rub his hands together, already anticipating the notoriety that would surely come his way after nosing out this nefarious drug ring, I added another trait—wild imagination.

This wasn't a bad thing. My imagination had helped me solve some pretty tough cases, so there was a time and a place when it could be useful. Other times it hindered clear thinking. I was firmly grounded by my mother's no-nonsense upbringing. I eliminated the chaff from my father's mental fantasies, looking for the whole kernel of truth.

Out of the corner of my eye, I saw Avery glance at his watch. Two things struck me. Avery wanted thirty minutes alone with me before the next guest arrived. My father said someone was at the cottage. Professionally, Avery had complete control over that cottage, but so far neither he nor the owner would take my offer.

I met Avery's gaze, and his eyes shifted uneasily away from mine. Disappointment brought a lump to my throat. I'd never pressed him. Not once had I demanded a decision. There were hard feelings toward me from the owner, and I'd hoped that if I bided my time, those old wounds would heal. But that hadn't happened. My intention to be a good-hearted, understanding person was about to be flung in my face.

The doorbell rang. Anger replaced my frustration. I

crossed the foyer, but I didn't open the door. Instead, I turned my back to it so I could tell Avery just what I thought. From the look on his face, my words were unnecessary.

"I assume this is my new neighbor," I said. "You knew I wanted that land because it's part of the original tract. And now you expect me to make this tenant feel welcome? To sit at my table and eat my food?" I gulped. "Gosh, Avery, I didn't think my day could get much worse."

I swept open the door and gasped.

Bailey Monroe stood on my doorstep. Since I'd returned from Branson, he'd haunted my thoughts. I almost reached out a hand to touch him, to see if he was real, but I quickly checked that impulse. "Bailey?" I whispered. "What are you doing here?"

The glance he traded with Avery said it all. I'd coveted the land. I'd coveted the man. Now both were tied together in one neat package.

Chapter Five

Since I'd last seen Bailey it would've been heartening to learn I'd magnified his fine points, exaggerated his good looks. No such luck. Six feet, two inches of muscle. Eyes the color of unpolished copper. Dark hair feathered with gray at his temples. When his lips slid into a lazy smile, my body reacted in a disturbing manner.

Carl had been as comfy as my house slippers—cushy to my soul. Bailey was that pair of stiletto heels you admire in a store window. Common sense says not to buy them—don't even bother trying them on—but the allure was there.

Feeling the need to say something, I repeated, "What are you doing here?"

"Who won the floral contest in Branson?" he said.

My eyes narrowed. He and I'd had a couple of these rounds where I'd ask a question and he'd answer with another. This was a different time and place, so perhaps it was only a coincidence. I tested him. "Won't you come in?"

The well-mannered response could have been "Thank you, Bretta." Or "Lovely home, Bretta." Or "Nice to see you, Bretta."

Bailey said, "Will I be a bother?"

I couldn't resist. "Are you usually?"

Bailey brushed past me. "Have you heard something I haven't?"

I gritted my teeth but fought foolishly. "Is this conversation going somewhere?"

Bailey didn't pause. "Life is trying, isn't it?"

I gave up. "But not as trying as you."

Avery and my father gaped as if they'd viewed a complicated vaudeville skit and hadn't gotten the punch line. No way was I going to explain.

"Let's eat," I said, waving the men into the dining room. I headed for the kitchen, where I could catch my breath. DeeDee looked up from the pot she was scraping.

"Is everyone here?" She turned her question into an explanatory sentence. "Everyone is here."

"Ha, ha," I said, grabbing the platter of grilled pork chops. "We'll discuss your part in this calamity later."

"Th-there's nothing to d-discuss. Avery is your f-friend, and it isn't m-my p-place to d-deny your father a meal."

"And Bailey? Where does he fit in?"

DeeDee met my gaze. "Wherever you let him."

Dinner passed rather well with my father monopolizing the conversation, telling about his flight from Texas. Under Bailey's artful questioning, I along with everyone else learned that my father had sublet his condo, had sold his interest in the cattle-branding tool manufacturing company, and was here to stay. Where he was going to live brought us to the hot topic of the evening—Bailey's takeover of the gardener's cottage.

We had moved into the library and were sipping coffee. DeeDee clattered dishes in the kitchen. My father lounged in one of the wingback chairs; Avery occupied the other.

Bailey sat on the sofa with his arm flung across the upper cushion. If I were to sit, he'd either have to move his arm or I'd find it draped across my shoulders. I stayed where I was, which was across the room near the fireplace.

Avery twisted around to stare at me. "Bretta, come sit down. Let's get this situation ironed out."

I moved to the sofa and perched on the arm. "What's to iron out? Seems to me every wrinkle is permanently set."

Bailey chuckled softly.

I turned my cool gaze on him. "What's so funny?"

"You're bent out of shape, and you don't know the details."

"Are you living in the cottage?"

"Yes."

"Are you buying it?"

"The contract is signed."

"So it's a done deal. I don't need to hear the details because they won't make any difference."

Bailey sighed and stood up. "If that's the way you want it. Thanks for dinner. I'll see myself out." He strode from the room. His footsteps clunked across the foyer. The front door opened, then closed with a sharp snap.

"Well," I said, "I don't know why he's upset. I'm the one who's gotten the short end of this situation."

Avery drummed his fingers impatiently. "This hasn't worked at all the way I had planned." He shook his head at me. "Which would you rather have in that cottage? Bailey Monroe or Fedora's Feline Care and Grooming Center?"

"You had *my* offer."

"But the owner wasn't going to take it regardless of the amount. I've warned you not to get your hopes up over buying that piece of property, but you ignored me. She doesn't want you to have it, and she doesn't want any ties here. I was given orders to find a buyer. I had two offers at the stipulated amount."

Avery raised his hands with the palms turned up. He lifted his right hand. "Here is Bailey, a retired federal agent. He wants a quiet place to write a book on his twenty-odd years of work." He lowered his left hand. "Here we have Fedora. A nice lady, but a fanatic when it comes to cats. I visited her home and was appalled at how she let her pets have free rein."

His hands seesawed. "Quiet man. Cat woman. You weren't in the equation, Bretta. I made my decision, and it's the right one." He smoothed his collar, then settled back in his chair. "If you think about it, you'll see I've done you a tremendous favor. You're planning a garden. Do you want cats running amuck over your seedlings?"

I pursed my lips, then finally said, "I guess not. Did Bailey tell you we'd met before?"

Avery nodded. "That's why he was out this way. He was hunting your address and saw the cottage. His inquiries brought him to my office. That piece of property was going to someone, other than you, and as I see it, Bailey was the best choice."

My father hadn't asked for an explanation but had apparently caught the main theme of what was going on. "I'll offer five thousand over Monroe's deal. With my name on the deed, who'll know—"

"I will," said Avery. "It's over."

"But if I—"

"No. I don't operate in that manner." Avery heaved himself out of the chair. He nodded to my father. "It was a pleasure meeting you again," he said, though his huffy tone sent a different message.

Avery's expression softened when he turned to me. "I worry about you in this rambling old house with only DeeDee for company. Put that cottage out of your mind and concentrate on finishing the rooms upstairs. Your plan for a boardinghouse is sound. Stick to it. Diversification is the right step for some people. You have plenty on your plate with the flower shop and this house. Don't be led into more than you can handle."

He gave my father a sharp glance before moving toward the door. Of course, Avery was referring to the idea of my becoming a partner in a detective agency. At the moment that plan was the last thing on my mind. I was exhausted. The day had been an emotional roller coaster with monumental valleys and peaks.

"Did you know Oliver Terrell?" I asked Avery as I opened the front door.

"Yes. I heard he'd passed away." Avery's walrus mustache twitched. "I also heard you were there, and a short time later you discovered a body in a beauty shop."

"How come you didn't say something?"

"I had my own agenda for this evening. The last thing I needed was you reliving your disastrous day when I was about to pile more on top."

"Did you know Claire Alexander?"

"I go to a barber, not a beautician."

"What about a Mrs. Dearborne?"

Avery stroked his mustache. "Would that be Doreen, Sharon, or Lydia Dearborne?"

"I don't know. What about the name Spade?"

"I can't know everyone in River City. Why? Are these people connected to that alleged murder?"

"There's nothing alleged about it. Claire Alexander was

hit over the head, her nose and mouth filled with herbal foam so she'd suffocate."

Avery shuddered and stepped out into the warm night air. "I don't want to hear another word, Bretta. I need a good night's sleep."

He gave my arm a squeeze and warned me to keep my wits about me. I waited until he had his car started and was headed down the drive before I closed the door and went back into the library.

While I'd seen Avery out, my father had made himself comfortable on the sofa and fallen asleep. His snores were a sonorous accompaniment as I spread an afghan over him. I stared down at him and shook my head. What was he thinking when he'd concocted the foolish notion that I would want to be part of a detective agency? I enjoyed dabbling in solving mysteries, but to make it a day-in-and-day-out job wasn't of interest to me. Like Avery said, I had the flower shop, and I had this house and the garden—minus the cottage.

"Bailey." I breathed his name softly. He was so close and yet so far away, held at arm's length by my frustration and disappointment at not being able to buy the cottage.

Sighing, I gathered up the used coffee service and headed for the kitchen, where DeeDee was putting away the last of the dishes. "Here's some more," I said, setting the tray on the counter. "You can leave these things till morning, if you want. I'm going to bed."

"I heard Avery say you f-found a b-body today. W-whose was it?"

"Her name was Claire Alexander. She had a beauty shop located in the old section of town."

"Claire's Hair Lair? That's where my m-mother g-goes."

"You knew Claire?"

"N-not really."

"Does your mother have a friend by the name of Dearborne?"

"L-Lydia Dearborne."

I opened a drawer and took out the phone book. After flipping through the pages I saw a number of Dearbornes, but all were male. "Do you know her address?" DeeDee shook her head. "Could you call your mother and find out?"

"I-I guess." She glanced at the clock. "She'll be getting r-ready for bed."

I pressed. "It won't take a second. I'd like to have this information to give to the police."

Her tone was droll. "You don't think th-they can get it on th-their own?"

I gestured to the phone. "Please call."

Reluctantly, DeeDee did as I requested. Ten minutes later she replaced the receiver. Her slender shoulders slumped. Her head drooped with despair.

I'd eavesdropped the first few minutes, then busied myself washing up the coffee cups and saucers. I'd heard only one side of the conversation, but DeeDee's answers had clued me in. Her mother was being her usual annoying, overbearing self.

"I'm sorry, DeeDee," I said. "I keep thinking your mother will change. That she'll see how independent you've become, and stop being so domineering."

"W-won't h-happen, B-Bretta. I can take most of it until she asks if I'm w-wearing clean underw-wear. Then I l-lose it. L-Lydia lives on C-Catalpa R-Road. Out b-by that g-garden c-center. M-Mother can't recall the n-name."

DeeDee's stuttering was always worse after a conversation with her mother. I wanted to kick myself for putting her through— Garden center? There wasn't any garden center on Catalpa Road, but there had been a gardener.

Again I grabbed the phone book, although it wasn't necessary because I knew what I was going to find. Yes. There it was. "Terrell Oliver 18807 Catalpa Road." I flipped back to Dearborne. "Dearborne Harold 18809 Catalpa Road."

With this bit of trivia cluttering my brain, I said "Good night" and went upstairs to my room. So Oliver and Lydia were neighbors. How did that piece of the puzzle fit into the scheme of Claire's murder?

I tried to think about it after I was settled in bed, but I kept seeing Avery's blue-veined hands weighing his choice for the new owner of the cottage.

I dropped off to sleep with the image of those hands rising and dipping. But in my dream I removed Bailey and Fedora from the formula. Avery's hands were replaced by an old wooden teeter-totter. A faceless Mrs. Dearborne straddled one end of the plank, with Oliver balancing her weight at the other. They seesawed back and forth like a couple of kids at a playground. Then, like the zoom lens on a camera, I took a closer look at the middle support.

Mrs. Dearborne and Oliver were teetering over Claire Alexander's body. Claire's green hair grew like tentacles, twisting and tightening its hold over Oliver and Mrs. Dearborne. I reasoned this was a ridiculous dream. I had only to open my eyes and the horror would fade, but those slithering tendrils were mesmerizing, drawing me in.

Chapter Six

🌸 The ringing of a bell prompted swollen buds to emerge from the tendrils of Claire's hair. Another shrill ring and those buds burst into a multicolored display of blossoms. Like the painting on the ceiling of the beauty shop, the flowers flourished around the girl's head. Only this time the girl was Claire.

"Bretta? There's a c-call for you."

I came awake in a rush of confusion. Sunlight shone through my bedroom window. DeeDee stood in the hall doorway, motioning to the telephone on my nightstand.

"What time is it?" I asked, wiping the sleep from my eyes.

"Seven on S-Sunday morning."

I made a face and picked up the receiver. "This is Bretta."

"Why didn't you call me about Claire?"

I recognized Sonya's voice though it was rough with grief. Sitting up, I swung my legs over the edge of the mattress. "I'm sorry, Sonya, but I never thought—"

"I heard the news from Evelyn. She said you found the— uh—" She stopped and blew her nose. "I can't believe Claire is dead. We were like sisters, staying at each other's house, walking to school. I've let my business take over my life. She called a month ago to see if we could meet for lunch, but I've been booked up. I should have called her back, but I knew we'd be seeing each other as we worked on this Montgomery wedding. I thought it would help renew our friendship. Now it's too late."

"Do the others know?"

"I told them, and they're as shocked as I am. What happened? Was she robbed?"

"I don't know."

"How was she—uh—killed?"

I dodged her question. "Don't think about that. Think of the good times. Claire remembered them fondly or she wouldn't have recited that poem in the park. Something about Royals being on the make? Sounds like the male population back then didn't stand a chance against the four of you."

Sonya's tone was distressed. "I have work to do." She hung up.

I put down my receiver. I'd mentioned the poem because I'd wanted to divert her from asking about the murder—a subject I'd been warned not to discuss. But I'd also been curious. Sonya, Dana, and Kasey had all seemed bothered when Claire had recited it in the park. I wondered how the other women would respond to my referring to that poem now that Claire was dead.

I looked up Dana's number. She answered after several rings, sounding as if she had a severe head cold. When I identified myself she let me know she'd been crying nonstop, which accounted for her stuffy, nasal tone.

"Why Claire?" asked Dana. "She was good, kind, and generous. Did you know she spent her days off at local nursing homes washing and curling the residents' hair? Or that for the senior prom she styled the hair of any girl who couldn't afford a trip to a beauty shop?"

"No. I didn't know that. I'd never met Claire until yesterday at the park, but I could tell she had a sense of humor. That poem she recited was—uh—cute. Something about the Royals being on the make, wasn't it? Is that part of a school song or something?"

Dana gulped. "Why are you bringing that up?"

"Just curious, I guess. Claire must've had a reason. Perhaps good memories were associated with it?"

"She shouldn't have said it. I have to go. I have a—uh—cake in the oven." Dana hung up.

Next I looked up Kasey Vickers's phone number. When I dialed it, the line was busy. I got out of bed and made a trip to the bathroom. I washed my face, brushed my teeth, and wondered why I was exploring the reactions of three women about a poem that most likely didn't have any relevance on any level.

But if I didn't think about the poem, I'd have to think about my father's arrival and his plans for a detective agency. Or about Bailey's purchase of the cottage and his close proximity to my house and my life.

I wanted to know both men better, but I'd been thinking small doses, not the chug-a-lug portions I'd gotten. I'd hoped for a quiet talk with Bailey—a time of discovery—who he was, what he liked, how the past had shaped him into the man he was today.

As for my father, a lengthy and honest discussion was in order. After said discussion, I assumed he would go back to Texas, and I could digest the information at my leisure.

In my room, I plopped down on the bed and dialed Kasey's number again. This time she answered.

"This is Bretta Solomon. We met yesterday in the park."

"Oh. Hi."

Not a promising beginning. "You've heard about Claire?"

"Yes."

"I was wondering about that poem she—"

"Dana warned me that you might call. Drop it. She's dead. Everyone is dead." Kasey's voice hit a hysterical note. " 'Wherefore I abhor *myself*, and repent in dust and ashes.' " She slammed down the phone.

I hung up, rubbing my ear. "Whew," I breathed. "That woman has some serious issues." In fact, all three women seemed strangely moved by that simple poem.

I picked up a pencil and paper and tried to remember Claire's exact words. When I was finished, I studied what I'd written:

> You can boil me in oil.
> You can burn me at the stake.
> But a River City Royal
> Is always on the make.

The words seemed innocuous. The kind of song a kid might sing while skipping rope. What I needed was an impartial viewpoint. I picked up the phone once again, but this time I dialed Lois. She answered in a dull monotone.

"Are you all right?" I asked.

"Not really. Kayla and I had a terrible fight."

"Are you ready to discuss the problem?"

Lois sighed. "Out of fairness to my sister, I'd better talk to her first, but thanks."

"I won't bother you," I said quietly. "I'll see you in the morning—or if you need time off, just give me a call."

"Speaking of a call, why did you?"

"Forget it. We'll talk tomorrow."

Lois chuckled. "Go ahead, Bretta, tell me. Is it another detail about this wedding?"

"No. I haven't heard from Evelyn."

"That's a blessing. The Lord does work in mysterious ways."

"I think I had a Bible verse quoted to me this morning."

"It *is* Sunday."

"True." Then I spilled the whole tale.

When I'd finished, Lois clicked her tongue. "That's one helluva story. And the dream you had is frightening. I'm looking at my English ivy in a totally new light. It's growing awfully fast. The tendrils trail a good three feet. Maybe I should take it out of the house in case it has lethal tendencies."

"Not funny."

"I know, but I've learned that in the face of adversity, it's better to laugh than to bawl."

"I suppose so. But what about the poem? Don't you think it's odd that all three women seemed put off by my reciting a portion of it? Kasey was nearly hysterical." I gave Lois the gist of what I could remember of the verse Kasey had quoted. "Do you recognize it?"

" 'Ashes to ashes and dust to dust' is well known if you've attended a funeral, but you said Kasey said 'dust and ashes,' so I haven't a clue. As for the rest, my opinion is they're justifiably distressed. Their childhood friend has been murdered. That would freak anyone. Why are you harping on this poem business?"

"Harping?" I repeated. "Mmm. I guess I am, but it's easier to think about something distant than what's going on under my nose."

"And that would be?"

59

"I have a new neighbor and a houseguest. Bailey and my father."

Lois's tone brightened. "Wow. I hope Bailey is the houseguest, and while we're having this useless conversation he's in your shower washing away a night of passion."

"Useless conversation is right. I'm hanging up."

"I need details. I need juicy gossip. I need—"

"Bye, Lois. See you tomorrow." I dropped the receiver into place, cutting off her bawdy cackle.

Speaking of gossip. My hand hovered over the telephone. I wanted to call Mrs. Dearborne and ask a couple of questions, but I knew if Sid found out my goose would be fricasseed. Feeling as if I was leaving an important stone unturned, I dressed in a pair of jeans, sneakers, and a T-shirt.

My plans for the day involved puttering around the house. Makeup wasn't called for, but with Bailey nearby, I applied my weekday regimen of powder, blush, and mascara. I was combing my hair, grimacing at the nearly all-gray strands, when a chain saw roared to life outside.

I strode to the window to see what was going on. Eddie's truck was parked in the driveway. I craned my neck and caught a glimpse of him in the garden. Muttering under my breath, I left the bedroom and hurried down the back staircase.

He saw me as soon as I'd opened the terrace doors and stepped out onto the paving stones. His chin rose defiantly, but he kept sawing at an old apple tree we'd said needed removing. The chain saw's engine dipped and rose in pitch as the blade bit into the decaying wood.

From the terrace the main focal point of the garden was a concrete water lily pool. The water was long gone, but a crusty scum fringed the cement walls like a lace collar. I walked closer, but stayed well away from where Eddie worked. Four brick paths led to separate areas of the garden. The house was at my back—to the north. The east path ended in what had once been a formal setting with statuary, stone benches, and an abundance of perennial plantings. The west edge of the property was covered with dense-foliaged trees. Nothing much grew under them except ferns, astilbe, lily of the valley, and a few stubborn bleeding heart plants.

The section of the garden that set my creative juices flowing was where Eddie was working at clearing away the apple trees. Oliver had taken me beyond the rotting orchard to show me how the land gently sloped to a creek. We hadn't walked very far because of his heart problem, but through his eyes, I'd seen the possibilities. Before I'd talked to Oliver, the garden had looked like a mass of rampant-growing vegetation that could only be tamed by an experienced hand. Hearing the way Eddie gunned the chain saw, I wondered how knowledgeable his hands would be without Oliver to guide him.

The area below the terrace needed more brawn than brains to give it order. Rambling roses had grown unchecked for years. The thorny branches had caught weeds in a stranglehold, binding them together seamlessly like a woven cloth. Mingled among the dried thatch was a new growth of plants trying to make headway. It was in this area that I'd depended on Oliver for guidance.

I looked back at Eddie. He was bent over his task, ignoring me. As I watched, the final cut was made, and the tree crashed to the ground, reduced to a heap of brittle branches. Eddie hit the choke, and the chain saw spluttered and died.

Before I could say "Good morning," he spoke. "If you

don't want me here just say so, but I can't stay at home. Everyone is bringing food to the house." He grimaced. "As if a casserole is going to make Dad's passing any easier."

"People want to show their support. Taking food to a bereaved family is a gesture of love and respect."

He kicked the pile of wood. "I know it, but I don't have to like it. I need to work."

"Fine, but at some point you're going to have to deal with Oliver's death and the people affected by it."

Eddie's handsome jaw squared, and his blue eyes narrowed. "I don't need any lectures. I've already had my quota from my wife. Molly says I should be honored that Dad was so well liked." He grabbed a pitchfork and stacked the broken limbs. "This wood is too rotten to burn in your fireplace. The branches will have to be hauled off. Just another mindless job for me. I told Dad we should hire more people, expand our business. But he wanted to keep it in the family—a mom-and-pop operation. Mom is gone, and now Dad. Surprise. Surprise. Guess who's left?"

Eddie's attitude wasn't a good sign. Hurt or even anger would have been healthier. I didn't want Eddie to be bitter at Oliver's memory or his shortcomings. "Your father did what was right for him. Now you can do what you want."

"Oh, sure, like I have the capital to make major changes. Dad didn't have a business sense. When Mom was alive, she kept the books. She bid the jobs because Dad charged what he thought the customer could afford, not what the work was worth."

I faked a wide-eyed gaze of alarm. "You mean he didn't gouge people? He didn't take advantage of their ignorance? Gosh, Eddie, that's terrible."

"You don't get it. We're scrounging along. Dad was brilliant. He'd forgotten more facts about plants and shrubs and trees than I'll know in a lifetime. He could've cashed in on that knowledge, but he chose to be more of a handyman than a true landscaper."

Eddie leaned on the pitchfork. "He knew instinctively which plants were compatible, which ones needed shade, sun, more moisture or less. He wasted his talent. He could've been famous like those guys on PBS. He could've been rich."

"Let me get this straight. You think Oliver wasted his life because he wasn't on television or wasn't wealthy?"

Eddie didn't answer, but then I didn't give him much of a chance. "Your father was a sweet, generous man. You came here today, not because of the food that was being brought to your home, but because you couldn't stand hearing people tell you what a wonderful man your father was. You're resentful, Eddie, and probably jealous, too."

Eddie had a short fuse, and I was prepared to duck if he decided to throw that pitchfork. To my surprise, he blushed. "Yeah. I'm jealous of Dad's ability. I'm also mad because he should've placed a higher value on his talents and made people pay for his services."

I waved my arm, indicating our surroundings. "Who came up with the bid on my garden?"

"Me."

"According to what you're saying, I'm going to pay dearly for this work?"

"No. I wouldn't do that to you, Bretta."

I raised an eyebrow. "Really? And why is that?"

"Because it'll be a pleasure putting this area back to its original beauty. Dad said that in its heyday this estate was one of the most beautiful private gardens in Missouri. Once I get these trees cut and hauled out, I'll do a controlled burn to get rid of the thick layer of weeds and grass thatch that's been allowed to grow. Plants that have struggled to survive will be set free to reproduce and, I hope, to flourish."

He smiled. "Then I can get at the true spirit of this land. Taking advantage of what nature has lain out is what landscaping is all about. Once I get this useless vegetation out of the way, you won't believe the change."

"So you're doing this work because you want the satisfaction of a job well done and not just for the money?"

Eddie jerked around to stare at me. "Molly's good, but you get the gold star. You've made your point—loud and clear. Just for the record, I will make money on this project or I wouldn't be doing it. Dad would've done it for free."

"Oliver mentioned something along those lines to me, but I told him I could afford the bill."

Eddie rolled his eyes. "And that's *my* point."

He reached for the chain saw, but I forestalled his action. "Eddie, did the coroner rule Oliver's death was from natural causes?"

"Of course. Massive coronary." Pain flashed across his face. "I could have given Dad the entire bottle of pills and it wouldn't have made any difference."

I breathed a silent sigh of relief. I was sorry Oliver was gone, but if there had been a hint of foul play connected to his death it would have been devastating.

Eddie made another move toward the chain saw, but again I stopped him. "Before Oliver passed away, he looked up at me and said, 'Bretta ... Spade.' Did you hear him?"

"Nope. I had other things on my mind."

"What do you suppose he meant?"

Eddie lifted a muscular shoulder. "I don't know."

"Do you have his spade with you?"

"Yeah. It's in my truck."

"Can I see it?"

"Why? Do you think Dad was giving it to you?"

I could tell he didn't like that idea. "No. The spade is unequivocally yours, but I'd like to see it again."

Eddie strode across the garden to his truck and opened the passenger cab door. I hid a sad smile. For all of Eddie's tough talk, he'd given Oliver's spade a place of honor up front instead of rattling around in the truck's bed with the other garden implements.

I took the spade and stood it upright. It was about my height, coming almost to my shoulders. I ran my hands down the handle. Years of heavy use had refined the wood to a satiny sheen.

Eddie said, "I'm thinking I'll take the spade to the cemetery and use it to put the first scoop of dirt on Dad's grave." He glanced at me. "Do you think that's sappy?"

It took me a moment to find my voice. "No, Eddie, I think Oliver would have liked the idea."

"Dad did it whenever someone close to him passed away, so I guess he'd approve if I do it for him." Emotion made Eddie's voice husky. He tried to clear his throat, but tears filled his eyes.

Embarrassed, he grabbed the spade out of my hand and spun on his heel. His long strides took him back into the garden. After a few minutes, I heard the chain saw start up.

Oliver had said, "Just as the twig is bent, the tree's inclined." It was heartening that Eddie's grief hadn't killed his love for the work he and his father had shared. My garden project was the best thing for him right now.

I moved toward the house, leaving Eddie to vent his anger and frustration in the best way he knew how. I, on the other hand, wasn't sure what to do with my day. Slowly, I climbed the veranda steps, making plans, and eliminating each as uninteresting or uninspiring.

The front door was locked. I'd brought my hand up to press the doorbell when, from behind me, Bailey said, "Bretta, I'm gonna talk—and you're gonna listen."

Chapter Seven

I froze at the sound of Bailey's voice. I couldn't move, but my stomach lurched. My feelings for Bailey were confusing. I was upset that he owned the cottage, but the attraction I'd felt for him in Branson was as strong as ever. He'd come to River City looking for me. While this thought was exciting, it was also frightening. It meant that he was interested in me, interested enough to purchase a home that made him my closest neighbor.

Slowly I turned and faced him. He was dressed in blue jeans and a plain white T-shirt. Each time we'd met, I'd been impressed by his good looks. But it was more than his appearance that had kept him in my thoughts these last few weeks. He possessed an air of knowing what he wanted and having the ability to go after it. Nothing seemed to daunt him.

But he sure confused me. "Bailey," I said, "how nice to see you. Isn't this a beautiful morning?"

"I'm not playing that game."

I raised an eyebrow. "What game?"

"Twenty questions." He came up the walk and settled on the steps. Patting the space next to him, he said, "Sit here and listen. It's time to even the score."

"Even the score" sounded like revenge, and I wasn't in

the mood to match wits with him. Fact was, I'd probably be out of my depth before the first insult was hurled. And anyway, revenge for what?

"No thanks. I've got things to do." Before I could do the first—press the doorbell for admittance into my own home—Bailey grabbed my ankle.

"Nothing is more important than what I have to say."

The solemnity of his tone carried more weight than his hold on my ankle. After two years of doing as I pleased, coming and going as I saw fit, I didn't like being ordered about, especially on my own front porch. But curiosity has always been my downfall. I gave in as gracefully as an independent woman could.

"This better be good," I said, plopping down. I put four feet of porch between us. "And for the record, I didn't know there was a score to even."

Bailey, having gotten his way, relaxed and stretched his long legs out in front of him. He folded his arms across his chest. "Your mother's name was Lillie McGinness. Your father is Albert. He left you and your mother when you were eight years old. It wasn't until last Christmas that you renewed your relationship with him. You were brought up on a farm near a small town called Woodgrove. You never had children, but you were married for twenty-four years to Carl Solomon. He has a brother and a mother in Nashville, but you never see them. You own your own business—a flower shop. You have many friends, one of whom is the current sheriff of Spencer County. Sidney Hancock doesn't miss a chance to belittle your talents for meddling, but I think he has a high regard for you."

He cocked an eyebrow at me. "Shall I go on?"

Because of Bailey's career, I didn't question how he'd gotten this itemized account, but the *why* made me glare. "You forgot my weight and IQ."

Bailey chuckled. "I have it on good authority that I'd better not mention the former. As to the latter, I know from past experience that you're damned smart."

"Am I supposed to be impressed that you've taken the time to look into my background? Don't expect me to swoon from the attention. Frankly, it's an invasion of my privacy, and I don't like it."

"Ah, but that's where evening the score comes in. I know all these details about you. I'm ready to bring you up to speed on me."

To say I was interested was an understatement, but I played it cool. "I'm sure you've led a fabulous life."

Laughter rumbled in Bailey's throat. "Subtlety is definitely your style. You're a clever woman. I admire that." His tone grew serious. "I'm too impatient to fool with some convoluted male/female flirtation. I'm laying it on the line. I'm attracted to you. I came specifically to River City with you in mind. We had the beginnings of something special in Branson, but my job called me away. That part of my life is finished now. I'm ready to begin another."

His words made my skin prickle with excitement. What was he proposing? My pulse raced. He was free. I was free. We were of an age to do as we wished, and yet my upbringing reared its fundamentally moralistic head.

I couldn't leap into bed with this . . . this stranger, no matter how handsome and intriguing he was. Besides, I had all those ugly stretch marks that crisscrossed my body like a road map. Before I disrobed, I had to make sure the man I was with wouldn't take one look and run screaming from the room. My ego couldn't take such a beating. Neither could my heart.

But I was getting ahead of myself. Bailey had merely said he was attracted to me. "Just what are you suggesting?" I asked.

"How about a date? We can go to whatever restaurant you like. Or you can come to the cottage for dinner. I'm a good cook, though not too fancy. When my wife died, I had to learn my limitations the hard way."

"And this would be your first wife?"

Bailey smiled. "My one and only wife. That line I fed you in Branson about having three spouses was part of the plan to get information from you."

"As I remember, it didn't work particularly well."

"Depends on how you view the outcome. I'm here, and so are you. Dinner tonight? Say six thirty?"

He was rushing me. I wasn't sure how to take this sudden bout of honesty. I was suspicious, and my guard was up. Maybe everything he said was true, but what if he was in River City for a different reason? What if he wasn't retired from the DEA? What if he was feeding me another line?

He'd bought the cottage. I still hadn't gotten used to the idea that it would never be mine. But was the title of that piece of property more important than getting to know him?

I could tell him to dry up and blow away, but I'd wanted the chance to get to know him better. Here he was, offering me that chance. I'd be a fool not to take it. Or was I a fool for considering it?

Bailey said, "I can hear the wheels turning in your head. Are you willing to take a chance?"

I was startled at his use of the very same word I'd been thinking. "I . . . uh . . . guess dinner wouldn't be a bad idea."

His coppery eyes teased me. "Love your enthusiasm. I'll try to live up to your expectations."

I glanced sideways at him. "You have an advantage. You've had time to think this all out, but I haven't." Something had been nagging at me since he'd started this conversation. Now seemed a good time to check the degree of his candor. "I saw you yesterday—in the old part of town. I called out, but you walked away. What's the deal?"

"No mystery. I was taking a drive, looking over River City. I saw a crowd and stopped to see what was going on."

"How long have you known Claire Alexander?"

"Isn't that the name of the woman who was murdered?" Bailey's full lips turned down. "You're trolling for something, but I'm not biting."

He pushed up off the steps and stared at me. "I'll have dinner ready at six thirty. I can eat it alone or I can eat it with you. If you decide to come to the cottage, please leave your suspicions at the door. I've spent the last twenty-seven years screening every word I say. In my line of work, I had to be circumspect or it could mean my life or the life of my partner. I'm tired of it. Take me at face value, Bretta, or don't take me at all. The choice is yours."

With that, Bailey walked off. As I watched him go, I was mad, then I was sad, and finally I was resigned. The next move was mine, but thank goodness I had the rest of the day to make my decision.

Sundays are usually laid back, unless I have to go to the flower shop to do sympathy work for a Monday funeral. In the newspaper's area obituaries, I'd learned that Oliver's graveside service was to be Tuesday morning at ten o'clock. That left today free to do as I wished. It could have been pleasant except for two things—my father and Sid Hancock.

It was mid-morning when Sid arrived. I'd gone to the

garden to give Eddie a message from his wife, Molly. She thought it was time for him to come home, but first she wanted him to order the flowers for his father's casket. Eddie liked my idea of assorted foliages with just a few flowers. Once I'd seen him on his way, I went back into the house to find my father and Sid chatting in the library. Or rather Dad was chatting. Sid was doing a slow burn.

"—no such thing as a private investigator's license in Missouri." Dad delivered this bit of wisdom with a so-there attitude. "I'll locate office space, have business cards printed, and it's a done deal."

Sid heard my step in the doorway and swiveled around. "Well, if it isn't Ms. P.I. herself. Is it your goal in life to send me to an early grave?"

I smiled sweetly. "Right now my goal is food. DeeDee has refined her talent in the kitchen. How about scrambled eggs, sausage, and a biscuit topped with homemade strawberry preserves and a glob of butter?" I was in no mood to entertain Sid, but if his stomach were full, perhaps he'd be less inclined to be obnoxious.

"Trying a new tactic—stuffing my arteries with cholesterol and grease?" Sid grimaced. "Make that two biscuits and you've got yourself a victim."

I found DeeDee in the kitchen squeezing oranges for juice. When I told her there would be three for breakfast, her face lit up.

"Can do. I've got the b-biscuits in the oven. Won't take but a s-second to s-scramble more eggs." She flew into high gear, and I reluctantly went back to the library, where a stony silence greeted me.

I looked at my father. Our relationship was still at that "getting to know each other" stage. I was glad he was back in my life, but I wasn't sure I was ready to find him in my house each morning when I came downstairs. Opening my home to strangers, who were paying for their accommodations, would be easier than having a relative under my roof.

This morning my father wore a pair of mocha dress pants and a plaid sports shirt. His wavy gray hair gave him a distinguished look. The mulish gleam in his blue eyes gave me a bout of queasiness.

I settled next to him on the sofa but directed my comment to Sid. "Breakfast is on me, but it's gonna cost you. For the next half hour let's have pleasant conversation. No nasty remarks or harsh accusations." Out of the corner of my eye, I saw Dad open his mouth. I hurried on. "I know you have a reason for driving out here, but unless it's an emergency, it'll have to wait until we've eaten."

Sid struggled to hold in his usual caustic remarks. He finally muttered, "No emergency, but I never eat breakfast. I'll call this lunch."

And with that, the mood was set.

When DeeDee announced "B-brunch is s-served," in her most dignified manner, we filed silently into the dining room. To say this was a friendly occasion would be an out-and-out lie. Sid's business with me or his need for food must've been powerful because he behaved rather well. "Pass the jam" and "Anyone got dibs on that last sausage?" was hardly titillating conversation, but at least there was no open hostility at the table. At least not until Sid wiped his mouth and tossed the linen napkin on his grease-smeared plate.

"Thanks," he said, gesturing to the leftovers, which were scanty. He looked at my father. "You're excused. Close the door on your way out."

Dad bristled. "You, sir, may be a law enforcement officer,

but you don't know peanuts from pecans when it comes to getting information."

"And you don't know shit from Shinola. You'd better make sure you don't step out of line in my county. I'll be watching you so close you'll think you're casting a double shadow."

"Whoa," I said. My head wobbled back and forth as I stared at the two men. "Did I miss something? What's with you guys?"

Dad regally rose from his chair. "The sheriff and I understand each other, Bretta. When he arrived, I offered him our services in his latest case—the murder—but he tossed that offer back in my face."

"I never tossed nothing," said Sid. "I laughed. I thought he was joking. But hell no. He's having a sign painted. Haven't you heard that's the first qualification for going after a killer?" He turned a fierce glare on me. "Put an end to this nonsense, Bretta, but do it later. I want to go over your statement. I've got a couple of questions."

I gave my father a placating smile and nodded to the door. He took my suggestion, but he had the last word. "This is an election year. If we decide against the detective agency, perhaps I'll look into the sheriff's position." He swept Sid with a contemptuous stare. "The *qualifications* surely aren't too rigorous."

He walked quietly out of the room, pulling the door closed behind him. I shut my eyes, praying for a giant hole to open so I could painlessly disappear. The floor remained firmly in place, even as Sid noisily scraped his chair back from the table. I took a deep breath and faced him.

"Well," I said, not quite able to meet his gaze. "DeeDee's cooking skills have improved. She can caramelize with the best of them. She made a chiffon cake the other day that was—"

"Cut the food review. I want to hear again why you went to that beauty shop. Why did this Alexander woman call you? If you only met her that morning, why'd she pick you to confide in? Why didn't she call a crony?"

"Look, Sid, all I know for sure is what she said to me. I can draw conclusions, but you hate that. Right?"

"Right. Draw a couple anyway."

I couldn't hide my amazement. In the past Sid has over-emphasized that if I didn't know something to be God's own truth, I was to keep it to myself. Yet here he was inviting me to give him my theories. Maybe Bailey was right. Perhaps Sid did have a high regard for me. However, he hid it well behind a face flushed with anger.

He whirled his hand in a "get with it" motion. I settled in my chair and gave him my best uneducated guess.

"Claire made the comment that I have a reputation for getting to the bottom of suspicious doings. Yeah, yeah. Don't give me that look. You asked. Something was bothering her. At the park she made reference to a hot bit of gossip. She hoped Mrs. Dearborne would confirm what she suspected. If I were in your position, I'd ask Lydia Dearborne a few pointed questions."

"Been there, done that."

"What did she say?"

"A bunch of gobbledygook that's insignificant."

"How do you know that? You're still missing a big piece of the puzzle—the motive behind Claire's murder. Tell me what Lydia said, and maybe it'll trigger something."

Giving information wasn't easy for Sid. He acted as if he were choking on a chicken bone. He hacked a couple of times and consulted his notebook. "According to Lydia Dearborne, the topic of conversation while she got her hair done was nostalgia."

"Nostalgia for what?"

"A time when people were friendlier, when life wasn't so fast-paced."

"That's strange. I got the impression from what Claire said in the park that she had a particular subject in mind. There must have been more to their conversation."

"I wouldn't know. Lydia wasn't in the right frame of mind for doing any heavy-duty remembering. When I arrived at her house, she'd already heard about the murder. She'd called her doctor for a sedative, as well as a horde of relatives to hold her hand. It wasn't easy getting anything out of her. She kept saying she hadn't known Claire long, but she'd been a nice lady, though perhaps a trifle wild in her younger days."

"Maybe that's where the nostalgia comes in. Maybe they discussed some of Claire's adventures."

"The victim didn't have a record. I checked that."

"You saw Claire's hair and her contact lenses? Your average woman isn't prone to parading around town with green hair and strange eyes. When I see someone with a bunch of tattoos or body piercings, I always wonder what they're trying to compensate for in their lives. I didn't know Claire. Does she have a husband? Children?"

"Five ex-husbands, but no kids."

Now I understood Kasey's remark about Claire's track record. "That's interesting. Are the men still in town?"

"Nope. All are out of state except one, and he's serving time for criminal assault and armed robbery."

"What number was he?"

"Five."

I sighed. "None of this is helping, is it?"

"Nope." Sid came slowly to his feet.

I followed his lead and walked toward the dining room door. "I'll keep thinking on it. Can I talk to Lydia?"

Sid made a face. "You know where she lives?"

I nodded and would have opened the door, but he put a hand on the wooden panel.

"One more thing," he said softly. "Keep that father of yours in check. If you get the chance, send him back to Texas. He's a rich, bored old fart out to impress his daughter. That's a bad combination. He informed me that he's been a subscriber to the *River City Daily* newspaper since he left Missouri. Your snooping has made the front page, and he's aware of your . . . uh . . . luck."

Sid shrugged. "Poke around. Ask your questions, but keep me informed. Don't make me look bad. I want another term as sheriff in this county."

Abruptly, he opened the door, and my father nearly tumbled into the room. Dad recovered with aplomb.

Sid scowled. "This is the kind of crap I'm talking about," he said, stomping past my father. Sid crossed the foyer, but before he opened the front door, he looked over his shoulder at me. "Do what you gotta do." He slammed the door with such force the windows shimmied in their frames.

Dad harrumphed. "That man has the personality of a rock and the manners of an alley cat."

"Dad, we have to talk." I led the way to the library, and once we were seated, I said, "You can't antagonize people because you think you're helping me. They're my friends. Offering to top Bailey's bid for the cottage was very kind, but it was offensive to Avery. He has too much integrity to make what would've amounted to an underhanded deal."

"But you were disappointed about that cottage, and so was I. It would have worked as a wonderful location for our detect—"

I had to put a stop to this once and for all. "There isn't going to be a detective agency, Dad. At least none that will have my name attached to it. And I'd rather you didn't do it, either."

"Figured you was going to say that. You've let the sheriff bully you."

I perched on the edge of my chair. "No. Regardless of what Sid says, I'm my own woman. I make up my own mind, and I don't want any part of an agency. Besides, I have the flower shop. I love my work. There isn't room in my life for another vocation."

"Or room for me?" he asked in a morose tone.

"There's plenty of room for you in this old house."

He gave me a sad smile. "That isn't what I meant, and you know it."

He wanted reassurance from me, but I couldn't say the words. To lighten the mood, I said, "I can stir up enough trouble on my own. I don't think this town could handle the two of us."

He waved his hand to our surroundings. "I can't sit around here all day. I have to do something."

He was used to leading an active life, and besides, if he were busy he'd be out of my hair. I thought a moment. "How do you feel about overseeing the renovations of the rooms upstairs?" When he perked up, I added, "Let's take a tour, and I'll point out some of the things I want done. I have the names of some contractors, and you can—"

The phone rang, interrupting us. I said, "DeeDee, I'll get it." I stepped across the room and picked up the receiver. "Hello?"

A male voice edged with impatience asked, "You the one who found Claire?"

"I beg your pardon?"

"I said, are you the one who found Claire's body?"

"Who is this?"

"A simple yes or no," he said sharply.

"I'm not answering your question."

A deep, rough chuckle sent shivers down my spine. "I'll take that as a yes," he said. "So you're the florist. Maybe I should send flowers to her funeral. Didn't send them when she was alive, but what the hell? How much would a dandelion cost?"

"I don't know who you are, but I'm hanging—"

"Don't bother, lady. Claire was scared. Looks like she had good reason. History has a way of biting you in the ass. Everything can't be saved. It became extinct just like she is."

His laughter was cut off as he hung up the phone. I pressed the disconnect button, released it, and got a dial tone. I hit the numbers for the return call option. A recording identified the number as coming from within the state penitentiary at Jefferson City.

Sid had said one of Claire's husbands was serving time. I'd just been reach-out-and-touched by a man convicted of criminal assault and armed robbery.

Chapter Eight

I hedged my father's questions by saying the caller had been a newspaper reporter. He accepted this explanation dubiously before I switched his focus back to the house.

"I'm proud of the downstairs, Dad, but whenever I think about all the hard work and the headaches I had to go through, I lose interest in finishing the upstairs. When this house was originally built it didn't have the garages or the servants' wing. DeeDee is happy in her rooms next to the kitchen. I have the master bedroom, which is in fair condition, but the rest of the upstairs is in need of some heavy-duty work. Plastering, painting, cleaning, and of course, installing a couple of extra bathrooms." I sighed. "There are so many details that need attention."

"I'll have plenty of time. Where do you want to start?"

A balcony circled the upper floor with each of the seven bedrooms opening off it. I gestured for my father to take his pick, and trailed along behind him. My mind wasn't on the virtues of wallpaper versus paint, or if the hardwood floors under the old carpets would be worth refinishing. All I could think about was Claire's death.

From what Sid had said, I wanted to give Lydia Dearborne another day to recover. Perhaps by then the sedative the doctor had prescribed would have worn off and her relatives would have moved on.

Dad opened the door to the room that held the most potential. I'd dubbed it the Mistress Suite after its former resident.

"You should get a nice price for this room," he said, looking around. "It has its own bath, and this little sitting area is a good addition. It's larger than your room, daughter; don't you want it?"

Daughter? I frowned. Addressing me as such seemed rather formal, but his tone was kind, almost tender. "No. I like being able to see the front drive as well as the garden from my windows."

"I'd like to name each room. You know, the Green Room, Blue Room, but more inventive. Otherwise, we'll have to identify them by number, and that seems too much like a hotel."

"Good idea," I said absently. Who could I talk to about Claire? Dana was my most likely candidate. She'd always struck me as being gabby. I broke into Dad's commentary on the wonders of polyurethane. "I have to run an errand."

His face creased with a frown. "I thought we were going to make plans."

"Write down your ideas, and we'll go over them later. I won't be gone long."

"I could go with you, and we'll talk in the car."

"That would be nice, but you need time to get a feel for each room."

"True. True," he said, eyeing a crack in the ceiling like a doctor contemplating a seriously ill patient. "We've got a tough road ahead of us. These cracks could stem from a structural difficulty. A quick cosmetic cover-up will only hide the problem. What we want is long-term repairs."

He patted my shoulder awkwardly. "If that's the case, we're looking at a hefty chunk of cash. It's a good thing your old dad is here."

He looked at me expectantly, but again I couldn't say what he wanted to hear. So I teased him. "You'll have so much to oversee, you'll wish you were still in Texas."

"Won't happen, daughter." He rubbed his hands together briskly. "You go do your thing, and I'll do mine. I have to hunt up a measuring tape and some paper and a pencil."

"DeeDee can get whatever you need. I'll see you later."

I hurried downstairs, stopping in the kitchen to give DeeDee a brief explanation as to what my father was up to. "Keep an eye on him. I don't want him climbing any ladders." I took off down the hall.

From the kitchen doorway, DeeDee called after me. "Who's k-keeping an eye on you?"

I halted my retreat. "What's that supposed to mean?"

"I've s-seen that look. You might as w-well have a sh-shovel in your h-hand. You're d-digging for information on that m-murder."

Shovel—Spade.

Digging? Was that what Oliver had been trying to tell me? That I needed to dig for information? Claire had been murdered *after* Oliver had passed away. What had been on the dying man's mind?

"I'll see you later," I said, going out the door.

Dana lived on Mossy Avenue. I hadn't taken time to look up a house number, but I hoped her catering van would be parked in plain sight at the curb. Luck was with me. The van was in the garage, but the door was up. On the concrete pad, a man tinkered with a lawn mower. I parked and got out of my car.

"Hi," I said, coming up the drive. "Is Dana home?"

"She's in the kitchen. Go around back and knock on the door. Step light," he warned. "She has cakes in the oven."

I nodded and took the well-worn path around the side of the garage. I lifted the gate latch on a chain-link fence and stepped into the backyard. The front of the house had been bland, without personality. Here the place came alive. An aboveground pool dominated the area with a number of brightly colored deck chairs that invited a relaxing break from a hectic schedule. A gas grill stood near a picnic table covered with a red-checkered cloth. A couple of glasses and an almost empty pitcher of what looked like lemonade had attracted a swarm of insects. Flies buzzed happily as they sipped the nectar. The air smelled of grilled meat, chlorine, and some profound baking going on nearby.

I rapped on the screen door.

"You don't have to knock, Jonah," said Dana over her shoulder. "Just don't come clopping in here and make my cakes fail."

"It's me, Dana."

She whirled from the sink, soapsuds dripping off her hands. "Bretta? You startled me." She tiptoed across the floor and opened the door. "Come in, but walk easy. I've got my first batch of wedding cakes in the oven."

"Getting a head start?"

"With so much to do, I have to. Once these have cooled, I'll freeze them. No one will know they're eating week-old cake." A look of horror crossed her plump face. "Don't tell Evelyn. If she knows I'm doing this, she'll throw a fit. I'll be baking the day before the ceremony."

"My lips are sealed."

She pointed to a chair. "Have a seat. I can use a break. I'll fix us a glass of lemonade." She glanced out the window at the picnic table. "Oops. I forgot to bring in the pitcher. How about iced tea instead?"

"Don't go to any trouble. I'm not staying long."

Dana bustled around, brewing tea, filling two glasses with ice cubes. The legs of her blue jeans were dusted with flour, and her face was flushed from the heat that radiated from the dual stack ovens. The kitchen had been remodeled to accommodate her catering business. The refrigerator was monstrous. Mixing bowls were oversized, as were the pots and kettles that hung from hooks above an island.

By leaning back in my chair I could see into a formal living room that impressed me as being more froufrou than comfortable. The furniture was Queen Anne chairs and a sofa that looked as inviting as an oak log. Table lamps had shades trimmed in beaded fringe. The farthest corner caught my eye. A megaphone imprinted with the River City Royals' logo sat on a shelf. Near it were framed snapshots of Dana in a cheerleader's uniform. Blue and gold pompoms clashed with the room's formal decor, so I assumed this corner meant more to her than maintaining a fashionable theme.

"I thought my daughter and her family were coming for dinner," said Dana, "but Kyle, her youngest, has the sniffles, so it was just me and Jonah. I put steaks on the grill. It's an easy meal, and his favorite. He'll mow the yard, and I can clean up my mess. Tomorrow I'll bake another batch of cakes. And the next day another. By Wednesday, I should have them done, and I'll start on the main course menu."

She glanced at the refrigerator. "The shrimp arrived by special courier yesterday. I've cleaned them, and they're marinating. I'll drain them this evening and put them in the freezer." She shook her head. "Evelyn wants me to deep-fry them at the park. She's even brought me a special cooker. Everything has to be freshly prepared. I've never seen anything like it, or her, for that matter."

"She has specific ideas, that's for sure."

"What about the flowers? Can you do any early preparations?"

"Not a lot. We'll have the containers ready by cutting the floral foam to size. The bows for the corsages are made. But working with flowers is like working with food. Both are perishable, and it's the last-minute rush that's a *killer*."

It was a sly way to introduce the subject of my visit, and I hoped it would jar Dana's preoccupation with the wedding. The word had the desired effect. Apparently, Claire's death wasn't far from her thoughts. Dana's hand trembled as she set my glass of tea on the table. Liquid slopped over the rim.

She grabbed a paper towel to mop up the spill. "I still can't believe Claire's dead. If she'd been sick—"

"But she wasn't."

Dana pulled out a chair and sat down. "Maybe it was a random killing," she offered hopefully. "The paper didn't mention a motive."

"It's a safe bet she was killed for a reason. She knew something. You heard her in the park. She had a 'hot piece of gossip' she wanted confirmed. How many people do you think she teased like that?"

Dana propped her elbow on the table and cupped her chin. "Knowing Claire, it could have been her entire clientele or no one. When I saw her green hair, I should have suspected something was going on."

"Because it was green?"

"Not so much the color but that her hair had been changed. If Claire was upset or out to prove a point, she'd try a new style, but I've never known her to go for weird colors."

"Do you think the green was significant?"

"I doubt it. This hair business goes back to when we were sophomores in high school. Claire had the most beautiful auburn hair. It hung to her waist in gorgeous waves. When she discovered girls weren't allowed to take shop class, and boys weren't allowed to take home ec, she went to the administration and told them they were discriminating. According to Claire, young men needed to know how to cook and sew on a button. Young women needed to know how to change a tire, use a hammer, or anything else that would make them self-sufficient."

"That's sensible. Did she win them over?"

"No, and Claire was furious. In retaliation she whacked off her hair and took to wearing boys' jeans. From the back she looked like a guy."

"And how was this supposed to help convince the administration to change their school policy?"

"Remember, I'm talking about the sixties. Radical actions were the order of the day. Free love was the rage, along with bell-bottom trousers, miniskirts, and Beatles' haircuts. On a more dramatic note, we had the Vietnam conflict, riots, and demonstrations. Acid, not antacid, was in heavy use, and yet we were a naive society. We still thought we could save the world."

"I suppose that's true. I was about eight or ten, but I remember the hype. Save the rain forests. Save the whales. Feminist groups. Power to the people. Flower power." I grinned at Dana. "I must have been influenced even at that tender age." I expected her to give me an answering smile, but she stumbled to her feet.

"My cakes are about ready to come out of the oven."

As if on cue, the buzzer sounded. She waited for me to move, and when I didn't, she stepped to the ovens. She turned off the timer, twisted a couple of dials, and then opened the doors. A rush of hot, vanilla-flavored air wafted out.

Instead of reaching for a hot pad, Dana faced me. "I have work to do. You'll have to excuse me."

"Had you talked to Claire recently?"

"Just on the phone, the night before I saw her in the park."

"And she didn't say anything about knowing something that might have devastating results?"

"If she had, I'd have warned her to be careful. Claire wasn't always cautious. She wanted to right wrongs, to compensate for any injustice, and she was good at it. She had this built-in radar. She instinctively zoned in on wickedness."

"Her radar must have hit a snafu on the day she was murdered. Or maybe she thought she had the upper hand?"

Dana's face crumpled. "Please. I don't want to think about Claire anymore. I just want to do my part of this wedding and have it over."

I could relate to that. I stood up. "Did you know any of Claire's husbands?"

"Just Howie. He's in prison."

"Howie Alexander?"

"Oh no. Claire always took back her maiden name after each of her divorces. Howie's last name is Mitchell. His mother is my granddaughter's Girl Scout leader."

Mrs. Mitchell. The name was another thread in the tapestry of people who had a connection to Claire. I thanked

Dana for the iced tea and left the house. I drove to the flower shop, where a quick hunt in the phone book revealed eight River City residents with the name Mitchell. I dialed the first three numbers without success but hit a bull's-eye on number four.

"Mrs. Mitchell?" I asked hopefully. "Are you a Girl Scout leader?"

"Yes, I am. What can I help you with?"

"My name is Bretta Solomon. We've never met, but I'd like to stop by your house and talk with you."

"Is this about one of my Scouts?"

"No, ma'am." She sounded nice, and I wasn't going to lie. "Your son, Howie, called me today. He said some rather . . . uh . . . unpleasant things."

Her voice trembled. "My son is thirty-seven years old. I'm not responsible for his actions or what comes out of his mouth."

"I understand, but I'd still like to speak with you. I can be there in about five minutes."

Mrs. Mitchell's tone lacked enthusiasm. "Very well. You have my address?"

I told her I did, and we hung up. Before I left the flower shop, I grabbed a bouquet from the cooler. I'd made the arrangement several days ago and had included three lavender roses. The blooms were past the bud stage, which meant salability was chancy at best. But the roses still had a wonderful fragrance. Since I have a hard time tossing discards into the Dumpster, I hoped Mrs. Mitchell would appreciate the unexpected gift, and cooperate.

What I wanted from her still wasn't clear in my mind when I rang her doorbell some eight minutes later. The house was small—a two-bedroom bungalow dating back to the early fifties. The windows next to the porch were open. A breeze filled the lacy curtains. When they billowed away from the screen, I got the impression of a tidy living room with several silk arrangements and a floral-patterned sofa.

Good, she likes flowers, I thought to myself as I pressed the bell again. This time the chimes set off a riotous barking from inside. The timbre wasn't the annoying *yip-yip* of a lapdog but a deep *woof-woof* that carried the threat of bodily harm.

I shuffled my feet. I'd done enough delivering for the shop to have an aversion to house dogs. Most guarded their property with aggression. Lew kept a big stick in the van and carried pepper spray with him at all times. I had neither.

The door opened a crack. A pair of brown eyes peered at me through the screen door.

"Mrs. Mitchell?" I shouted above the din. From what I could see of her, she was about my height with dyed brown hair and exaggerated penciled eyebrows. One was arched higher than the other, giving her a perpetual look of skepticism.

She nodded primly, then turned and bellowed, "Down, Aristotle. Stop that racket or I won't give you a puppy morsel."

Puppy? The dog sounded like a mammoth canine with years of experience ripping flesh from bones. Instead of quieting the animal, her command provoked him. He hit the wooden door panel with a solid thud. The impact slammed the door in my face. I should've taken it as an omen to leave. I leaned closer to the windows, listening to Mrs. Mitchell admonish her pet for having "a nasty temper tantrum."

After another moment, she wrestled the door open to a six-inch gap. "I'm sorry. I don't understand what's wrong with him. He usually isn't so—" She saw the flowers in my hand. "Oh. That's the problem. He hates anything with a floral scent. Goes positively berserk when he smells roses."

Raising my voice, I said, "I'll put the flowers in my car."

"But you'll still have their scent on you. I can't wear perfume. I can't spray a room deodorizer, but he's as docile as you please when we go for a"—she quickly spelled—"w-a-l-k."

The barking had quieted, but deep menacing growls raised the hairs on my neck. "I'd really like to speak with you. Could you step outside for a minute or two?"

She glanced down. "I don't know. He seems quieter now. I can try."

She opened the wooden panel farther, giving me my first glimpse of the dog. His black-and-brown head was massive. His eyes were filled with evil intent. Lips curled back to expose fangs that dripped doggie drool. While I gave him a quick appraisal, he did the same to me. His expression seemed to say, "A snack is only a screen door away."

I shuffled the bouquet behind my back, then checked to see if he was fooled. Aristotle took a step closer and dropped to a crouch. I tore my gaze away from him and suggested to Mrs. Mitchell that we go to a restaurant. I added my own personal incentive: "I'd be glad to buy you a cup of coffee and a piece of pie."

Her eyes brightened at my suggestion. "I don't get invited to go out—"

The moment she said "out" Aristotle leaped at the screen. My high-pitched squawk of alarm intensified to an unadulterated scream of terror. The flimsy screen gave way. Aristotle's head and shoulders were suddenly on my side of the door. Snapping and snarling, he lunged, trying to widen the opening. His sharp toenails scratched and clawed the aluminum panel. He wanted a piece of me, and I wasn't about to accommodate.

I heaved the bouquet, hit him square on the head, and ran lickity-split to my car. I didn't have the notion that I was being chased, and once I had the door open, I glared at the house. Aristotle had made his escape, but he'd lost interest in me. He chomped on the flowers like they were a carcass to be devoured. Mrs. Mitchell stared down at her pet, shaking her head.

She looked so forlorn I was moved to say, "I'm sorry."

"So am I." She gestured to the dog. "He's named after the Greek philosopher Aristotle, who believed that reason and logic are what separates humans from animals. My pet has a high intelligence, and if my son hadn't mistreated him, I think I could have taught him rudimentary logic."

"Mistreated him how?"

"Howie doused Aristotle with perfume, then tied him to a rosebush without food or water. I was gone for three days. By the time I got home, Aristotle was dehydrated and almost starved. The chain had gotten tangled with the brambles, driving the thorns into his skin. That happened five years ago, but if I run my hand over his shoulders, I can still feel the scars under his fur."

"That's terrible," I said, staring at the dog with newfound understanding. If Aristotle had gone after his human tormentor with the same malice as shown him, he'd have been put to sleep. With no other recourse, the dog had sought revenge by transferring his hate to an inanimate object—the rose.

Mrs. Mitchell said, "That emotional trauma rules his life. When he smells any floral scent, he proves his namesake's theory. Logic and reason are beyond his capabilities."

I might have sympathy for the dog, but not an all-out forgiveness for his scaring me half to death. I ducked to get into my car, but Mrs. Mitchell's next words stopped me.

"I don't know what Howie said to you. It wouldn't matter if I did. I can't explain him. I've often thought my being involved in Scouts should've given me a special wisdom when dealing with youths, but that could be hubris."

"Hubris?"

"Excessive pride." Pain twisted her face. "I'm no psychologist, but I've had plenty of experience studying adolescent emotions and behavior. Even so, I couldn't help my own son."

I leaned on my car, staring across the rooftop at her. "What was Claire like?"

"Needy."

"In what way?"

"All ways. Claire followed her desires against reason and more often without logical forethought. Her marriage to my son is ample proof of that. But in the last few months I'd noticed a change. Everyone wants to feel special, unique. Claire dyed her hair and wore those strange contacts. Everyone wants a sense of being useful. She lavished attention on anyone who walked through the doors of her beauty shop. She donated her time and talents wherever they were required. Everyone needs to feel an emotional bond. We need to have a sense of belonging in this world."

Mrs. Mitchell shook her head sadly. "From what I understand, Claire's earlier years were spent eliciting attention. What she got was a reputation for being a rabble-rouser."

Aristotle had finished massacring the flowers. He stepped to the edge of the porch and stared at me.

Mrs. Mitchell grabbed his collar. "You'd better go."

I didn't have to be told twice.

As I drove away, I looked in my rearview mirror. Amid the flower stems, petals, and chunks of floral foam at her feet, Mrs. Mitchell hunkered down to the dog, her arms wrapped around his neck. Aristotle's thick pink tongue slurped her face with adoring kisses.

I might have smiled. On the surface it was a charming picture—a woman and her faithful companion. I shook my head and pressed on the accelerator. Aristotle wasn't the only one in that household who carried emotional scars.

Chapter Nine

I drove up my driveway, keeping my eyes straight ahead. I would not look over at the cottage. It wasn't any of my business if Bailey was home. Besides, I'd know soon enough if I decided to join him for dinner.

If? Who was I kidding?

Since I'd met him in Branson, I'd tried picturing him going about his daily life, but it was hard forming a mental image when I didn't have a shred of information. Would we have things in common? Did he listen to the radio while he drove? Were the lyrics important to him—that unique phrase that can strike a chord, bring forth a passionate thought? Was he a sports fanatic? Did he like walks in the woods? Was he content to lean against a tree to marvel at nature?

I knew the cottage and could imagine him in this setting. The vaulted ceiling with its rough-hewn beams seemed like it might suit him, as did, perhaps, the multicolored braided rug on the glossy hardwood floor. Would he use the fireplace? Or see the necessity to cut wood and clean ashes from the hearth as a tasteless chore?

I had hundreds of questions, and if I'd understood Bailey correctly, he was willing to answer them. Anticipation made my stomach quiver. I felt as giddy as a schoolgirl about to go on her first date.

What was I going to wear? My weight had stabilized, but only because I was prudent and DeeDee cared enough about me to not keep high-calorie snacks under my nose. It wasn't a blue jeans evening, but nothing too dressy. I had that pair of black slacks. I could top them with a shirt and my favorite vest. Catching sight of my expression in the rearview mirror replaced my enthusiasm with guilt.

"I'm sorry, Carl," I said as I pulled into the garage. I shouldn't feel guilty. I hadn't gone looking for someone. I still wasn't sure I was doing the right thing, but spending one evening with Bailey was an opportunity I didn't want to pass up.

I'd been gone from home longer than I'd planned. Had my father found something to occupy his time? In the hallway, I stopped. White particles danced and swirled, cloaking the air like a fine mist. At first I thought it was smoke. I sniffed, but only smelled something cooking in the kitchen.

A crash from above brought my head up. I charged into action when my father yelled, "Stand back! There's more gonna fall!"

"What's going to fall?" I demanded as I took the stairs two at a time. I was about halfway up the steps when another loud crash rocked the house.

On the second floor the dust was like a fog. "Dad? DeeDee? Where is everyone?"

"Bretta?" answered my father, stepping into the hall from the Mistress Suite. An embroidered dresser scarf was tied over his mouth and nose. He carried a fine ebony walking stick topped by a pewter knob. He brandished the staff like a classy bandit about to rob me.

"You hadn't been gone fifteen minutes when I discovered we've got one hell of a problem. But I've remedied it. That wasn't just an ordinary crack in the ceiling, daughter. I poked at it with my stick, and a huge chunk of plaster fell. It hit the light fixture, and we had fireworks. Sparks were shooting out like it was the Fourth of July. DeeDee replaced the blown fuse. She's a smart young woman. Can't figure out how she knew what to do, but she did it. While I caught my breath, we did some evaluating over diet-style slices of key lime pie. When we came back upstairs I put in a new bulb, and everything is in working order."

I went past him, but stopped at the doorway. DeeDee was on the far side of the room. Her eyes were like two pee holes in the snow. I couldn't speak, but stared in utter confusion at the chaos.

Three quarters of the ceiling had been reduced to rubble on the floor. The falling pieces of plaster had hit a lamp, and it lay smashed. A curtain had been ripped from the window. A marble-topped table had one corner broken. But what rocked me back on my heels was the dust. I could feel it in my nose, my eyes, and my mouth. The white grit sifted over everything, coating the interior of the house as effectively as pollen stuck to a bee's belly.

My gaze traveled from the floor to the twelve-foot-high ceiling. "How did you get up there?" I asked.

"DeeDee said you don't have a ladder—which is on my list to buy—so I improvised." Dad rapped his knuckles on a wooden highboy. "They don't make furniture like this anymore. I used the open drawers for steps and climbed up."

He stared at the ceiling with a small smile, as if reliving some great adventure. "Just before you arrived, I knocked down the rest of the ceiling. That corner over there is being stubborn, but I'll get it. We'll have this fixed in no time."

My temperature shot to a dangerous level. Three quick thoughts—He's an old man; he's trying to help; he's my father—kept me from combusting. "We'd better get this cleaned up," I said, trying not to clench my teeth.

"H-he meant w-well," said DeeDee, picking her way across the floor. "I'll go get some cardboard b-boxes from the g-garage."

"I know this is upsetting, Bretta," said Dad, "but you have to tear down before you can fix up. I remember the time we papered the living room at the farmhouse. We had to peel off eight or ten layers of old stuff before we could put on the new." He chuckled weakly. "Off with the old. On with the new."

"But I didn't plan to do any major plastering. The contractor had spotted the crack and said he'd take care of it."

"You didn't mention that."

"I didn't know you were going to poke it."

"True. True. We're both at fault."

I nearly choked. "Let's not talk. Breathing this dust can't be healthy."

My father gestured to the cloth that covered his face. "Shall I find you a mask?" Using the toe of his shoe, he rooted in the debris. "Seems like I saw another one of these doohickeys on a table."

"Here comes DeeDee with the boxes." She handed me a large carton, and I picked up pieces of plaster. My father continued a running review on his afternoon. I let his words flow around me, but I didn't pay any particular attention.

I filled one box, left it sitting where it was, and then filled another and another. We were making headway, but the bulging cartons were in the way. I bent to heft one and groaned. I couldn't budge it. DeeDee was trying to drag a box across the carpet.

I straightened, rubbing my back. "We've done all we can. I'll have to call in a cleaning company. Even if we got these cartons downstairs, I don't know what I'd do with them." I waved a hand. "Let's call it quits. I need to shower and change. I have a dinner date at six thirty."

"You do?" said Dad. "I thought we'd spend the evening together."

It wasn't an unreasonable idea, but I wanted to wail like a banshee at the added pressure. He expected me to conform to his agenda, and I had my own. Even when Carl was alive I was free to come and go as I pleased. If I needed a break from the frantic pace of the flower shop, I could buzz off to Springfield without any pangs of guilt. If Carl's schedule let him, he'd go with me. If it didn't, I went on my own.

I liked that freedom, and I realized I'd been guarding it zealously. I'd made it clear to DeeDee, when she took the job of housekeeper, that I might be home or I might not, depending on my mood.

Maybe the curtailing of my freedom was another reason why I'd put off renovating these rooms. People in the house could tie me down. Make me feel that I had to put in an appearance. Having my father here was even more complicating. With strangers, I could be the eccentric landlady. My father expected to be included in my life, and with each passing hour I felt the pinch of responsibility in a relationship.

"I've g-got to stir the b-bouillab-baisse," said DeeDee. "The ingredients are too exp-pensive to let scorch. I'll b-be r-right b-back." She dashed out of the room.

"Who are you having dinner with?" asked Dad.

"Bailey."

He cocked an eyebrow. "Oh, really. I didn't get the impression the two of you were friends."

"We have a few things to straighten out." I looked at the antique clock on a dust-shrouded table. We hadn't been cleaning as long as I thought. There was still plenty of time to get ready. Then I remembered the fireworks. "How long was the electricity off?"

Dad glanced at the clock, compared it to his wristwatch. "Looks like about thirty minutes. What time is Monroe picking you up?"

"He's not picking me up. I'm walking over to the cottage."

"Hmm. A private dinner party. Monroe's a good-looking man, and his former life could be viewed as glamorous—righting wrongs, rubbing out drug deals. I could see where a woman would be attracted to him, but discretion might be the better part of valor. Don't you think it would be more sensible to go to a restaurant or come here? DeeDee has that pot of fish soup simmering on the stove."

"No thanks. I can take care of myself."

"Carl's been dead, how long?"

I was rapidly losing my cool. "It's been two years, but I don't see—"

"I *do* see. You're lonely. You'd like to find someone to . . . uh . . . spend time with." He tugged off the mask to expose a crimson face. "Are you ready to take this step?"

With a studied effort, I kept my tone even. "What step? I'm having dinner with him. I'm not promiscuous, Dad. I never was, and you'd know that if you'd been around. Now, if you'll excuse me, I have to wash away this dust."

Alone in my room, I forced myself to take a couple of deep breaths, then I treated myself to a hot bubble bath. I shaved my legs, plucked a stray hair or two from my eyebrows, and did the things women do when they want to impress a man. I added a lavish spray of cologne, and I was ready. The black slacks were snug in all the right places. The blue vest brought out the color of my eyes.

"This is as good as it gets," I said as I turned away from the mirror. I opened my bedroom door and hurried down the front staircase.

DeeDee stepped out of the kitchen. "You l-look nice," she said. "Have a g-good time."

I grabbed a jacket out of the front hall closet. "Gotta rush. I don't want to be late."

DeeDee glanced over her shoulder. "It's not quite s-seven-th-thirty."

I froze in the act of slinging the jacket over my shoulders. Slowly I turned. "What did you say?" When she opened her mouth to repeat it, I said, "Never mind. Where's my father?"

"He t-took a cab into t-town. He's th-thinking about b-buying a car."

My expression must have been frightening, because DeeDee's stuttering intensified. "W-what's w-wrong? He's t-trying to f-fit in. H-he s-said if h-he h-has h-his own v-vehicle he w-won't be a b-burden to y-you."

I opened the front door and stepped out on the veranda. I could see the cottage driveway if I went to the farthest end of the porch. By stretching my neck and peering around a grouping of pine trees I saw Bailey's black-and-silver truck was gone.

"I'm only an hour late," I said, going back into the house. "Doesn't the man have patience? Doesn't he know that stuff happens?" Stuff like an interfering father. But maybe Dad hadn't done it on purpose. Yeah, right. He knew he was giving me the wrong time, and then to make matters worse, he skipped out so he wouldn't have to take the heat when I discovered what he'd done.

I draped my jacket over the stair railing. In the library, I plopped down in a chair and folded my arms across my chest. After a few minutes, DeeDee peeked around the doorway.

"I'll be eating here tonight," I said. "Bring me whatever is left of that key lime pie, and you might as well haul out the crème brûlée. It's going to be a long, long evening."

DeeDee has a stubborn streak that often flares up when I try to eat something that I shouldn't. I didn't get the pie until after I'd eaten a bowl of the low-cal bouillabaisse. The fish was succulent, the shrimp plump and pink.

At regular intervals, I called the cottage armed with an explanation. Over and over, I rehearsed what I was going to say. Sometimes I thought I should be formal, not give a specific reason, but an ambiguous "I lost track of the time." In the next instant, I decided to tell the truth. That I had an overprotective father who was proving to be a pain in the tushie.

At a quarter after ten, my father still hadn't returned, but Bailey finally answered his phone. When I heard his voice, I blurted, "I would've figured a drug agent had a world of patience. I was only an hour late."

For a minute all I could hear was his breathing, then he said, "Ex-agent. I'm retired, remember? So what happened? An emergency call for flowers?"

"No, it's a bit more complicated than that. The electricity went off, and the clocks weren't set with the right time."

"I didn't lose power over here."

"This was an in-house catastrophe." I sighed. "You wouldn't believe me even if I told you."

"Try me."

So I gave him a spirited account of what I'd found when

I came home. His laughter put the irritating event into a different perspective. "It wasn't funny at the time," I finished with a smile. "If you aren't doing anything, you can come see for yourself."

I'd thrown out the invitation with no real hope of his accepting. When he replied "I'll be right there," I was surprised. As good as his word, he rang the doorbell in less than three minutes. I was ready. I opened the door and we stared, looking quietly into each other's eyes. Not once did he make a move to touch me, but his expression told me he was thinking about it.

Suddenly shy and unsure of what I wanted, I broke eye contact and moved toward the staircase. "I'll give you a quick tour, then we'll go to the kitchen. DeeDee always keeps the cookie jar full for guests."

As I led the way up the stairs I could feel Bailey's eyes on my backside. I fought the urge to tug at my slacks. Perhaps they were too tight in the derriere department. I glanced back at him, and he winked. This was no playful eye maneuver. It was stimulating and damned sexy. I gulped and scampered up the remaining steps, talking a mile a minute.

"I'll have to call in a cleaning company to get rid of the mess. In fact, I'm wondering if they'll need to clean the entire house. The dust was unbelievable. I'm sure it's penetrated every nook and cranny." I opened the Mistress Suite door, thinking that in my irritated state I might have overplayed the details. Nope. It was bad.

Bailey's whistle was low and sharp. "And your father did this with only a walking stick and a chest of drawers? I'm impressed."

His quirky comment made me giggle. Before long I was doubled over with laughter. When I could speak, I said, "Thanks. I needed that."

Bailey took my hand and kissed it. Goose bumps the size of ostrich eggs puckered my flesh. "I aim to please," he said.

Oh, yes, I breathed to myself. Please . . . please me.

Out loud I gasped. "Cookies."

He raised an eyebrow. "I beg your pardon?"

I eased my hand out of his and hurried toward the stairs. "I offered you cookies and here I am going on and on about—"

Bailey had caught up with my mad dash. He put a hand on my arm and turned me on the stairs to face him. "Cookies are fine—if that's all I'm being offered. But if I had my druthers"—he bent toward me, his eyes steady on mine, his lips a scant inch away—"I'd rather have a kiss."

"Oh," I squeaked. "Well . . . uh . . ."

I closed my eyes. Every sensory organ in my body was primed for his touch. My nose was filled with his scent—something woodsy and clean. His hand on my arm was warm and provocative. His breath was sweet and smelled of peppermint. His lips—

Where the hell were his lips?

I moved my head to the left and then to the right. Nothing. Opening my eyes, I found Bailey's attention had wandered. Not a good sign.

"What's wrong?" I asked. "Changed your mind?"

He brushed a quick kiss to my cheek, then galloped down the stairs. "Can't you hear it?" he called over his shoulder. "Something's going on outside."

I couldn't hear anything over the rapid beat of my heart. But now that he mentioned it, there was a hullabaloo out on my drive. Horns were blaring.

Horns? Car horns?

It had to be my father.

Trying not to whimper, I shuffled down the stairs and out on the veranda. Parked in the driveway were five vehicles with their headlights aimed at the house. Nearly blinded by the glare, I brought my hand up to shield my eyes. Bailey stood on the porch. I yelled, "What's going on?"

"Looks like a car show. Damned fine assortment, too. That's a Dodge Viper on the end. I've always wanted to see one up close." He leaped the steps and made for the yellow car on the far left.

"Viper?" I shivered. Sounded too much like a snake to me.

The horns stopped and peace reigned. Four men, whom I took to be salesmen, stepped from their vehicles. My father climbed out of a silver something or other. I didn't have a clue what make or model it might be, and frankly, I didn't care.

"Well, Bretta," said Dad, coming up on the porch. He waved his arm expansively. "What do you think?"

"Nice," I murmured, my eyes on Bailey. I was envious of that yellow car. He caressed the upholstery with a slow, lingering touch. I watched his chest rise and fall as he sighed wistfully.

"Take your pick, daughter. You can have whichever one you want."

Being called "daughter" was wearing on my nerves. It implied a closeness that just wasn't there. And being offered a car only agitated me more. I didn't want a car. I didn't need one. But I had been gypped out of Bailey's kiss.

Resentment and disappointment bubbled in me like Alka-Seltzer in a glass of water. Before I got carried away on an effervescent tide, I turned on my heel and went into the house.

Chapter Ten

🌺 I arrived at the flower shop Monday morning with the feeling I was running fast and furious from home. Turning down Dad's offer of a new car hadn't been as difficult for me as it had been for him. He couldn't accept the fact that I didn't want expensive gifts.

When I repeated my previous request for a heart-to-heart conversation about the past, he'd stalked into the library. I'd followed, but only to suggest that he take my room for the night. He'd replied that the sofa was good enough for him. He didn't mind living out of a suitcase.

This morning I found his signed blank check on the carpet outside my bedroom door. A notation stated that the money was to be used for cleanup. Since he was still asleep on the sofa, I'd placed the check on the end table next to him and left for work.

I took a swig of coffee. He wasn't getting it, and I didn't know how to be more explicit. Fancy cars or money wasn't going to buy my love—or my benevolence.

Footsteps coming from the alley entrance interrupted my thoughts. I turned, expecting to see Lois or Lew. But it was Evelyn who marched toward me. Frowning, I asked, "What are you doing coming in the back door?"

"You haven't unlocked the front, and I don't have time to wait."

Her attitude—that what concerned her had to be of utmost importance to me—really bruised my petals. I said, "We've been over each and every detail of your daughter's wedding until they're ingrained on my brain."

Evelyn smiled. "Let's hope so. I'm not here about Nikki's wedding. I want to place an order for flowers to be delivered to Oliver's funeral. He was a gentle, thoughtful man, and I want a fitting tribute sent from me."

She brought out her checkbook, dashed off the information, and then ripped out the slip of paper. Handing it to me, she said, "He believed in nature's own beauty. Keep my bouquet simple but elegant."

I shook my head in amazement. This from a woman who wanted foliage sprayed gold.

As the back door closed behind Evelyn, I looked down at the check. "Two hundred dollars?" I said aloud. "How much does she think 'simple but elegant' costs?"

The alley door opened again. This time it was Lois. "Hi," she said as she came into the workroom. "Did I see Evelyn leaving? Kind of early for a rout with her, isn't it?"

"No rout. At least, not this time." I studied Lois. Usually she bustled in babbling about something that had happened at home before she left for work. Today her shoulders drooped; her smile trembled around the edges. Was Kayla still causing problems?

Hoping to perk Lois up, I showed her Evelyn's check, explaining that it was for Oliver's funeral. "Got any ideas about what would please her?"

Lois didn't pause to think. "I'm uninspired. What's on for today?"

We discussed the orders. Lew arrived. The phones started ringing, and our day was off to a fast start. While we worked, I kept an eye on Lois. Twice I saw her dab at her eyes. Desperate to pique her interest, I brought up the subject of Bailey and how my father had sabotaged our dinner plans.

Her bland comment, "That's too bad," stabbed me with anxiety. Whatever was going on with her niece really was serious if Lois didn't have a speck of advice to give about my social life.

Lew had followed my account, and when Lois didn't offer any wisdom or insight, he put his own spin on the situation. "You and your father are too much alike," he said in that know-it-all tone.

I stiffened. "What's *that* supposed to mean?"

"Whether you like it or not, you have a combination of your mother's and father's genes. Perhaps the things about him that annoyed your mother are annoying you. He, on the other hand, sees your mother in you. He's trying to pacify you, maybe even make amends with her in the only way he has left."

I asked Lois. "What do you think? Is Lew right? Do you think my father—"

Lois picked up her purse. "I have to leave for an hour."

"What's going on?" I asked.

In a gloomy tone, Lois said, "I have a meeting with Kayla's principal. School is out, but the problem hasn't been resolved. I know we're busy. I should've said something when I came in this morning."

I glanced at the clock. It was after eleven. I looked at the orders that needed to be done. Some were for patients at the hospital, others for Oliver's funeral. I made a quick decision when I saw the distress on Lois's face.

I put two phone lines on hold. Picking up my purse, I said, "None of these deliveries have to be made right away. I'll take you to the school."

"You can't do that."

I touched her shoulder. "You're in no shape to drive, and besides, I'm the boss. I can do as I please."

Giving Lois a minute to compose herself, I told Lew to hold down the fort. Taking my friend's arm, I walked her out the back door and into my car. We were silent on the way to the school. I parked in the lot and turned off the ignition.

"You don't have to stay," said Lois. "Noah is joining me. He'll drop me off at the shop when this mess is cleared up."

Noah was Lois's husband. I was glad she wasn't facing this problem alone. "That's good," I said, then grinned sheepishly. "I brought you because I wanted to, but I also had another reason. Claire Alexander graduated from River City High School in nineteen sixty-six. I thought I'd nose around."

Lois reacted to my explanation like her old self. She snorted. "Lately my life has been topsy-turvy. Thank God I can depend on you. At least you never change."

"That's a compliment, right?"

Lois rolled her eyes, and we got out of the car.

Inside the school, the lingering odor of vegetable soup, sweaty bodies, and disinfectant layered the air. A bell rang. The sound triggered a rush of adolescent emotions that made my stomach flutter. For an instant I was once again that shy, unsure teenager, looking for acceptance among my peers. Irked, I shook off the image, but I was amazed that at my age, the clanging of a school bell could rouse such memories and make me feel vulnerable.

Aristotle, Mrs. Mitchell's dog, had gone berserk when he'd

caught a whiff of the roses I'd taken to her. Oliver had said, when he touched the wooden handle of his spade, "Memories of bygone years flash into focus."

The school bell had triggered my reaction. The roses had set Aristotle off. Had the spade stimulated a remembrance that was so important it had stayed in Oliver's mind while he'd had his heart attack?

I left Lois at the door to the principal's office, then wandered down the hall. River City High School showcased its students' achievements with photos, trophies, and banners displayed on walls and in glass-fronted cabinets.

The awards were in chronological order, with the latest near the front of the building. Since information on Claire was my goal, I skipped recent decades, looking for 1966—the year she and her friends had graduated.

From the amount of pictures and awards, the class of '66 had been outstanding in both athletics and academics. Bold captions depicted the highlights: RIVER CITY HIGH SCHOOL TRACK TEAM ENDS SEASON WITH HONORS.

Above a picture of young men in football uniforms were the words WE WERE DETERMINED, TOUGH AND FINE . . . ROUGH AND READY ON THE LINE. Conference champs in 1966. I grinned but kept reading and searching.

Candid photos of River City cheerleaders were next. I looked for Dana, but she wasn't there. That's odd, I thought, then shrugged. Perhaps she wasn't at school the day they took the picture.

DEBATE CLUB NAILS OPPOSITION. I searched the photo for Claire but found Sonya's name as a member, only she wasn't in the group picture. BOTANY CLUB MEMBERS PLANT TREES—WIN CITY'S BEAUTIFICATION AWARD. All four women—Sonya, Dana, Kasey, and Claire—were named as members, but none were pictured.

Peculiar that all four girls were missing the day photos were taken. Randomly, I picked three students, who seemed to be overachievers since they were in all the snapshots. A close inspection showed that in the Botany Club photo the two guys wore short-sleeved shirts. In another they had on V-necked sweaters. A girl named Tina had gone from a brunette to a blonde. Sweaters could be added over a shirt, but I was sure Tina hadn't gone for a dye job between photo sessions.

I meandered farther down the hall, looking in classrooms, but all were either empty or in session. Since I didn't have a specific question in mind, I gave up and went out to my car.

Driving across town, I kept wondering why all the girls had been absent each time pictures had been taken.

It was food for thought. Since I could chomp on this morsel and not gain a pound, I gnawed away like a frustrated dieter eating a celery stick. I'd found a bit of nourishment, but it lacked substance. What I needed was a glob of pimento cheese for my stalk of celery. Translation: I needed more information.

Chapter Eleven

When I returned to the flower shop I found a pile of new orders. The work was expected, but Evelyn seated on a chair wasn't. Before I put my purse up, I dug out an antacid tablet. The chalky, fake-fruit taste made me grimace. Lew caught my expression and sidled over.

In a low tone, he said, "I needed her help. She answered the phone and took orders while I waited on customers. It was a madhouse for a while, but she did a great job. Besides, what was I to do? I thought you would drop Lois off at the school and be right back."

"I'm here now." The smile I gave Evelyn was mere lip action—no warmth behind it. "Thanks for helping Lew. What can I do for you?"

"If I remember right, you said Nikki's fresh flowers would arrive today. I want to look them over."

This wasn't a good idea. Flowers were shipped without water. The foliage would be limp, blossoms tight. The flowers needed to be conditioned—stems cut and put in warm water. "The delivery is running late," I said. "I can call you after we've unpacked the flowers and they've had time to take up water."

Evelyn leaned back in her chair and crossed her legs. "If you don't mind, I'll wait."

I minded very much. Watching a florist struggle to get her work done isn't a spectator sport. I tried another tactic to get her to leave. "We're very busy. No time for chitchat."

Evelyn gestured to the ringing telephone. "I'm well aware of that. Shall I get it?"

"No thanks." I picked up the receiver. "The Flower Shop. Bretta speaking."

"I just talked to Mrs. Mitchell to see if she knew when Claire's funeral service would be, and she says you're asking questions about Claire."

"Dana?"

"Why can't you leave things alone? Don't tarnish Claire's memory."

"Tarnish it with what? We all have areas in our life we're not proud of. Are you thinking about a specific event?"

"I shouldn't have called," she said, gulping back a sob. "A wedding and a funeral. I'm not thinking straight."

I tried a soft, subtle approach. "Dana, something is bothering you. I'm trying to help. Tell me what it is. It often helps to talk to a stranger, someone unbiased, unconnected to the present circumstances."

"Time's supposed to blur the memories, not make them clearer. We were so young and so full of— I have to go. My cakes are burning."

"Dana, wait. Don't—" But she'd already hung up. I replaced the receiver and turned to find Evelyn smiling.

She nodded to the deliveryman who was unloading four big boxes from the alley. "My daughter's flowers have arrived," she said, clasping her hands. "Isn't that wonderful?"

God, but this woman was exasperating.

The day went down as the longest on record with no time for food to soften the edges. It was one o'clock before Lois came back to work. With Evelyn at our elbows, we didn't do much talking. It was three before the wedding flowers were processed and the mother of the bride had departed. The day's orders were finished and delivered around four o'clock.

By the time we'd cleaned the shop and I'd locked the doors and counted out the cash drawer, it was after five. The others had already gone. I schlepped out to my car with my tail dragging, only to find Sonya waiting. She didn't waste time with niceties.

"You've lost your focus, Bretta. The Montgomery wedding should be your prime objective. I understand from Dana that you're asking questions about Claire. Leave it be."

"She was murdered."

Sonya winced but didn't lose momentum. "That isn't your problem."

"Then why did she call me? Why didn't she call you or Dana or Kasey? After all, the three of you were her friends."

"We don't have your reputation for amateur detecting. But in this case, you should leave the investigation to the professionals. Your skill as a florist is on the line. Surely you don't want any unfavorable comments about your work?"

"I could ask you the same thing."

Sonya peered at me. "Explain that statement."

"You came all the way over here to put me in my place, so your mind isn't entirely on the wedding either." I gave her a tight smile. "Why are you really here? Is it because I might be close to discovering what happened all those years ago?"

Of course, I didn't know jack. I was bluffing. Dana's words "We were so young and full of—" were fresh in my mind. I used that as the basis for my bamboozling.

Sonya's eyes narrowed. Her lips thinned into a grim line. I'd pricked her composure, but with her experience at placating neurotic brides, Sonya had all the stress-reducing tools close at hand.

She flashed me a firm smile. "This conversation is going nowhere. Let's start over. I understand the flowers have arrived and are absolutely gorgeous. Evelyn is very pleased."

"That's good, because at this late date, there's not much we can do."

Sonya glanced at her watch. "And speaking of late, I really must be going." She went around to the driver's side of her car, but before she got in, she looked back at me. "Claire's death is a tragedy, but it can't interfere with our obligation to Evelyn and her daughter. Nikki deserves the best because that's what her mother is buying."

"Have you met Nikki?"

"No, but I'm looking forward to it. From her picture she's a lovely young woman. Working with a beautiful bride makes my job and yours easier. Anything we do will only enhance the final picture."

"That reminds me. I was at the high school this morning, and I saw that you were a member of the Debate Club in nineteen sixty-six. But you weren't in the picture of the team. And Dana wasn't in the picture of the cheerleaders. All four of you belonged to the Botany Club, but none of you were in the photo. What's the deal? Mass influenza?"

"That's right," snapped Sonya. Without saying good-bye, she got into her car and drove off.

I smacked my hand against my forehead. "Dummy!" I'd given her an easy out.

Boy, this questioning thing really sucked. If I was too blunt, I hacked people off. If I was too subtle, I didn't get anywhere. I had to find a happy medium, maybe adopt my own persona. With Sid, a suspect knew exactly where he stood if he didn't come across with the truth.

I climbed into my car. I didn't want to be as belligerent as Sid, and besides, I didn't have a badge to back me. Carl had switched between the direct method and the "I'm your buddy" approach. Both had worked for him. He'd tried to teach me how to recognize which one to use in different situations. I'd practiced interrogating him at our kitchen table or in bed, but that usually ended in a strip search with the lesson abandoned for more important activities.

I reached for the ignition but didn't turn the key. Bailey's way had been to fabricate giant tales that might elicit an emotional response. Making up all that stuff took too much brainpower. If I got befuddled, I'd never keep the facts straight.

I licked my lips. He'd also held my hand, stared deep into my eyes, and kissed me. Not exactly a formula he could employ every time he needed answers, but he'd sure gotten my attention.

"Are you okay?"

I jerked upright at the sound of Bailey's voice. Turning, I saw him leaning against my car. "I'm . . . uh . . . fine. What are you doing here?"

"Are you going to ask me that each time I see you?"

I shook my head. "Is something wrong?"

"Questions . . . questions. You sure have a bunch."

Bailey leaned closer. The coppery color of his eyes had stayed in my mind all these weeks. It was an effort to meet his gaze because I had so many emotions tugging at my heart, and yet, it was harder to look away.

"Have dinner with me," he said quietly.

I didn't need to think about it. "My car or your truck?"

"Come with me. You look too tired to drive."

I was, which probably meant it showed. I glanced in my rearview mirror and groaned. My nose was shiny. My hair was a mess. I'd known we'd be busy at the shop, so I'd worn a comfortable pair of sneakers and blue jeans that were too big.

Bailey opened my car door and held out his hand. "Come on. I can see you're having second thoughts."

"Where are we going? I'm not dressed very well."

"You look fine to me."

"Oh," I breathed. Suddenly I didn't care that my jeans were baggy. I slipped my hand in his and watched his fingers curl around mine. His touch was strong and warm and comforting. He held my hand all the way to his truck, where he opened the door so I could get in.

For a moment, I hesitated. If I turned and looked up at him would he kiss me? I wanted him to, but I was shy, and I was afraid. His lips on mine could unleash a passion I wasn't ready to handle. So I climbed into his truck and watched him close the door, hoping I hadn't missed an opportunity.

Bailey pulled out of the alley. "What are you hungry for?"

I gulped. "Whatever you want."

"Mexican? Oriental? A juicy steak?"

"Steak sounds good. But nothing fancy. Okay?"

Bailey nodded and drove to a restaurant that advertised family dining. It wasn't romantic, but the informal atmosphere put me at ease. We sat across from each other in a booth. After a waitress had taken our order, I said, "Even the score."

"Where do I start?"

"No particular place. Tell me whatever pops into your head."

Bailey settled back, one arm on the table, the other at his side. He glanced around the restaurant and suddenly smiled. "See that kid? The one giving his mom trouble?"

I followed his gaze. A boy I guessed to be eight or ten was arguing with a woman. She thumped his bulging jeans' pocket and then pointed to the table. With a disgusted expression the boy pulled out a fistful of sugar packets.

"But they're free, Mom," he said in a loud voice.

"Free to use. Not free to steal."

"But I was going to use them—at home."

Bailey said, "That's me, umpteen years ago. I always had something in my pockets, and my mother was always making me empty them. That woman is lucky it was only sugar packets. My mom was confronted with wooly worms, earthworms, toads, frogs, and once, a garter snake."

The waitress put our salads in front of us. I picked up my fork but didn't take a bite. "Did your mother make you toss out the snake?"

"No. She let me keep it at the barn. Along with a crippled rabbit, three turtles, a horse, and an assortment of cats and dogs. The number changed often. We lived on a gravel road that was a convenient place for people in town to dump their unwanted pets. In my younger days I saw myself as a healer and a protector of those animals. But sometimes they were beyond my help, and we couldn't afford to take them to a vet. Mom didn't have the heart to put them down. Dad didn't have the time. So the chore was left up to me."

"That's a pretty heavy load for a kid."

"It was the only humane thing to do. I could shoot a rifle as soon as I was big enough to hold one. The kill was quick and clean." Bailey's expression darkened. "Unlike some."

"Tell me what you're thinking."

"This isn't pleasant dinner conversation."

"Please?"

Bailey hesitated, then spoke quietly. "My brother was hooked on drugs by the time he was eighteen. He suffered as a human never should. He served time for dealing. He was in rehab more than he was at home. He was my brother, and I loved him, but I couldn't do a damned thing to help."

"Is that why you became a DEA agent?"

"To avenge my brother's death? To fight the bastards who used his weakness for their gain? It sounds heroic and noble, and if I was trying to impress you, I'd say sure, but it wouldn't be the truth."

"Is something wrong with your salads?"

We looked up at the waitress. Our steak dinners were on her tray, but she hesitated setting them down.

"Can you make our meal to go?" asked Bailey. He turned his gaze on me. "I need fresh air."

The waitress frowned. "I guess I can wrap everything in foil."

Bailey removed a money clip from his pocket and handed her a folded bill. "That should cover our tab. The rest is yours. We'll wait up front."

Five minutes later we walked to his truck with two foil-wrapped packages. Bailey opened the passenger door and stashed our dinner behind the seat. When he turned to me, his eyes were troubled. "Are you all right with this?"

"Leaving? Yes. Let's put the windows down, turn up the music, and just drive."

He ran a finger down my cheek and across my lips. "Thanks," he said before moving back so I could get into the truck. He shut the door and went around and got behind the wheel. "I was listening to this CD when I stopped by the flower shop. I hope you like Kenny G." He poked a button.

I grinned as the first notes of a familiar instrumental song filtered from the speakers. "I have this same tape in my car. He's bad. B-b-b-bad to the bone."

Bailey chuckled as he put the truck in gear, and we headed out of the parking lot.

We traveled up one street and down another, commenting about a house or a yard. Our conversation was easy and comfortable—no earth-shattering revelations or emotional remembrances. Our rambling took us to the outskirts of town, where the heat from the pavement was absent and the air cooler.

"This is nice," I said, taking a deep breath. "I haven't been this relaxed in days."

"Something bothering you?"

"I have a big wedding at the end of the week, but I don't want to think about that right now."

Bailey nodded that he understood, and turned onto a gravel road that edged the limestone bluffs that overlooked the Osage River. I feasted my eyes on the view. The multitude of trees swayed as if a chorus line of beauties vied for my attention. A June breeze fluttered the leaves, giving the impression of feathery plumes on elaborate chapeaus.

Bailey turned off the music. "I left you up in the air at the restaurant. You went along with my need to get out of there without question. I'm ready to finish my tale."

"Only if you want to."

"It's part of evening the score," he said. "I was one of those guys who went to college because he didn't know what else to do. I played with the idea of becoming a veterinarian, but after the first semester my grades were terrible. I knew I wasn't cut out for the medical field. For my second term, I enrolled in classes where I thought I might succeed. One was a firearms course. I aced it, and my skill caught the instructor's interest. He told me I should get a criminal justice degree. It seemed as good a major as any other, so I did as he suggested. I graduated college. Got a job as a security officer in the federal building in St. Louis. I changed jobs but stayed within the system. Federal work interested me, but I wasn't sure which branch to pursue."

"You became a drug enforcement agent. Some people would say that subconsciously you were striving for that goal all the time."

Bailey flashed me a lopsided smile that made my knees quiver. "Have I ever told you that you're too smart for *my* own good?"

"Not yet, but I'm sure you will."

"How about if I told you that we're being followed?"

I didn't look around, but accepted what he said as fact. "Really? When did you notice?"

"When we left the restaurant parking lot."

"You're kidding." I looked at his dashboard clock. "But that was over an hour ago."

"I know. He or she is persistent but not skillful. A tail doesn't drive a cherry-red SUV. Nor does he stick like glue to your bumper even in heavy traffic. Out here, he could have dropped back, but he's eating our dust." Bailey cocked an eyebrow. "What do you think? I can try to get a look at the license plate"—he tapped his chrome cell phone, which was on the console between us—"and call it in. Or we could confront our stalker."

"Let's confront. This tailing business sounds like something my father might do. It would serve him right if we embarrassed him. Turn left, and then right. The road dead-ends at Make Out Point."

Bailey waggled his eyebrows. "That sounds interesting."

"It's also known as Kegger Canyon and Drug Bust Bluff. He'll have to turn around, and we can nab him—or at least make an ID."

Bailey followed my directions to a deserted tract of land that was a sinner's paradise. Trash was caught in the brush at the edge of the road. The dirt lot was littered with bottles and cans that had been tossed out car windows. A rustic rail fence was the only barrier between wide-open spaces and us. Bailey pulled his truck around, parked parallel to the fence, and cut the engine. Out my window was a fantastic bird's-eye view of the treetops.

Bailey unbuckled his seat belt. "Here he comes."

I didn't bother turning. This was humiliating, but my father had to be taught a lesson.

"What the hell?" shouted Bailey. "He's gonna ram us."

My mind was still tracking on my father. "He wouldn't—" I looked past Bailey, and my eyes widened. The SUV veered toward the back end of the truck.

Bailey grabbed my hand. "Hold on, sweetheart."

The SUV plowed into the rear fender. The impact whipped the lightweight truck bed into the fence. The back tires dropped, touched nothing, and the truck flipped like a tiddly-wink chip.

Bailey's hand was jerked out of mine. The front of the truck took a nosedive. The air bags inflated. Windows shattered. Metal screeched with outrage at the abuse. The truck careened down the embankment and then came to an abrupt stop that rattled my teeth and jarred my bones.

My body had taken a beating, but I was secure in my seat belt, cushioned by the bag of air.

Seat belt.

The word shot through my brain like a piercing arrow. Bailey had unfastened his seat belt so he could confront the driver of the SUV. There hadn't been time for him to secure it again before we were hit.

"Bailey!" I screamed, clawing at the bag that protected me but blocked my view. "Bailey!"

The air bags were deflating. I pushed the wad of material out of my way. The driver's door had been wrenched off its hinges. Bailey was gone.

Chapter Twelve

I was dizzy and nauseous, like I'd been on a carnival ride gone berserk. My hands shook so badly it took several tries before I could unsnap my seat belt. I blessed the safety apparatus that had saved me, but cursed the fact that Bailey hadn't been wearing his.

The console lid had popped up, and the interior of the truck was littered with CDs, maps, papers, and notebooks, as well as leaves and twigs. Filling the air was the overpowering aroma of the grilled steaks we hadn't eaten.

I gagged and tried my door. It wouldn't open. Swallowing the bile that rose in my throat, I worked my way over the console, pushed aside the driver's air bag, and climbed from the truck.

I saw the giant tree that had stopped the truck's descent, then looked beyond it into nothingness. The sight made me puke. When I was finished, I leaned weakly against a crumpled fender and used the tail of my shirt to wipe my mouth.

I ignored the bumps and bruises that throbbed all over my body. Turning my back on what might have been, I searched the hill above me for Bailey. I called his name, but there was no answer. The truck had mowed a path down the slope. Bent almost double from the steep incline, I worked my way up, trying not to cry, trying not to imagine the worst.

The sight of Bailey's chrome cell phone, lying on some leaves, gave me a ray of hope. I picked up the phone absently, still searching. Then I saw him, and nearly strangled as panic gripped my throat. He was so still.

I flew to his side and dropped to my knees. I was afraid to touch him. Afraid of what I'd find. I looked him over. He was on his back, eyes closed; one leg, twisted at an odd angle, was obviously broken. Blood oozed from a gash on his forehead.

I leaned over him, peering into his face, willing him to be alive. Slowly I lowered my head to his chest and heard soft, shallow breathing.

I dialed 911 and begged them to hurry.

"Are you Mr. Monroe's next of kin?"

The doctor stood in front of me, his hands thrust deep into the pockets of his white coat. I focused on the stetho-scope that hung around his neck, and licked my dry lips. "If it's bad news, you have to tell me."

We were in the waiting room at River City Memorial Hospital. I'd been checked over, my cuts had been treated, and I'd been released. I'd spoken with two Missouri High-way Patrolmen, giving them a description of the SUV that had followed us and rammed Bailey's truck.

My mouth tasted like caffeine-flavored vomit. I'd gotten some coffee from a vending machine and had waited and waited. Information concerning Bailey's condition had been sketchy up till now. This was the first time I'd been ap-proached by anyone who might have answers. I wasn't sure I could deal with the news. "Next of kin" sounded too om-inous, too foreboding.

The doctor sat in a chair next to me. "My name is Dr. Watkins, and I'm going to be honest with you. Mr. Monroe is in critical condition. We set his broken leg, treated his abrasions and contusions, but he hasn't regained consciousness. The blow to his head has left a portion of the brain swollen."

"Oh, no," I said softly. Tears filled my eyes. I tried to blink them away, but was unsuccessful.

"Now, now," he said. "Mr. Monroe is in good hands."

"Can I see him?"

"He's in the unit where only family members are permitted."

"I *could* be his sister."

The doctor eyed me. "Yes, you could. Since I'm not acquainted with Mr. Monroe, I can't dispute your claim." He nodded down the hall. "Tell the nurse at the desk that you have my permission to visit Mr. Monroe. Keep it short. Five minutes—tops. Don't be afraid to touch him. Talk to him, but be calm and reassuring. Let him know that he's going to be fine."

"But you said he was unconscious."

"That's true, but sometimes comatose patients can hear, and they're often aware of what's going on around them even though they can't respond. In this case, I think it might be helpful if Mr. Monroe heard optimism in your voice."

I thanked him with a smile that wobbled around the edges. The nurse didn't question my request to see Bailey after I'd mentioned Dr. Watkins's name. She looked at some papers on her desk and said he was in Cubicle 7b.

"Cubicle? Doesn't he have his own room?"

"This is the Critical Care Unit," she explained. "No walls, no doors, just curtained cubicles and seriously ill patients.

Don't be alarmed by the tubes and wires. Each has a purpose and is important. You may go in, but keep your visit to five minutes."

I found 7b and pushed the curtain aside. I hesitated for only a moment before I took a deep breath and walked to the bed. Bailey's arms were straight at his sides. His right leg was in a cast, and a bandage wrapped his head. A crisp white sheet was smooth over his stomach. His chest was bare except for electrodes attached to a machine that kept up an encouraging *beep, beep, beep.*

I touched his hand. "Bailey, it's Bretta. You're going to be just fine." Tears threatened, but I forced myself to talk quietly. "You have to come back to me. We have too much to do. I want to sample your cooking. I want to slow dance with you. I want you to meet my friends."

I kept my eyes on the monitor as I leaned closer. "I want you to hold me in your arms." Saying those words made my own heart's rhythm increase. Did his? I scanned the peaks and valleys on the screen.

"What are you doing?"

I turned to see a nurse standing at the foot of Bailey's bed. My cheeks felt hot. "Dr. Watkins said I should talk to Bailey. So I am. Is that wrong?"

She looked from me to him to the electrocardiograph. "Mr. Monroe's heart changed rhythm, and we were alerted at the nurses' station."

"Changed in a bad way?"

"No. Just a hiccup in the pattern."

"Should I go?"

Again, she studied Bailey's handsome face. "No. If the doctor told you to talk, that's what you should do." She lowered her eyebrows. "Just watch what you say. Don't make

126

any promises you aren't prepared to honor." She left the cubicle chuckling lightly.

Gingerly, I picked up his hand. Speaking softly, I said, "Looks like I'd better not try any more rousing experiments. But you get better, and we'll—" I dropped my voice to a husky whisper and said something that deepened my blush.

I looked at Bailey's heart monitor, then glanced behind me. No one appeared in the doorway, but his fingers curled ever so gently around mine.

"It was not a muscle spasm," I said to myself. I limped back and forth in front of the hospital, waiting for my ride home. It was late. The parking lot was deserted, which gave me freedom to vent my frustration. When I'd felt Bailey's fingers move, I'd rushed to the nurses' station with the encouraging news. After he'd been examined, I'd been told there wasn't any change and that it was time for me to go.

I'd left the Critical Care Unit, but had gotten only as far as the nearest phone. My car was parked behind the flower shop in the alley. I couldn't drive it anyway. My purse was in Bailey's truck, which had been towed away and impounded for an evidence search.

I'd thought about calling Sid, but I didn't have the stamina to face him. I'd thought about calling Lois, but she had enough on her mind. I'd thought about calling DeeDee, but I didn't want her out on the roads at this time of night. I had settled on my father.

When he answered the phone, I'd simply said I was without a car and needed a ride home from the hospital. He'd promptly replied, "I'm on my way." Twenty minutes after my call, he rolled into the parking lot.

Leaning across the seat of his new blue truck, he pushed

open the door. "Are you all right, daughter?" The dome light accentuated the wrinkles on his face and the concern in his eyes.

"I'll be fine once I get into bed. I'm exhausted." I started to climb in but saw my purse on the seat. I touched the familiar bag. "Where did you get this?"

"A deputy brought it out to the house. He said there had been an accident, but he assured me you were all right. I've been waiting by the phone, hoping you'd call."

"Accident?" I muttered, as I settled on the seat. I slammed the door with more force than necessary. "It wasn't an accident. We were rammed by an SUV."

"Rammed?" My father studied me. "Why would anyone ram your car?" His eyes narrowed. "We? Who was with you?"

"I was with Bailey in his truck."

"Ah," said my father. "That would explain it. I'm sure Bailey Monroe has made plenty of enemies over the years. A drug dealer who's been brought to justice would have irate customers wanting to even the score."

I winced at my father's choice of words—"even the score." They brought back happy memories of the first part of my evening with Bailey. The last half had been disastrous.

As we pulled away from the hospital, I said, "Please, take me by the flower shop. Since I have my purse and keys, I'll drive my car home. I'll need it in the morning."

"You're still shaky. Tomorrow you'll be stiff and sore. I'd be glad to take you to work."

"Thanks, but I'd rather have my car so I can come and go as I please."

"Always the self-sufficient one, aren't you?" Under his breath, he added, "You're so like your mother—intimidating and damned frustrating."

I stared at him. "What do I do that intimidates you? More importantly, what did *she* do?"

"I'd rather not discuss it."

"How did Mom intimidate you? I don't remember any fights. There weren't shouting matches. You simply took off. Why?"

"How is Bailey? Was he hurt?"

"Talk about frustrating. You could give lessons on the subject." I shook my head. "Bailey is in critical condition. He's in a coma."

We stopped for a red light, and I felt my father's steady gaze on me. "So your heart's bruised as well as your body," he said quietly.

My chin shot up. "My heart? Good heavens, no. Bailey is just a friend."

The light turned green. Dad didn't comment, just pressed on the gas pedal. We rode in silence. The lie I'd told hung in the air, begging me to recant it. But I couldn't find the courage to speak about my feelings for Bailey to my father. The subject was too personal.

After a moment, Dad said, "When I was in Texas and you were here in Missouri, I took comfort in the fact that the same sun that shone on you was shining on me. I wanted to see you. I missed you until the ache in my heart was almost too much to bear, but I stayed away. Sometimes, you have to be cruel to be kind."

I turned to him, relieved at the subject change. "What was kind about leaving me?"

"I'm not talking about the leaving. I'm talking about the staying away."

"I don't get it. Either explain what you mean or drop it."

"I knew when I left without saying good-bye your heart

would be broken, but I also knew it would mend. Time does that, you know. It heals all wounds."

I hugged my purse to keep from trembling. "That's a crock."

"No it isn't, Bretta. You had your mother. You had school and other activities to keep you occupied. As time passed, the hole I'd left in your life would grow smaller and smaller."

I fought tears that were close to the surface. "What you don't understand is that you left me with all the reminders. You went on to a new and different life. But everywhere I looked, I expected to see you. Coming in the back door. Sitting at the dinner table. Holding me on your lap and reading me a story. Once I was older, I'd think about conversations we'd had. I kept looking for something I'd said that would keep you from picking up a phone and calling me."

"But if I'd called you, it would have renewed our relationship."

"But that's what I wanted. That's what I needed."

"I know. But it wasn't something I could handle. I couldn't chance talking to you. I couldn't see you. The sight of your face, the way your smile lights your eyes—" He sighed. "I would've been back in your life—and your mother's."

We'd come full circle. I still didn't understand, and I was too tired to pursue it. A block later, I pointed to the alley entrance. "Turn there," I said, searching in my purse for the keys. They always settled to the bottom.

"Oh, my Lord," said Dad. He slammed on the brakes.

I pitched forward, and the seat belt dug into my bruised shoulder. I moaned at the pain. "Dad, that hurt," I said, frowning at him. He stared straight ahead.

I followed his gaze and caught my breath. My car had been vandalized. Tires slashed. Windows smashed. Fenders battered.

Dad's theory about a drug-related hit was shot all to hell when his truck's headlights picked out the writing on the driver's side of my car.

"STRIKE 2!"

Chapter Thirteen

My father got a flashlight out of his truck, and while we waited for the police to arrive, I inspected my car. I was careful to not get very close, but I couldn't stop staring. I'd been too upset since the SUV rammed Bailey's truck to give thought as to why it had happened. My father's explanation had sounded viable, but to realize I'd been the intended victim was mind-blowing.

The devastation to my car made me heartsick, but the message painted on the driver's door panel shocked me. "STRIKE 2!" The unwritten words crept through my brain—strike three, and I was out.

I played the beam over the interior, wondering if I'd left anything in the front seat that I might need. Amid the twinkling bits of glass, I saw something lying near the accelerator. Leaning closer, I stared at a small bundle of flowers and leaves tied together with a piece of orange twine.

"Look at that," I said.

My father took a step forward and peered over my shoulder. "What is it?"

"It's a tussie-mussie. It's a custom that dates back to pre-Victorian times. From what I've read, people didn't bathe regularly, so the women carried these little bouquets made from fragrant leaves and flowers to mask body odor. In later years the language of flowers evolved, and blooms and foliage were given individual meanings. The tussie-mussie was sent to a special person to convey a message of love. Each leaf, each flower, even the way the blooms were placed in the bouquet had a meaning, and they were all tied together with a piece of twine."

I frowned. "But I doubt this combination means I have an admirer. That dried white rose represents death. I wish I had a camera. Someone more knowledgeable than me will have to identify each leaf and the placement of the flowers."

"Why don't we take it? The police won't know anything about a tussie-mussie, and you'll have—"

"I can't do that. It's evidence—and important, too."

"Why so important?"

"Not just anyone would know how to construct a tussie-mussie. That in itself is a clue."

"I don't have a camera, daughter, but I could make a sketch."

"There isn't time—" I stopped speaking when he ignored me and went to his truck. He came back with a tablet and a pencil. With swift, sure strokes, he etched in the general outline of the nosegay. When I saw the bouquet come to life under his expert hand, I leaned closer to the car so I could better aim the flashlight at the floorboards.

"Make each leaf as accurate as possible, Dad. Isn't that a milkweed bloom in the center?"

"Could be," he mumbled, leaning through the broken window. "Smells funny in here. Pungent."

I sniffed, but a squad car pulling into the alley drew my attention. "Are you about done?" I asked.

"Need a few more minutes." He took the flashlight out of my hand and made another quick study of the tussie-mussie before he turned off the light. As he stuck the flashlight into his back pocket, he said, "Stall."

"How?"

"Hysteria might work."

I rolled my eyes, but moved away from my car and down the alley. Before the officer had climbed from behind the steering wheel, I was wringing my hands. I put on a good act—or was it an act? The fear and confusion came awfully damned easy.

Last night I'd said a sad farewell to my car as I watched the police tow it away. This morning I was behind the wheel of a cherry-red SUV, not unlike the one that had plowed into Bailey's truck.

When my father had offered to arrange transportation, I'd gritted my teeth and accepted. Only this time I'd given him a description of what I wanted. I didn't know motor size, make, or model, but I knew big and red.

My new set of wheels outclassed me in the color department. I was dressed in black. Oliver's funeral was at ten o'clock, and I planned to attend. But first, I made a trip to the hospital. I asked at the desk if Bailey was conscious and learned that his condition was unchanged.

My mood was glum when I arrived at the flower shop. Lois had the doors unlocked, the lights on. I didn't have to ask how she was doing. She gave me a quick grin as she carried a bucket of flowers to her workstation.

"I've taken another order for Oliver's service," she said. "The bouquet is to be in a large basket, so I guess you won't be able to haul it in your car. Lew can—"

"I've got plenty of room."

Lew strolled in. "Who owns that hunk of hot metal in the alley?"

I waved a hand. "Dad bought it after my car was van-dalized last night."

Lois looked from me to the back door. "I wanna see what you're driving, then you can tell the tale."

"I don't have much time, and neither do you if you're going to do an arrangement for Oliver."

She nodded and took off. In a flash, she was back. "Wow. Why didn't you get a tank? That thing's as broad as it is long. Are the highways wide enough?"

I admitted that it was huge but that it drove like a dream. "Or a nightmare, if the wrong person is behind the wheel. I don't want to go into detail, but Bailey and I were rammed last night by an SUV that looked like the one in the alley. His truck went over Make Out Point with us in it. I had my seat belt on, and I'm fine. Bailey is still in a coma."

Accustomed to the task, Lois's hands flew as she designed the bouquet. "Rammed. SUV. Make Out Point. You're fine, but Bailey is in a coma." She tossed the order form at Lew. "Type the sympathy card." She handed me a bolt of yellow ribbon. "Make me a bow."

I drew the satin ribbon through my fingers. "Is that all you've got to say?"

"Are you kidding? I'm about to explode with questions. You didn't mention how or why your car was vandalized." She shot me a frown. "Though, since I know you so well, the why is obvious. You've been poking into that beautician's murder."

"The few inquiries I've made hardly warrant the type of destruction that was done to my car. It was bashed and bat-tered."

"By a vengeful hand," said Lew.

I didn't comment, but folded the ribbon back and forth,

creating even loops. "Vengeful hand" was an apt description.

Right now the big question was—did I back off? My shifting emotions ran as hot as my new car and as cold as a well digger's ass. Anger surged through me each time I thought about the devastation to my car, but the thought of Bailey lying in that hospital bed because I'd been the intended victim was enough to freeze me in my tracks.

I reached for a pair of scissors and saw Lois watching me. "You aren't telling us everything, are you?" she said.

"You've been pretty tight-lipped yourself. How's it going? Are you ready to talk about Kayla's problem?"

Lois gave me an exasperated glare at the subject change, but relented and spilled the beans. "Raising children can be rewarding, but it's also nerve-racking." She cut the stalk of a yellow gladiola. "I'm sorry for my sister. Kayla is a brat, but now she's my responsibility, and I'm not going to shirk it."

"Send her back to Cincinnati," I said.

Lois shrugged. "I could, but I know I can make a difference in her life. I just have to find the right approach."

"What did she do?"

"My niece and two of her new friends thought it would be a great joke if they put a mud turtle in the principal's aquarium." She poked the gladiola stem into the floral foam. "Cute, huh?"

"Where'd they find the turtle?"

"Does it matter? Suffice it to say they picked the nasty thing up on some road. It had crud and leeches on it, but my finicky niece put it in her backpack and took it to school."

"So?" said Lew. "What's the big deal?"

I ignored him to ask, "Was it a large aquarium?"

"Fifty gallons."

"Expensive fish?"

"Oh, yeah, to the tune of three thousand dollars."

"I still don't see the problem," said Lew, typing fast and furious. "A turtle can live in water, especially if it's a mud turtle."

A clueless Lew was awesome. If we'd had more time, I'd have played on his ignorance, but Oliver's funeral was in forty-five minutes. However, I couldn't resist putting Lew's own brand of pomposity in my tone: "A mud turtle can live in water, but it has to eat. I'm guessing that old reptile had a rich banquet."

"Oh," said Lew as understanding dawned. He rolled the card out of the typewriter and carried it to the worktable. "You say this was the *principal's* aquarium?"

Lois took the finished bow from me and attached it to her arrangement. She plucked the card from Lew's fingers and pinned it to the ribbon. "That's what I said. The principal is thoroughly pissed. Two of the fish she raised herself. She'd had the others for ages, and they were like family to her. I wanted to tell her to get a life, but figured that wouldn't help the situation. We've been waiting for her to decide the girls' punishment."

I picked up my purse and removed the keys. "Now you know?"

Lois stood back and stared at the arrangement. "I'm done. Does it look okay? My mind wasn't on what I was doing."

I assured her the bouquet was fine, and then asked, "So? Tell us what's going to happen to Kayla, but make it the condensed version."

"During the next school year each girl has to earn a thousand dollars without a parent or guardian contributing so much as a dime. The money, once it's earned, is to be donated to an animal rights organization."

"That's not so bad," said Lew.

I agreed and picked up the bouquet, ready to head out the door.

"There's more," said Lois.

I stopped and waited.

"When school begins this fall, Kayla and her friends will start the year with ISS—in-school suspension—for the first six Saturdays." Lois sighed. "It could have been worse. The principal had the right to expel the girls, which would've gone on their permanent records."

Oliver was laid to rest in a small country cemetery that was about eight miles from where he'd lived on Catalpa Road. It was a beautiful day to be alive, and I silently gave thanks, sending up an additional prayer for Bailey's speedy recovery.

Across the road prairie grass waved in the breeze like an undulating tide. A wrought iron fence enclosed the cemetery. Cedar and pine trees sparked the hope that life was everlasting. Carrying the bouquet Lois had made, I dodged marble markers, crossing the uneven ground to Oliver's gravesite, where I put the flowers next to the casket.

The turnout for the service was small—thirty adults and his two grandchildren. The minister was frail and had to be helped across the rough ground to the grave. His hands trembled, but his voice was firm.

"From Second Corinthians, chapter nine, verse six, the Good Book says, 'But this *I* say, He which soweth sparingly shall reap also sparingly; and he which soweth bountifully shall reap also bountifully.' "

The minister closed his Bible and lifted his head. "We

have evidence of Oliver's caring for others right here in this cemetery. He kept the graves mowed and trimmed, without pay. He planted trees and flowers in memory of those who have gone before us. Oliver sowed bountifully, but it us who have reaped the benefit of his compassion, his love, and his charity. Let's bow our heads in prayer."

Eddie seemed composed and in control during the brief eulogy. Once the final prayer was said, his jaws clenched. I'd been watching him because I knew what was coming. Oliver's spade leaned against a tree.

The casket was lowered. The vault lid moved into place. Eddie reached for the spade, taking the handle in a firm grip. For a second or so, he stood with his head bowed. It was a poignant moment—not a dry eye among us.

The funeral director moved a piece of green carpet aside, exposing the soil that had been taken from the grave. Eddie stooped and picked up a clod. As he crumbled the lump, he shook his head. "This stuff won't grow nothing." He sighed. "But then I guess it don't have to."

He stood and plunged the spade into the dirt, then gently sprinkled the dirt over the vault. "Bye, Dad," he said quietly before turning to his family. "Son?" he asked, holding out the spade.

Both of Oliver's grandchildren took a turn, as did Molly, Eddie's wife. Then he offered the spade to me. "Bretta?"

I didn't hesitate. My fingers wrapped around the wooden handle. It hurt to move my shoulders when I lifted the scoop of soil. In the past, I'd heard the comment about "planting" someone and thought it unfeeling and crude. But in this case, planting Oliver was exactly what we were doing—as an act of love and respect for a man who'd earned both.

After mourners had been given the opportunity to place

dirt on Oliver's casket, all meandered toward their cars. I hung back so I could have a private word with Eddie. He saw me waiting and came over.

"It was a nice service," I said. "Your father would have approved."

"I think so. Anyhow, it felt right. When Mom died, my kids were too small to hold the spade. I was proud of them today, but I never thought about others wanting a turn." He chuckled. "Dad would've gotten a kick out of prissy Mrs. Dearborne handling a spade."

"Dearborne? Lydia Dearborne? Which one is she?" I asked, craning my neck.

Eddie scanned the area. "That's her," he said, pointing. "The red-haired woman getting into the car parked nearest the exit."

"I want to talk to her, Eddie. I'll see you—" I took a step, but the heel of my shoe had sunk into the sod. I stumbled. If I hadn't been stiff and sore, I might've regained my balance, but my reflexes were slowed by strained muscles. Eddie made a grab for me, but I went down on one knee.

"Bretta, are you all right?"

"Help me up, but do it slowly."

He took my arm. I tried not to wince, but he'd grabbed a tender area. I got to my feet as quickly as I could to relieve the pressure. Rubbing the spot, I looked around for Mrs. Dearborne. "She's gone?" I asked.

"Lydia? Yeah." He dismissed her with a wave of his hand. "I'll be at your place this afternoon. I've lined up some guys to help remove the tree limbs. The weatherman forecasts showers for the weekend. I'd like to get the area cleaned up so I can do a controlled burn of the thatch—"

I'd been inspecting the grass stain on the knee of my panty hose. "Rain?" I said. *This* weekend?"

Eddie grinned. "I see it as poetic justice for the witch. I hope it rains like hell on her parade."

"That's not nice," I said. "Don't forget I'm part of that parade."

We visited a while longer about my garden. I got directions to Lydia's house, then crawled into my SUV and headed down the road.

I knew I wouldn't like Lydia Dearborne from the moment I set eyes on her property. Eddie had called her prissy, and if her yard was any indication, the word was apropos. The house was pristine white. There wasn't a flower or a weed in sight. The grass had been given a crew cut—no blade longer than an inch. Branches had been lopped off trees so they resembled lollipops spaced in tidy rows.

I knocked on the front door, but received no answer. The clatter of a metal bucket drew me around to the back of the house. Lydia didn't see me, so I watched her in fascination. The smell of ammonia perfumed the air as she scrubbed the trunk of a tree.

The chore itself was unique, but the woman had tackled the job dressed in white slacks, a green blouse, and matching green shoes. Not your average tree-trunk-scrubbing uniform. But then, scrubbing trees was hardly your average person's idea of garden work. Rubber gloves encased Lydia's arms up to her elbows.

She walked around the tree, inspecting her endeavors. That's when she spotted me. "Oh," she said. "Mrs. Solomon. You startled me."

"Have we met?"

"Not formally, but my friend Darlene's daughter works for you." Her expression turned to pity. "How is poor little DeeDee?"

The hairs on the back of my neck bristled like the brush in her hand. "She's doing wonderfully. I couldn't ask for a more competent housekeeper."

"I'm surprised. She was such a shy, delicate child."

"She isn't a child."

"No, of course not." Lydia lifted a shoulder. "Oh, well, at least she's doing something appropriate." She clicked her tongue in distaste. "My, my, the things women do nowadays are amazing. I had my car serviced last week and a woman dressed in filthy coveralls took care of it. Just a little while ago, when I came home from Oliver's funeral, a lady was here from the Gas Service Company."

Lydia frowned. "We didn't talk long because I was in a hurry to change out of my funeral clothes. She seemed familiar, but I don't know anyone who'd have her job. She crawled under the house without a qualm. Came out with cobwebs in her hair and dirt under her fingernails."

I could have said a number of things in reply, but I plunged into another topic. After her comment about DeeDee, I happily employed the shock method of questioning. "Did Claire act like a woman about to be murdered?" I asked.

Lydia blinked. "How does such a person act, Mrs. Solomon? She was Claire. Talking and laughing while she curled my hair."

"She told us in the park that she had a hot piece of gossip she hoped you'd confirm. What did she ask?"

"She didn't ask anything. We just visited."

"She said if she phrased her questions right you wouldn't know what she was after." I smiled coolly. "Since you don't have a clue, I guess she was good."

"I'm not a fool, Mrs. Solomon. I know when I'm being

pumped for information." She gave me an arch look as she stripped off her gloves and laid them on a chair. "Claire and I talked about the passage of time. How people move away and you lose track of them. I told Claire I've always been lucky to have caring neighbors. Oliver's land connects with mine on the west. I've heard that someone is interested in the property that lays to the east. There isn't a house anymore, but the site would make a lovely place to build a new home."

"Do you think Claire was interested in buying that land?"

"Not at all. Why would she want property out here when her business was in town?"

I hadn't heard anything that could be termed a "hot piece of gossip." My frustration made my tone sharp. "You must be forgetting something. Claire expected you to tell her a piece of important information."

"Don't be snippy, Mrs. Solomon. Since Claire's murder I've had a difficult time. I haven't slept without medication. My sister and my daughter came to stay with me, but they left this morning to go back to their lives. Now I'm coping alone."

"I didn't realize you and Claire were such close friends."

"I wouldn't call us friends, though I saw her once a week. She began doing my hair when I won a contest she held at her shop. My name was drawn as the winner of a wash and set, though I never registered for the prize. Hadn't stepped foot in her shop."

"How did she get your name?"

"I never win anything, so I didn't ask. She was excellent with my hair. I told my friends about her work, and they switched to Claire." Lydia touched her henna-colored curls. "I'm going to miss her. She was clever. Have you seen the mural on her ceiling?"

"Yes. It's very nice."

"Claire did the work herself. A month or so ago, I was tilted back in my chair, and she told me she'd been thinking about painting a picture on the ceiling. She asked my advice, and we tossed ideas back and forth. Claire hit upon the idea of a woman with flowers sticking out of her head like hair."

"Is the girl on the ceiling a real person?"

Lydia started to speak, then stopped. After a moment she mumbled, "Now, isn't that strange?"

"What's strange?"

"I haven't thought about that family in years."

Totally confused, I said, "What family?"

"Shh," she said sharply. "I'm thinking."

I watched Lydia, who was acting more than weird. When she finally looked at me I said, "Well, what's going on?"

A sly smile twisted her lips. "That's my secret."

"There aren't secrets in an ongoing murder investigation. If you have information, you have to give it to the authorities."

Lydia sniffed. "Which you are not."

From the stubborn twist of her lips, I could see I wasn't going to convince her to talk to me, so I switched gears. "What about the flowers?"

Lydia lifted a shoulder. "Claire said that by painting Missouri wildflowers on the ceiling she might be able to achieve a total state of . . . uh . . ." Lydia stopped and thought. "Now, what was that word?" Her face brightened. "That's it—a total state of catharsis."

"Catharsis?" I murmured, studying Lydia. "What did Claire mean?"

"I couldn't tell you." At my look, she snapped, "Because I don't know, Mrs. Solomon. When Claire was in one of her analyzing moods, she'd quote her ex mother-in-law, who in turn quoted this Aristotle." Lydia shook her head. "Seems silly to me. What did Aristotle Onassis ever say that was so profound?"

Chapter Fourteen

I turned my head to hide my amusement. How could I expect Lydia to know about a Greek philosopher who had believed in logic and reason? Where was the logic and reason in the idea that a woman's place was only in the home?

I mumbled something about getting back to the flower shop and went around the house and climbed into the SUV. After I'd cranked over the engine, I smiled at the powerful sound. I'd never owned anything remotely like this vehicle. I zipped down the drive, whipped out onto the road, and then applied the brakes. A sheriff's car was headed my way.

Sid pulled alongside me. He gave my new wheels a sharp study and grunted. "Looks like a rich father has its dividends. Why red?"

"Why not? Any news on who rammed Bailey's truck?"

"Nothing on who, but a red SUV was found abandoned out near the River City waste plant. It was reported stolen from a strip mall. The owner went into a store to get cough syrup and left the motor running. Our suspect got in and drove away. No one saw who it was, so we don't have a description. There's damage to the left front fender complete with flecks of black paint."

"What about my car? Did you find anything?"

"Not much. It was beat to hell with a baseball bat. I read

in the officer's report that you called that wad of wilted flowers on the floorboard a tussie-mussie. I saw it. Looked like a bunch of leaves and dead blooms to me. Why do you think it was put there?"

"I told the officer that each leaf, each flower, even the placement of them, is important. It contains a message, and it isn't good."

"A message?"

I explained about the language of flowers, but Sid lost interest. When I took a breath, he said, "I hear you're a regular visitor to Monroe." He reached down beside him and held up a plastic bag. "Here's the personal items that were in the truck—CDs and the ring of keys that were in the ignition. We kept the notebooks and papers for a closer inspection. I'd give this stuff to his family, but so far they haven't been located. His daughter is on some cruise ship with her grandmother." He passed the bag out the window.

I took it, placing it on the seat next to me. I hadn't thought about Bailey's having children. "What's his daughter's name?" I asked, trying to keep my voice casual. "How old is she?"

"Jillian Monroe is all I know. I didn't ask for her life history." He stared at me. "I heard he bought the cottage next to your house." He raised an eyebrow. "That's convenient."

I wasn't going to discuss my relationship with Bailey, so I asked, "Are you on your way to talk to Lydia?"

He studied me a moment, then said, "Yeah. I assume that's where you've been. Did you get anything out of her?"

"Nothing much."

Sid's eyes narrowed. "I'll be the judge of that. What'd she say?"

I shrugged. "Changing attitudes of neighbors. The property to the east of her place is for sale. Claire herself painted the mural on her beauty shop ceiling." The devil in me added, "She's keeping something to herself, and I think it has to do with the painting."

"Is it important?"

"I don't know, but she says it's her secret. She was snooty about it. Lydia also said that Claire painted Missouri wildflowers so she could achieve 'a total state of catharsis.'"

Sid's eyebrows zoomed up. "Aristotle's theory of catharsis? Interesting."

When he saw my mouth hanging open, he said, "Don't look so damned surprised. I read more than deputies' reports. Philosophy exercises my brain in other areas."

He drummed his fingers on the steering wheel. "Aristotle believed that pity and fear were the extremes of human nature, and for a person to attain virtue these emotions should be avoided. According to him, by viewing a tragedy there could be a kind of purgation or purification from these feelings—a catharsis."

"I'm impressed. But wasn't Aristotle talking about a tragedy represented by a stage enactment, not real life?"

"If you're scared you look for comfort anywhere you can find it." Sid tilted his cap back and scratched his head. "But I don't see how flowers painted on a ceiling could be called a tragedy, unless she was an artist with my talent."

"Claire's ex-husband, Howie, told me she was scared about something, but I didn't get that impression when I talked to her. She seemed more excited than frightened." Sid's expression stopped my palavering.

His chin dropped, and he glared. "When did you talk to—"

Kaboom!

Lydia Dearborne's house exploded into a fireball, altering the bright yellow sunlight into a surging, unnatural, orange glow. The concussion slammed me into the steering wheel before the SUV's suspension rocked me like a baby.

"Holy Mother of God," said Sid.

I twisted around in my seat and stared in horror. The upward escalation had blown the house debris sky-high, where it maintained a sort of suspended animation. Hunks and chunks appeared to burst into flame against the blue background. As gravity took hold, charred bits of unidentifiable materials slammed to earth. Ashes floated on air that was thick with black smoke. Where the house had been, flames leaped and danced like demons intent on total destruction.

While Sid called in the emergency, I thought out loud. "She has to be dead. She couldn't have lived through that explosion even if she was outside scrubbing trees."

"What?" shouted Sid.

I raised my voice. "Lydia must be dead, but shouldn't we check?"

Sid shot me a disgusted glare. "Which part of her are we gonna look for? That was either a bomb or a gas leak. See how the flames are roaring straight up? They're being fueled by something. I've called the gas company to come turn off the main valve. Until they do their job, we're gonna sit tight."

Gas company.

With my eyes on the fiery scene, I said, "Lydia told me a woman from the gas company had gone under her house for an inspection." I glanced at the dashboard clock. "That was approximately an hour ago."

Sid looked at the house and then back at me. "Holy shit! Are you thinking this was intentional?"

"Carl never liked coincidences. It's more than a fluke that after an inspection the whole house would go up."

His mouth pressed into a grim line. "If you're right—and I'm not saying you are—tell me what Mrs. Dearborne knew that would make her a threat."

"I think she knew something, but she didn't know she knew it."

"Double talk," said Sid. "I hate it. Be clear."

"In the park, Claire said she wanted Lydia to confirm a piece of information. When I saw Lydia just now her hair was freshly curled. When I was in the beauty shop I smelled fresh perm solution. A permanent takes time to complete. They chatted. Claire maneuvered the conversation and got what she wanted. Lydia didn't have a clue until I asked her some questions. She started thinking, and up came this 'secret,' which she wouldn't share with me."

I thought a moment, then added, "I bet the killer has been waiting for a chance to kill Lydia, but delayed the deed until Lydia's company left."

"Why? If you've killed once and plan on killing again, what's a few more bodies?"

I didn't have an answer. Fifteen minutes later a group of rural volunteer firefighters arrived. Sid jumped out of his car and motioned for me to move on.

"I know where to find you," he said.

I put the SUV into gear and drove back to River City, meeting emergency vehicles on my way. As each one passed, I shook my head and murmured, "Too late. Much too late."

Bailey had been moved out of the Critical Care Unit into a private room, but he hadn't regained consciousness. I'd been told his vital signs were good and the swelling to his brain was going down.

A nurse had patted my hand and said it would only be a matter of time before he opened his eyes. When I pressed her to be more specific, she had smiled and said, "He'll come around when the time is right."

"Time?" I grumbled as I dragged a chair up to Bailey's bedside.

What was time, anyway? We gain time, kill time, do time, are behind the times, or pass the time of day. Old folks look back and say they had the time of their life. Young people want to be ahead of their time. There are instances when we'd like to turn back the hands of time. And sometimes, we're simply out of time.

When Lydia went to Oliver's funeral, she probably thought she had plenty of time left. She'd been scrubbing tree trunks, for God's sake. Surely if she'd known her time was almost up, she would have done something more worthwhile.

I picked up Bailey's hand and tenderly wrapped his fingers around mine. "Open your eyes," I said quietly. "It's time."

No one would've been more surprised than I had Bailey done as I'd directed. But he didn't, and I wasn't. I sat with his hand in mine and talked.

"This really sucks. I can feel your warmth, but you aren't here with me." I leaned closer. "I have a major problem. Well, I guess it isn't really my problem, but Claire did call me. She thought I could help her. I have all these thoughts waltzing around in my head. Help me, Bailey. Help me figure this mess out.

"If I start with the park where I met Claire, then I have to consider Oliver's dying words—'Bretta—Spade.' I'm not sure if they belong with the rest of the scenario. Oliver had a heart attack. Claire was murdered. Both were in the park. Both knew Lydia Dearborne. Oliver heard Claire say Lydia's name. Before Oliver's heart acted up, I noticed he had his head cocked to one side as if he were concentrating on remembering something. He said, 'So long ago.' He had his spade in his hands. Earlier he'd told me 'whenever I touch this wood, memories of bygone years flash into focus.' "

I rested my cheek against Bailey's hand. "Bygone years. Claire and Lydia talked about neighbors and how times change." I grimaced. "Dana said, 'Time's supposed to blur the memories—' There's that word again. *Time.* My father believes that time heals all wounds. He seriously thought, when he left all those years ago, I'd get over the pain. That I'd simply forget him and go on with my life. I did to a certain extent. I married a man I adored and who adored me. I started and maintained a successful business, but at odd moments I'd think about my father and wonder what he was doing. And more importantly, I wondered if he ever thought of me."

I sighed deeply and sat up. "You're not helping, and I'm getting off track. I wanted to talk to you about this murder case, and here I am going on about my personal life."

I glanced over my shoulder. "Before someone comes in and tells me visiting hours are over, I want you to hear the latest development. Lydia Dearborne's house blew up. It was murder, Bailey. I'm sure of it. When Sid questions the Gas Service Company, he'll find they didn't send an inspector out to Lydia's house.

"Lydia has had someone with her since Claire's murder. She's been on medication, too. This very morning her family leaves, and Lydia feels well enough to go out—out where she could talk. About what, I'm not sure, but our killer feared she had something to say. If I'd stayed another five minutes, I'd have been blown to bits." I shuddered. "I left her house in the nick of time."

I sat quietly, thinking, then said, "Lydia told me it was a woman inspector and that she seemed familiar. Why didn't I ask for a physical description?"

I snorted. "Because at that *time* I didn't know it was important. *Time.* That word sure does crop up—time after time. It's time for me to go. Time for you to wake up."

I stood and leaned over Bailey so I could whisper in his ear. "What's it going to take to bring you back to me? A hug? A kiss? I can supply both, but you have to ask."

I'd have been thrilled with a muscle spasm, but Bailey lay quietly. Tears threatened, but I winked them away, forcing a bright note in my voice. "You think over what I've said. I'll drop by later to hear your theories."

Before I left the hospital, I called the flower shop to check in with Lois. "How's it going?" I asked.

"Manageable. Where are you?"

"At the hospital." Anticipating her next question, I added, "Bailey isn't conscious, but he's improving."

"That's good news. I have three messages for you. One is from DeeDee. She says the cleaning crew is at the house, and they're doing a wonderful job, but your father is wandering around the estate like a lost soul. Eddie called. He and his crew are hauling brush out of the garden." Lois heaved a sigh. "I've saved the worst for last. Evelyn was by."

"Do I want to hear this?"

"Probably not, but *I* had to listen to her. She has too much time on her hands. While looking through some bridal magazines she saw a picture of an arch made of twisted grapevines."

I heard paper rustling. Lois said, "She left the picture with me. If we had another month, we could do it, but we've got four days. I told her no way. She told me to give you the message."

"Message received. Now, forget it. I'm not adding another thing to this wedding. As it is we're going to be hard-pressed to get everything done and delivered and set up. Eddie says it's going to rain."

"It wouldn't dare."

"I'll be at the house if you need me, but don't tell Evelyn. I'm almost out of antacid tablets and patience."

"Speaking of patience. How do you feel about hiring Kayla to do odd jobs here at the flower shop? I can't give her money outright, but I could give it to you, and you could give it to her."

"Sounds complicated. Can we talk about it after this wedding?"

"Yeah, sure. I want her under my thumb for a while. If this escapade had gone on her permanent record, it could haunt her for the rest of her life."

I shook my head. "It was a turtle, Lois. A year or so down the road, what possible difference could it make?"

"I don't know, but some people could view her as a troublemaker. She trespassed into the principal's office. She had a disregard for someone else's property. If she was up for a job and her prospective boss called the school to ask what kind of student she'd been, would that boss hire her if he or she found out she'd been in trouble?"

"Depends on the trouble. A turtle is pretty tame compared to some of the pranks kids pull."

"I suppose, but she's so young. Here comes a customer. Gotta go."

I hung up the receiver and walked slowly out of the hospital. On automatic pilot, I started the SUV and left the parking lot. Dana had said, "We were so young and full of—"

Full of what? Hopes? Dreams? Plans for the future? Somehow I didn't think she'd been talking about aspirations and goals. When I'd tried bamboozling Sonya about what had happened all those years ago, I'd been left with the impression that I'd touched a nerve.

I drove to River City High School with the idea of probing for that nerve ending. Sid had said Claire didn't have a police record. But there were other paper trails.

My inquiry into obtaining information from the school's permanent records hit a brick wall in the form of a Mrs. Florence Benson, secretary. When I walked up to her desk, she smiled pleasantly. Her hair was gray, eyes blue. She looked like someone's sweet little grandmother, the kind that bakes sugar cookies and never forgets birthdays.

After I'd made my request, she said, "I'm sorry, Ms. Solomon. This isn't a public library. Our records aren't part of a free-reading program. Besides, I'd need maiden names. Do you have those?"

"I can get them."

She glanced at the clock on the wall. "My break is in thirty minutes."

I raced down the hall to the 1966 display. Hunting and mumbling, I searched out Dana, Sonya, Kasey, and Claire's last names. Kasey Vickers had never married, so that was simple enough. Claire had returned to her maiden name, Alexander. Dana Simpkin Olson. Sonya Darnell Norris.

Huffing and puffing, I arrived back at Miss Benson's desk. I'd used five minutes of my allotted time. "Alexander. Vickers. Simpkin. And Darnell. Now will you help me?"

"Up to a point."

I expected her to click some computer keys on the machine next to her. Instead she got up from her desk and frowned at the clock before disappearing down a back hallway. I waited and waited and waited. Finally, when I'd decided she'd sneaked out a side exit, she came back with a stack of ordinary folders.

She tapped them. "If you'd been looking for students who'd graduated in nineteen sixty-nine, I could have brought the names up on the computer. But since we're talking nineteen sixty-six, I had to find them in the vertical files. What do you want to know? You have twelve minutes."

"I'm not sure. Something they all had in common."

She raised her eyebrows. "Could you be more specific? Same classes? Same bus route? What?"

"Did they get into trouble?"

"Trouble? What kind of trouble?"

"That's what I'm looking for."

She sat down and opened the first folder. Running a finger down the page, she scanned and muttered. I strained my ears but couldn't make out a word. She took another folder off the stack and gave it the same perusal. When she reached for the final report, she slid me a glance, and I knew she'd found something.

I waited as patiently as I could until she'd flipped over the last sheet. I asked, "What did they do?"

"Is this the Claire Alexander who was murdered a few days ago?"

I nodded.

Mrs. Benson pointed to a yellow tab stuck to the folder. "Her file has been flagged, meaning she had trouble while in our River City school system. Claire's career as instigator goes all the way back to kindergarten. From that time, and including eighth grade, her teachers attached personal notes to her record outlining different capers, fights, and disruptive behavior."

"What kind of disruptive behavior?"

"The usual kid stuff. Picking on others. Cutting in line. Chewing gum in class. Arguing with the teacher." Mrs. Benson tapped the folder. "It wasn't until high school that she found her niche."

"And that would be?"

"Agitator. I realize it was the sixties and everyone was protesting everything, but the way her file reads, Claire Alexander jumped on the bandwagon with both feet. She organized boycotts, strikes, and demonstrations about too much homework, bad school lunches, and the right to wear miniskirts. From what I get here, most of her demonstrations were orderly, not violent. Minor annoyances to the administration. Claire and Kasey Vickers are named as the founders of the Botany Club, which is still in existence today. In fact, all four girls were members."

Mrs. Benson scanned Claire's file again. "Claire and her cohorts picked the wrong person to tangle with when they upset Ms. Beecher—God rest her soul. The home ec teacher had taken enough of Claire's foolishness."

Mrs. Benson chuckled. "Kids can find the strangest ways to get into trouble. Claire and her three friends were denied taking part in the photo sessions for the school's yearbook because—here's the corker—they stole four bottles of lemon extract from the home ec kitchen."

That explained the girls' absence from the club pictures. But why would four high school girls want bottles of lemon extract?

Chapter Fifteen

When I pulled up the lane to my house I wasn't sure where to park. Three vans with "River City Cleaning Company" painted on their sides blocked my entry into the garage. Four trucks piled with brush were lined up caravan-style, headed down the drive. My father had apparently been watching for my arrival. He limped out the front door and down the steps, waving me to a space near the veranda.

I nodded and brought the SUV to a stop in the shade. Before I climbed out, my father launched a conversation through the closed window. The only words I caught were "—stay close to home until this maniac is caught."

I opened the door. "Are you talking about me staying close to home?"

"Of course, daughter. Your safety is my concern." He gestured to his dusty clothes and green-stained fingers. "I've spent the day investigating your gardens, searching for plants and flowers that would match those of the tussie-mussie. In your personal library I found a book on the language of flowers. I've got it nailed down."

I assumed he hadn't nailed the book down, so he must be talking about what the tussie-mussie represented. I was skeptical. "You've figured out the message?"

"Damned straight, and it isn't good. Someone is hell-bent

on bringing you grief. Come into the dining room; I have it laid out."

He took off for the house. I followed more slowly. Since I had the sketch in my purse, I couldn't quite believe that my father had found each leaf, each blossom, and put it together from memory. But the project had kept him out of trouble. That by itself deserved a few minutes of my attention.

DeeDee met me at the door. Her eyes sparkled with excitement. "The c-cleaning crew is d-doing a great job. The boxes of p-plaster chunks are gone. The d-dust has been s-sucked up. They're f-finishing in the b-ballroom." She leaned closer. "It's g-gonna cost you a f-fortune."

I grimaced. "It's money well spent if the dust is gone." I stood in the foyer and looked around my home. Above me, the crystal prisms on the chandelier sparkled. All the wooden surfaces gleamed from a recent polish. Each riser on the horseshoe-shaped staircase glowed as if lighted from an inner beauty. The air had a clean, lemony fragrance.

I sighed softly. "Money well spent, DeeDee. Tell the foreman to bring me the bill before he leaves, and I'll write out a check."

"He s-said he'd mail you a s-statement."

"Whatever." I nodded to my father, who shuffled his feet impatiently in the dining room doorway. "Have you seen what he's been doing?"

"E-earlier this morning, we m-moved his s-stuff into a bedroom. While I made his b-bed, he took a walk around the es-estate. When I b-brought him lunch, he was m-messing with a b-bunch of weeds on the d-dining room t-table."

"Weeds." I shook my head. "That's what I'm afraid of, but I'll still have to be appreciative."

"And nice, Bretta," she added softly. "You're always p-patient with me. Give h-him the s-same respect. He is your f-father."

I winked. "My, aren't you the little pacifist? Make love, not war. Next thing I know you'll be wearing flowers in your hair reminiscent of the sixties."

"Flower power. I've heard about that." She giggled and raised her hands above her head. "Flowers sticking out to h-here. I'd l-look like a b-blooming idiot."

"Or the painting on Claire's ceiling," I said.

A buzzer went off in the kitchen. "Gotta go," DeeDee said. "Th-that's my timer."

Flower power. Someone in history had once said, "Knowledge is power." While in high school, Claire had organized strikes, boycotts, and demonstrations. All represented acts of power. She'd told Lydia that by painting Missouri wildflowers on the ceiling of her beauty shop she might be able to achieve "a total sense of catharsis."

Wouldn't that be power, too? A power over what had been troubling her? She'd dyed her hair green—which, according to Dana, meant Claire was bothered by something.

"Bretta," called my father. "Please come into the dining room. I want to show you what I've discovered."

I moseyed across the foyer, my mind trekking on Claire. Lydia had said she hadn't registered for the prize she'd won from Claire's shop. Had Claire made up the contest so she could meet the woman? Why? What had Lydia known?

My father gestured to the dining room table. I dropped my gaze but didn't focus on the items. Going back to this catharsis business. If Claire needed catharsis she was looking to be purified—which translated to me that *she'd* done something wrong. But if she were the culprit, then why had she been killed?

"Don't you see it?" demanded my father.

I squeezed my eyes shut. "I'm trying."

When I'd been in Dana's kitchen, she'd said that Claire had "this natural radar when it came to wickedness." Whatever had happened had been in the past. Kasey, Dana, and Sonya had been Claire's friends in high school. If something were about to come out, would one of them try to stop Claire from telling it? The girls had gotten into trouble for stealing four bottles of lemon extract. So many years later, why would it matter?

"If you're not interested, just say so," said my father in a disappointed tone.

Reluctantly, I abandoned my thoughts and stared at my father's labors. As I took in the assembled tussie-mussie, I gasped. "Where did you get this? Is it the one that was in my car?"

"Nope. Made this one myself. Do you still have my sketch?"

I pulled the paper from my purse and laid it on the table next to the small bouquet of leaves and flowers. My gaze Ping-Ponged back and forth. "Damn," I said. "This is excellent." I bent and sniffed. "It even smells the same as the interior of my car."

"I worked my way through your garden using my nose and my eyes." He touched some dark green fernlike leaves. "This is tansy."

"What does it mean?"

"Before I get to that, let me say I had a heck of a time finding a source for negative meanings. Like you said, flowers are supposed to convey a message of happiness, flirtation, and love. This bouquet is a deadly warning, daughter. The tansy is an herb and was put in coffins in ancient times because of its strong odor and its use as an insect repellent. If the leaves are crushed, they release a scent that reminds me of pine. According to the book I used, the tansy means 'I declare against you.' "

"I'm not surprised. I told you in the alley that the tussie-mussie hadn't come from an admirer. I knew that as soon as I saw the dried white rose."

Dad touched leaves that were elliptical with slightly toothed edges. "This is pennyroyal. It's part of the mint family and was also used as an insect repellent. It means 'You had better go.' "

I touched a leaf that had a patent leather feel to it. "This looks familiar. It isn't an herb."

"No. It's from a rhododendron bush. It means, 'Danger. Beware. I am dangerous. Agitation.' "

"There's evidence of that. This other is a milkweed flower. What does it mean?"

"Let's skip that for the moment. I want you to notice that the bundle is tied together with a vine, not twine as you first thought."

I leaned closer and saw a bright orange cord about the size of a stout thread with hairlike tendrils. "What is that?"

"I had to ask Eddie. I described what I'd seen by flash-light." He pointed to his sketch. "I put those little hairs on my drawing because I'd noticed them, but I didn't know what I was seeing. Eddie told me the plant is dodder. He'd seen it attached to some weeds at the back of your property. I went hunting and was amazed at how it grows. It's a member of the morning glory family. It doesn't have leaves, roots, or chlorophyll, but has these special suckers that draw nourishment from its host. 'Meanness' is what the book tells me it represents."

"And now the milkweed?"

My father scratched his head. "That's the odd part. I've spent the last hour thinking and thinking, but I can't figure out how it fits into the rest of the message."

"What is it?"

"Milkweed means 'hope in misery.' " He motioned to the tussie-mussie. "After all the threats—death, danger, beware, meanness, I declare against you—this seems out of place. If you remember, the milkweed flower was right on top, above the dried white rose. As you said, placement is as important as the plants. So if that's the case, it's almost as if the giver was saying the milkweed flower negates the rest. 'Hope in misery,' " repeated my father. "If he's miserable, then why continue?"

Slowly, I answered, "Because *she* has hope that *her* plan will succeed. Perhaps she is suffering but has an urgent need to finish what she started." I closed my eyes and whispered, "A type of catharsis—a purging of the soul."

My brain was overworked. I needed fresh air. I went out the terrace doors to have a look at the garden. A smile of appreciation came easily to my lips. Having those old decayed trees gone had made a huge difference in the landscape. Eddie had made a wonderful start on the renovation, and I moved in his direction to tell him. He was alone, a notebook in his hands and a faraway gleam in his eyes.

I recognized that look. He was plotting my garden, letting his imagination soar over the mundane details. If he concentrated only on the necessary work, what was needed to complete the project, he'd get bogged down. But to stand back and visualize the final results brought a fresh vigor and anticipation to the job.

Eddie had buried his father that morning. He needed this time alone. I quietly went back into the house. I told DeeDee I was leaving for a couple of hours. I wanted to check on Bailey, but I also wanted to go to the park. Eddie's big job was my garden. My big job was the Montgomery wedding. Maybe if I went back to the park I could recapture the enthusiasm I'd first felt when Evelyn had outlined her plans.

As I drove into town, I made a conscious effort to put Claire's and Lydia's deaths out of my mind. I lowered the windows and turned up the radio just as a meteorologist gave his weather report: "The Ozarks are ten inches short on rainfall for the month of June. And folks, it looks like we're going to miss a good shot at precipitation for the weekend. Highs will be in the eighties, with lows overnight in the sixties. If you have plans to go out on our many lakes and streams, take plenty of sunblock."

"Sorry, Eddie," I said with a smile. "No rain on Evelyn's parade."

I pushed buttons until I found a song I liked, then settled back. I didn't know Nikki, but she was a woman in love, about to marry the man of her dreams. The shipment of flowers had arrived in excellent condition. The weather was cooperating. I could count on Lois and Lew for assistance. My heart gave a little skip of confidence. I had the ability to bring my part of this wedding off with panache.

Twenty minutes later, I strolled down the path the bride would take. Seeing the shrubs Eddie had planted reminded me that I had to order several cases of gold paint so I could spray the foliage. Just the thought of doing this ridiculous chore made my blood pressure skyrocket again.

Quickly I dismissed the foliage from my mind and let the serenity of the park soothe me. After a few minutes the colorful mental pictures that frolicked in my head reaffirmed my conviction. I would do my best to make this a gorgeous wedding. My mood had mellowed, so I even felt a bit more benevolent toward Evelyn. After all, she was the mother of the bride, and she obviously loved her daughter.

I stopped in the area where the guests would be seated, and squinted at the gazebo. I'd learned early on in my career that for an event to be impressive, the senses—taste, sight, smell, hearing, touch—had to be titillated. The brass and copper baskets would catch the last rays of sun. Five hundred flickering candles would add to the ambience. I didn't like the idea that my fragrant flowers would have to compete with Dana frying shrimp, but the food-preparation tent was some distance away from the main festivities.

I pondered each point of the wedding. Taste, sight, and smell would be well covered. Evelyn had hired a woman to play the harp. The lilting music would calm any frayed nerves. I frowned. Touch was the one impression left undefined.

"What can we do for touch?" I murmured, walking toward the gazebo. Then I spotted an unlikely vision. I hadn't seen Evelyn crouched on the steps. She hadn't heard me because she was crying. The sight of this arrogant, self-possessed woman weeping was disconcerting.

"Evelyn?" I said. "What's wrong?"

She jerked upright and dashed a hand across her eyes. "I'm a mess. I never thought anyone would be here this time of evening."

"I was thinking about the wedding and wanted to have another look."

"Me, too, but I let my guard down."

"Nikki is okay?"

"Oh, yes. She's fine. As far as I know, everything is falling into place. I should be happy, but what will I do when Saturday is over? I've dedicated so much effort to planning and anticipating this day that once the candles are lit, it's the beginning of the end."

I leaned against the railing. "I know what you mean. There's a letdown after you've come through a big event. You want to relax, but you're still pumped, and there's nothing left to do." I paused. "Maybe it will help if you keep in mind that once our duties are over, your daughter will be starting a new life as a married woman."

Evelyn sighed. "I lose sight of that sometimes. I keep thinking of what I need to do to make it perfect for her."

"It will be perfect."

Briskly, Evelyn stood up. She smoothed her dress and tucked a stray black curl behind her ear. "Now, about that grapevine arch. I hope you've had the chance to study the picture I left with your employee. I think we should—"

My earlier feelings of benevolence for Evelyn dissolved into a mist. Nothing had changed. She was still as irritating as bird droppings on a freshly washed car.

Chapter Sixteen

The coroner released Claire's body the next morning. By ten thirty, Harriet Mitchell was at my front counter, placing an order for a spray of flowers to grace her ex-daughter-in-law's casket.

"Claire had no family," explained Harriet. "Her mother died when she was a baby. Her father drank himself to death a few years ago. Claire was always kind and thoughtful to me. Giving her a decent burial seems the right thing to do. My son is throwing a fit, but that's his problem."

"Why should he care?"

"Money. I have a little nest egg set aside. He has his eyes on it. Claire's funeral expenses will deplete the balance by several thousand dollars."

"It's very generous of you. I've gotten the impression, from things people have said, that Claire admired you. She quoted you often."

Harriet blinked. "Quoted me? Whatever did I say that was noteworthy?"

"Maybe not you per se, but Aristotle."

"Oh, yes. I tried to help her. She had a burden on her heart. She wouldn't talk about it in specific terms, but occasionally she tossed out odd comments. Her most recent observation has stuck in my mind, given the way she died.

Claire admitted she didn't think there's a God because He allows evil in our world."

"In my line of work, I deal with bereavement on a daily basis. Nothing is more heart wrenching than to help a family choose a suitable memorial for a child who's been killed or a young mother who has died from cancer. Evil people continue to live and wreak havoc on others, and yet the good die young."

Harriet's eyes sparkled. I could see the Scout leader in her emerge before she opened her mouth. "Aristotle believed that reason is the source of knowledge. Each time we see or hear of evil, we use our ability to reason, to use logic to evaluate the situation. If this world were perfect, if everyone lived long, wonderfully productive lives, then where's the challenge? By allowing us to see others make mistakes, God has given us the chance to learn and grow. As each generation comes along, the lessons learned by the previous generation are passed on."

"But what can we learn from the death of a child?"

"Each tragic event in our life makes us stronger. Are you familiar with the word *heterosis*?"

I shook my head.

"It's a phenomenon resulting from hybridization in which offspring display greater vigor, size, resistance, and other characteristics than the parents. A properly developed hybrid will have any weaknesses bred out and optimum values enhanced."

"I get the gist of what you're saying, but where does Claire's death fit in? What have we learned from her murder?"

Impatience threaded Harriet's voice. "You're expecting a revelation from one circumstance. You have to view Claire's death from a general outlook. How her life touched others. How her death affected those around her. How she lived. Where she lived. What she did."

"And this will give me insight into God's plan?"

Harriet laughed. "Not at all, but it will make you question. We can't begin to understand the why, but to grow intellectually we have to question, to reason, and to think logically. Events from our past shape the people we are today. If Claire had been raised with a functional mother and father, would she be dead today at age fifty-four? Is this cause and effect? When her parents passed away was Claire's fate sealed?"

My brain was spinning. "It's too early in the morning for this conversation. I'm out of my depth."

"Not at all. You have a logical mind, and being a florist augments your capabilities to reason through a situation."

"I don't understand."

"It's another of Aristotle's theories. He defines the imagination as 'the movement which results upon an actual sensation.' As a florist, you're attuned to receiving sense impressions. You see details that others might overlook or ignore. You listen carefully to what is needed and use your talents to deliver."

Last night while in the park, I'd had these thoughts about the senses, but had been stymied by one. Curious, I asked, "How does touch come into play with respect to my being a florist?"

"I'm sure you've physically comforted someone by giving them a hug. However, to advance my theory, I'd substitute feel for touch. You *feel* the pain of others. You *feel* the need to be involved."

She cast me a smile. "You also have good taste. Claire

liked bright colors. I'll leave the choice of flowers to your discretion. Send me the bill." She turned and walked away.

"Wait," I called. "There are five senses. You left out smell. Is it obvious?" I waved my hand to our surroundings. "Flowers have a scent?"

Harriet cocked her head and studied me. "And good cigars have an aroma. Skunks have an odor. All can be smelled, but a sensory perceptive person will categorize rather than make a blanket analogy."

I watched Harriet leave the shop. My forehead puckered with thought. I fingered the lines, smoothed away the ridges, but my mind rippled, stirred by Harriet's theories.

I was especially struck by the phrase "cause and effect." I squeezed my eyes shut so I could recall her exact comment: "Events of our past shape the people we are today."

If my father had stayed home, would I have turned out differently? I credited my mother and Carl as having the biggest influence on me. My father's absence had shaped my life, too. But which had the most effect on me? His leaving or his staying away? I had no way of knowing for sure, even though his abrupt departure had been as traumatic as a death. But even death doesn't end a relationship. Memories, often scarred and battered from constant use, plague the mind and the heart.

I opened my eyes. The first thing my gaze landed on was the plant display by the front window. A dracaena had missed getting a drink of water. The leaves were limp, the plant wilted. From experience I knew once it received moisture it would revive, but there was a good chance the leaves would develop brown tips. I could trim away the damage, but the plant would never be the same. Cause and effect.

"That was quite a conversation," said Lois.

I grimaced. "The one in my head or the one with Harriet?"

"Both. The way your mind works has always been a mystery to me." She nodded to the door. "I had a hard time following what she said. I liked the part about a florist using her senses, but she lost me on the scent, aroma, and odor thing. What did she mean about 'blanket analogy'?"

I glanced at Lew to see if he was going to jump in with a lengthy explanation. He widened his eyes at me in a fake innocent stare. Well, fine. I'd give this philosophy a shot. If I got it wrong, I was sure he'd bulldoze in to correct me.

"Okay. Here goes," I said. "Scent, aroma, and odor are categories of smell. Most people only smell." I giggled. "You know what I mean—use their noses. They don't consciously apply the correct word. Harriet says that as florists we classify things more specifically."

I thought for a moment. "She's right, you know. Take, for instance, how we distinguish color. To some, brown is simply an earth tone. As florists we categorize by fine-tuning—cocoa, toast, toffee, and fudge. When I named each one, didn't you have clear mental pictures of each color?"

Lois nodded. "I get it, but it sounds to me like you need a snack."

I waved away her suggestion as excitement throbbed through my veins. It was as if I'd exchanged a low-watt bulb for a brighter one. It's funny how an image or an idea changed when a speck of knowledge or a new perspective came into play.

"Claire was an artist as well as a beautician. She was creative. She painted that mural on the ceiling of her shop and called it a way of achieving 'a total sense of catharsis.' Doing the work might've been rewarding, but I'd lay you odds it was the picture that was important and suited her purpose."

"And that would be?" asked Lew.

"She used Missouri wildflowers for the hair. The girl looks sweet, innocent. Her eyes are closed as if she's sleeping. But I can't figure out where the tragedy fits in." My mouth dropped open. "Oh, my gosh. She's not asleep. She's dead."

Lois gasped. "Claire painted a dead girl on her ceiling? That's morbid."

"Not that kind of dead. She looks angelic." I bit my lip. "I have to see that painting again."

"How?" asked Lois. "According to the story in the newspaper, Claire didn't have a partner or any family. The shop will be locked up. It's a crime scene." Her eyes narrowed. "You aren't thinking about breaking in?"

"Of course not." I fluttered my eyelashes. "I have more *sense* than that. If I was in jail, you and Lew would have to do this wedding by yourselves."

"God forbid." Lois sighed. "I suppose we could do it, but I'd probably end up your cellmate. I'd kill the woman."

"Evelyn isn't so bad," said Lew. "I feel sorry for her."

"Why is that?" demanded Lois.

He lifted a shoulder. "We've had extra people help at holidays, and they make mistakes. Evelyn walked in the door, watched me take an order, and took five more without a problem. She thrives on challenge. Once this wedding is over, I think the woman will fall apart."

I nodded. "She said as much to me last night when I saw her in the park. In fact, she was crying."

"That's just great," said Lois. "When a woman cries, that means someone's gonna pay. You just wait. It'll be us. Before this day is over, Evelyn will be in here wanting to add something totally off the wall to this wedding."

I went to the phone. "That's an excellent reason for making myself scarce. I talked her out of the grapevine arch. But if she has another brain cramp, tell her she'll have to discuss anything new with me."

"Are you calling Sid?" asked Lois.

"No way. I don't want him glaring at me while I study that painting. Besides, he's county. I'm calling River City's police chief, Jean Kelley. She'll be a bit more tolerant." I crossed my fingers. "At least, I hope she will."

Once Chief Kelley was on the line, I said, "This is Bretta Solomon. Would it be possible for you to meet me at Claire Alexander's beauty shop?"

"What for?"

"I want another look at that painting on the ceiling. I've had a couple of thoughts."

"And they would be?"

Her indifference gave me an inkling as to how the conversation I hoped to initiate would be received. She might not be as blunt with her contempt as Sid, but I doubted she would be enthusiastic at the idea of exploring Claire's sensory perception.

Beating around the bush, I asked, "Could this wait until I've had another look at the painting?"

Reluctantly, Chief Kelley agreed, and we settled on a time. After I'd hung up, I dialed another number. When Eddie answered, I said, "This is Bretta. Can you meet me in half an hour at 3201 Marietta Avenue? I need your expertise in identifying some Missouri wildflowers."

"Guess I can. That's down in the old part of town. I don't remember any garden plots."

"This is a painting."

"Hell's bells. I don't know nothing about art."

"But you know flowers, and that's what I need."

Eddie grumbled and groused. I cajoled and cajoled until he finally agreed to meet me. I hung up the phone and said, "Boy, the things you've got to say and do to get a little co-operation really bite."

Lois pointed to the front of the shop. "I see a familiar white BMW pulling into a parking spot." She huffed on her fingernails and polished them on her shirt. "Golly, I'm good." She leaned across the counter, peering intently. "Oh, hell. Evelyn is carrying another magazine."

I sprinted for the back door.

Chapter Seventeen

🌼 "This better have some bearing on the case, Bretta," said Chief Kelley, getting out of her car. She crossed the sidewalk to the door of the beauty shop. "I've got a pile of paperwork that needs my attention."

"I think the painting is important, I'm just not sure how."

"Well, that's encouraging," she said, inserting a key in the lock. She turned the knob. "I'd hate to think you had all the answers."

"Not even close." At her hard look, I added, "But I've got a couple of theories, if you'll be patient."

She pushed open the door and motioned me in. "Not one of my virtues, but I'll walk the walk." Looking past me to the street, she said, "I see a man headed this way. From the expression on his face, I'd say he's as happy to be here as I am. Who is he? What's going on?"

I made the introductions, then asked, "Can Eddie come in with us? He's here to identify the flowers in the painting."

Chief Kelley agreed. We moved into the shop and stood under the painting, studying the artwork in silence. The picture was as colorful and distinctive as I'd remembered. When I'd first seen it, I'd concentrated on the flowers. Today that was Eddie's department. This time I focused on the girl. As I stared at her I kept thinking she looked familiar, but was it merely a scrap of leftover memory from when I'd first set eyes on the painting?

The face was a smooth, unblemished oval. Thick, dark lashes fringed her closed eyelids. Her lips were slightly parted, as if she were about to speak. Tiny hands were folded in prayer; the tips of her fingers rested against her chin. She appeared to be wearing a robe. Soft brush strokes had created the effect of draped material that flowed gracefully.

What made me think that Claire had depicted her as being deceased was the strange aura that surrounded the portrait. I'd seen the same dramatization used when the subject had a religious theme.

Chief Kelley said, "What's the deal with the radiating light? Is she supposed to be an angel?"

"A girl who has passed away."

"Who was she?"

"Lydia Dearborne knew but wouldn't tell me. I have a feeling her identity is important." I turned to Eddie. "Do you know who she was?"

"No, but then I probably wouldn't recognize my own mother if her face was two feet wide, painted on a ceiling, and had flowers sprouting out of her head."

"Okay. How about the flowers? Do you know their names?"

"Sure. You would too, if you took a book and drove down a country road." He pointed. "That pink daisy is echinacea— coneflower. Pink evening primrose is curled around her ear. That huge bloom is from the rose mallow family. Elderberry is the cluster of white. Orange butterfly weed. Goldenrod, purple asters, and over to that side are ironweed and milkweed."

"Milkweed?" I murmured. "Hope in misery."

"How's that?" asked Chief Kelley.

"Just thinking out loud." I pointed to the one blossom Eddie hadn't mentioned. It stood above the others as if Claire had given it preferential treatment. The cluster consisted of eight flowers and was yellow-green, tinged with purple. The individual flowers had five tubular hood-shaped structures with a slender horn extending from each.

"What's the name of the yellow-green flower up at the top?"

"I'm not sure. I'm thinking it's in the milkweed family because of the shape of the leaves and blossoms, but the color is off. I've never seen anything like it around here."

Chief Kelley was losing interest. "Maybe Claire got a wild hair to be inventive."

Eddie said, "Why would she do that? All the other flowers have been painted accurately, complete with stamens, pistils, and sepals. I have a book in the truck that was Dad's. I'm gonna get it."

Uneasily, I watched Eddie leave. With just the chief and me in the shop, I knew what was coming. I felt her gaze and tried to ignore it, but she wasn't having that.

"All right, Bretta. What is it about this painting that made you ask me down here? Something has put the wind in your sails. Give it over." She flashed me a wicked smile. "Or would you rather tell Sid?"

That was a threat if ever I heard one, but I wasn't alarmed. Fact was, now that I'd seen the painting, I wondered if Sid might've been the better choice over Chief Kelley. Sid had known about catharsis, but the chief had accommodated me by letting me into the beauty shop. I owed her an explanation. Whether she understood or believed me was up to her.

I gave it a shot. "Claire painted this picture because it represented a tragedy. By giving form to whatever was bothering her, she hoped to be purged—a catharsis."

Chief Kelley glanced at the ceiling. "You're saying that girl died tragically."

"That's my guess."

"So we need to match her picture to some fatal event that happened—how long ago?"

"I think you'll need to look back to nineteen sixty-six."

"Nineteen sixty-six? You've lost me. If Claire needed to be purged, why'd she wait so long?"

"The painting is new, but Claire's needs weren't. From all accounts, she spent her entire life looking for acceptance. She tried finding it with men, but had five failed marriages. She donated her talents as a beautician to help others, but that probably wasn't enough. In her younger days, Claire changed her hairstyle if she wanted to make a point. Dyeing her hair outrageous colors and using those weird contacts were ways of disguising her appearance."

The chief perked up. "She's been hiding out from someone?"

Slowly, I nodded. "Yes, but not the way you're thinking. She's been hiding from herself. Something traumatic was bugging her. When she looked in the mirror she saw the person she had been, so she invented a new image."

"I don't understand how dyeing her hair green would make her feel any different, but I'll give it thought. Let's skip on to the flowers coming out of the girl's head. What does that mean? If she died tragically, did she eat something poisonous?"

"I suppose that's possible, but you're being objective, thinking only about what you're seeing—the flowers. Try being subjective—look beyond the painting to Claire's thoughts and feelings. The flowers are important. I'm just not sure why. Claire put this girl's image on the ceiling because Claire regarded her as the heart of the problem. Up there, in plain sight, she was a daily reminder."

"Of what? Guilt?"

Eddie banged the door shut. "I've got it, Bretta. And I was right. It is in the milkweed family." He put the open book under my nose. "See? *Asclepias meadii.* Mead's milkweed. According to this, the plant is listed as endangered by the Missouri Department of Conservation and is classified as threatened by the U.S. Fish and Wildlife Service."

"Really?" I looked from the picture in the book to the painting on the ceiling. It was an excellent rendition. "Why is it endangered?"

"This article doesn't say, but the Mead's milkweed's natural habitat is grassy prairie. From that I would guess agriculture and residential development have eliminated it. You know how it goes. Heavy machinery comes in and plows up native ground. Plants are destroyed. Once concrete is poured any roots or seeds that escaped the excavation are history— and, on that note, so am I. I have to get to work."

Once Eddie had left, Chief Kelley turned to me. "What does this extinct milkweed have to do with your theory?"

"It fits, but I'm not sure where. Someone said something to me about extinct, but I can't remember who or the context of the conversation."

"Well, if you remember, give me a call. In the meantime, I'm sending a photographer over to get a shot of this painting."

"What for?"

"I don't have time to search back to nineteen sixty-six for

a might-have-been tragedy. I'll cut to the chase and run the picture in the newspaper. If that girl is local, someone might recognize her if the painting is accurate. It'll be like a composite drawing. Something about the girl might give us a lead." The chief motioned toward the door. "Let's go," she said. "I have work to do, too."

I gazed up at the painting. If Chief Kelley followed through with her plan, River City residents would soon stare into that angelic face. It didn't seem right for her to be on public display. And yet, here she was on the ceiling of a beauty shop. But only Claire's clientele had seen her. Once her picture was printed in the newspaper, she'd be fair game for any and all observations.

Half an hour later, I was seated at Bailey's bedside, trying to explain what was bothering me. "It's just a painting," I said, picking up his hand. "But something about it has caught my heart. She looks so defenseless. I feel as if I should protect, not exploit, her, but that's exactly what will happen. Once her photo hits the paper, there will be speculation. If she's recognized, her whole life will be opened up. I hope her memory can take the scrutiny."

Massaging each of his fingers, I said, "I've never told anyone this, but after Carl died, I'd hear his voice in my head." My cheeks felt hot. "Don't think I've lost my mind. Carl and I were close. When he was alive, I knew what he was going to say before he said it."

My throat tightened so I could barely speak. "Once he was gone, I was lonely. It was as if a part of me had died, too. Most of the time I went about my life as usual, but other times, especially if I was alone, I'd lose it."

A tear rolled down my cheek. In order to wipe it away,

I tried to pull my hand out of Bailey's, but his grasp was tight. I leaned closer. "You can hear me, can't you?"

His fingers tightened around my hand.

"Are you playing possum so you can be privy to all my tawdry secrets?"

No answering pressure.

I chuckled. "Ah. You already know them, right?"

His fingers moved.

I should have hunted up a nurse or a doctor, but for a moment I wanted to keep Bailey's improvement to myself. "I wish you could talk to me. In the last two years when I needed insight into a problem, Carl would speak to me, but I haven't heard his voice for weeks."

I sat up straight. "I haven't heard Carl's voice since I met you in Branson. Do you think there's a connection?"

His fingers moved against mine.

"Oh, Bailey." I moaned quietly as it registered how deeply I cared for him. "I think I'm falling in love with you. I love the way you hold me. The way you touch me. The way you kiss me. But I loved my husband. Can you love two people at the same time?"

His fingers moved.

"What's wrong with me? It's only been two years since Carl's death. That doesn't seem like enough of a trade-off for twenty-four years of marriage. Shouldn't I still be grieving?"

I tugged my hand out of his and stumbled to my feet. "I have to go."

I left the hospital in a rush, hoping to leave my confusing thoughts behind. But they hung around like an unwanted guest, invading my space. I was amazed at how easily I'd fallen in love with Bailey. We'd had a few conversations. We'd shared a kiss, a touch.

"How could I substitute Bailey for Carl?" I asked aloud.

"Babe, he's there. I'm not."

The unexpected sound of Carl's voice made me jump. I jerked the steering wheel and ran off the pavement. Horns blared. I quickly gained control. "Carl?" I whispered. "I'm scared."

"No wonder. Driving like that would terrify anyone."

"Don't be silly. This is serious."

"What you feel for Bailey doesn't take away from your love for me. I might be gone, but I'm not forgotten. I'll always be in your heart, Babe."

Perhaps it was my imagination, but instant warmth enveloped me. It was as if I'd been gathered close by a pair of loving arms and given a hug.

I wiped the tears from my eyes. "Stay with me, Carl," I said quietly. "I'm going detecting, but my questioning technique needs work. I've had good results in the past, but this time everything I do seems purely amateur. I'm not getting much when it comes to hard facts."

"I don't believe that. I trained you. You just aren't putting everything you know in the right order. Think it through, Babe."

I turned into the high school parking lot. "I'll do that later. Right now I want to talk to the botany teacher. Maybe he or she can fill me in on the extinction of the Mead's milkweed plant."

"And if you're lucky the teacher will be a fossil who'll remember Claire and her cohorts from their younger days."

"That would be too much to hope for, Carl," I said as I walked through the school's front door. And it was.

Miles Stanford was seated at his desk when I knocked on his classroom door. He motioned for me to come in. In the first few minutes of our conversation I learned this past year had been his virgin voyage into academic employment. He was fresh-faced and self-conscious of a huge pimple on his chin. He kept a hand over it as we made polite chitchat.

I'd only given him my name, so maybe he mistook me for an interested parent. With an enthusiasm that exhausted me, he outlined his plans for the upcoming school year.

"As I teach my students about plants, their structure, growth, and classification, I'm learning right alongside them. Not the botanical information, but how to get under their skins." He rubbed the pimple and winced. "Each class, each student, is a personal challenge. I spent too much time this year on botanical names. I won't do that next year."

He used his free hand to flip a stack of papers. "I have here a syllabus that will interest even the most unresponsive kid. I want to raise moral consciousness about the world around us. If I have my way, no one will leave my room without having gained something that will make this planet a better place to live."

Was I supposed to applaud? I was tempted. It sounded like a portion of a speech he might have delivered—or was he practicing on me?

I smiled politely. "The reason I'm here is to get information on an extinct plant. The Mead's milkweed."

"Really? That's interesting. It's been on the endangered list for years. Is this the local club's new project?"

"What local club?"

"The Missouri Save the Wildflowers Association. You need to speak with Kasey Vickers. She's the chapter's president."

"I know Kasey. I might give her a call, but since I'm here, do you mind telling me about the plant?"

"There's nothing particularly impressive about it. It flourished in most of Missouri, but erosion, herbicides, and overgrazing threatened its existence. Baling hay in September would've allowed the Mead's milkweed time to disperse its seeds. Manipulating the land could've saved the species, but then human intervention was originally the plant's downfall."

"Is it valuable?"

"Only from an ecological point of view."

"Did it grow around here?"

"Yes. Mead's milkweed is native to dry prairies and igneous glades of the Ozarks."

"Igneous?"

"Formed by volcanic action." He grinned. "I don't suppose you want a lesson in geology, so suffice it to say that from the molten slag, rocks solidified and over time were covered with a thin topsoil. Mead's milkweed found a home. Here, let me show you."

He walked to a laminated map of Spencer County that hung on the wall. "See this area?" He pointed to the southwest corner of the map. "If your group is planning a field trip, I'd start here. The rock formations and the open prairie are prime locations. I doubt that you'll find the plant, though stranger things have happened."

I leaned closer, squinting at the tiny printing. My heart thudded with excitement. The tract of land he indicated was east of Lydia's house on Catalpa Road.

Stranger things, indeed.

Chapter Eighteen

I wanted to zip on out to Catalpa Road and do some looking around, but I wasn't dressed for hiking through igneous glades and grassy prairies. I went home to change out of a dress and hose.

There was no sign of my father, but DeeDee was in the kitchen. The food channel blared from the television in the corner of the room. Lined up on the table were bottles of rum, whiskey, and vodka.

"Hey-ho," I said, eyeing the liquor. "What have we here? A party for one?"

DeeDee whirled around. "I-I didn't h-hear you come in."

I adjusted the sound on the TV. "I'm not surprised. What are you doing?"

She nodded to the television. "Earlier this m-morning th-there was this program about f-flaming f-foods. It was f-fantastic." She moved away from the counter, and I saw three saucers. Each contained six sugar cubes piled in neat triangles. "I t-tried wine, but the f-flame wasn't b-blue. I went to the l-liquor s-store and bought a variety so I c-can experiment."

"I hope your mother doesn't hear about your purchase. She'll have your suitcase packed before we can say Harvey Wallbanger."

"Who is h-he?"

"It's the name of a very potent drink." I walked to the counter. "What are you flaming besides sugar cubes?"

She took a deep breath and spoke slowly. "I'm checking to s-see which liquor works best. A b-blue flame is the most elegant when making a presentation. I can add the liquor to b-bananas, grapefruit, anything I want."

I made a face. "Roasted grapefruit. That sounds divine."

DeeDee giggled. "I've got more imagination than that. I'm d-doing Cherries Flambé served over low-fat vanilla ice cream. I f-found some s-silver goblets in the attic. At our n-next d-dinner party, I'll lower the l-lights and—" She flung out her hands. "Ta da. You'll be impressed at the s-sight."

I touched her shoulder. "I'm already impressed that you drove your car to the liquor store and bought the stuff. How did that go?"

"Great. I p-picked out what I w-wanted and took the bottles to the cashier. She asked to s-see my ID."

I laughed. "Cool. That hasn't happened to me in years."

"Do you have t-time to watch me compare which liquor p-produces the p-prettiest f-flame?"

"No. I'll leave you alone. Just don't hurt yourself or set fire to the kitchen."

DeeDee pointed to a small fire extinguisher. "I w-went to the hardware s-store, too. Martha says to be p-prepared."

Martha Stewart. I rolled my eyes. At the flower shop, customers were always quoting her. I was tired of hearing the name, but DeeDee was one of Martha's faithful followers. I kept my comment to myself, but DeeDee saw my expression.

"Sh-she has great ideas. Tomorrow she's g-going to show how to s-sculpt a block of ice into a bear using a piece of nylon fishing line and a chain saw."

Chain saw? Yikes!

I quickly left the kitchen and went upstairs to change clothes. I was proud of DeeDee. A few weeks ago I couldn't get her out of the house. Now she was going to a liquor store and buying booze.

I grimaced. Not exactly what I might have wanted, but at least she was showing a degree of independence. I couldn't fault that. Maybe I should look into enrolling her in a gourmet cooking class. It would broaden her horizon beyond the television, and she'd have a chance to meet people who shared her interest.

Dressed in blue jeans, a T-shirt, and sneakers, I went downstairs and peeked into the kitchen. DeeDee was carefully spooning rum over a pile of sugar cubes. The fire extinguisher was close at hand, but so was a box of wooden matches. I cringed, but didn't say anything. She wasn't a child, but she was a bit naive. Could I walk out the door and leave her alone? If she was to gain maturity I had to hope for the best and let her learn.

I started to step away, but she reached for the matches. I had to know that she was all right. I waited. She struck the match and applied the flame to the mound of sugar. I heard a soft *poof*, and the cubes burned blue.

"Hot damn," said DeeDee, her stutter gone. "I did it." She turned, caught sight of me, and grinned. "I'm fine, Bretta. Watch this." She picked up an aluminum lid and put it over the saucer, smothering the flames. "See? I'm prepared."

I drove into River City, stopping in at the flower shop to see if I was needed. I found my father seated on a stool. He was entertaining Lew and Lois with a story from my childhood.

All were enthralled, and my entrance from the alley went unnoticed. I stood in the doorway and listened to my father.

"—made Bretta crazy because that mother cat had hidden her kittens. Bretta was about five, maybe six, and I'd told her she couldn't go up in the hayloft, but that didn't stop her. As soon as my back was turned, she was up that ladder, poking among the hay bales. If I'd told her an old black snake made his home up there, she'd never have gone."

"Bretta doesn't have a high regard for snakes," said Lew.

Lois chimed in. "She had a narrow escape with one not long ago."

My father nodded. "I read about it in the paper. Anyway, she climbed up there looking for those kittens."

I knew what was coming, and so did the others. I shivered as I remembered the sly rustle of movement over the hay. I had leaned down, expecting to see bundles of silky fur. Instead, I'd come nose-to-nose with that old snake.

"—screamed like a pig stuck in a fence," continued my father. "I don't think her feet touched a single rung of the ladder as she came down. She tore past me, slipped in a pile of manure, and landed flat on her back." He shook his head. "Lord, but she was a smelly mess. She was crying and reeking when I took her to the house to get cleaned up."

I waited for him to finish the story, but he stopped and Lew swung into a remembrance from his life. I stared at my father's profile. That moment when I'd entered the house, all those years ago, was as vivid as if it had happened only yesterday.

My mother was at the sink. I'm sure she heard my bawling before she saw me. Perhaps it was fear that I'd been mortally wounded that prompted her to place the blame for what had happened on my father. Her verbal rebuke had been delivered in a soft tone, but as I recalled her words, I flinched.

"Alfred, your carelessness will be the death of our daughter."

My father hadn't replied. He'd hunched his shoulders and walked quietly from the room. While my mother cleaned the poop off me, I'd asked her what "carelessness" meant. She'd said, "Having no thought for the safety of others." I worshiped my father and had taken up for him in my typical outspoken way. My mother didn't approve of "talking back." My punishment had been to pick green beans until supper.

Mom had never screamed insults. She'd spoken quietly, but the words—*careless, ineffective, wasteful, imprudent,* and *head in the clouds*—had been applied often to my father. For a child they'd meant nothing because my mother never raised her voice. Mom was just talking, and Dad was just listening.

I felt a chill as the implication of what I was thinking registered. When spoken on a daily basis the constant belittling would be intimidating and devastating to a person's self-esteem. I studied my father. I saw the proud tilt of his head. The confident way he carried himself. He had dignity and seemed self-assured.

A small voice inside of me murmured, Only because he got away.

I gasped and everyone looked my way. "Hi, all," I said, trying to smile. "Just dropped in to see if I would be missed if I took time off." My glance slid over my father's face. "Dad, if you aren't busy, I'd like for you to come with me."

His smile went from ear to ear at my invitation. It was a simple gesture on my part, but the fact that my father showed overwhelming delight reminded me I had some serious holes to mend in our relationship.

Lois said, "Tomorrow is Thursday. Are we going to start on the wedding?"

"We have no choice. We can't leave everything until Friday. The next three days are going to be horrendous. That's why I'm taking the rest of the day off." I motioned to my father that I was ready, and we went out and got into the SUV.

My father patted the dashboard. "Now that you've been driving this beauty, how do you like her?"

My first impulse was to downplay my feelings—be reserved. But I stopped myself and was totally honest. "It's a helluva machine. I love it."

If he'd had a tail it would have wagged. "Good, good. I'm glad I could give it to you." He glanced at me. "But more importantly, I'm glad you accepted the gift."

"It wasn't easy. I'm used to working for everything I get. It still doesn't feel right, but I'm not giving it back."

"I don't want it back. Just enjoy."

We were silent for a few blocks. I kept asking myself how I was going to broach the subject of my mother. I finally decided to use the story my father had told to Lois and Lew. After all, that had been the source of my enlightenment.

"I heard you telling about that old snake in the hayloft."

"As a child you didn't get addlepated very often. It's one of my favorite memories."

"I'm surprised you remember it fondly, considering how Mom blamed you."

"She was right. I should have watched you more closely."

"I was pretty strong-willed. I thought those kittens were in the hayloft. Come hell or high water I was going to check."

"Even if I'd told you about the snake?"

"I'd have taken a hoe with me, but I'd probably have gone up there."

"Yeah. You're probably right."

I swallowed my nervousness. "Mom did that often, didn't she? Blamed you for stuff that did or didn't happen."

His gray head swiveled in my direction. "I had faults that irritated your mother. Let's leave it at that."

"Not this time, Dad. Because you and Mom never argued or had rousing shouting matches, I thought you got along. But your marriage was too silent. When Carl and I had a dispute, we'd get vocal. We'd air our problem, make up, and move on. As I remember, Mom did all the talking. You listened or walked away."

"She was usually right."

"I don't think right or wrong has anything to do with it. I think you took her abuse as long as you could and that's when you left."

"Abuse?" His eyes widened. "Your mother wasn't abusive. She was an exceptional woman. We were just mismatched. She had her way of doing things, and I had mine. It's funny how the very traits that attract you to a person can turn out to be the most frustrating. Your mother was strong of spirit and firm in her convictions. When I first fell in love with her, I admired the way she always seemed to know what was right. I always seemed to make the wrong choice. She had no patience with my ideas. I liked to make changes, try something new, even if it failed. She wanted everything to stay the same."

"Such as?"

He thought a moment. "The vegetable garden comes to mind. She was pregnant with you and as big as a barrel when it came time to plant. I worked and worked that soil until it had the texture of flour. I sowed the seeds, putting the corn near the pig lot. I thought that as the corn grew tall it would hide the dilapidated building. When we sat on the porch we wouldn't have to look at it. I admit it was an aesthetic concept, but what difference would it make? The ground was the same in both places."

"Mom didn't want the corn there?"

"Hell no. She got so upset she nearly went into premature labor. She said the hogs would smell the corn ripening and would tear down the fence to get to it."

"Did she raise her voice?"

"Of course not. That wasn't her way."

"But you were made to feel inferior. That you'd screwed up, right?"

"I had."

"No, Dad. What you did wasn't wrong. What Mom wanted wasn't wrong, either. It was just a difference of opinion."

"We had those differences often, daughter. After a while, it gets to where you can't trust your own instincts. You begin to question whether you have a working brain. I'd had this cattle-branding-tool idea spinning around in my head for years. I'd tried talking to your mother, but she wouldn't listen. She only saw the here and now, not what could or might be. Those months before I finally left were hell. Nothing I did suited her, so I took off."

I turned onto Catalpa Road and slowed the SUV. "I can better understand now why you left, but what about me? You sent a yearly check, and Mom deposited it into an account for me. After she died you started sending me a birthday card and a box of grapefruit at Christmas. Dad, I don't even like grapefruit."

He stared at me. "Well, I'll be damned. I didn't know that."

"There's so much about me you don't know. Mom's been dead for over fifteen years, but you waited until last Christmas to come see me. Why?"

"How did I know if you'd want to see me? I didn't really think your mother would speak ill of me to you. Fact is, I figured once I was gone she'd simply never mention me again. But I couldn't be sure. Time has a way of slipping by. Before I knew it you were grown. You had a life here in River City. You had a husband, who from all accounts was kind and loving to you. Then when I read Carl's obituary in the paper, I thought of returning."

"Thought must have been all you did. He's been dead for two years."

"Give it a rest, Bretta. I'm weak. I'm shy. I'm old. I'm scared. Take your pick. I didn't feel I could intrude on your grief. I came at Christmas because DeeDee called and said you needed me. *You needed me.* I got on the first plane. We spent a few days together. I went back to Texas, but I wasn't satisfied. I wanted more."

"More what?"

He whispered, "I wanted revenge."

"On whom?" I squawked.

Wearily, my father said, "Let's drop this. I've said too much."

"No. No. I think we're finally getting somewhere."

He stared out the window. "I wanted revenge on your mother. I wanted to prove her wrong. I'm not a fool. I'm not lazy. I have amounted to something. In this world, money spells success. I have money, and I've made it using my abilities, my imagination, and my skills."

"You don't have to prove anything to me. I credit you with my creative talent, my imagination, and my penchant for 'what if.' Mother's influence grounded me so I give it some thought before I go off the deep end. I got the best from both of you, with my own personal quirkiness tossed in to keep life interesting."

I topped a hill, and my lips turned down in a frown. Sid Hancock stood in the middle of the road at the end of Lydia's driveway, waving me to a stop. "And if my life gets too humdrum, I have Sid to annoy the hell out of me."

I slowed the SUV, pulled alongside him, and put down the window. His pale complexion was blotchy from the sun. His eyes shot sparks when he saw my passenger.

"Take your joyride somewhere else, Bretta," Sid said, keeping his gaze off my father. "We're working a crime scene."

"So Lydia's death wasn't an accident?"

"Nope. Murder. There was no gas inspector. The fire marshal says the gas line was tampered with. Gas leaked and filled the house. When Lydia flipped the switch for the kitchen light, the spark triggered the explosion. You've got your information, now buzz off."

"I'm *buzzing* on my way to the property east of here."

Always suspicious, Sid demanded, "What for?"

"I'm looking for a flower."

"A flower? Don't you have a shop full of them? Now you're out scrounging the fields and ditches." He shook his head. "Jeez. You can do the damnedest things." He waved me on, but hollered, "If you haven't passed back by here in half an hour, I'm coming to look for you."

"Be still my heart," I muttered under my breath, but I put up a hand to show I'd heard.

My father chuckled. "That was quick thinking about the flower."

"It's the truth. I *am* looking for a flower, but not because I'm a florist. On the ceiling of Claire Alexander's beauty shop is a painting of a girl. Among the flowers surrounding this girl is a bloom that's been identified as Mead's milkweed."

"Milkweed? Like what was in the tussie-mussie?"

"Same family, but an extinct cousin. From what I understand, it grew in this area. An area where Oliver and Lydia used to live."

My father glanced over his shoulder. "So we're investigating the murder right under the sheriff's nose? I like that. He's entirely too arrogant."

"Forget Sid," I said, pulling into the first driveway that was east of Lydia's place. The lane was rutted, grass and brush waist-high. "This is as far as I want to take the SUV, Dad." I glanced at his neatly creased trousers, knit polo shirt, and dress shoes. "There's rough terrain ahead. You might want to wait here."

"Not a chance, daughter. I'm with you on this mission."

"Sid gave us thirty minutes. Let's make the most of it."

We got out and pushed our way through the thicket. I tried not to think of ticks, chiggers, and other creatures hiding in the grass.

"Where are we going to find this Mead's milkweed?" Dad asked.

"In an igneous glade," I said, then explained what the botany teacher had told me. "I doubt we'll find the plant, but I want to see where it could have grown. I'm not sure if that's important, but something about this area is."

Dad stopped a few feet ahead of me. "Here's what's left of a foundation," he said. "It was either a shed or a very small house."

"Lydia said there used to be a house here." I pointed. "Look at those old trees. They're ancient. Wonder how come they died?"

Dad squinted, then moved so the sun wasn't in his eyes. "Dutch elm disease swept this part of the country and took plenty of victims. But I don't remember the trunks turning black like that."

Dad wandered on, but I stayed where I was. Parts of the concrete foundation had crumbled until it was no more than a pile of rubble. Saplings as thick as my arm had taken over the area. A plump toad hopped out of the grass and scuttled into hiding under the rocks. Mother Nature had reclaimed this spot as her own, rubbing out nearly all traces of human inhabitance. The trees, their trunks rotted hulls, stood like decrepit sentries. I gazed at them, wondering what they were guarding.

Off to my right, my father shouted, "Bretta! You have to see this." He motioned to me.

"I'm coming," I said, but I didn't move. I kept staring at the foundation. Carl had said I needed to put everything in the right order. I knew that Claire had been a rebel. The sixties were a time of revolution—of social reform. People were looking for answers. They wanted to preserve and often took up causes.

"Bretta?" called my father.

I hurried forward and stopped at his side. He flung out his arm and stared at the ground. "Would you look at that? Can you believe it?"

I looked and saw a tangle of plants. He picked a leaf, and after he'd bruised it with his fingers, held it under my nose. The aroma was powerful, and memorable.

"Tansy?" I asked.

"And that's pennyroyal," he said, pointing. "Over there are rhododendron bushes. And unless my eyesight is failing, I see orange dodder wrapped around those weeds yonder." He turned again. "There's the milkweed. Everything needed for the tussie-mussie that was left in your car."

"Except for the white rose," I said.

"Are you going to call the other River City florists and ask them—"

I shrugged. "What? Did they sell a single white rose in the last day or two? Why would they remember that?"

"I guess you're right."

I turned and stared at the grassy prairie, and heard Carl's voice in my head.

"Put it together, Babe. Use logic and reason to figure it out. If the Mead's milkweed was the cause, then what was the effect?"

Chapter Nineteen

Early the next morning, I called the hospital to check on Bailey. A nurse told me he was stirring, and mumbling, but he hadn't opened his eyes. Next I searched the newspaper for the picture of the girl from Claire's beauty shop ceiling. No mention or photo in today's paper. I drank another cup of coffee, and then gave it up. There wasn't any way around it. I had work to do.

I drove to the flower shop, but I dreaded going inside. I hadn't slept well. My mind had tossed and turned all night long, running over and over what I knew about Claire. As I unlocked the shop door, I squared my shoulders, prepared for battle. Murder investigations would have to be put on hold. I was a florist, and the wedding adventure was about to begin.

Sometimes it's nice to be the boss, but today I just wanted to be an employee. I knew that by the end of the day I'd be sick and tired of my name.

"Bretta, where's the ribbon?"

"Bretta, what do you want me to do now?"

"Bretta, is this arrangement too big?"

"Bretta, how many roses should we save for the bride's bouquet?"

I couldn't blame my help. On a big job everyone wants

reassurance that they're doing the right thing. No one wants to screw up. But to whom could *I* turn? Who was going to tell me if I was making the right decisions? And each judgment call had to be made off the top of my head. We didn't have guidelines.

During my floral career, I'd never undertaken an event that involved so many picayune details. For each section of the Tranquility Garden either a unique bouquet or a display had to be fabricated from the tools of my trade and one hell of an imagination. This last was my department, too. Lois and Lew would offer suggestions, but once again the final decision would be mine.

By quarter till nine my crew had gathered in the workroom. Lois and Lew knew what to expect. The three women I'd hired were oblivious. They'd helped us out on Valentine's Day, when the Flower Shop had been a madhouse, but that holiday would be nothing compared to what was ahead of us.

Besides doing the wedding work, we had our regular duties. Evelyn might think River City would come to a halt for her daughter's nuptials, but that wasn't the case. We had Claire's funeral flowers to do. Lydia's memorial service was pending. Then there were the usual assorted hospital, birthday, and anniversary bouquets to design.

I'd worked out a game plan for what needed to be done and when. I'd assigned specific tasks to each person, leaving myself free to gallop around the shop, available to be at their beck and call, while doing my own work.

By noon we were honking on. Twenty Boston ferns had been cleaned of any dead leaves and repotted into brass containers. The morning deliveries had been made. I thought everything was coming along, but apparently I had a touch of hubris. My pride took a beating when Lois finished a prototype of the wreath that was to float on the reflection pool at the base of the gazebo.

She bellowed from the back room. "Bretta, you gotta see this."

I went to the tub of water and stared at the drowned flowers and candles.

"It sank like a stone," she said, trying not to snicker.

On paper the plan had seemed feasible. The ring of Styrofoam had floated when I'd given it a test run, but the added weight of the flowers and candles was too much for it to remain buoyant.

"Hell and damnation," I muttered. "Now what?"

"Bretta?" called Lew from the workroom. "How are you going to attach this tulle to the gazebo?"

I'd bought one hundred yards of white gold-shot tulle. The netting was to frame all six of the gazebo openings and hang in gossamer folds like a tent under the peaked roof. According to Evelyn, I had to achieve the impression that Nikki was taking her vows among wispy clouds.

I turned to Lois. "Should we use ribbon to tie the tulle to the posts? Or tendrils of ivy and wire?"

"I don't know. What are we gonna do about this sunken treasure?"

"Bretta?" said Gertrude. "There's a woman here to see you. She says the mother of the bride wants preparation photos. You know what I mean? Some behind-the-scenes candid shots."

I peered around the doorjamb and saw Kasey at the front counter. Her blond hair was limp. She looked thinner and more retro sixties than she had at the park on Saturday. Her camera was focused on Lew.

I'd given him the job of measuring the tulle into accurate lengths for each of the six gazebo openings. He was such a perfectionist, I knew he'd get the numbers correct, but he wasn't used to working with the flimsy material. The hundred yards of tulle had slipped and slid into a filmy lake on the floor. He'd gathered it up in his arms but had succeeded in draping his body diaphanously. The man looked totally inept.

"Don't take that picture," I said, but I was too late.

Click!

Kasey spun in my direction with the camera aimed at me. "Don't even think about it," I said sharply.

Click!

I was seething. "Dang it, Kasey, don't take another picture."

Click! Gertrude picking her teeth.

Click! Eleanor eating the last jelly doughnut.

Click! Marjory turning over a vase of roses.

In four quick strides I was at the front counter. "What do you think you're doing?"

"My job."

"No. Not here. Not now. We're under enough pressure. We don't need this distraction."

"Evelyn wants photos of Sonya, Dana, and you at work."

"I don't care what she wants."

In a low voice, Kasey said, "How does it feel?"

"How does what feel?"

She brought up the camera and took my picture. "To not get what you want. Sonya and Dana both asked you to back off from Claire's murder investigation, but you keep asking questions. You keep snooping and prying into things that aren't any of your business."

My eyes narrowed. "Is that what this is about?" I waved a hand. "Fine. Take your pictures—and while you're doing it, let me ask you this. In your environmental work have you come across any Mead's milkweed?"

Kasey's lips parted in an *O* of astonishment. She stared at me for a full minute, then picked up her equipment and walked out.

"Whatever you said to her really worked," Gertrude said. "She hightailed it out of here like a duck in a hailstorm."

"Let's get back to work," I said. "Lew, we're using wire and ivy. Eleanor, help him get that tulle under control. Marjory, you missed a puddle of water over by that table leg. We don't have time for an emergency run to the hospital if someone should slip and fall. Gertrude, please answer the telephone. It has rung three times."

"And me?" called Lois from the back room. "What about this floral submarine?"

I gritted my teeth, stared into space, willing an answer to come to me. Finally, I said, "We'll double the ring of Styrofoam. I bought spares. Attach another under the one you already have. If you need to, add a little more greenery so the extra thickness doesn't show."

"Can do," she said.

I glanced around the workroom. Everyone was intent on his or her tasks. Maybe I'd have five minutes to concentrate on what I had to do. I consulted my notes. Two massive bouquets set on pedestals were to flank the reflection pool. I filled the copper containers with water and grabbed the bucket of flowers I'd reserved for the arrangements.

White larkspur for height. I used my florist knife to barely cut the stem end. I needed as much stalk as possible. My bouquets would be in competition with the twilight canopy.

And yet, I had to keep in mind that once these bouquets were completed, they had to be hauled in the delivery van to the park. I'd considered making the arrangements on-site, but there would be enough to do on Saturday.

The rest of the day passed without incident. I finished the two bouquets and the arrangements for the reception tables, then called a halt at six thirty.

"We'll have to work later tomorrow night. Let's go home." I didn't have to say it twice. Before I could draw a breath, Gertrude, Marjory, and Eleanor had grabbed their handbags and were out the door.

"I'm pooped," said Lois, dropping into a chair. She eyed me. "You don't look like you have the energy to drive home."

"I'm tired," I admitted, "but the show is just starting. Tomorrow we have to make the corsages, the boutonnieres, and the bridal party flowers. And I can't forget that I have to go to the park and spray the shrubs gold before everyone gets there for the rehearsal." I had a heart-stopping thought. "Those cases of paint were delivered, weren't they?"

"Yes," said Lew. "Three big boxes. Talk about your environmental hazard. All that aerosol paint fogging the air can't be good. Do you have a mask to wear over your nose and mouth?"

"I'll figure out something," I said. "I'm scheduled to paint the shrubs before the rehearsal. Paint the shrubs? Gosh, I can't believe the things I do."

Lois struggled wearily to her feet. "By the way, what did you say to Kasey to make her 'hightail it out of here like a duck in a hailstorm'?" Her eyebrows drew down in a frown. "Are ducks afraid of hail?"

I grinned. "I haven't a clue as to what ducks like or dislike, but Kasey wasn't pleased when I asked her about Mead's milkweed."

While we turned out the lights and gathered up our belongings, I brought Lois and Lew up to speed on what I'd discovered. When I'd finished, both were too tired to offer more than a feeble "Good night."

As I drove home, I wondered if we were getting too old for this stuff. If we were exhausted now, how would we make it through two more days?

I woke up Friday morning to the smell of smoke. I tried to leap out of bed but I'd done too much lifting and stooping yesterday. Shuffling across the floor like a decrepit woman, I peered out the window. It was early, not even light yet, but I didn't need the sun. I had flames.

"Omigod." I gulped. "The garden's on fire."

I grabbed my robe and struggled into it. I made two tries to find the belt, then realized I'd put the robe on wrong side out. I didn't stop to change it. I stuffed my feet into a pair of loafers and hurried downstairs with my robe flapping about me like the Caped Crusader.

"DeeDee!" I shouted. "Dad! Come quick. The garden's on fire."

I didn't pause, but headed out the terrace doors and nearly took a fall when I tripped over a rubber hose. I traced it to the water faucet at the side of the house.

"Bretta?" called someone from the shadows.

I thought I recognized the voice. "Eddie, is that you?"

"Yeah. Sorry about the drifting smoke. The wind has shifted, but now that I've started the fire, I don't want to put it out until I get this controlled burn finished."

My heart eased its rapid beat at the word *controlled*. "You set this fire on purpose?"

Eddie said, "Jerry, keep a close eye over here. I don't want heat anywhere near this old ginkgo tree."

I watched Eddie walk toward me. He had a small tank strapped to his back. A black hose with a perforated nozzle was connected to the receptacle.

Once he had joined me on the terrace, he said, "I told you we had to get this heavy thatch out of the way. A rapid fire will burn the grass but won't damage the plants underneath. I should be able to start moving soil tomorrow."

I nodded. "Now I remember, but the smoke woke me from a sound sleep. I panicked when I thought my garden was on fire."

Eddie grinned. "It is, but it's under control. I told the fire department and the Missouri Conservation Department that I was doing a burn. I didn't want your neighbors calling in an emergency." He pointed to the hose. "We have water close at hand. I have three men with shovels and wet burlap to smother any flames that spread farther than I want."

My father opened the terrace door, and he and DeeDee stepped out. I told them what was going on.

Dad asked, "Why so early? The sun isn't even up."

"For exactly that reason," said Eddie. "Any wayward spark will be spotted in the dark."

Dad nodded. "Makes good sense."

Now that my eyes were accustomed to the dusky light, I saw Eddie's men. They wore heavy overalls, long-sleeved shirts, and stout boots, but none of them had a tank like Eddie's. "So what's this?" I said, pointing to the apparatus on his back.

"Propane tank." He turned away from us and twisted a valve. I heard a clicking sound, a roar, and flames flashed from the nozzle.

DeeDee said, "W-wow. I wonder if M-Martha has one of those. You could brown a h-hundred m-meringue pies at one t-time with that b-baby."

Eddie touched the flame to some blades of grass growing in a crevice of the sandstone terrace. The blades shriveled and dissolved into ash. "Petroleum has too much vapor that can lead to unpredictable explosions," he explained. "It's too combustible. Kerosene or diesel fuel leaves a residue in the ground. Since I'm planting this area, I don't want that. This propane torch gets the ball rolling. If I see a spot that needs added heat, I only have to touch it and—*poof*—the thatch is gone."

"Eddie," shouted one of the men. "The fire is almost to the southwest corner. You wanna check it out?"

"Gotta go," he said. "I'll be around all day to make sure everything is saturated with water. We don't want any flare-ups. I hoped it would rain tonight or tomorrow, but I guess that isn't going to happen."

The sun popped over the horizon, showering the landscape with flecks of gold. Looking at the light, I said, "I can't forget to paint those shrubs in the park."

Eddie snorted. "Better you than me." He took a couple of steps, stopped, and hollered, "Jerry, I said I didn't want the fire close to that tree. Put your eyes back in your head and pick up a shovel."

I looked at Jerry and saw him staring at me. Under my breath, I said, "Wonder what his problem is?"

DeeDee giggled. "B-baby doll p-pajamas show p-plenty of leg."

My father said, "We have enough heat around here, Bretta, without you adding to it."

Embarrassed, I wrapped my robe around me and marched into the house. What a way to start the day.

Chapter Twenty

Friday was a repeat of Thursday with two exceptions. The morning paper ran the girl's picture from Claire's beauty shop ceiling. The photo was less imposing in black and white and only the width of two columns. I asked Lois, Lew, and my three extra helpers if they recognized the girl. None did. I thought about calling Chief Kelley to see if the picture had generated any new information, but didn't. As Avery, my lawyer friend, had said, I had "enough on my plate" with this wedding.

At four o'clock, the hospital called. Bailey was awake and asking for me. Tears of relief filled my eyes, but my heart was heavy.

"Go see him," urged Lois. "According to your schedule, we're doing fine."

"I can't."

"Why not? While he was in a coma you visited him. Now that he's awake, don't you want to be there?"

I sighed. "I do, and I don't."

Lois grabbed my arm and hauled me to the back room for a private grilling. "I'm not getting this," she said. "What's going on? I know you like the man."

"That's the problem. I don't just *like* him. I think I may love him."

Lois rocked back on her heels. "Well, I'll be damned. You finally admitted it. I'm impressed. I thought it would be at least another six to eight months before you figured that out."

I made a face. "Are you saying I'm slow?"

She grinned. "No, just conservative, and loyal to Carl's memory, and timid, and scared, and you think too much, and—"

I held up my hands. "Stop. Stop. I get the picture. I'm a neurotic mess, but only where Bailey is concerned. He boggles my mind."

"Everyone should be so boggled. What's the problem?"

"I miss Carl, but I'm adjusting. I like my life the way it is. I have DeeDee. Dad is here, and our relationship is progressing. Bailey could complicate everything. I don't know what he expects. He said he's interested in me. He bought the cottage." I gave her a meaningful look. "He might want *more* than I'm ready to give."

Lois knew me well and tracked my thought explicitly. "Bretta, the man just woke up from a coma. I doubt that he's recovered his libido this quickly."

"I don't know. He's danged sexy."

Lois rolled her eyes. "If he has that kind of stamina, hook him and reel him in. He's a keeper."

Grumbling, I said, "I never was much of a fisherman, but I'll think about it while I'm spraying the shrubs. Help me load those boxes of gold paint into the SUV. I'm going to the park. Can you keep everyone in line while I'm gone?"

"On the straight and narrow," she said, hefting the first box. "They won't know you've left the building."

Painting foliage was a mindless chore. Shake the can, aim, and press the nozzle. A light first coat. Another application and a final touch-up. Move on to the next bush.

Ho hum. This area of the park was quiet and secluded. In a few hours the wedding rehearsal would begin. I wanted to be done with this painting and out of here, but if I could be a leaf on a tree, I'd stay. I wondered if Evelyn would order her daughter around like she'd ordered us.

Another ho hum. I could think about Bailey, but what was the use? I could plan, and dream, and fret, and stew, but until I faced him, I didn't have a clue how I should act. A small part of me wanted to rush to his side and fling myself into his arms. But I wasn't the flinging type. Carl used to tease me that when it came my time to pass on, I'd have it planned down to my last breath.

I couldn't help it. I had to think everything through to what I thought might be the correct conclusion. I called it "covering my ass." I didn't have to be right, but I had to use my brain.

I hadn't always been like this. The flower shop had changed the way I approached life. Every hour of every day I had to anticipate any eventuality. Should I order extra flowers? Would people want red roses this week or yellow or pink? Most of the time it was guesswork based on experience, but I still had to plan, to think, to reason.

I tossed another empty paint can into the box and uncapped a fresh container. My arm moved steadily back and forth, giving the foliage the Midas touch. The motion was hypnotic, and I was tired. My eyelids drooped. I jerked upright. Or maybe I was sucking down paint fumes. I giggled. Good thing I wasn't a smoker. If I lit up, I might *poof* like the sugar cubes DeeDee had saturated with liquor.

I eased my finger off the spray button. *Poof!* In my mind I saw Eddie's torch burst into flames and burn the blades of grass.

I shook my head to make the thought clearer. When that didn't work, I put the paint can on the path and walked away from my work. I went to the gazebo and sat on the steps. Taking deep breaths, I concentrated on that fragment of thought.

Liquor. Alcohol. *Poof!*

Cause and effect.

Mead's milkweed.

I put my elbows on my knees and cupped my chin in my hands. Staring at the ground, I ordered myself to concentrate.

Claire had been the activist. Sonya had won honors in the Debate Club. Dana had cheered her team to victory. Kasey had been president of the Botany Club. In fact, all four girls had been members.

The preservation of our natural resources would have interested Kasey. It would also have made a good debate topic for Sonya. From past information, Claire had been hot and ready to take on any and all causes. Dana would've tagged along because that's the kind of person she is.

Was the Mead's milkweed extinct back in the sixties?

I sat up straight. Howie, Claire's ex-husband, had been the one to use the word *extinct*. I closed my eyes so I could remember his exact words: "History has a way of biting you in the ass. Everything can't be saved. It became extinct just like she is."

"Everything can't be saved," I said out loud. During the sixties groups were formed to save the whales, save the rain forests, save the—flowers?

Had the girls tried to save the Mead's milkweed? How? Eddie had said a rapid burn would get rid of the thatch but would leave the plants underneath unharmed. Had the girls tried a controlled burn? Eddie used a propane torch to set the fire. What would the girls have used as an accelerant to set fire to an entire glade?

Something combustible. Gas? Diesel fuel? Kerosene? No. All were environmentally unsafe, and would have gone against ecological preservation.

My eyes binged open. "I'll be damned." It had to be the lemon extract. Wasn't it made up of alcohol? Wouldn't it burn?

"Bretta, are you all right?"

I jerked around. Dana, Kasey, and Sonya stood off to my left.

Dana said, "Bretta, you're pale. Are you sick?"

"Inhaled too many paint fumes," I said, getting up from the steps. I brushed past their united front, then turned and asked, "What brings all of you to the park? Kind of early for the rehearsal, isn't it?"

"There isn't going to be a rehearsal," said Sonya.

I looked from one to the other. "Why? What's going on?"

"Evelyn says the ballet company has been held over in St. Louis for an encore performance."

I shook my head. "I bet Evelyn is fit to be tied."

Sonya said, "She's handling it well. She says Nikki is an intelligent woman. She can find her way to the altar."

"I'm glad Evelyn is confident. I haven't liked this tight schedule since the first time I heard about it." I looked at the women and repeated, "So what brings you to the park?"

Sonya seemed to be the trio's spokeswoman. "Dana called the flower shop and was told you were here. We've tried talking to you one-on-one, but that hasn't worked. Perhaps if we're together, we can persuade you to leave Claire's memory intact."

I raised an eyebrow. "Claire's memory or your reputations?"

The women traded looks. Sonya said, "You obviously have something on your mind. Say it, and let's be done with it."

I wasn't ready to speak my theory aloud. There were still too many leftover pieces of the puzzle. But I couldn't let this opportunity pass. I felt my way along. "Something was bothering Claire on the day she was murdered. She hinted at a secret while we were here at the park. Later she called me. Why me? Why not one of her friends? Unless she knew none of you would help her."

"That's not true," said Dana. "We would have done anything for Claire."

"I'm sure you would. Right down to stealing four bottles of lemon extract from the high school's home ec kitchen."

Sonya laughed. "That was a long time ago. What does a childhood prank have to do with Claire's murder?"

"You tell me."

Kasey started to speak, but a look from Sonya silenced her.

I nodded. "Okay, if that's the way you want it. As you said, it was a long time ago, but not if the memory of what happened plays in your head daily. The mind keeps events fresh, and the pain doesn't go away, especially if you continue to probe it. I think that's what Claire did. She was the organizer of your little group. She decided to take the lemon extract, but only after Kasey expressed an urge to preserve the Mead's milkweed plant.

"I'm assuming you learned about the plant's extinction in botany class. Perhaps you took a field trip and saw it growing in its natural habitat, which is out on Catalpa Road."

Sonya scoffed, "I don't see what you're driving at. We used the extract to make lemon squares."

I shook my head. "No, you didn't. You set fire to that

glade. You wanted to do a burn. Get rid of the heavy thatch of grass so the Mead's milkweed would have a chance to survive."

Sonya looked at her two friends, then turned back to me. "This is all very interesting, but again I'm asking, what does it have to do with Claire's death?"

I didn't answer right away. I sensed a change in the trio facing me. When they'd arrived at the gazebo, I'd felt the tension in the air. Now they seemed more at ease. In fact, the longer I'd talked the more relaxed they'd become. That meant I was missing something. What?

Softly I recited, "You can boil me in oil. You can burn me at the stake. But a—"

The tension was back. Sonya's spine stiffened. Dana's knuckles turned white as she clenched her hands.

"No!" shouted Kasey. "Stop it. Don't say another word."

"Why does that poem upset all of you so much?"

Sonya took a step in my direction. Her eyes were narrowed. "I'm telling you for the last time to drop it, Bretta."

I was fully aware of my vulnerable position. I was in a secluded area of the park with three women, any of whom could be a murderer. In my head I heard Carl whisper, "Use the buddy approach, Babe, and if that don't work, run like hell."

I softened my tone. "Your childhood friend has been murdered. A killer is walking around free. Doesn't that bother you? If any of you knows something, you need to tell me."

Sonya said, "We don't have to tell you anything. I'm leaving, and if you ladies have any brains, you'll come with me."

Without hesitation, Kasey went to Sonya's side. I looked at Dana. She was my best bet for information. I waited hopefully, wondering if she'd meekly follow Sonya's lead.

Dana licked her lips and fought back tears. "We aren't bad women, Bretta. We weren't bad girls. We most surely aren't murderers."

Her words and tone touched me, but if I believed her, then who had killed Claire and Lydia? Who had driven the SUV that plowed into Bailey's truck? Who had constructed the deadly bouquet that had been left in my car? Who had the most to gain by bringing the past into the present?

Chapter Twenty-one

❧ Nikki Montgomery's wedding day had arrived. It was Saturday, and the ceremony was to begin at eight o'clock that evening. My crew and I were in the park by ten A.M., ready for some intense decorating and beautifying. We wouldn't bring the flowers until later in the day, but there was plenty of preparation to do before we set the bouquets in place. My SUV was packed with everything I'd need— hammers, nails, tacks, florist knives and nippers, wire, tape, a ladder, and a box of Band-Aids.

Lois would stay at the flower shop until twelve, when the store closed. She had several sympathy arrangements to make for Lydia's memorial service, which was scheduled for two o'clock this afternoon. Gertrude was answering the phone, doing whatever needed to be done. Once the shop was locked, both women would join us in the park. I'd left money for them to buy us lunch. By noon we would be in need of sustenance.

I had begun my day by tackling the tulle. Working with the filmy material was like fighting a phantom opponent. My nerves were already shredded. I'd spent another sleepless night, worrying and wondering. I'd juggled thoughts of the wedding with the murders until I thought I'd go bananas. Bananas had made me think of food. I'd raided the refrig-

215

erator. At the very back of the freezer, I'd found DeeDee's stash of Blue Bunny ice cream—tin-roof sundae, my favorite. I'd eaten half the carton, and had indigestion the rest of the night.

Lew, Marjory, and Eleanor unpacked the twenty Boston ferns from the delivery van. Each person was armed with a sketch I'd made that showed where the bouquets, ferns, hanging baskets, and displays were to go.

From my roost on the ladder I watched the goings-on in the park. Kasey and Evelyn were outside the reception tent. Both women were smiling, which was a good sign. In another section Sonya played ringmaster, directing her twelve helpers with clear, precise orders. She caught me watching and gave me a curt nod.

In the far corner of our arena, Dana and her group were unloading supplies into another smaller tent that would serve as the food-preparation station. For easy entry into the tent, the side flaps were up. I watched Dana set an ice chest on one of the tables, then rub her stomach.

I was on intimate terms with that gesture. Dana had a belly full of nerves. Maybe I should offer her one of my antacid tablets. I'd brought along a new supply. I could share, and perhaps ask a question or two.

I started down the ladder, saw the tulle in a wrinkled wad on the gazebo floor, and went back up. First things first, old girl, I said to myself.

For more time than I cared to think about, I folded and looped, wired and tied the tulle into a floating, gossamer gob of shimmering clouds.

"Bretta, that is absolutely fabulous," said Evelyn from the gazebo steps. "It's just the way Nikki and I had it pictured. Thank you."

I rubbed my neck, trying to get rid of the crick. My legs and feet ached from climbing and standing on the narrow rungs of the ladder. It helped ease my pain that I'd accomplished what I set out to do, and the work had been approved.

"How's everything going?" I asked.

"Wonderful," said Evelyn. She glanced at her watch. "Nikki and the rest of her bridal party should be here in another few hours. I can't wait."

"She's cutting it pretty close."

"I know. I spent a horrible night last night. But things are going to work out just as I've planned. I'm leaving in a few minutes to check on the hotel rooms. My guests will need snacks to help them recuperate. I want them to have whatever they need."

"Will they be coming out here?"

"Not right away. The limo will deliver them to the park later this evening."

I started to say that they ought to get a feel for the garden, but at this point I didn't care. I just wanted my part done.

"Did you see the shrubs?" I asked.

"I'm glad you brought that up. I saw them, and they aren't shiny enough."

"Really?" My eyes narrowed. "What would you suggest?"

"I have a case of aerosol lacquer in my car. It's on the backseat. The doors aren't locked. Have your man unload the box and give each bush a quick touch-up. I want those leaves to gleam in the candlelight."

My jaw dropped. Before I had recovered, Sonya called, "Evelyn, could you come over here? This lamp oil has an unusual odor."

Evelyn touched my arm. "You're doing an excellent job,

Bretta. Now, see to those shrubs." To Sonya, she said, "I've checked the oil. It's what I ordered. Nikki loves the smell of clematis blossoms. I had the oil specially blended even though the cost made me blink twice."

I'd never noticed a scent from the blossom of a clematis vine. I started toward the group so I could have a whiff, but my path crossed Lew's. I explained about the case of lacquer in Evelyn's car.

"I'll get it," he said, "but you might want to go to the hospital. I have my cell phone with me, and Lois called from the shop. Mr. Monroe is pitching a fit. He wants to see you immediately."

"Bailey?" My heart skipped a beat. "Why? What's wrong?"

"Haven't a clue, Boss. I'll go get the lacquer, and I suppose you want me to do the spraying?"

"Yes. You, Marjory, and Eleanor spray the shrubs. The rental company has finished setting up the chairs for the guests. Now I can attach the satin bows. After that, I have to do the display by the entrance into the reception tent. White satin is to cover the wire stands that are to be at different heights for the bouquets."

I thought a moment. "Did I put that tall pedestal in the SUV? Yeah. Yeah." I nodded. "I remember taking it out of the closet." I shrugged. "Anyway, by the time we finish these jobs, it'll be after twelve, and Lois and Gertrude will arrive with lunch and the helium for the balloons. For the rest of the afternoon, you'll be trundling back and forth from the park to the shop hauling bouquets. Our extra helpers will be inflating balloons."

"What about Mr. Monroe?"

I raised my chin. "What about him?"

"Are you going to the hospital?"

"I just gave you a rundown on what I'm doing. Did I mention leaving the park?"

Lew pursed his lips. "Fine. I'm turning off my phone. If he should get my number, he might call me. I don't need to be harassed by a man I've never met. I have people closer at hand doing an excellent job of that."

I grimaced. "I'm sorry. Don't you feel the pressure we're under? Am I the only one worried about details?"

A wail of displeasure rose from the food-preparation tent. Lew cocked his head in that direction. "Sounds like another nervous Nellie. Marjory, Eleanor, and I will be spritzing bushes if you need us."

The conflict in the tent subsided quickly. I went over anyway, and met Evelyn as she was leaving. She brushed past me without a word, headed for the parking lot. I stepped into the tent and saw Dana kick an ice chest. Instantly, she dropped to her knees and lifted the lid to see if the contents of the chest had been harmed by her temper.

"What's going on?" I asked.

Dana spoke over her shoulder. "That woman and I don't jive. Nothing I do suits her."

"It isn't an exclusive club. I'm a founding member. What's her problem now?"

Dana stood up and moved to a cart that held a huge deep-fat fryer. "She doesn't want me to start frying the shrimp until eight o'clock, when the ceremony begins. That gives me thirty to forty-five minutes to have everything ready for the guests. I told her if there's one glitch, then everything will be thrown off this tight schedule. Evelyn has assured me there *will not* be any glitches."

I shook my head. "I have problems, too. Maybe we need

a break." I looked at the boxes, sacks, and ice chests sitting on the tables. "Have you got anything to drink?"

"Nothing cold, but I have a thermos of coffee. Want some?"

"Oh, yes, if you have enough to share."

She nodded, got out some Styrofoam cups, and filled two. As she handed mine across to me, she said, "I'm telling you upfront, I'm not discussing Claire's death. We can chat about other things but not her murder."

I led the way to a table near the front of the tent. We sat and sipped. It was an effort, but I didn't say a word. After a while, Dana began to talk. I hid a smile. When something is on your mind, it's hard to keep still.

"I hit my stride in high school," said Dana. "I was forty pounds lighter. I was a cheerleader. I was dating three guys at one time. I thought I had the world by the tail. I could do anything, be anything I wanted." She glanced at me. "I didn't care about the extinction of a stupid milkweed plant. But I liked stealing the lemon extract from Ms. Beecher, the home ec teacher. She was such a crab. Said my cooking lacked skill and finesse."

I laid it on thick. "This Ms. Beecher should see you now." I sniffed the air. "It smells wonderful in here. You're a true professional, Dana."

Dana looked pleased, but demurely said, "I don't know about that."

"I *know* you ladies need to get into gear," said Sonya. "You don't have time to sit and gossip."

I stood and faced Sonya. "I'm well aware of my responsibilities. If you'll excuse me, I have to attach satin bows to chairs." I walked off but glanced over my shoulder. I expected to see Sonya giving Dana hell for talking to me, but

Sonya had moved on and Dana had gone back to work.

I tied the bows to the chairs. I inspected the shrubs, which now looked artificial with their sheen of lacquer. I positioned the wire stands for the display by the entrance into the reception tent, then draped the stands with white satin cloth.

Lois and Gertrude arrived with food and the helium tank. After we'd eaten, I put the three extra helpers to work inflating the latex balloons, then I sent Lew to the shop for the first load of bouquets.

Finding a spare minute, I sat on the gazebo steps and said to Lois, "I'm exhausted. Remind me of this day when I'm asked to do another wedding."

Lois leaned against the railing and grinned. "You wanted the kudos. Can't get them without showing your talent."

"I feel more like a pack animal than a florist. Do you have any idea how many trips I've made to the SUV for tools and materials?"

"Nope. Have you made any trips to the hospital?"

"Don't even start on Bailey."

"I talked to him. He doesn't understand why you won't come see him."

"Did you tell him I'm busy with this wedding?"

"Yes, but we both agree you could find the time to make a quick visit."

I glared. "I don't need you siding with him." I waved a hand, dismissing the subject of Bailey Monroe. "I'm not discussing him. Let's talk about something else."

Lois curtsied. "What's your pleasure, madam?" She raised an eyebrow. "Murder?"

My tone was dry. "That's a safe topic." But I couldn't resist filling her in on the conversation I'd had yesterday in the park with Sonya, Dana, and Kasey. "Those girls set fire to that glade using lemon extract as an accelerant. Can you believe that?"

"I not only believe you, but I remember that fire." Lois shook her head. "Damn, Bretta. How have they lived with this all these years? At least with Kayla's prank, the only things destroyed were fish. What a horrible tragedy." She frowned. "But as I remember it, nothing was reported about the fire being arson."

"What's so tragic about a field burning? And why do you remember that particular fire?"

"Because I was pregnant and emotional. The idea of a woman and her child trapped in their house was terrible. They burned to death. The family had nothing. One grave, one casket; they were buried together. A neighbor supplied the cemetery plot and the grave marker."

I closed my mouth when I realized that I was staring at Lois like a slack-jawed idiot. This news changed everything. No wonder the tension had disappeared as I talked to those women in the park. I'd merely scratched the surface of their juvenile high jinks when I'd accused them of setting fire to that glade.

I had a hundred questions, and there was only one person I could think of who might crack if I exerted a bit of pressure. "I need to speak to Dana," I said, staring at the food-preparation tent.

"It better be a speedy conversation," said Lois. "Here comes Lew with the first load of bouquets."

Lois took off for the van. I got up from the steps and went in search of Dana. I found her stacking a wedding cake layer on pillars. Once she had the cake safely in place, I didn't waste time with subtlety.

"A mother and her child died in that fire the four of you set."

Dana whirled around. She met my gaze full on, then crumpled like a wet dishcloth. "Go away, Bretta. Please."

"I want to hear what happened."

"But I don't want to talk about it."

"I don't understand how you could have kept it a secret. Wasn't there an investigation into their deaths? Were none of you suspects?"

Dana held up her hands. "I'm trembling so badly I won't be able to pipe icing onto these cakes. Why are you doing this now?"

"Clear your conscience, Dana. Maybe then you'll find peace."

"Peace?" She tried to laugh, but it was a feeble effort. "That would be wonderful, but I doubt that telling you will bring me peace."

I kept still.

Dana closed her eyes. When she spoke her voice was low, and I had to lean closer to hear. "When the fire spread to the prairie, it went like the speed of sound through that dry grass." She blinked away tears. "We were shocked, but there wasn't anything we could do to put it out. We got in our car and left. It wasn't until the next morning that we learned the woman and her daughter had died."

Dana took a shaky breath. "Everyone thought of the fire as a tragic accident. That's the way it was reported in the newspaper. The glade was used back in the sixties like Make Out Point is today. It was a hangout for the kids. There was talk of dope smoking. A dropped cigarette, but nothing more."

My blood boiled. "Which one of you rammed Bailey's truck?"

Dana frowned. "Who's Bailey?"

I studied her puzzled expression. Her confusion seemed genuine. Impatiently, I motioned for her to continue.

"The day before Claire died she called me to talk about what happened the night of the fire. I cut her off. Hung up on her. When I saw her green hair in the park the next day, I knew we were in trouble. Then she said that horrible rhyme. We made it up before the fire. It was our credo. We were 'on the make,' upholding our rights as citizens. When that woman and her daughter died, we swore never to utter those words again. I thought Claire was being mean, reminding us of our secret. But I never dreamed she'd die."

"She was murdered, Dana. What happened in nineteen sixty-six might have been an accident, but Claire's death was homicide."

Dana licked her lips. "In our own way we've tried to atone for what we did that night. We were young and scared. The mother's name was Alice. The fifteen-year-old daughter was Erica. According to reports, the house went up like cardboard. Neighbors saw the blaze but couldn't pull them to safety. If the younger daughter, who was ten, hadn't spent the night away from home, she'd have died too."

"I doubt she took much comfort in that. Her mother and sister were dead. What happened to her?"

Dana lifted a shoulder. "I heard she went to live with relatives. After a year, Claire tracked down her address and sent a gift. A few months later, Claire sent another."

"Did she write the girl a letter explaining the reason for the presents?"

Dana stared at me. "Gosh, no. She'd never do that." A look of uncertainty crossed her plump face. "Or would she?"

"Claire might," I said. "The girl must have wondered why someone was sending her presents. Did Claire hear back? Get a thank-you card?"

"No. Claire couldn't be sure the girl had even gotten the packages, but they weren't returned. A couple of gifts could hardly make up for the loss of her family, but Claire felt she had to make contact in some way."

Dana rubbed her arms and spoke quietly. "After Sonya, Kasey, Claire, and I graduated, we went our separate ways. We'd see each other around town, but our friendship wasn't the same. We never talked about what happened that night, but in our own way we each tried to compensate for what we'd done. Kasey has her environmental work. Sonya spends all her free time volunteering in the pediatric wing at the hospital. My being a clown and making children laugh at birthday parties isn't much, but even if we'd come forward with our story, the woman and her daughter would still be dead."

"But Claire might not," I said quietly. "For years she was able to go on with her life. Then all of a sudden she needed catharsis. Why? What happened? What was the gossip Claire needed confirmed by Lydia Dearborne?"

"I don't know, but I think she's the lady Claire got the little girl's address from."

"But you said that was a year after the fire."

Dana nodded. "I've told you all I know. The others are going to be furious with me. Please don't say anything to Sonya or Kasey until after this wedding. We're already stressed enough as it is."

I left the food-preparation tent without making any promises. I wanted to find a quiet corner to mull over what I'd discovered, but the hustle and bustle around me was too distracting. I couldn't concentrate.

The next hours passed in a final flurry of frustration. While unloading one of the massive gazebo bouquets, Lew

broke the tallest flower head from its stem. I did some fi-
nagling—tape and wire are a florist's best friends. We
checked lists, checked bouquets, and checked twinkle lights.
We smoothed tulle, smoothed satin cloth, and smoothed ruffled feathers. Finally, at six o'clock, I called a halt. We'd done
what we'd been paid to do.

Evelyn hadn't arrived, so I hunted up Sonya to tell her
the exact location of the bridal party flowers. I found her
fighting to keep her composure. Her power suit was rumpled
and smudged. Her eyes held a "help me, Lord" expression.

Was the wedding getting to her? Or had she learned that
her past had finally caught up to her?

I asked, "Have you talked to Dana?"

"Why?" Sonya squawked, craning her neck. "What's happened now? She forgot the oil for the deep-fat fryer and her
husband had to bring the jugs from home."

"Nothing like that," I said. "I just wanted to tell you that
the corsages and boutonnieres need to be kept in the ice
chests until time to pin them on. We've labeled each, so there
shouldn't be any confusion as to who receives which one."

Sonya nodded. "Evelyn called. You're to leave the helium
tank."

"Why?"

"She has a special heart-shaped balloon she wants inflated
to tie to the limo."

"This has gone way beyond ridiculous. Have you met any
of the wedding party yet?"

"No."

I flipped my hands, absolving myself from the event. "I've
had it. No rehearsal. Everything on a schedule. I'm out of
here."

Sonya looked longingly at the path that would take her

away from Tranquility Garden. Deliberately, she looked away from freedom and squared her shoulders. She asked, "You aren't coming to the wedding?"

"No. I've seen enough. I'm taking a hot bath and going to bed."

"Evelyn assumes you'll attend."

"I'm not under that obligation. I've done my work. You're the coordinator."

"I'm surprised you don't want to see and be seen. It's good advertising for your shop. This wedding will be the talk of River City for weeks and months. Anyone who is anybody is coming."

I looked around at the serenity and beauty. Soon this place would be filled with River City families. The previous Saturday, when we'd met in the park, Sonya had said the mayor was attending, as well as doctors, lawyers, and councilmen— the elite of our society.

A twinge of unrest caught me by surprise. I tried to analyze the feeling, but I couldn't get a handle on it. I finally told myself it was because my part in this gala was finished. After the candles were lit there would be no turning back for Nikki and her groom.

I chewed my lower lip. Evelyn had said something along those lines. I searched my brain for her exact words: "Once the candles are lit, it's the beginning of the end."

Sonya asked, "What's wrong? Have you changed your mind about attending the wedding?"

I ran a hand wearily through my hair. "You've made valid points for me to stay, but I'm tired. When I get tired, I get cranky. The best place for me is home."

It might have been the best place. But thirty minutes later, I found myself in the hospital parking lot.

Chapter Twenty-two

✿ I didn't analyze why I'd come to Bailey. I only knew that I had to talk to someone. I couldn't shake the feeling that I was on the edge of a precipice and any wrong move could be disastrous. Since I'd left the park, my chest ached with anxiety. I was antsy—filled with apprehension. I needed professional feedback. But I couldn't face Bailey until I was able to relate the facts in a rational manner.

I paced the parking lot, pondering what I knew, filling in the blanks with what I suspected.

Events of our past shape the people we are today.

In 1966, four girls had the righteous idea of saving a plant from extinction. Their good deed had resulted in the deaths of two innocent people. Lois had said, "One grave, one casket; they were buried together. A neighbor supplied the cemetery plot and grave marker."

I was sure Oliver had been that neighbor. Before he'd suffered his fatal heart attack, he'd seemed confused. Perhaps in his befuddled state, he'd thought the park was the cemetery, hence his question: "Where are the markers?" As for the "Bretta—Spade," I could only guess at what had been in the dying man's mind. Eddie had said that whenever anyone close to Oliver had passed away, he used his spade to sprinkle soil on the grave. If Oliver had donated the cemetery plot, I had to assume he'd cared about that mother and her child.

The puzzler was—what had prompted him to have that particular thought at that particular time?

I blinked. One grave. One casket. One little girl's family wiped out. I ran my fingers through my hair. One daughter had been spared. That child had been ten years old.

Everyone who'd been in the park the morning Oliver died had been involved in some way or other with that fire. Everyone except Evelyn. I grew still, staring, visualizing, and remembering.

I'd been so caught up in the details of this wedding that I hadn't considered it anything more than an extravaganza brought about by an indulgent mother doing a bit of River City social climbing. Now I wasn't so sure. My theories were conflicting, but my gut feeling said something wasn't right.

Who was Evelyn Montgomery? What did we know about her? Why had she chosen River City for her daughter's wedding?

I'd thought it strange that an environmentalist was taking the wedding photos. I'd thought it odd that Dana had been given the entire responsibility of such a lavish banquet, when her expertise was birthday parties and anniversaries.

Was the choice of the women—Kasey, Dana, Claire, and Sonya—a coincidence? Or was it an elaborate scheme to get all four women together in one place at one time? River City had other caterers, other photographers, but none of them were linked to a terrible secret—a fire that had killed a mother and her daughter.

Oliver hadn't met Evelyn until she came into the park. Had he seen a glimmer of the child she'd been but couldn't quite make the connection? He had made the association with a grave marker. But wouldn't that traumatic episode supercede any gentler memories of this orphaned child?

I pictured Tranquility Garden, and my agitation grew stronger. The hurricane lamps set at strategic spots around the gazebo, five hundred candles strewn throughout the area, specially blended oil for lighting. Paint and lacquer on the shrubs, delicate wisps of tulle, a helium tank, and a deep-fat fryer to be used at a specific time.

Was I way off track? I took a deep breath. It was time to air my theory.

I charged into the hospital and punched the button for the third floor. On the ride up, I added everything together, and I came up with a four-letter word: *fire*. What better way to seek revenge for your mother's and sister's deaths than to bring all the guilty parties together for one big . . . *burn*.

The elevator came to a stop. I stepped off the car and turned toward Bailey's room. But why would Evelyn choose her daughter's wedding for such a dastardly act? This was the conflict. This was why I needed to talk to Bailey.

I pushed open the door to his room and found my father seated at Bailey's bedside. They were visiting compatibly. My father had one leg crossed over the other. Bailey's smile was a welcome sight. Emotional tears filled my eyes. I couldn't control the sob that worked its way up my throat and past my lips.

"Bretta?" said both men at the same time. My father came to his feet, grabbed his walking stick, and limped toward me. "You're as pale as a turnip, daughter."

"Sweetheart," said Bailey. "What's wrong?"

My fears were unleashed by their concern. In a torrent of words, I said, "Evelyn was in the park. She heard Dana's comment about the hot piece of gossip from Mrs. Dearborne. Oliver's overworked heart couldn't take the strain. He was stressed trying to remember. Add in Evelyn's and Eddie's argument and Oliver keeled over. Three people are dead. I think more victims are to come."

I grabbed my father's arm. "I don't know what to do. Maybe I'm wrong, but what if I'm right? Five hundred guests are supposed to attend that wedding."

Bailey patted the side of his bed. "You're not making sense, Bretta. Sit here and tell us what's going on. Start at the beginning."

"I can't sit." My gaze went to the clock above his bed. "Soon those candles will be lit. Evelyn said it was the 'beginning of the end.'"

My father put his arm around my waist. "We'll do whatever you say, but you have to calm down so we can get the gist of your worries."

Talking to myself, I muttered, "Evelyn said she had the lamp oil specially blended with the fragrance of clematis blossoms. Dad, when you looked up the meaning of those flowers in the tussie-mussie, did you come across clematis?"

"Yeah. Recognized the name right off. When we lived on the farm your mother had a vine growing up the clothesline pole."

"What does clematis mean?"

"Artifice—deception and trickery. Lousy definition for such a beautiful—"

I broke out of my father's grasp. "I've got to go back to the park. I don't know what I'll do, but I've got to do something."

Bailey called, "No, Bretta, don't—"

But I was already on my way. The stairs were closer than the elevator. I figured I'd have to wait for a car, so I took the steps, thinking this route might be quicker. I clopped down three flights, and then wound my way through a maze of corridors until I finally made it out of the building and across the parking lot.

Irritated at the delay, I revved the SUV's engine and headed for the exit. My father stepped from behind a parked car, and I nearly clipped him with my bumper. Tires squealed as I slammed on the brakes. I unlocked the door and watched him climb in.

"I don't know about this, Dad. Maybe you should go home."

"Don't talk. Drive."

There wasn't time to argue. I stepped on the gas and asked, "How did you get down here so quickly?"

"The elevator was still on the third floor. I got on, pushed the button, and here I am. No mystery there, but I am mystified by what you think might be happening at the park. Can you explain while you drive?"

"I can try." Grimly, I began, "Evening weddings normally have candles, but this ceremony is teeming with flammables. Back in nineteen sixty-six—"

While I talked, I took advantage of the SUV's power. I ignored yellow lights, and when the intersections were clear, I crossed against red. I prayed for an officer to appear, but none did. The trip seemed to take forever, but according to the clock, we were making good time. I drove by instinct— braking and accelerating as the need arose.

The exit ramp I wanted loomed ahead. I switched lanes and decreased my speed, but only until I was on the road leading to the park. I took the sharp curves at an excessive rate. When we got to the park entrance, I slowed to a crawl.

"Good Lord above," said Dad. "Look at the cars. You say Evelyn only came to River City eight months ago. How'd she get such a following of people so quickly?"

"Money, is my guess. A donation here, a donation there. She's lovely to look at. She can be charming. I myself tried to please her because she was the mother of the bride—and paying big bucks for my service."

I edged my way past the cars, knowing there wouldn't be a legal place to park. As we drew closer to Tranquility Garden, I put the SUV's windows down. I didn't hear anything except the rustling of leaves in the treetops. It was getting dark early. The gathering clouds had blocked the setting sun's rays.

"A front is moving in," said Dad. "The wind has changed. It's blowing from the north."

With one hand on the steering wheel, I leaned out the window. The faint, lilting notes of the harp drifted on air currents. I almost smiled. "Music," I said. "Maybe I'm wrong."

The words were barely out of my mouth when I saw the path that led to Tranquility Garden. Where was the limousine? Where was the bridal party? Where was the bride?

I slammed the SUV into park and left the vehicle blocking traffic. Jumping out, I said, "Dad, stay here in case you need to move my car. I have to see what's going on."

I sprinted across the tarmac, my gaze on the path. I didn't see Evelyn until she stepped from the shadow of a tree. She wore a flannel shirt, jeans, and boots. I tried to be calm, gesturing to her informal attire. "Has the theme of this elegant wedding been changed?"

"Don't come any closer, Bretta," Evelyn warned softly. "You're not going to stop me."

No need for pretense. "You're Alice's daughter. Your sister was Erica. Both were killed in a fire."

"You've been busy."

"Evelyn, think about what you're doing. Think about Nikki."

"There is no Nikki. It's a hoax."

"But why a wedding?"

"Because Sonya, Claire, Dana, and Kasey's professions made that seem the most workable solution. If they'd been nurses, teachers, secretaries, I'd have made their acquaintance, then planned a huge party toward the same end."

"How did Claire figure out you were the sister of the girl who died?"

"Family resemblance. I think Oliver saw it, too, but he died before he could say too much. He was kind to my sister and me. He taught us the meaning of flowers and showed us how to plant an herb garden. But most of all, he helped me get through the funeral by letting me—"

"—use his precious spade to put dirt on their grave?"

Evelyn nodded. "I feel bad that Oliver died. As for Claire, I didn't go to the beauty shop with the intention of killing her. I only wanted to find out what information she hoped to get from Lydia Dearborne. But Claire made me furious. She pointed to my sister's picture on her ceiling and told me she'd painted it because it was cathartic—a way of purging her past indiscretions."

Evelyn's voice rose in outrage. "That woman classed the deaths of my mother and sister as an indiscretion."

"And you killed Lydia because—"

Evelyn regained control and spoke quietly. "She was a loose end from the past. I couldn't be sure what Claire might have told her. I wanted to go to Lydia's house immediately after I'd killed Claire, but you came into the shop. I had to see what you were up to. By the time I got to Lydia, her sister and daughter had come to visit. They were innocents. I couldn't kill them. So I took a chance and waited until Lydia's company had gone away."

"Did Claire come right out and ask if you were the daughter who'd escaped the fire?"

"Not in so many words. For weeks now, she'd tried to trip me up. She asked hundreds of questions, but I always had pat answers. Many times I thought I'd thrown her off my trail by talking about this bogus wedding. But Claire kept prying and prying. I'd drop into her shop every so often, just as I did with you and the others. The rest of you were oblivious, but Claire was different. All those years ago, she sent me gifts. Once she even called, to see if I was happy and settled in my new life."

Evelyn stopped to look at her wristwatch. "I was a child, but as I grew older, I'd think about the woman in River City who had seemed so concerned but wouldn't tell me her name other than Claire. In her letter she said she was graduating high school with three of her closest friends. I kept the letter because it was a tie to River City and to the family I'd lost."

Evelyn glanced at her watch again and said hastily, "Last year my aunt passed away. As I was going through her belongings and mine, I came across the letter. When I read those words with adult eyes, I had this horrible feeling that Claire's concern was motivated by guilt. I had to know the truth, so I made the decision to move to River City. From the first time I met Claire, she said I looked familiar. Then she painted my sister's picture on the ceiling of the beauty shop. Putting my sister's image up there was cruel."

"Why cruel?"

"Because Claire was my sister's killer."

"It was an accident, Evelyn. Those girls were burning off the field to preserve an endangered plant."

Evelyn laughed bitterly. "Save the plant. Kill my family. It was a lousy plan."

I waved my hand to our surroundings. "All this work, all the money you've spent, was for revenge?"

Evelyn nodded. "Yes. To bring grief to the girls who killed my mother and sister. To wreak havoc on a town that didn't care enough to investigate the deaths. I've looked at back issues of the newspaper. Do you know my family's murder didn't rate more than a tiny story at the bottom of the front page? They were dead. My life was forever changed. But this town didn't care."

Evelyn bent down and carefully picked up an open container. "Tonight, River City will care. They'll see the light."

Before I could draw a breath, she hurled the can under a cedar tree. I saw the arc of liquid. I smelled the gasoline vapors. She struck a match.

"Nature's own bomb," Evelyn said, tossing the flame.

The gas ignited with a whoosh. The fire leaped up the cedar tree, found dry tinder, and exploded into an inferno. Sparks leaped and whirled on the rising wind. With choreographed precision, the blaze spread to the shrubs I'd painted and Lew had touched up with lacquer. The natural moisture trapped in the leaves was no contest for this heat. The flammable material combusted and the shrubs were aflame.

In horror, I said, "Are you insane?"

Evelyn shook her head. "Not at all. I'm well aware of what I'm doing." She cocked her head. Screams came from the area where the guests had been entertained by the music.

I started in that direction but glanced back at Evelyn. She was on the move. With everything else so well planned, she would have to have an escape route. But Evelyn didn't head for the parking lot. She took off into the woods.

In the midst of this heat, an icy finger of fear crawled up my spine. Evelyn had years of hatred bottled inside. Was the wedding in the park her only scheme? Did she intend to burn all of River City?

I ran after her.

I wasn't sure where we were headed, but I crashed into the underbrush about twenty yards away from the wedding fiasco. This part of the park hadn't been tamed. I caught a shadowy glimpse of Evelyn ahead of me, off to my right. I angled that way and found a hiker's path. Picking up speed, I gained on her, but the climb grew steeper. Before long I was huffing and puffing.

The fire raged at my back, but off in the distance I heard sirens. Damage control was headed for the park, courtesy of Bailey or my father. However, Evelyn was still on the loose. I hoped my being on her trail might keep her from committing another horrendous act.

I've run for my life before, but I've never been the aggressor. I wasn't comfortable with the role. What would I do if I caught up to her? What was her strategy? I believed she had one. She'd plotted an entire wedding, down to the minutest detail, with the thought of achieving this devastating finale.

Fear forced me to put one foot in front of the other. Behind me, in the direction of Tranquility Garden, was a series of explosions. I assumed this was the specially blended oil for the hurricane lamps.

I quickened my pace, and the trail began to level out. I looked up and saw Evelyn silhouetted against the night sky. She posed there briefly, seemed to stare straight at me, then she disappeared over the horizon. I plugged onward until I came to the spot where she'd vanished.

I turned and saw Evelyn hadn't been staring at me but at her handiwork. Fueled by an insatiable appetite, the fire leap-frogged from treetop to treetop. Sparks sprinkled the earth, igniting the underbrush. Like ground troops, the flames advanced at a rapid rate, energized by the rising wind.

I started down the hill, lost my footing, and made the journey on my butt. My ungainly passing raked up moldy leaves. The musty odor mixed with the acrid smoke made my eyes water. When I hit the bottom of the gorge, I wiped my eyes on my shirttail. With my vision cleared, I searched for some landmark that would tell me where I was in relation to the park.

The night seemed brighter, and I thought the moon had come out. But it had a surreal glow. I looked up at the ridge. The fire had spread at a heart-stopping rate. It was above the gorge. I blinked, and the flames swooped toward me. Stumbling to my feet, I wanted to shout—*I'm not the enemy*—but this army knew no friend or foe. It would take no prisoners. Its mission was death and destruction.

I ran down the gorge, unsure of where I was going, but I didn't have a choice. I couldn't see what lay on the other side of the embankment. I couldn't see what was ahead of me. Suddenly the terrain changed. Waist-high blades of grass grabbed at my jeans, sliced into the flesh of my arms. My feet sank into spongy soil.

I stopped in my tracks to take stock of where I might be, and saw Evelyn. I'd temporarily put her out of my mind in my haste to get away from the fire. She was huddled at the base of a giant tree. Her eyes were closed.

I fought my way over to her. "Evelyn, the fire is headed our way."

"I know."

"Let's go."

She opened her eyes. "This old tree looks like the ones that used to stand near our house. My sister and I played for hours under their branches. I'll die here."

Evelyn spoke so calmly, I didn't immediately grasp her meaning. When I did, I was infuriated. "You led me on this merry chase so you could die at this spot?"

She stared at me. "I didn't invite you to follow me."

"What would you expect me to do? Let you escape?"

She didn't answer, but closed her eyes. Her posture was that of a martyr—a Joan of Arc in blue jeans.

Well, fine. Let her stay. I was leaving. I took two steps past the tree. I couldn't do it. I swiveled on my toe and grabbed her arm. "You're coming with me."

Evelyn jerked away. "I'm tired. I've done what I set out to do. Just let me die."

Grimly, I stooped until we were nose to nose. "Not on your life." I pulled her upright. "Let's go."

She stared at me. "Why are you doing this? Why should you care what happens to me?"

I didn't answer, because I didn't know. She'd killed twice. Her fate should be to burn in hell, but that was for a higher court to decide. I tightened my grip on her arm.

Evelyn sighed and stood up. "At this point, I really don't care what happens to me."

Encouraged but not completely convinced of her change of heart, I kept hold of her arm, and we loped down the gorge. The tall grass and the mushy ground were a hindrance. The fire was about fifty yards behind us. I could feel the blaze of heat breathing down my neck.

The cattails in our path were a surprise. The tall marsh plants with their fuzzy, cylindrical flower spikes batted us about the shoulders and face as we forged on. I kept moving, but Evelyn tried to hang back. I demanded, "What's your problem?"

"The lake is straight ahead. I don't know how to swim."

"The lake?" I said. "If we can make it to the lake, we can jump in—"

"Not me," said Evelyn.

I nodded behind us to the wall of fire. "And you're afraid of drowning?" I didn't give her a chance to reply. I towed her along, but finally had to let go of her arm. It took all my energy to get through the jungle of cattails. Evelyn limped next to me, mumbling about the water.

I glanced over my shoulder. The damp ground and green foliage had slowed the raging fire, but we were being attacked from a far greater danger. The slopes of the gorge—or, as I now knew, the spillway from the lake—contained driftwood, decayed trees. The wind whipped up the flames, making the dried wood burn like a funeral pyre. If we didn't hurry, the fire would edge past us and cut off our escape.

I needed more energy, more stamina for this dash to safety, but I floundered. My chest ached from sucking in the smoke. Each breath I took seared my lungs. The soggy ground tugged at my feet, slowing my progress. We were getting closer to the lake. But out of the corner of my eye, I saw the flames.

Embers rained down on us. Sparks showered us with pinpricks of pain when they landed on our flesh. In a dead heat, we raced the fire. For every step we took, the flames advanced two yards. Tears filled my eyes. We weren't going to make it. I thought of DeeDee. I thought of my father. I thought of Bailey.

I took another step and sank into knee-deep water. The

cattails thinned out. We were at the lake's edge. There wasn't time for hesitation. I took Evelyn's arm and said, "I can swim, but you can't fight me."

She nodded, and we took the plunge. My lifesaving skills wouldn't win an award. My swimming technique wouldn't get me into the Olympics. But at least we were out of the fire's deadly grip.

Behind us, there was a thunderous crash. I glanced back and saw a flaming tree had fallen across the spillway. Fiery projectiles splattered the water, sizzling on contact.

I didn't try to identify the tree's exact location. At some point I'd been in its path. My immediate problem was how to contend with Evelyn's stranglehold on my shirt. She kicked her feet ineffectually. I ordered her to stop. "Take a deep breath and float," I said. "We aren't going far."

The lake covered three acres. I had no intention of crossing it, but simply prayed for enough strength to get us to the closest shoreline. The will to live drove me through the inky water. I might be a smaller size than I was two years ago, but I've never been in good physical shape. My body had taken a severe beating when I'd chased Evelyn over hill and dell. Towing her through the water was almost more than I could endure. Sheer exhaustion forced me to stop swimming. I couldn't paddle another inch. I straightened my legs under me and felt the lake bottom.

I could barely get the words out. "Evelyn. Stand up. We're safe."

She knelt in the shallow water and stared across the park. "Safe from what, Bretta?" she asked softly.

I followed her gaze. A patrol car with flashing red lights barreled toward us.

Epilogue

It had been five days since the fire in the park. Evelyn had been indicted on two counts of homicide—Claire and Lydia—as well as arson, public endangerment, and a few other charges. There were multiple civil suits filed against her by wedding guests, citing pain and suffering and mental anguish. Evelyn had been denied bail and was awaiting trial in the River City jail. I'd thought about going to see her, but I was a witness for the prosecution. Besides, what would I say if I saw her?

I was at the Flower Shop, watering plants, watching the clock. Bailey was being discharged from the hospital at noon. DeeDee had helped his daughter, Jillian, clean the cottage, making it ready for his homecoming. I'd stayed away. Jillian seemed like a pleasant young lady. She was twenty years old, full of youthful thoughts and ideas, and extremely possessive of her father.

Tipping the water can spout over the dracaena plant, I was happy to see it had survived its wilting episode without any visible sign of damage. I'd escaped the fire with only a few minor cuts and blisters. Since that night, I'd thought about cause and effect in relation to my father, and to Evelyn, and to life in general. I'd even bought a book on philosophy, trying to get a perspective on human morals, character, and behavior.

I was still waiting for enlightenment, though the words of Aristotle played often in my mind.

The quality of life is determined by its activities.

After my close encounter with death, I figured I'd better curb my pastime of detecting. I revised that thought once I'd done some soul-searching.

Where would be the quality of life if I didn't care enough to get involved?

If I didn't make a difference in my corner of the world?

If I minded my own business?

NOTHING DAUNTED

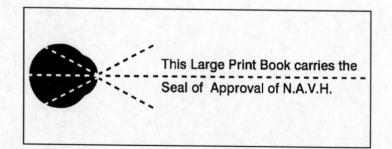

NOTHING DAUNTED

THE UNEXPECTED EDUCATION OF TWO SOCIETY GIRLS IN THE WEST

DOROTHY WICKENDEN

THORNDIKE PRESS

A part of Gale, Cengage Learning

Detroit • New York • San Francisco • New Haven, Conn • Waterville, Maine • London

GALE
CENGAGE Learning®

Copyright © 2011 by Dorothy Wickenden.
Chapter 1: Hayden Heritage Center. Chapter 5: Carpenter Ranch.
Chapter 9: Denver Public Library, Western History Collection.
Photographer: L. C. McClure. Chapter 11: Perry-Mansfield Archives.
Chapter 13: Courtesy of Ruth Perry.
Thorndike Press, a part of Gale, Cengage Learning.

Thorndike Press® Large Print Biography.
The text of this Large Print edition is unabridged.
Other aspects of the book may vary from the original edition.
Set in 16 pt. Plantin.

LIBRARY OF CONGRESS CATALOGING-IN-PUBLICATION DATA

Wickenden, Dorothy.
    Nothing daunted : the unexpected education of two society girls in the West / by Dorothy Wickenden. — Large print ed.
        p. cm. (Thorndike press large print biography)
    Includes bibliographical references.
    ISBN-13: 978-1-4104-5635-9 (hardcover : large print)
    ISBN-10: 1-4104-5635-8 (hardcover : large print) 1. Woodruff, Dorothy. 2. Underwood, Rosamond. 3. Teachers—Colorado—Biography. 4. Education—Colorado—History—20th century. 5. Large type books. I. Title.
LA2315.C59W53 2013
371.100922--dc23
[B]   2012044220

Published in 2013 by arrangement with Scribner, a division of Simon & Schuster, Inc.

Printed in the United States of America
1 2 3 4 5 6 7 17 16 15 14 13

for Hermione and Caroline

Rosamond and Dorothy, "Stranded for a day on the Moffat Road"

CONTENTS

PART THREE: WORKING GIRLS

PART FOUR: RECKONINGS

PROLOGUE

Miss Underwood (left), Miss Woodruff, and Elkhead students, 1916

One weekend afternoon in the fall of 2008, at the back of a drawer in my old wooden desk at home, I came across a folder I had forgotten. "Dorothy Woodruff Letters, Elkhead 1916–17." My mother had given me the file when my children were young, and I had put it away, intending to look through it, but life had intervened. I glanced at the first letter. Dated Friday, July 28, 1916, it was written on the stationery of the Hayden Inn. At the top of the sheet was a photograph of a homely three-story concrete-block house with a few spindly saplings out front. The inn advertised itself as "The Only First-Class Hotel in Hayden." Dorothy wrote: "My dearest family: Can you believe that I am actually far out here in Colorado?"

She and her close friend, Rosamond Underwood, had grown up together in Auburn, New York. They had just arrived after a five-day journey and were preparing to head into a remote mountain range in the Rockies, to teach school in a settlement called Elkhead. Dorothy's letter described their stop overnight in Denver, their train ride across the Continental Divide, and their introductions to the locals of Hayden, whom she described as "all agog" over them "and *so* funny." One man could barely be restrained "from showing us a bottle of gall stones just removed from his wife!" She closed by saying, "They are all so friendly and kind — and we are *thrilled* by every-thing. We start now — four hours drive. Goodbye in haste. . . ."

Dorothy Woodruff was my grandmother. As I began reading the letters, I recognized her voice immediately, even though they were written by a young woman — twenty-nine years old, unmarried, belatedly setting out on her own. An avid correspondent, she captured the personalities of the people she met; the harsh landscape; her trials with a classroom of unruly young boys; and her devotion to Rosamond, known to my brothers and me as "Aunt Ros." I also was struck by their unusually warm friendship with two men: the young lawyer and rancher who hired them, Farrington Carpenter; and Bob Perry, who was the supervisor of his father's coal mine. They were eighteen hundred miles away from their families, and from decorous notions about relations between the sexes.

The letters revealed the contradictions of Dorothy's upbringing. She was a daughter of the Victorian aristocracy. Her forebears, like Rosamond's, were entrepreneurs and lawyers and bankers who had become wealthy during the Industrial Revolution. In 1906, the young women were sent to Smith, one of the earliest women's colleges, and afterward, they were indulged for a year with a grand tour of Europe, during which they saw their first "aeroplane," learned how

11

to blow the foam off a mug of beer, expressed disdain for the paintings of Matisse, and watched Nijinsky dance. Then, like other girls of their background, they were expected to return home to marry, and marry well.

Yet they had grown up surrounded by the descendants of some of the most prominent reformers in American history, including the suffragists who organized the first women's rights convention in Seneca Falls, fifteen miles west of Auburn; and the man who overturned barbaric penal practices at the Auburn state prison, Sing Sing, and penitentiaries across the country. Auburn was a stop on the Underground Railroad, and some of the families they knew had hidden runaway slaves in their basements. Dorothy's grandfather lived next door to William Seward, President Lincoln's secretary of state. One day when she was visiting my family in Weston, Connecticut, she recorded an oral history, speaking with unerring precision about her childhood and about her time in Colorado. Retrieving the transcript of the tape, I was reminded of the breathtaking brevity of America's past.

I remember Dorothy as white-haired, impeccably attired, and sometimes stern. The second youngest of seven children, she grew up in a big hipped-roof clapboard house staffed by servants. Her bedroom and that of her younger sister, Milly, were in the nursery, reached by the back stairs. Raised largely by their nursemaid, they rarely stepped into the kitchen. When Dorothy's four children were growing up, she didn't know how to cook anything except creamed potatoes and hot cocoa. Every night she brushed her hair a hundred strokes with a French boar-bristle brush. She joked to us about her height — four feet eleven and shrinking every year. To reach her high mahogany four-poster bed, inherited from her parents, she had to use a footstool upholstered in needlepoint.

She gave me tips in etiquette: how to file my nails, how to set a formal table, how to avoid acting "common." When I was a slouching teenager, she showed me how she had been taught to walk across the room with a book balanced on her head. On my eighteenth birthday, she wrote to me: "To be happy it is necessary to be constantly giving to others. I do not mean to give in work alone — but all of your self. That means interest in other people — not only by affection — but by kindness." She didn't like the fashions of the 1970s — curtains of hair, tie-dyed T-shirts, and tight bell-bottoms — and once told me haughtily, "I never wore a pair of trousers in my life."

For all that, she was spirited and funny — not at all the deferential young woman she had been brought up to be. After she and Ros returned from Europe, they attended friends' weddings, along with traditional luncheons and balls, but six years later, they were still uninterested in the suitors who were interested in them. Chafing at the rigid social routines and not getting anywhere with the ineffectual suffrage work they had taken on, they didn't hesitate when they heard about two teaching jobs in Colorado. The nine months my grandmother spent there seemed to have shaped her as much as her entire youth in Auburn. She was full of expansive admiration for the hardworking people of Elkhead, and when she faced great personal difficulties of her own, she called to mind the uncomplaining endurance she had witnessed in the settlers and their children.

She and Ros, like other easterners going west, were time travelers, moving back to the frontier. Although they ventured out after the first settlers, and went by train rather than covered wagon, their destination felt more like 1870 than 1916. They took with them progressive ideas about education, technology, and women — and post-cards from their travels abroad. The home-steaders — motley transplants from across the country, Europe, and Russia — lived almost twenty miles north of Hayden. Effectively cut off from modern life by poverty and the Rocky Mountains, the pioneers found the two women as exotic as Dorothy and Ros found them.

Although World War I was looming, such a cataclysm was unimaginable to Americans who knew nothing of combat. Dorothy sometimes talked disparagingly about her grandfather's brother, who had avoided service in the Civil War by paying a substitute to take his place — a common practice among wealthy families in the North. Just weeks before Dorothy and Ros left for Colorado, President Wilson averted war with Mexico. The prevailing spirit among the elites of Auburn, the industrialists of Denver, and the homesteaders of Elkhead was an exhilarating optimism about the future.

These people were swept up in some of the strongest currents of the country's history: the expulsion of native tribes; the mining of gold, silver, and coal; the building of a network of railroads that linked disparate parts of the country and led to the settlement of the West; the development of rural schools; the entry of immigrants, African-Americans, and women into the workforce and the voting booth; even the origins of modern dance. Their lives were integral to the making of America, yet the communities they built, even their idioms, had all but vanished.

As I got to know the children and grandchildren of the people my grandmother told us about, I began to see her story as more than a curious family history. It was an alternative Western. There were strutting cowboys and eruptions of violence, but the records the residents left behind turned out to be full of their own indelible characters and plot twists. Dozens of descendants in Denver, Steamboat Springs, Hayden, Elkhead, and Oak Creek had kept their family memorabilia from that year. Rebecca Wattles, a rancher in Hayden and the granddaughter of the secretary of the Elkhead school board, showed me the 1920 yearbook of the first five graduates of the school, all of whom had been Ros's students. They wrote: "It isn't the easiest thing in the world to buck trail for two or three miles when the trail is drifted and your horse lunges and plunges; nor yet to ski, when the snow is loose and sticky. But, if as we are told, it

16

is these things that develop grit, stick-to-it-ive-ness, and independence — well, the children who have gone to school in Elk Head, ought surely to have a superfluous amount of those qualities."

One Sunday in early October 2009, my husband and I pulled up to an old white Georgian house on a cul-de-sac in Norwalk, Connecticut. We were greeted at the front door by Peter Cosel, one of Ros's grandsons. He appeared to be mildly amused by my mission: a search for the letters that Rosamond had written from Elkhead. For a year I had been pestering him about going through the boxes he had in storage there. Peter called his brother Rob, also a lawyer, who arrived just as we finished a cursory examination of the attic treasures, including a trunk filled with papers dating back to the 1850s from a branch of the Underwood family that had settled in Chicago.

I sat on the floor in front of a sagging box, blackened on the bottom from mildew and eaten away in spots by a squirrel, and began to unpack it, setting aside a stack of five-year diaries — fastidious chronicles by Ros's mother of her family's daily life in Auburn. Peter absently combed through some business documents of his great-grandfather's, a man named Sam Perry, who — I soon learned — was one of Denver's "empire builders," a financier of the railroad that Dorothy and Ros rode over the Continental Divide. Rob sat on the edge of the bed and talked about childhood visits to their grandmother's rustic summer cabin in the hills of Strawberry Park outside Steamboat Springs. Then my husband handed me a two-page typewritten letter. In the upper-right corner, it said, "Saturday Night. Aug. 6." I looked at the closing: "Dotty and I can hardly believe that this school is really ours to command! . . . Lovingly ROSAMOND."

Ros's entire correspondence was there, each letter typed, folded, and numbered by her mother. The letters had been written to her parents, who, like Dorothy's, had left them for her children and grandchildren. Unwinding the string of a thick legal envelope, I looked inside. It contained dozens of articles and letters from October 1916. They confirmed the most improbable of all the tales my grandmother had told us, about the violent kidnapping of one of their friends. Sensational headlines were spread across the front pages from Denver to Los Angeles: HOW THE MILLIONAIRE'S SON WAS KIDNAPPED AND HELD FOR RANSOM; EXTRA! KIDNAPPER IS SLAIN.

All of these papers and recollections, with

their idiosyncratic details about the "set-tling up" of northwestern Colorado, pro-vided a backstory to America's leap into the twentieth century. And they filled out the saga about two cosseted women from New York who shunned convention to head out to what was still, in many ways, the Wild West.

■ ■ ■ ■

PART ONE:
BEGINNINGS

■ ■ ■ ■

Dorothy in 1899, age twelve

1
OVERLAND JOURNEY

Hayden, c. 1913

July 27, 1916

A passenger train pulled into the Hayden depot at 10:45 P.M. with a piercing squeal of brakes, a long whistle, and the banging of steel shoes against couplers. The ground shook as the train settled on the tracks, releasing black plumes from the smokestack and foggy white steam from the side pipes. The Denver, Northwestern & Pacific Railway, popularly known as the Moffat Road, had reached Hayden just three years earlier. Until then, Colorado's Western Slope was accessible only by stagecoach, wagon, horseback, and foot. Despite the hulking locomotive, the train didn't look quite up to the twelve-hour journey it had just made over some of the most treacherous passes and peaks of the Rocky Mountains. It consisted of four cars with an observation deck attached at the end. Inside the parlor car, several passengers remained. Hayden was the second-to-last stop on the line.

Dorothy Woodruff and Rosamond Underwood, seasoned travelers in Europe but new to the American West, peered out the window into a disconcerting darkness, unsure whether it was safe to step outside. Then the door of the compartment opened, and a friendly voice called out, "Are you Miss Woodruff and Miss Underwood?" The voice belonged to their employer, Farrington Carpenter. Just a few weeks earlier, he had hired them to teach for the year at a new schoolhouse in the Elkhead Mountains, north of town. His letters, written from his law office in Hayden, were full of odd, color-

24

ful descriptions of Elkhead and the children — about thirty students, from poor homesteading families, ranging in age from six to nineteen. Carpenter had assured them it was not a typical one-room schoolhouse. It had electric lights, and the big room was divided by a folding wooden partition, so that each of them could have her own classroom. The basement contained a furnace, a gymnasium, and a domestic science room. Notwithstanding its remote location, he boasted, it was the most modern school in all of Routt County — an area of two thousand square miles.

Ros observed with surprise that "Mr. Carpenter" was a "tall, gangly youth." He wore workaday trousers, an old shawl sweater, and scuffed shoes. She subsequently discovered that he had graduated from Princeton in 1909, the same year she and Dorothy had from Smith. But when they were traveling around Europe and studying French in Paris, he was homesteading in Elkhead. In 1912 he had earned a law degree at Harvard. He retrieved their suitcases from the luggage rack and helped them down the steep steps, explaining that the electricity in Hayden, a recent amenity, had been turned off at ten P.M., as it was every night.

The baggage man heaved their trunks onto the platform, and Carpenter assessed the cargo. Dorothy and Ros had been punctilious in their preparations for the journey, packing suitcases full of books and the two "innovation trunks," which stood up when opened and served as makeshift closets, holding dresses and skirts on one side and bureau drawers on the other. Although they had consulted several knowledgeable people about the proper supplies and clothing, their parents kept urging them to take more provisions. Ros later commented that they were treated as if they were going to the farthest reaches of Africa. Their trunks were almost the size of the boxcar in front of them, which, the women could now make out, was the extent of the depot. Carpenter told them that a wagon would come by the next morning to retrieve the trunks. As he picked up their bulging suitcases and set off, Dorothy suggested sheepishly that he leave them with the trunks. He replied, "Well, no one would get far with them!"

Dorothy and Ros liked him immediately. He staggered down the wooden sidewalk along Poplar Street to the Hayden Inn, followed closely by the ladies. Ros wrote to her parents the next morning, "Why he didn't pull his arms out of their sockets before reaching here, I don't know." There was no reception desk at the Hayden Inn, and no proprietor. Putting down the suitcases inside the cramped entryway, Carpenter turned up a kerosene lamp on the hall table and promised to meet them at breakfast. They found a note by the lamp: "Schoolteachers, go upstairs and see if anyone is in Room 2. If they are, go to Room 3, and if 3 is filled, go to Room 4." When Dorothy cracked open the door to Room 2, she could see that it was occupied, so they crept along the hall to the back of the house and found that the next room — "the bridal suite" — was empty. "We went to bed," Ros said, "glad to be there after that long trip."

They had said goodbye to their parents at New York Central Station in Auburn five days earlier. Auburn, a city of about thirty thousand people in the Finger Lakes district, was one of the wealthiest in the state. Ros's father, George Underwood, was a county judge, and Dorothy's, John Hermon Woodruff, owned Auburn Button Works, which made pearl and shellac buttons, butt plates for rifles, and later, 78-rpm records. The Button Works and the Logan silk mills, jointly owned by Dorothy's father and a maternal uncle, were housed in a factory about a mile north of the Woodruffs' house. They were two of the town's early "manufactories." Others produced rope, carpets, clothes-wringers, farm machinery, and shoes. Auburn's main arteries, Genesee and South streets, which formed a crooked T, were more like boulevards in the residential neighborhoods, lined with slate sidewalks and stately homes. Majestic old elms arched across and met in the middle. The ties within families and among friends were strong, and the local aristocracy perpetuated itself through marriage. Men returned from New York City after making money in banking or railroads; opened law practices and businesses in town; or worked with their brothers and fathers, cousins and uncles. Some never left home at all. Sons and daughters inherited their elders' names and their fortunes. Most women married young and began building their own families. One chronicler observed, "Prick South Street at one end, and it bleeds at the other."

Dorothy, less composed and orderly than Rosamond, had arrived at the station only moments before the train left for Chicago, and as she climbed aboard, she could almost hear her mother saying "I told you so" about the importance of starting in plenty of time. Her last glimpse of her parents was of her father's reassuring smile. He and Ros's mother championed their adventure. Her mother and Ros's father, though, were convinced their daughters would be devoured by wild animals or attacked by Indians. When Ros showed her father one of Carpenter's letters, he turned away and put up his hand, saying, "I don't want to read it."

The girls prevailed, as they invariably did, when their parents saw they were determined to go through with their plans. As Mrs. Underwood put it, "They were fully competent to decide this question." Although intent on their mission, they had bouts of overwhelming nervousness about what they had taken on. During the ride to Chicago, they took notes from the books on teaching that Dorothy had borrowed from a teacher in the Auburn schools. They also reread the letter they had received the previous week from Carpenter:

My dear Miss Woodruff and Miss Underwood,

I was out to the new school house yesterday getting a line on how many pupils there would be, what supplies and repairs we would need etc. . . . I have not heard from you in regard to saddle ponies, but expect you will want them and am looking for some for you. . . .

I expect you are pretty busy getting ready to pull out. If you have a 22 you had better bring it out as there are lots of young sage chicken to be found in that country and August is the open season on them.

With best regards to you both
I am very truly
Farrington Carpenter

They were met at the Chicago station by J. Platt Underwood, an uncle of Ros's, who was, Dorothy observed, "clad in a lovely linen suit." A wealthy timber merchant, he did much of his business in the West, and when they told him that Carpenter had advised them to bring along a rifle, he agreed it was a good idea. The next morning he took them from his house on Lake Park Avenue into the city to buy a .22 and a thousand rounds of shot. It was already 90 degrees downtown and exceedingly humid. Dorothy wrote to her mother that everyone laughed when she tried to pick up the rifle. "I could hardly lift the thing. . . . Imagine what I'll be in Elkhead!" She had better luck at Marshall Field's, where she found a lovely coat: "mixed goods — very smart lines & very warm for $30.00." She and Ros bought heavy breeches at the sport store and got some good leather riding boots that laced up the front.

The oppressive heat wave followed them as they left Chicago, and it got worse across the Great Plains, clinging to their skin along with the dust. Although transportation and safety had improved since the opening of the West, and there were settlements and farms along the railway, the scenery, if anything, was starker than ever. When they were several hundred miles from Denver, there were few signs of life. The riverbeds were cracked open, and there was no long, lush prairie grass or even much sagebrush, just furze and rush and yucca. The few trees along the occasional creeks and "dry rivers" were stunted. The Cheyenne and Arapaho and the awkward, hunchbacked herds of buffalo that had filled the landscape for miles at a stretch were gone. From the train window, Dorothy and Ros caught only an occasional glimpse of jackrabbits.

They had not been aware of the gradual rise in terrain, but they were light-headed as they stepped into the Brown Palace Hotel in Denver. Ros was tall, slender, and strikingly pretty, with a gentle disposition and a poised, steady gaze — "the belle of Auburn," as Dorothy proudly described her. Dorothy's own round, cheerful face was animated by bright blue eyes and a strong nose and chin. People tended to notice her exuberant nature more than her small stature. Under their straw hats, their hair had flattened and was coming unpinned.

Half a dozen well-dressed gentlemen sat in the lobby on tufted silk chairs, reading newspapers or talking; women were relaxing in the ladies' tearoom. A haberdashery and a barbershop flanked the Grand Staircase, and across the room was a massive pillared fireplace made of the same golden onyx as the walls. The main dining room, with gold-lacquered chairs and eight-foot potted palms, was set for dinner. As they approached the reception desk, they saw that the atrium soared above the Florentine arches of the second story. Each of the next six floors was wrapped in an ornate cast-iron balcony, winding up to a stained-glass ceiling. The filtered light it provided, along with the high wall sconces, was pleasantly dim, and it was relatively cool inside.

Ros signed the register for both of them — Miss D. Woodruff and Miss R. Underwood — in neat, girlish handwriting, with none of the sweeping flourishes of the male guests who had preceded them from Kansas City, Philadelphia, Carthage, and Cleveland. On a day when they would have welcomed a strong rain, they were courteously asked whether they preferred the morning or afternoon sun. A bellman showed them to Room 518, with a southeastern exposure and bay windows overlooking the Metropole Hotel and the Broadway Theatre. They were delighted to see that they also had a private bathroom with hot and cold running water. Each of them took a blissful bath, and despite Dorothy's assurances to her mother after her purchases at Field's ("Nothing more for nine months!"), they went straight to Sixteenth Street to shop. They had no trouble finding one of the city's best department stores, Daniels & Fisher. Modeled after the Campanile at the Piazza San Marco, it rose in stately grandeur high above the rest of downtown.

Denver was up-to-date and sophisticated. Its public buildings and best homes were well designed, on a grand, sometimes boastful scale. The beaux arts Capitol — approached by paved sidewalks and a green park — had a glittering gold-leaf dome. There was a financial district on Seventeenth Street known as "the Wall Street of the West"; a YMCA; a Coca-Cola billboard; electric streetcars; and thousands of shade trees. Under the beautification plan of Mayor Robert Speer, the city had imported oaks, maples, Dutch elms, and hackberries, which were irrigated with a twenty-four-mile ditch carrying water from the streams and rivers of the Rockies. The desert had been transformed into an urban oasis.

Dorothy and Ros had heard about the Pike's Peak gold rush of 1859, and they could see how quickly the city had grown up, but beyond that, their knowledge of early Western history was hazy. It was hard to imagine that not even sixty years earlier, Denver City, as it was then called, was a mining camp with more livestock than people. Still part of Kansas Territory, it consisted of a few hundred tents, log cabins, Indian lodges, and shops huddled on the east bank of Cherry Creek by the South Platte River. The cottonwoods along the creek were chopped down for buildings and fuel. Pigs wandered freely in search of garbage. Earthen roofs dripped mud onto the inhabitants when it rained, and they frequently collapsed. The only hotel was a forty-by-two-hundred-foot log cabin. It had no beds and was topped with canvas.

The more visionary newcomers looked past the squalor. One of them was twenty-eight-year-old William Byers, who started the *Rocky Mountain News*. In his first day's edition of the paper, he declared: "We make our debut in the far west, where the snowy mountains look down upon us in the hottest summer day as well as in the winters cold here where a few months ago the wild beasts and wilder Indians held undisturbed possession — where now surges the advancing wave of Anglo Saxon enterprise and civilization, where soon we fondly hope will be erected a great and powerful state." Already Byers was Colorado's most strident advocate, and he became part of the business and political class that made sure his predictions came true. Thousands of prospectors, stirred by exaggerated tales about gold discoveries, imagined the region as "the new El Dorado."

Few valuable minerals were found at Pike's Peak until long after the gold rush had ended. Nevertheless, in the winter and spring of 1859, the first significant placer deposits were found, in the mountains at Clear Creek, thirty-five miles west of Denver; they were soon followed by finds at Central City, Black Hawk, and Russell Gulch. By the end of the year, a hundred thousand prospectors had arrived.

Denver City became an indispensable rest and supply stop for gold diggers on their way to and from the Rockies, as it was for trail drivers and lumbermen. Wagon trains from Missouri and Kansas came to town filled with everything from picks and wheel rims to dry goods, whiskey, coffee, and bacon. Gold dust was the local currency, carried in buckskin pouches and measured on merchants' scales. There was enough of it to start a building boom in everything from gambling halls to drugstores.

With the accumulation of creature comforts in Denver, some speculators were confident that they could domesticate the mountains, too, with dozens of towns and resorts. In the meantime, men returned with stories of suffering and gruesome deaths in the wilderness. In June 1859 a forest fire swept through the dry pines on gusty winds, killing over a dozen people. Horace Greeley, the editor of the *New York Tribune,* had recently stopped in Denver during his famous "Overland Journey," and he made some harsh but titillating assessments of what he had found. "Within this last week," he reported on June 20, "we have tidings of one young gold seeker committing suicide, in a fit of insanity, at the foot of the mountains; two more found in a ravine, long dead and partially devoured by wolves." A month earlier, a man from Illinois, Daniel Blue, had stumbled into Station 25 of the Leavenworth & Pike's Peak Express, skeletal and nearly blind. He said that he and his brothers and the others in their party had lost their way along the Smoky Hill Route, and their packhorse had wandered off. In mid-March, they had used up their remaining ammunition and food, subsisting for a week on grass, boiled roots, and snow. When one of the group died of starvation, the Blue brothers resorted to cannibalism.

One entrepreneur with grandiose ideas about Colorado's future was Henry C. Brown, a tenacious carpenter who opened a workshop by Cherry Creek and eventually owned and ran the *Denver Tribune* and, with a partner, the Bank of Denver. In 1867, when Denver's power brokers were competing with their counterparts in Golden to be the capital of Colorado Territory, Brown settled the issue by donating ten acres of his 160-acre homestead to the city. He stipulated that the capitol be built on the highest point, envisaging the neighborhood as both the city's commercial center and its finest residential district. The Civil War was over, and influential Coloradans, many from northern states, were firm Republicans. Brown gave the new streets resonant pedigrees: Broadway was surrounded by Lincoln, Sherman, Grant, and Logan.

When Brown was ready to build a luxury hotel, he hired Frank Edbrooke, a young architect from Chicago who had designed Denver's spectacular Grand Opera House and one of its earliest office buildings, which was fronted with plate-glass windows. Edbrooke planned the hotel to fit a large triangular plot that Brown had used as his cow pasture. The project took four years and cost $2 million, including the furnishings and fittings. The Brown Palace opened in 1892, sixteen years after Colorado became the thirty-eighth state.

By the time Dorothy and Rosamond arrived, the hotel presided over Denver's business and theater districts. The Union Pacific Railroad delivered passengers to Union Station at the northwest end of Seventeenth Street, near the original site of Denver City; and automobiles — along with trolleys and bicycles — were replacing horses along Broadway. The new "machines" were unreliable and noisy but left behind none of the bacteria, odors, and mess of manure. Colorado, with its high altitude and dry air, was the Baden-Baden of the United States. Hospitals in Denver specialized in the treatment of tuberculosis, and spas had been built in mountain towns known for their mineral waters. Thanks to the boosterism of the *Rocky Mountain News* and other newspapers, the aggressive advertising campaigns of the railroads, and stories of medicinal miracles in Colorado Springs, Manitou, Steamboat Springs, and Hot Sulphur Springs (a town owned by William Byers), tourism had replaced gold as the state's biggest lure.

The two women from the East were surprised to find themselves gazing at the white peaks and blue skies of the Rockies through a heavy haze that was just as bad as the air in Auburn. The pollution was less noticeable in the summer, when coal wasn't needed for heat, but coal fired the electrical generator of the Brown Palace and other businesses, and half a dozen smelters ran year-round, processing mountain ore into gold and silver and emitting their own noxious odors. As in other industrial cities, plumes of gray-black smoke rose throughout downtown; the Brown Palace already had been sandblasted to remove a dark residue that had settled on its facade. The Denver Tramway Company provided service to the "streetcar suburbs." Businessmen who wanted to escape the grit and crowds at the end of the day moved their families south, east, and west of the city, away from the prevailing north winds.

Rosamond and Dorothy had dinner that evening with Palmer Sabin, the son-in-law of Platt Underwood, and his family. The Sabins must have been charmed by their visitors' gumption and social graces. They were worried, though, about how well the two women would manage in Elkhead. The Western Slope lagged decades behind the Front Range of the Rockies. Although the region had fertile valleys and mineral deposits that exceeded those on the eastern side, an 1880 tourists' guide called it "an unknown land." Denver society referred to it as "the wild country." The mountains where they would be living were far from Hayden and the railroad. Elkhead was not a town; it barely qualified as a settlement. It had several dozen scattered residents, no shops or amenities of any kind, and a brutally punishing climate.

Farrington Carpenter had arranged for them to stay with a family of homesteaders. He wrote to them, "I dropped down onto Calf Creek and took dinner with the Harrisons about 2 miles from the school and

Mrs. Harrison said she would take you to board if I would explain in advance that they do not run a regular boarding place, but are just plain ranch folks. They have a new house and can give you a room together for yourselves. . . . They will charge you $20 per month apiece for board and room. You will be expected to take care of your own room and that price does not include washing. . . ." Palmer's mother, Rosamond said, "was very discouraging about our adventure." She told them, "No Denver girls would go up there in that place. It will be terribly hard."

Friends at home believed they were wasting yet another year. Unlikely to find worthy suitors among the cowboys and merchants of Routt County, they were apparently dooming themselves to be old maids. Dorothy and Ros, however, were more bothered by the idea of settling into a staid life of marriage and motherhood without having contributed anything to people who could benefit from the few talents and experiences they had to offer. The notion of a hard life — for a limited time — was exactly what they had in mind.

"We were nothing daunted," Ros recalled, "and spent the night in grandeur at the

Brown Palace Hotel . . . the hottest night I
ever spent in my life."

2
THE GIRLS FROM AUBURN

Dorothy (front) and Rosamond on Owasco Lake

Dorothy and Ros met in Miss Bruin's kindergarten in 1892. The school, started ten years earlier, was one of the first kindergartens in the United States. Miss Bruin was kind to the children, but they shrank from her hugs and kisses because, Dorothy said, "her face bristled with stiff hairs." Dorothy briefly attended a public school on Genesee Street, but when her parents heard about the outside toilets and the unsanitary water pail with a tin cup fastened to it with a chain, they moved her to a private school that Rosamond was attending. Happy to be with Ros again, she didn't mind her solitary mile-and-a-half walk through the village, but her trips home from the primary school on North Street unnerved her. She had to pass through the business district, which was lined with saloons. They had old-style swing doors and smelled strongly of stale beer. Occasionally in the afternoon, she and her friends saw men stumbling out onto the street, and they would run down the block as fast as they could.

Dorothy had six siblings. Anna, the oldest, was followed by Carl, Hermione, Carrie-Belle, Douglas, Dorothy, and Milly. Their mother, Carrie, Dorothy later said, didn't really understand how babies were conceived. Consumed by her many domestic and philanthropic duties, she had little time for the fancies of young children. "I used to beg my mother to tell me stories about what life was like when she was a little girl and how she lived and what Auburn was like," Dorothy said. "But she never seemed able to do it." She revered her mother, and worried about how frequently she displeased her. One spring day, Dorothy was walking by her older cousin's house on South Street, and noticed the garden was full of blooming hyacinths. "I thought they were perfectly beautiful, and how much my mother would like them," she said. "So I walked up and picked every one, took them home, and proudly gave them to Mother. She was absolutely horrified." Carrie insisted that Dorothy go back and apologize to her cousin. In July 1897, when she was ten years old, her parents went off on an extended holiday, and she and her siblings were left with their nursemaid, Mamie. She wrote a winsome note: "My dear Mama . . . I can't imagine that a week from today you will be away out at sea. I do hope that you won't be seasick and that Papa won't have any occasion to put an umbrella over him. . . . I promise to try my best to mind Mamie, so that when you come back you will find me improved. With millions of love, Dorothy."

Carrie, the image of Victorian rectitude in ornate, high-necked dresses, closely watched the household budget, though immigrant labor was cheap. The staff included several maids, a cook, and a gardener. Carrie lived to be ninety-three, one of her daughters-in-law wrote, "in spite of the vicissitudes of a big family." And she never cooked a meal in her life. "Her theory was that if she didn't know how, someone could always be found to do it for her."

Dorothy's father, a commanding figure with a receding hairline and a bushy walrus mustache, was known in Auburn for his quick wit and his generosity. On his birthday every year, all of the guests would find twenty-dollar gold coins in their napkins. Dorothy looked forward to the formal family dinner each night, seeing it as an opportunity to spend uninterrupted time with her parents and her older brothers and sisters. She particularly liked sitting next to her handsome brother Carl, despite his occasional offhand cruelty. One evening she showed him her new pair of white button boots, and when he teased her about her baby fat, she burst into loud sobs and was sent to her room. There was no discussion about who was to blame. Mrs. Woodruff was a strict disciplinarian, and the children were forbidden to interrupt or ask questions at the table. Nevertheless, Dorothy, the product of a pre-psychoanalytic culture, looked back on her childhood in almost idyllic terms. She said of her father, "We just swallowed everything he said and thought it was perfect."

She spent much of her time with her maternal grandmother, Anna Porter Beardsley, a short, erect woman with a strong but embracing personality. Anna had four colonial governors in her lineage, and Dorothy was expected to know their histories. That branch of the Beardsleys lived in a rambling clapboard Greek Revival house, with extensive formal gardens and a level expanse of lawn on which the family gathered to play croquet. The grounds were kept by a gardener who had a square-trimmed beard, a strong Irish brogue, and always kept a clay pipe in his mouth.

On cool days, Dorothy often found her grandmother reading on her bedroom sofa, a wood fire burning in the fireplace. The room contained a bed, a bureau, and a dressing table, painted a pale green, that Dorothy's grandparents had bought soon after they were married. She was told that the furniture had been made by Italian inmates at the Auburn state prison on the other side of town, and she noticed that they had decorated it in delicate brushstrokes with butterflies, trees, and flowers. In the summer, the gardener lined up tomatoes and peaches to ripen on the railing of a porch off the dressing room.

The drawing room, with a white marble

fireplace and tall windows covered by embroidered French white curtains, was used only for formal occasions, such as funerals and the Beardsleys' holiday dinners. "The Beardsley family and its connections by marriage had grown so large," according to one account of early Auburn, "that when the family Christmas dinner was eventually reduced to twenty-five, it seemed to some of the members so small [as] to be hardly worth having."

Dorothy's mother and father were married in the Beardsley mansion in 1872 near a wooden full-length mirror set on a low marble stand. Her father told her that the only thing he remembered about the wedding was looking into the mirror and seeing the shine on his boots — "not very romantic to my young ears." To Dorothy, the dining room was memorable chiefly for the heating register in the floor, where she and her sisters liked to stand and feel the warm air billow their skirts around their legs. Her grandfather had his own use for the heating vent: a servant warmed his pie on it before it was served to him.

Alonzo Beardsley had an aquiline nose, very blue eyes, a bald pink head with a fringe of white hair, and a trailing white beard on which he was apt to spill food. He and his brother Nelson were among the richest men in Auburn. In 1848, along with several colleagues, they had invested in a cornstarch factory nearby. The many uses for cornstarch — from stiffening shirt collars to thickening blancmange — were just being discovered, and in the decades after the Civil War, the Oswego Starch Factory became the most extensive factory of its kind in the world. Each year it burned six thousand tons of coal and used 701,000 pounds of paper and five million board feet of lumber. After dinner, Alonzo retired to his library, which had a floor-to-ceiling mahogany bookcase with glass panes in the door. The only books Dorothy ever took out were James Fenimore Cooper's novels, and she read them all.

She was happiest when she was with Rosamond. The Underwoods' good spirits were contagious, and Ros, who had three brothers but no sisters, cherished her companionship. Ros's mother, Grace, was almost completely deaf — the result of an attack of scarlet fever when she was thirty. No one took much notice of her handicap, despite the ear trumpet she sometimes used. "Mrs. Underwood was a remarkable mother," Dorothy said with unintended poignancy, "because she was so understanding of children and used to play games with us." Mr. Underwood called her "Dotty with the laughing eyes."

Judge Underwood had a keen sense of humor and was a gifted musician who had taught himself to read music and play the piano. At family gatherings, he produced jingles and poems he had written, and Rosamond loved the evenings "when Papa sat alone at the beautiful Steinway piano, sometimes for hours, roaming over the keyboard. He could pass from jazz to grand opera, from hymns to Gilbert and Sullivan's productions, singing the latter with his good voice." Dorothy remembered that one night, after the judge and Ros and her brothers returned from a musical at the Burtis Opera House, he sat down and played the entire score by heart.

As Dorothy grew up, she absorbed the city's spirit of entrepreneurship and noblesse oblige, along with some of the radical thinking about the rights of blacks and women and the working class that had infiltrated an otherwise conservative stronghold. The children of Auburn's gentry learned most of their American history through stories their parents and grandparents told about the city's prominent citizens. William H. Seward had moved to Auburn as a young man and married the daughter of the judge he had worked for before starting his own law practice. Dorothy's great-uncle Nelson Beardsley later became a partner of Seward's at Seward & Beardsley. One of her aunts, Mary Woodruff, was a good friend of Seward's daughter Fanny.

Seward, the foremost of the Auburn radicals, was short and clean-shaven, with red hair, a raspy voice, and a sharp, swooping nose that prompted Henry Adams to refer to him as "a wise macaw." In 1846, after serving two terms as governor, Seward represented a twenty-three-year-old black man named William Freeman who was charged with stabbing to death a white family of four in nearby Fleming. The victims were a pregnant woman, her husband, her son, and her mother. People in Auburn were stunned by the crime and warned that whoever defended Freeman could expect retribution. As Freeman was escorted to jail, he was almost lynched by a mob.

Seward's wife, Frances, was passionately interested in abolition, women's rights, and her husband's work, and she helped him with his research. Freeman's family had a history of mental illness, but the Sewards believed that he became deranged after repeated beatings in the Auburn prison, where he was held for five years for horse stealing, a crime he almost certainly did not commit.

During the trial, Seward made an early use of the insanity defense. His library on South Street, which today is filled with the pleasant smell of moldering leather bindings, contains a dense volume published in 1845 called *Principles of Forensic Medicine.* One of the passages that Frances marked in the margins with two heavy lines in black ink was "*Non compos mentis* is one of four sorts." In Seward's summation to the jury, he argued: "I am the lawyer for society, for mankind, shocked beyond the power of expression, at the scene I have witnessed here of trying a maniac as a malefactor."

Although he lost the case, he appealed to the New York Supreme Court, which reversed the conviction. Freeman died in prison before a second trial could take place. Seward was out of town, and Frances wrote to him with the news: "Poor Bill is gone at last — he died alone in his cell was found dead this morning. . . . I am glad the suffering of the poor benighted creature is terminated. . . . The good people of Auburn can now rest quietly in their beds 'the murderer' has no longer the power to disturb them."

Seward had earned a national reputation as a man of unimpeachable integrity. Three years later, he began the first of two terms in the U.S. Senate, and after contending unsuccessfully against Lincoln in the 1860 presidential contest, he became the secretary of state. Lincoln liked to call him "Governor," but when Seward returned from Washington, his once disapproving neighbors referred to him respectfully as "the Secretary."

The Sewards provided financial backing for the abolitionist newspaper *North Star,* published out of Rochester by their friend Frederick Douglass. In the 1850s — along with half a dozen or so other Auburn families — they harbored fugitive slaves in their basement. Through their work with the Underground Railroad, they became close to Harriet Tubman, and after the Civil War, they convinced her to settle in Auburn, selling her a wooden house and seven acres a few miles down South Street for her and her relatives. She also looked out for other African-Americans in town, opening the first home in the country for indigent and elderly blacks. When Dorothy and Ros were small, the elderly Tubman rode a bicycle up and down South Street, stopping to ask for food donations. If she had specific needs, she sat on the back porch and waited for the lady of the house, with whom she would chat and ask for bedding or clothing for her residents. One of Ros's nieces said, "Mother had coffee with Harriet and would always leave a ham or turkey for her for the holiday."

The Woodruff fortune rose and fell according to the demand for buttons, so Dorothy's family did not have all of the luxuries the wealthiest families had, such as a summer cottage on Owasco Lake. But Ros's parents did, and Dorothy spent most summers with them. One of the Finger Lakes, Owasco was a few miles south of Auburn. About eleven miles long and three-quarters of a mile wide, it was surrounded by lush and hilly farmland that dropped sharply to a wooded shore. In the summer months, the women and children of Auburn society took advantage of the fresh air and clean water, and the men commuted to Auburn by steamboat or train. People came all the way from New York City to escape the "vapors" and epidemics. The lake also was a popular spot for entertaining U.S. presidents and other dignitaries. In the mid-1800s, there were legendary parties at Willowbrook, the family compound of Enos Throop, New York's tenth governor. Presidents Johnson and Grant and General Custer were among the guests, stopping for a banquet in their honor during Johnson's "Swing Around the Circle" tour in 1866, an unsuccessful effort to boost support for his Reconstruction policies.

Ros's father taught the children to swim, row, and sail. When the girls swam, they wore the heavy bathing costumes of the day: short-sleeved wool dresses to their knees, over drawers and black stockings, and bathing slippers — all topped with oversize caps to protect their hair. The picturesque "Lady of the Lake" steamboat made two round trips a day, delivering groceries, mail, and guests to the cottages. Residents hoisted flags on their docks when they wanted the boat to stop, and, Dorothy said, "No ocean voyage was more thrilling than those trips on our little twelve-mile-long lake."

One summer Dorothy's extended family rented Willow Point, a spacious two-story shingle house owned by a particularly esteemed Auburn couple, David Osborne and his wife, Eliza. The tracks of the Lehigh Valley Railroad ran behind the houses on the lake, and Dorothy remembered that when the freight trains went by, transporting anthracite coal from Pennsylvania to Ontario, they rattled the house.

David Osborne, a friend of the Woodruffs, Underwoods, and Beardsleys, was one of the city's most influential entrepreneurs. His business, D. M. Osborne & Company, sold harvesters, mowers, and other farm equipment. Its phalanxes of factory buildings along Genesee Street had thirty-five hundred employees, and by the turn of the century, it had become the third largest enterprise of its kind in the country.

Eliza Osborne was one of the most prominent suffragists in Cayuga County. Her mother was Martha C. Wright, whom an Auburn neighbor referred to as "a very dangerous woman." Martha Wright organized the 1848 Seneca Falls Convention for women's rights, along with Eliza's aunt Lucretia Mott and Elizabeth Cady Stanton. Eliza was a tall, regal woman whose glorious black eyes, according to Stanton, were brimming with "power and pathos." Ros's mother considered her a close friend, even though Eliza was a generation older. Eliza's father, David Wright, worked with Seward on the defense of William Freeman, and the Wrights, too, hid runaway slaves. Beginning in the 1860s, Eliza Osborne hosted her own meetings with Stanton, Susan B. Anthony, and other feminist leaders at her home on South Street.

When Dorothy was seven years old, Eliza bought her grandfather Woodruff's former property next to the Seward House. For two decades Eliza was the president and principal financial patron of the local chapter of the Woman's Educational and Industrial Union, a group devoted to the moral and social welfare of local working girls. She greatly expanded the house, turning it into the Osborne Memorial Building, an august four-story structure of red brick, for the growing activities of the Woman's Union. It contained a dressmaking classroom, a cooking school, a gymnasium, and a day nursery. Before long, a "swimming tank" was added in a new wing. Many of Auburn's socially prominent women donated money and time to Eliza's undertaking. Eventually, Dorothy and Ros were among them.

Eliza doted on her son Thomas Mott Osborne, who inherited his elders' commitment to political reform and social justice. In middle age, he befriended and advised young Franklin D. Roosevelt. In 1911, when FDR was a twenty-nine-year-old state senator, they worked together to fight the corruption of Tammany Hall. They were also active supporters of Woodrow Wilson's 1912 presidential campaign, lobbying behind the scenes at the Democratic convention in Baltimore; Wilson secured the nomination on the forty-sixth ballot. Osborne was gratified when the new administration appointed Roosevelt assistant secretary of the navy, but he abandoned politics in disgust after many federal appointments went to Tammany Hall and its sympathizers. Instead, Osborne convinced the governor of New York to appoint him chairman of a long overdue state commission on prison reform.

The young ladies of Auburn were mostly protected from the uglier outgrowths of the industrial age, but the state prison, a vast complex on State Street across from the train station, was unavoidable. Auburn's rapid growth from a quiet village on the edge of the American frontier into a major industrial center would not have been possible without it. Two octagonal stone towers framed the main gate, and the high, long walls enclosed a grim collection of cell blocks, workshops, and the administration building, heavily hung with untended ivy.

The prison opened in the early 1800s, and four years later, inmates began providing cheap contract labor — an attraction for fledgling industries. Convicts made steam engines, sleighs, shoes, nails, furniture, and other products. Factories quickly sprang up nearby, along the Owasco Outlet, an excellent source of hydraulic power. Auburn's officials promised an innovative approach to rehabilitation, and their methods, known as "the Auburn system," were admired throughout the country and Europe. So was the prison's intimidating architecture, which became the model for most U.S. penitentiaries.

The Auburn system was designed to instill good behavior through confinement in individual cells, strict discipline, and work at various trades. Silence was maintained at all times. The inmates marched in striped uniforms to workshops in the Auburn-invented "lockstep." Anyone who broke the rule of silence was flogged with the "cat" — a cat-o'-nine tails, with lashes eighteen inches long, made out of waxed shoe thread, which were said to "cut the flesh like 'whips of steel.' " Eventually, the cat was replaced with a three-foot wooden paddle covered with leather. Others were subjected to the "shower bath": stripped, bound, and placed inside a barrel. A wooden collar was fastened around their necks to immobilize their heads as a spigot dispensed ice-cold water. The shower bath was discontinued in

1858 after a prisoner drowned during treatment.

Thomas Mott Osborne often hosted elaborately costumed theatricals at his home, and he had a gift for impersonation. In 1913, a few months after taking the job as prison reform commissioner, he posed for a week as Tom Brown, Inmate #33,333X. When he got out, he and a former prisoner founded the Mutual Welfare League, devising a form of limited self-government in the prison and helping to prepare inmates for life outside. Osborne's work put an end to the rule of silence and secured prisoners the right to go out into the yard for an hour each evening. He wrote a book about the experience, *Within Prison Walls,* and his exploit as an inmate and his reforms were recounted in papers around the world.

Dorothy never fully reconciled the two Auburns. She told her grandchildren about a horrifying early memory: the execution of William McKinley's assassin, Leon Czolgosz, who in 1901 was put to death in the prison, in the world's first electric chair. She was fourteen years old at the time, and some eighty years later, she said she had been upset to hear that there would be no funeral for him; he was to be buried in Fort Hill Cemetery in a far corner in an unmarked grave.

Fort Hill Cemetery, set on eighty-three verdant acres, played a vivid role in her imagination. Fort Street was only one block long, and the Woodruffs lived by the cemetery's entrance. In the sixteenth century, Fort Hill — the highest spot in the vicinity — was a fortified area in a Cayuga Indian village. Dorothy's grandmother Anna had her own story of back-door visitors when she was a child in Auburn: hungry Indians who occasionally appeared outside the kitchen asking for food. The road was steep and winding as it entered the cemetery, and during Auburn's heavy snows, Dorothy and her siblings went sledding there. On weekends in warmer weather, Dorothy and Milly explored the cemetery. Mamie packed their lunches in shoe boxes, which they supplemented in the fall with ripe beechnuts that dropped from the trees. Their sister Hope had died of whooping cough in 1884 when she was six weeks old, and the girls were sentimentally drawn to the graves of children. As soon as they could read, they wandered among the tiny tombstones, making out the dates and the weathered inscriptions.

Dorothy's favorite stop, on a mounded crest of the highest hill, was a fifty-six-foot obelisk, a monument to a Cayuga Indian chieftain known as Logan who was widely admired in the East. Chief Logan was born Tahgahjute, ostensibly on Fort Hill, which the Cayugas called Osco; when he was a young man, his name was changed to Logan, apparently as an homage to Governor William Penn's secretary, James Logan. Judge William Brown of Pennsylvania, reflecting the romantic Victorian view, called Logan "the best specimen of humanity I have ever met with, either white or red." In 1774 Logan's family had been murdered by colonists in Virginia. He organized a retaliatory attack that turned into a series of bloody battles between the settlers and area Indian tribes. Logan refused to attend the peace conference, although he sent an eloquent statement for the occasion, which was described in a history of Auburn as "that masterpiece of oratory which ranks along with the memorable speech of President Lincoln at Gettysburg." Dorothy never forgot the haunting inscription on the Logan memorial, taken from the address: "Who is there to mourn for Logan?"

During Auburn's military funerals for its fallen soldiers, she and Milly sat on the curb in front of their house and watched the aged veterans of the Civil War marching solemnly by in faded uniforms. Dorothy remembered that Brigadier General William H. Seward, Jr., led "a fife and drum corps which used to wail famous funeral marches which I can hear to this day."

Dorothy and Ros were separated for the first time in their third year of high school, when Ros went to Germany with her family. The Underwoods asked Dorothy to join them, and she desperately wanted to go, but she thought that if she didn't apply herself to her schoolwork, she might not get into Smith College, which she and Ros had long planned to attend together. Dorothy's oldest sister, Anna, a brilliant, serious girl with a long, heavy braid down her back, had gone to Smith in 1893 — a major event in the family. Few women went to college, and Dorothy was prepared to sacrifice for that experience. Nevertheless, she came to rue her decision to stay home.

While Ros was becoming worldly — learning German, traveling to Greece, and journeying up the Nile in a dahabeah — Dorothy was attending Rye Seminary, a girls' boarding school on the Boston Post Road in Rye, New York. The school gave its students a sober Christian education, with an emphasis on college preparatory work. Although it eventually morphed into the well-appointed Rye Country Day School, it was a spartan place early in the twentieth century. At mealtime, the girls clattered down the iron stairs into the basement, where the French teacher presided over one table and the German teacher the other, and no English was spoken. As a result, conversations were halting and garbled. Dorothy shared a large bedroom with two other girls. Each had an iron bed and a washstand, and there was also a piano in the room. Girls were excused from class for their weekly baths. A schedule was posted on the bathroom door at the end of the hall.

In her letters home, Dorothy wrote about extracurricular activities off school grounds. In 1903, when she was sixteen, she described a day in New York, where she and her classmates went to Wagner's *Die Walküre*. "Oh, Grandma," she wrote, "I have just come home, and the opera was the most wonderful thing I have ever seen. I was afraid that it would be deep and perhaps it was, but I never enjoyed anything so much in all my life." The next fall, she told about a trip with her friends to Lakehurst, New Jersey. The girls stayed at a beautiful inn where, she wrote, "the spirit is so lovely that it doesn't seem a bit like a hotel." They played tennis, danced, and took walks in the woods.

At Thanksgiving, Dorothy and three other girls were invited to a friend's house near Port Chester, and she wrote to her mother on November 27 about their trip into Manhattan, where they shopped at Altman's, had lunch, and went to the Hudson Theater to see *Sunday*. "Ethel Barrymore is simply perfect," she announced, "and I am crazy about her."

Although Dorothy said she didn't learn much at Rye, she was strongly influenced by one teacher who sometimes invited her to her room, where she served little cakes and pastries and gave her books of poetry by Shelley and Keats. "I just loved her," Dorothy said, "and this is a perfect example of what a good teacher can do to stimulate a growing young person's mind and imagination."

3
"A Funny, Straggly Place"

Ferry Carpenter in his law office

On the morning after their arrival in Hayden, Dorothy and Ros woke up early. They would be leaving in several hours for Elkhead, in the mountain range that abutted the Yampa Valley, and as Dorothy recalled, "We could hardly wait to see what was in store for us." When they walked into the dining room, half a dozen cowboys were seated at a large round table. "Of course nobody got up or anything, they simply stared at us." As they sat down, the man next to her said, "Good morning, ma'am." He was wearing a boiled white shirt with no collar, and a diamond stud in the neckband. The table was covered with hot cereals and biscuits and jams and coffee, and she and Ros ordered eggs, "once over, in the most approved manner." Then "started a great procession of right and left," as the men passed the food around, so persistently that it was hard to eat. The women tried to make conversation, "but all we got out from anybody was 'Yes, ma'am' and 'No, ma'am' or 'I wouldn't know, ma'am,' " and when they handed a dish to a neighbor, he would say, " 'I wouldn't wish to care for any, thank you, ma'am.' "

Their breakfast companions bore no resemblance to the refined young men they were accustomed to. Nor did Farrington Carpenter, who soon came in, introduced them to the cowboys, and said he had two ponies for them, as well as a conveyance to take them to the Harrison ranch. "We are tremendously impressed by Mr. C., who is a big man," Dorothy wrote that morning.

"He has a gentle, kindly manner, with keen eyes, a fine sense of humor and a regular live wire along every line." He took them to his office to talk everything over, and Dorothy — not wanting to confirm her mother's preconceptions about the uncouth West — avoided any mention of the office's history as a one-lane bowling alley, the electrical cord dangling from the ceiling to Carpenter's desk lamp, or the homely floral curtains.

Instead, she wrote: "His library was perfectly amazing, it showed such broad up-to-date interests, and we are certainly going to have to work night and day to keep up our end." His books included a complete set of Shakespeare, *The Life of David Crockett, An Autobiography,* a collection of Ralph Waldo Emerson's essays and lectures, *The Greek View of Life,* a biography of Walt Whitman, a six-volume edition of the poetry of Robert Burns, several biographies of Abraham Lincoln, *The Colorado Justice Manual,* and a book called *Swine,* a breeding and feeding guide. They spent two hours discussing their work at the school, and Ros wrote that morning with undisguised relief: "He is anxious to have us run the whole thing as we want to run it — and says we don't have to teach Domestic Science if we don't want to — or Sunday School either." She and Dorothy, having grown up in households staffed by maids and cooks, were more nervous about teaching domestic science, a turn-of-the-century precursor to home economics, than any other subject. "We didn't know anything about domestic science," Ros later admitted.

As for Hayden, Dorothy wrote, it was "a funny, straggly place," and its residents "snappy and entertaining," their good manners "as surprising as the kind of English they speak." Neither of them mentioned the cowboys in the dining room. Ros wrote, "The air is like tonic — and we are cool at last after dreadful heat in Denver. The country here is flat — with blue mountains in the country towards we go." Dorothy's pony was a sorrel called Nugget, on loan from Carpenter. She said he "is so little that I can hop off and on with the greatest ease." Ros's horse came from Steamboat Springs, and she was to name him herself.

At Earnest Wagner's saddle shop, they rented saddles and bought bits, bridles, ropes, spurs, and ponchos, then shook hands with all of the townspeople in the street. "We were introduced to each one, who gave us a terrible grip with their horny paws," Dorothy wrote innocently. As they were about to embark on their long, dusty ride to Elkhead, Ros scribbled: "Mr. C. has just telephoned that he is coming to lunch with us, and start us on our way — so no more now. Rosamond."

Straggly Hayden, like so many western towns, had come into being quickly and violently. Among its first settlers was the extended family of Porter M. Smart, the superintendent of the Western Colorado Improvement Company. In December 1874, the *Rocky Mountain News* referred to Smart as "one of that peculiar and persevering class of pioneers who are always in the van of civilization." He had built his house in "the remotest settlement of Western Colorado." That winter, his son Albert took in a few families who had been unable to provide for themselves, and one man began to steal flour, bacon, and groceries. The "culprit was arrested, tried, convicted, tied up to a tree and 'larruped' with long switches, and then given forty-eight hours to leave the country. He left." The *News* declared, "The company of which Mr. Smart is the representative is doing a world of good in thus extending family altars into the wilderness."

The Smarts and their few neighbors were

sometimes visited by Ute Indians, members of a nomadic tribe whose name for the Rockies was "the shining mountains." They had inhabited the land for over five hundred years. In return for dinner and a few sacks of potatoes, the Utes offered game and buckskins. But relations with the Utes became difficult over the next several years, as miners and merchants began to settle in the region.

Like the early gold prospectors in Denver, people rushed out after learning of the region's natural resources. This time the riches were publicized almost single-handedly by one man: Ferdinand Vandeveer Hayden, the world-famous geologist who in 1871 had led an expedition to survey all of Yellowstone country, and helped convince Congress to establish it as the first national park. Hayden spent the summers of 1873–75 conducting a similarly exhaustive study of the Colorado Rockies. One of his teams of surveyors, photographers, and scientists, working for the Department of the Interior, camped by the Bear River, near where the Smarts lived; the surveyors' mail was addressed simply to "Hayden Camp."

A thin, obsessive scholar with dark pouches under his eyes and an irascible disposition, Hayden had a genius for transforming highly technical geographical and geological data into popular science. He also was an outspoken advocate of development, writing to the secretary of the Interior Department about how rapidly the region would grow with the coming of the railroads, thus rendering it "very desirable that its resources be made known to the world at as early a date as possible." He gave lectures in Washington and New York in the mid-1870s about his discoveries of fantastic geysers and bubbling gray mud pots in Yellowstone, and hidden valleys with thriving communities in the Rockies. The talks included slides by a member of his team, the renowned photographer William H. Jackson, projected on a stereopticon. Hayden's *Atlas of Colorado,* published in 1877, was glowingly written about in both the United States and Europe. William Blackmore, a British investor in American ventures, claimed that English schoolboys couldn't name the presidents, but "all knew intimately the stories of Dr. Hayden's expeditions in to the wild Indian country of the far West."

The atlas gorgeously laid out every feature of the state in a succession of oversize maps showing its topography, drainage, geology — and its economic resources, including

"Gold and Silver Districts" and "Coal Lands." The region west of the Divide was densely speckled with prospective mining sites. The atlas also revealed how much of that land the Utes controlled, according to a treaty signed in 1873: twelve million acres on the Western Slope — over half of the Colorado Rockies. Two pages of the atlas, showing northwestern Colorado, were marked with large capital letters crossing the book's gutter and filling almost the entire map: RESERVATION OF THE UTE INDIANS.

By the late 1870s, Colorado's second mining boom was well under way, and Leadville and other camps were built on Ute territory. The Utes rebelled, setting fires to settlers' homes and to timber and prairie grass. This fueled a propaganda campaign in the pages of the *Denver Tribune,* with the slogan "The Utes Must Go!" Governor Frederick W. Pitkin emphatically shared that view, and did his part to encourage the growing public uproar.

The most serious trouble between the settlers and the Utes was precipitated by Nathan Meeker, head of the White River Agency, forty-five miles southwest of Hayden. Meeker was attempting to build a model agricultural community, teaching the

Indians to become good farmers and Christians; educating their children; and disabusing them of numerous uncivilized practices. The Ute men, though, believed that farming was women's work and that horses were not meant to pull a plow but to be ridden and raced. They despised Meeker, with his arrogant paternalism and his threatening claim that the U.S. government owned their land.

The Utes in Yampa Valley appealed for help to Major James B. Thompson, who ran a trading post by the Bear River and had won their trust. In response, Thompson, Smart, and the other settlers sent a petition to the Interior Department, asking for an investigation of Meeker and for protection for their families. Troops were sent, but to Hot Sulphur Springs, the closest town, about a hundred miles southeast. Porter Smart's daughter-in-law Lou, the mother of four children and pregnant with her fifth, was visited repeatedly by Utes in June 1879 when her husband, Albert, was away. She wrote in a letter afterward that they demanded food and matches, and that one of them wanted to trade back a gun that Albert had given him in exchange for a pony: " 'The gun no good. Would not kill buckskin, wanted trade back, give five dollars take pony go away no trouble squaw.' "

That summer, she said, she had "another dreadful miscarriage, worse even than the last." For ten days she couldn't sit up in bed. The Utes returned, camping near the house. When they heard that a company of Negro soldiers — Company D of the Ninth Cavalry — was not far away, waiting for orders, "They said they didn't care how many white men came but they wouldn't stand Negroes (that was too great an insult)." They set fire to two houses before riding off.

In August, after an altercation with the Utes' medicine man at the White River Agency, Meeker, claiming serious injuries, requested that Governor Pitkin send troops for his protection. Pitkin, a former mining investor and one of the more unscrupulous proponents of Manifest Destiny, had long argued that, treaty or not, the situation with the Utes was untenable. A few weeks later, three cavalry companies crossed onto Ute land at Milk Creek, the northern border of the reservation; about a dozen soldiers were killed and many more injured. The ambush came to an end when Company D arrived to rescue the men, but the White River Utes turned on Meeker, shooting him in the head, burning his farm to the ground, and abducting his wife and daughter.

Major Thompson, anticipating disaster, had already left. The Smarts and other families hurriedly packed their belongings and moved out. They stopped at Steamboat Springs, which consisted of little more than the homestead of James Crawford, the town's founder. They barricaded themselves in at the Crawfords' cabin for a few days, continuing on to Hot Sulphur Springs when it seemed safe. They arrived ten days after leaving home. Lou Smart and her husband learned that their house had been robbed of everything edible; chicken bones and feathers were scattered about inside. She said she feared that the Ute war had only just begun, yet she went on, "The only thing that worries me is the children not having any schooling, especially Charlie. There is no school here and they say there is to be none this winter." Lou Smart died a few months later of complications from her miscarriage.

The Meeker Massacre, as newspapers across the country labeled it, gave Governor Pitkin an opportunity to make a special announcement to the press about the Ute threat: "My idea is that, unless removed by the government, they must necessarily be exterminated." He pointed out "The advantages that would accrue from the throwing open of twelve million acres of land to miners and settlers. . . ." In August 1881 the U.S. Army force-marched virtually all of the Colorado Utes 350 miles to a reservation on a desolate stretch of land near Roosevelt, Utah.

As the Utes were being dispensed with, the settlement by the Bear River grew. A log school and a store were built on the homestead of Sam and Mary Reid, who had moved to the valley in 1880. Mary became postmistress the following year. The mail came by buckboard from Rawlins, Wyoming, three times a week, and the mailman crossed the river in a canoe. Sam Reid's brother-in-law, William Walker, moved from North Carolina; several years later, he was joined by his wife and children. They homesteaded on a parcel of land just north of town previously held by Albert Smart. A man named Ezekiel Shelton, trained as an engineer in Ohio, was sent to Yampa Valley by some Denver businessmen in 1881 to investigate stories of coal beds in the Elkhead Mountains. His reports were positive, and so was his response to the valley. Shelton helped establish the Hayden Congregational Church, to which one of the settlement's first three women, Mrs. Emma Peck, donated her organ. Shelton and Emma Peck even started a tiny literary society. Other pioneers followed, and the town of Hayden was incorporated in March 1906, when Farrington Carpenter and Ros and Dorothy were in their first year of college.

4
"Refined, Intelligent Gentlewomen"

Dorothy and Rosamond at Smith

One Sunday afternoon that month, Dorothy got a letter from her father, reminding her to dedicate herself to her studies at Smith. "We follow your life at College as reflected in your letters with deep interest & while you evidently enjoy the days as they pass I doubt not you are doing your work — I want you to master your French so that you can make it practical, learn to converse fluently. . . ."

Smith students were caught between the college's aspirations for them and the social mores of the day — some of which the school administration shared. Not all of the women made it through four years. Seventy-five of Dorothy and Ros's classmates, about a fifth of the class of 402, withdrew before commencement. One graduate wrote a "Senior Class history of 1909" for the yearbook, in which she coyly presented their dilemma as they entered the world: "We have not yet decided whether to 'come out' in society or 'go in' for settlement work." Jane Addams had started Hull House, the country's first settlement house, in Chicago in 1889. The underprivileged, regardless of race or ethnicity, took advantage of its social services, including school for their children and night classes for themselves. Addams had longed to go to Smith, to prepare for a career in medicine, but her father wouldn't allow it; he believed that her duty was to serve her family. In the years after his death, she became known across the country for her advocacy for civil rights, unions, female suffrage, and an end to child labor. To many college women, she was a model of enlightened thought and industry.

Yet, the Smith graduate continued in the yearbook, "Unlike our neighbor Holyoke 'over the way,' we have not troubled our busy heads over the right and wrong of woman suffrage, but are discussing whether psyches make long noses look longer and just who *are* the best-looking girls in the class. Some of us are hoping for an M.A., others, to quote a scintillating Junior, are hoping for a M.A.N. A few of us look, may look, forward to getting Ph.D.'s after our names, a few more of us, however, are looking forward to getting M-r-s. in front of them."

Smith College, started by Sophia Smith, a maiden lady who lived in Hatfield, near Northampton, was young: chartered in 1871, it opened in 1875. The only other full-fledged women's colleges in the country at that time were Elmira, Mary Sharp, and Vassar. Mount Holyoke and Wellesley were still known as female seminaries, where students attended Bible-study groups, church services, chapel talks, and prayer meetings. Twice a day they performed private devotions. Wellesley Female Seminary changed its name to Wellesley College in 1875, and Mount Holyoke, eighteen years later. The pastor of Sophia Smith's church had repeatedly urged her to pursue the idea of a college for women, and three months before her death, she made a codicil to her will in which she declared her belief that a higher Christian education for women would be the best way to redress their wrongs and to increase their wages and their "influence in reforming the evils of society . . . as teachers, as writers, as mothers, as members of society."

This belief — that women and men should be educated in separate colleges — was not widely shared among public intellectuals along the Eastern Seaboard. Henry Ward Beecher, for one, thought that the solution to higher education for women was to admit them to men's colleges, a practice already being followed in the Midwest and the West. (Oberlin became the first coeducational college in the country in 1837, when it enrolled four women. Two years earlier, it had admitted its first African-American students.) At Amherst's semicentennial celebration in July 1871, Beecher gave a speech in which he pressed his alma mater to admit women. So did the former governor of Massachusetts. Lengthy deliberations followed at Amherst and at Yale, Harvard, Williams, and Dartmouth, but the notion was not pursued at any of these colleges for another century. When Radcliffe College opened in 1879, it was known as "the Harvard Annex."

The president and trustees of Smith were clear about their mission. In June 1877, while Lou Smart was negotiating trades with the Utes in Yampa Valley, President L. Clark Seelye wrote in an annual circular in Northampton, "It is to be a woman's college, aiming not only to give the broadest and highest intellectual culture, but also to preserve and perfect every characteristic of a complete womanhood." He often said that one of Smith's missions was to teach its students to become "refined, intelligent gentlewomen."

The college intended to provide a curriculum just as rigorous as that of the best men's schools, but Seelye conceded that many of the students were not entirely ready for the academic demands. He and his successor expected Smith to stimulate students' intellectual curiosity and help them develop an appreciation of the scientific method. However, since most of them had "neither the call nor the competence to devote their lives to research," they were encouraged to work on "the development of the character and capacities of the personality."

The exceptions were notable. After graduation, Jane Kelly, Class of 1888, went to Northwestern University Women's Medical School and then to Johns Hopkins for a year of postgraduate work in medicine — there, she was required to sit in the balcony behind a curtain during lectures. She established both a medical practice and a family in Boston. After a week at Wood's Hole in the summer of 1902, she wrote to her classmates, "There was a large number of Smith girls working in the Laboratories, which speaks well for the scientific spirit fostered in our Alma Mater."

Dorothy did not have that calling. She had graduated from Rye Seminary with strong grades and managed to pass Smith's entrance examinations, which included translating English sentences into Greek, Latin, French, and German, and — in the English section — writing on the themes of *Julius Caesar, The Vicar of Wakefield,* and *Silas Marner,* and on the form and structure of *Macbeth, Lycidas, L'Allegro,* and other texts. She was not strongly motivated, though, and claimed that Rye had not taught her how to study. "The fact that I'd gone to Smith College to learn, I don't think made much impression on me," she said. The first semester, she got the equivalent of Ds in her two English classes, C- in French, B- in

German, C- in Latin, and C+ in mathematics. She was put on probation. Ros did better, with a C, two B-'s, a B, and two A's. Dorothy's record improved somewhat as the semesters wore on, but she never excelled and was not overly concerned about her grades.

She had warm recollections of one teacher at Smith, just as she'd had at Rye. In her junior and senior years, she took European history with Charles Hazen, whom she described as the first teacher she'd ever had who "could make you live the way those characters lived so long ago and the events in history seem so real." Dorothy's fascination with the past, sparked in Auburn and revived by Hazen, stayed with her throughout her life.

Admitting that her academic performance over her four years was undistinguished, she described herself as "romping" through Smith: "I loved every minute . . . I was invited to join all of the fun and social clubs that there were." She and Ros both belonged to the Phi Kappa Psi Society, the Current Events Club, and the Novel Club (its goals were to write a good novel and to have a good time, no one seemed to bother with the novel). She was a "tumble bug" at the Junior Frolic event at "the Hippodrome" and helped design costumes for the senior production of *A Midsummer Night's Dream.* Ros was a member of the Smith College Council. Their friendship was no less close in those years; it simply expanded to include others. "Life was very relaxed and easy," Dorothy noted. "Although of course we studied, we nevertheless had plenty of time to be with each other." They kept in touch with their Smith friends for sixty years.

When it came time to choose an "invitation house," Ros joined the White Lodge, and Dorothy agonized between that and Delta Sigma, which was, one of its founding members emphasized, not a secret society or a sorority — a distinction, perhaps, without a difference. The invitation houses cost more than campus housing, but along with an exclusive circle of friends, they promised single rooms, a housekeeper, a cook, a waitress, and some freedom not allowed on campus. Dorothy wryly described the choice between the two houses as "really one of the great problems of my young life — what I should do about this."

She joined Delta Sigma as a sophomore, and she idolized the juniors and seniors — "I thought they were the most beautiful and brilliant creatures on earth." The members had recently moved into a yellow clapboard house off Main Street, with a welcoming veranda and a spacious side porch that had two long wooden swings, cushioned in chintz and suspended from the ceiling by chains. The living room had a large fireplace, which was lit on chilly days after lunch. Sixteen students ate their meals at a long table in the dining room, presided over by the house matron. When they invited President Seelye or professors to dinner, dessert was the Faculty Cake, filled with macaroons, sherry, and whipped cream. The girls managed the household budget and were expected to observe the college's "ten o'clock rule" at bedtime. The college held dances, but they were women-only. Students were allowed to invite gentlemen to the Junior Promenade, the Rally on Washington's Birthday, and the Glee Club Concert.

Dorothy and Ros played gentle games of tennis in white skirts sweeping their ankles, and planned off-campus activities, including picnics. They took the trolley out Main Street to the end of the line in Greenfield, and walked through the woods to a brook, where they gathered twigs and built a fire. They roasted sausages called "bacon bats" on forked sticks, which they ate on buttered rolls, and they made coffee in a tin pail. For longer trips, they rented an old horse and wagon and rode out into the country, occasionally stopping for a night or two at one of the farmhouses.

Several weeks before graduation, Dorothy wrote to her grandmother. She and some friends had visited Deerfield's Memorial Hall, a museum that contained relics from the French and Indian Raid of 1704. Referring to the sacking of the town and the letters written from Canada by captured French officers to their families, she observed: "The village is so little and sleepy, and still so much in the country, that it required very little imagination to take us back to those times." The girls had supper by "that same brook, which has seen so many awful things," she wrote, "but I never saw more wonderful country. The mountains are so very green, dotted here and there with fruit trees and the air heavy with the odor of lilacs."

There is no indication that either Dorothy or Ros had in mind anything more taxing for their futures than the kind of charity work pursued by their friends and mothers in Auburn. Nor were they intent on finding husbands, not having met any young men whose company they liked nearly as much as they liked each other's. Dorothy told her grandmother how much she appreciated the privilege of attending college, then said, "Nevertheless, I am looking forward a great deal to being at home with you all next year." On a note of determined good cheer, she concluded: "I am sure I shall be very happy."

On the afternoon of June 13, 1909, the first of the four-day commencement events for Smith College, Northampton residents lined the streets and clustered by the First Congregational Church. "It was a fine opportunity," the *Springfield Republican* reported, "for the automobile experts to see a larger variety of automobiles than is often observed in Northampton and an equally rare opportunity, most appreciated by the women, to see a splendid display of handsome gowns and beautiful millinery." At four o'clock, the seniors marched in from the vestry, attended by the junior class, to the sight of masses of pink mountain laurel on the platform. President Seelye gave the sermon, telling the rows of serious young women, "[Y]ou will not become the useless members, but the benefactors, of society. Whatever be your employments, your lives then will be prolific of good deeds."

The congregation sang "Jesus Comes, His Conflict Over," and as Seelye gave the benediction, a light rain began to fall. It was pouring as they got ready to leave the church. The junior ushers rushed back to campus, returning with the girls' black rubber coats and hats and armfuls of umbrellas. They escorted the seniors and their guests into the hacks and carriages and automobiles outside the church.

The next morning, the heavy skies lifted in time for the Ivy Day procession. After chapel services at St. John's Church, the alumnae set forth by class along a white canvas carpet, past the gymnasium to Seelye Hall. The junior class — in brightly colored dresses and hats festooned with flowers — carried the ivy chains (actually long ropes made of laurel leaves) on their shoulders. The graduating class marched in pairs, their hair piled high in soft buns, in wasp-waisted, high-collared white dresses, carrying their roses. To Dorothy's great disappointment, her mother and father didn't see her graduate. They were in Europe and unwilling to interrupt their holiday. They returned with a present for her: a filigreed silver card case from Holland.

After the ivy song was sung and a class photograph taken, the graduates marched into the assembly hall for the class-day program. At the chapel exercises, President Seelye spoke of the first Smith class, of

1879: "There were eleven graduates and ten are still living, and seven of them are married. All of them hold honored positions. One of them is a professor in college; two are wives of college professors; one is at the head of an educational institution; a number of them are interested in educational work and are home-makers, and the same is true of graduates of succeeding classes."

■ ■ ■ ■

PART TWO:
OLD WORLD
AND NEW

■ ■ ■ ■

Rosamond, winter of 1916

5
UNFENCED

Steamboat & Wolcott Stage

Farrington Carpenter had a different kind of experience in college, and not only because it was a men's school. His jocular personality disguised a sensitive intelligence and a restless nature, and he was far more uncomfortable with the American class system than most of his peers. The old-line

East Coast students hastened to exploit his awkwardness. He had not been to Exeter or Andover. He was from Evanston, Illinois, a town that many of them had never heard of, and his father, although wealthy enough, was a shoe manufacturer. When he arrived at Princeton and read the "Freshman Bible," he realized that the stiff collars, vested suits, and neckties his mother had bought for him were hopelessly unstylish. "A freshman had to wear a black turtleneck sweater, corduroy trousers, and a little black cap called a 'dink' on the back of his head," he wrote in his autobiography, *Confessions of a Maverick.* When someone joked that Farrington sounded like the name of an English resort town, he told everyone his name was Ferry, but they dubbed him Skinny instead. It wasn't long before he turned his lack of social standing to his advantage. He took courses taught by the college's president, Woodrow Wilson, and made sure he got to know him.

Wilson's years at Princeton shaped his convictions about the purpose of education in a democracy — and Carpenter's beliefs were shaped alongside them. When Wilson assumed the job in 1902, his political views were conservative. In November 1904 he gave a speech in New York to the Society of

Virginians on "The Political Future of the South." Implicitly denouncing the populism of William Jennings Bryan, he declared, "The country as it moves forward in its great material progress needs and will tolerate no party of discontent or radical experiment; but it does need a party of conservative reform, acting in the spirit of law and of ancient institutions." At the university, though, Wilson was soon undertaking a radical experiment of his own known as the Quad Plan.

He officially introduced it to the Board of Trustees in December 1906. The idea was to replace the university's snobbish eating clubs or to absorb them into larger and less exclusive "quads." Ferry Carpenter acted as an enthusiastic student liaison. As conceived by Wilson and endorsed by some faculty and alumni, the quads would provide living and eating quarters for 100 to 150 students, from freshmen to seniors, thus encouraging them to enlarge their circle of acquaintances. Young faculty would live there, too, so that conversations, as Carpenter put it, would venture beyond sports and dirty jokes. The prospect of not getting into a club, he said, was appalling — one was deemed "a sad bird" and socially ostracized.

Wilson told Ferry, "Some of the wealthy

New York and Pennsylvania people with sons here would like to turn this college into a Tuxedo Institution, a country club. I refuse to head such an establishment." However, the board mostly was composed of wealthy easterners, and they vigorously opposed Wilson's idea. Over the next three years, as told by one of Wilson's biographers, Henry Bragdon, the press reported the controversy at Princeton as a fight between "college democracy" and social privilege. Wilson was depicted as a courageous progressive. "To the country at large, his dispute with the Princeton clubs was analogous to Theodore Roosevelt's struggles with the trusts, the meat packers, and the railroads." Infuriated though he was by the trustees' intransigence, Wilson found that the role of reformer suited him.

In June 1908 Ferry wrote to "Dr. Wilson" about his progress with potential supporters of the Quad Plan. He had joined the "middle-rated" Campus Club, to avoid the sad-bird taint, and become its secretary. Thanking Wilson for the clear grounding he had given him in his courses in jurisprudence and constitutional government, Ferry said that he had just read an article in the *Saturday Evening Post* that "sounded like a trumpet call to Americans to rally to Democracies' standard."

That fall, he invited Wilson to speak about the Quad Plan at the Campus Club. Wilson had just returned from a trip to the University of Wisconsin, where he had delivered a lecture on Abraham Lincoln. He was full of what he had seen there, telling his acolyte: "At those great state institutions, the gates are flung wide open. The wind of public opinion sweeps unobstructed through them. . . . But here at a proprietary institution, we are surrounded by a great high wall, which admits little from the outside world."

After dinner, Wilson instructed the students, "When you go out into the world and have to make your own living, you may have to sit at a desk next to a man who spits all over his own shoes, and you won't be able to take it because you have been so careful to avoid all unpleasantness in your college associations." In 1909 a majority of the trustees and a number of influential members of the administration at Princeton forced Wilson to drop the Quad Plan. The fight embittered him, but it also steeled him for a career in politics. Aristocracy, he informed a despondent Ferry Carpenter, was a fact of life even in democratic America.

Wilson and Ferry shared an interest in the American West. Wilson had gotten to know Frederick Jackson Turner in 1889, when Turner was a graduate student at Johns Hopkins University and Wilson a visiting professor. They lived in the same boardinghouse, and their conversations about the role of the West in American history helped Turner to develop his Frontier Thesis. Four years later, Turner made his renowned speech in Chicago, arguing that "The existence of an area of free land, its continuous recession, and the advance of American settlement westward, explain American development."

Carpenter chose to be inspired by Wilson's view of the West rather than bow to social realities in the East. He, too, believed that American democracy was born on the frontier. Growing up in Evanston, Ferry had idolized two of his father's cousins from Vermont who had become ranchers in North Dakota. They visited the Carpenters whenever they went to Chicago to sell their cattle at the stockyards. "They wore big black hats and buffalo robe overcoats that hung to their ankles," Carpenter wrote. When he begged his relatives to take him back with them, they told him there were Indians in North Dakota "just looking for a chance to scalp young boys." He couldn't get enough of these stories, and he twice convinced his mother to take him to Chicago to see Buffalo Bill's Wild West show.

He was a spindly youth. Injured in an ice-hockey scrimmage in high school, he was taken to New Mexico to regain his strength. After washing dishes and doing the family laundry at a twenty-thousand-acre ranch, he managed to get a job as a ranch hand in Colfax County, for a legendary pioneer named J. B. Dawson. At the age of fifteen, Carpenter had found his western role model. In the 1850s Dawson drove cattle fifteen hundred miles from Arkansas to California; during the Pike's Peak gold rush, he took his herds from Texas to the soon-to-be territory of Colorado. He served as a Texas Ranger during the Civil War and fought Indians on the Plains. Dawson had a disfiguring scar on his right hand, caused by an arrow wound. During a raid on Paint Creek, a Comanche who was no more than seventeen, having witnessed the death of a comrade, rode straight at Dawson and met him, Dawson told a journalist, "face to face about ten steps apart. We both started to shoot almost at the same time, I with my pistol, he with his bow. He was a little quicker than I was and his arrow went into my right hand . . . and into the lock on my pistol, disabling it and rendering me helpless." One of Dawson's companions shot the Indian, and he fell from his horse. "When we looked at his body," Dawson claimed, "we found he had one rifle wound and nine pistol wounds, besides the wound made by the shotgun. . . . His shirt was as bloody as if it had been dipped in blood." Dawson told people when recounting this story, Ferry doubtless among them, "He was the bravest man I ever met."

In 1905 Dawson sold his ranch and bought two thousand acres in Routt County, Colorado, an idyllic stretch of land by the Yampa River (formerly the Bear River), four miles outside the village of Hayden. The previous owner had added onto his cabin by putting four abandoned homesteads on some roped-together logs and pulling them over by mules. He put the cabins together like Lincoln Logs. As one of Dawson's granddaughters described it, "Floors met at different levels. . . . Ceilings jigged up and down, sometimes as much as three feet higher in the middle of a hallway; walls, butted together, refused to stand amicably side-by-side. . . . On the inside the rough logs or rough-sawn timbers were covered with a kind of construction paper which absorbed moisture. Brown stains like thin tobacco juice ran down the walls."

Carpenter was mesmerized by Dawson's description of Colorado: "the place for a young man to go. The hills . . . are full of deer and elk and antelope, and the streams are full of trout." The alfalfa was so high, Dawson told him, "that you couldn't see Ol' Coley's back when he pulled the mowing machine through it. And the bees made all the honey that you wanted. The public domain, open and unfenced, was available to any citizen over twenty-one. All you had to do was file on a homestead and, by living on it for seven months a year for five years, get title to 160 acres of free land." Dawson talked of a town (Steamboat Springs), twenty-two miles away, as a place that had every kind of mineral water, which could "cure anything from gripes to the hiccups . . . and you'd come out a new man."

In the Princeton library, Carpenter read about Routt County and learned that it stretched 150 miles west from the Continental Divide near Steamboat Springs to the Utah border. From the Wyoming line, the county made its way south almost to the Grand River — now the Colorado River. In 1900 the entire population of Routt County was thirty-six hundred people, and, Carpenter wrote, "for a hundred miles to the west, not a single town was shown on the map and the land was marked 'sage and bad lands.' "There was no railroad in the region, although he learned that David Moffat, a Denver tycoon, was building one from Denver to Salt Lake City.

Ferry asked if he could work for Dawson again that summer, and in June 1906, after his freshman year, he headed to Wolcott, Colorado, by train and, the final three days, by stagecoach. Carpenter trained Dawson's mares and watched over the wild elk, buffalo, and deer that Dawson had brought to the ranch. Ferry returned the following summer as well. He regarded the fertile Yampa Valley, he wrote, "as one of the most beautiful spots on earth."

On arriving that second summer, Ferry was asked to "take a letter to Dave Moffat," who wanted to run the tracks of his railroad through two and a half miles of Dawson's meadows, a few hundred feet from the ranch house. Old Man Dawson, Ferry said, had known Moffat ever since Moffat ran a little stationery store in Denver City. As Carpenter recalled, Dawson "could read, but he couldn't write. . . . [H]e used me as his amanuensis." The letter read:

Friend Dave,

I came over here to Northwest Colorado to get away from railroads. Now you've surveyed a railroad right in my doorstep. I can't stop civilization. When you get ready to build, I'll give you the right of way.

All Dawson asked in return was a flag stop and load-out facility, which he could use to get his cattle to market. The railroad stock cars were parked on a siding, with a chute for herding the cattle inside. The cars were then picked up by a passing freight train. Dawson and his wife, Lavinia, could ride the rails to Denver right from the ranch.

One of Ferry's jobs was to help Dawson's surveyor identify the borders of some state-owned land that Dawson wanted to lease. On one excursion into the Elkhead Mountains north of Hayden, the two stopped to eat lunch on a rise above Morgan Creek. Wolf Mountain was visible to the east, and the Flat Top Mountains about forty-five miles to the south. Consulting his calculations during lunch, the surveyor noted with surprise that the only water within miles, a flowing spring, was twenty-four feet from the state land. It was part of the public domain and therefore available for homesteading.

Carpenter said he felt as if he had stumbled on a gold mine, and he moved quickly. He was only twenty years old and barely broken into ranch life, but after consulting with Dawson, he put up a sign saying that the land was Farrington R. Carpenter's homestead. He took his camp supplies, bedding, and rifle to a spot by the spring and watered his horse there every day. Six weeks later, on the morning of his twenty-first birthday, August 10, 1907, at the Department of the Interior's land office in Hayden, he filed his claim for 160 acres under the Homestead Act of 1862. He called the property Oak Point, and five years later, when he received his certificate of approval from the Glenwood Springs land office, he felt that he was "a frontiersman at last, a citizen of the American fraternity of empire builders."

In June 1908 a childhood friend from Evanston, Jack White, with whom Ferry had spent some time in Taos and who longed to settle in the West, came to see Elkhead for himself. Carpenter suggested that they join forces. White filed on land near Carpenter's, and they began to plan their future together as partners in the cattle-ranching business. Carpenter asked his father for a loan of

$2,500 to buy twenty-five purebred Herefords. Carpenter Sr. agreed, with two provisos: he would receive one third of the profits, and Ferry would study law before settling in Routt County. The last thing Ferry wanted to do, he said, was "sit at a steam radiator and stare at a book all day long." Nevertheless, he complied, and Jack took care of the cattle while Ferry attended Harvard Law School, returning to Elkhead in the summers. In a 1909 photograph, Ferry sits very tall in his saddle in shirtsleeves, vest, bow tie, spurs, and bowler hat, in the center of Hayden. There is a mud path running by the false-fronted Hayden restaurant, and his horse, Nugget, stands up to his knees in weeds.

In August 1914 Ferry filed for an adjoining 160 acres under the Desert Land Act of 1877. One could obtain title to "desert land" by irrigating twenty acres, which he proposed to do by impounding the overflow from the spring into a reservoir he was building. He described the improvements he had made upon his first claim: a three-room house (30 × 30) and barn (18 × 20), three corrals, a branding chute, a squeezer ("all well-built"), a cellar, and four hundred feet of piping from spring to garden and house; fifteen acres grubbed of scrub oak, broke, and fenced; five acres of oats; four acres of potatoes, corn, "garden stuff, strawberries, raspberries, etc."; sixty apple trees, "the first to live in my altitude. About 20 of them are alive today, and thriving."

In answer to a question on the land office's form about whether he had any personal property elsewhere, he declared, "I have about $500 worth of books in Hayden, Colo." He wrote in his autobiography, "Part of my joy in that homestead derived from my feeling that I was playing a role in a unique historical process." It was as thrilling to him as the American Revolution. "I felt that this remarkable system of land distribution, in contrast to the feudal system in the rest of the world, was the keystone to the success of American democracy."

6
THE GRAND TOUR

Dorothy, Rosamond, and Arthur in Cortina, 1910

Dorothy and Ros took seriously President Seelye's admonition that they meet their full potential. He liked to ask students, "Are you a leaner or a lifter?" Life in Auburn, though, was highly ritualized and didn't allow for much lifting. Its social routines continued much as they had for generations.

Ros volunteered at the Auburn City Hospital, the day nursery at Eliza Osborne's Woman's Union, and the Ambulance Aid Society. Both joined the Young Ladies Benevolent Association, and Dorothy was a member of the Auburn College Club. Their parents held afternoon card parties, followed by suppers of grapefruit (a novelty fruit), pastry shells filled with chicken and mushrooms or sweetbreads and canned peas, hot rolls, and ice cream and cakes from Sherry's in New York. Many in their social circle were members of the Euchre or Whist Club and the Toboggan Club, to which they wore special suits made out of heavy Canadian blankets.

For young women, the principal diversions were luncheons, afternoon teas, the annual charity ball at the Armory, and dances every Saturday in June and July at the Owasco Country Club, where they were vigilantly chaperoned by parents. Dorothy and Ros went to their luncheons in the prescribed evening coats, dresses of broadcloth or satin, and large picture hats with plumes and flowers. The hostess's dining room always contained vases of freshly cut flowers, and the table was set with heavy damask, long rows of monogrammed silver, fine china, and crystal. Etched finger bowls were presented on dessert plates before the final course, with a flower petal or a slice of lemon floating in the water. Sometimes people who were new to such occasions picked up the bowl and drank from it.

French food was in fashion, and the cooks in Auburn's kitchens sometimes turned for guidance on formal entertaining to *The Epicurean,* a Franco-American culinary encyclopedia by Charles Ranhofer, the former chef at Delmonico's in New York. Dorothy's favorite part of these meals was dessert, and she was especially fond of Baked Alaska. William Seward had bought the territory of Alaska from the Russian empire in 1867, to widespread ridicule. Seward, though, was a loyal patron of Delmonico's, and Ranhofer commemorated the occasion by creating a variation on a dessert of hot pastry filled with ice cream that Thomas Jefferson had eaten at the White House. Ranhofer's version, which he called Alaska, Florida, involved hollowed-out Savoy biscuits, apricot marmalade, banana and vanilla ice cream, and meringue. The incomprehensible instructions in *The Epicurean* conclude: "A few moments before serving place each biscuit with its ice on a small lace paper, and cover one after the other with the meringue pushed through a pocket

111

furnished with a channeled socket, beginning at the bottom and diminishing the thickness until the top is reached; color this meringue for two minutes in a hot oven, and when a light golden brown remove and serve at once." In the accompanying illustration, it looks like a dunce's cap, but perhaps it was meant to resemble an iceberg rising from the ocean.

Arriving at one Wadsworth event, Dorothy and Ros decided to gauge how much they consumed. There was a bathroom off the bedroom upstairs where the guests left their coats and hats, and they got on the scale before they went down to join the other guests. After the epic meal, they weighed in again, and according to the scale — and Dorothy's memory — together they had gained four pounds. "I don't know why we weren't all big as houses," she said.

They were soon ready for a change. At their first Smith reunion, they learned that many of their classmates had married, and a few arrived with baby carriages. Several had begun teaching or had gone into nursing — two of the few careers open to women; social work was just getting started as a profession. "None of those appealed to either Ros or me," Dorothy said. There was only one other avenue of escape available to unmarried, well-educated women. They conspired to spend a year in Europe, accompanied in the initial months by Ros's family. After their travels, they would live in Paris on their own, perfecting their French and broadening their cultural sensibilities. Ros persuaded her parents to take them, and Dorothy announced to her mother and father, "I am just going, and that is all there is to it."

On the morning of June 18, 1910, the low, echoing horn of the S.S. *Lapland* sounded as the ocean liner glided out of New York Harbor, on its way to Dover and Antwerp. Dorothy and Ros were on board, accompanied by Ros's parents; Mrs. Brookfield, an elderly cousin from Manhattan; and Ros's fifteen-year-old brother, Arthur. "He was . . . very much bored with us and we certainly were bored with him," Dorothy remarked. The two girls rushed to claim their deck chairs, which were in a secluded section in first class. There was a strong wind blowing, and Dorothy put on a heavy coat over her suit. Before long she noticed an acquaintance from Auburn whom she hadn't seen in years. The girl, dressed in deep mourning, was alone in the world with the exception of a brother she was traveling with. Dorothy was sorry about her loss but commented, "She has been abroad so much that she is very blasé, and it makes me tired."

After lunch, they made a dive for their stateroom, and, Dorothy wrote to her family, "It was more exciting than any Christmas, opening all the things." Friends and family had sent a tremendous box of fruit, enough candy to make them ill, and more than a dozen books, including new novels by G. K. Chesterton and Mrs. Humphry Ward, a popular English novelist who was a good friend of Henry James. Dorothy's favorite gift was a bottle labeled "Sure cure for homesickness," which contained a furled silk American flag. Mrs. Brookfield, who had made the crossing many times, had brought along a selection of new magazines that she shared with them. Far less austere than she looked, she was a generous and humorous companion.

Both girls suffered from seasickness the first several days and treated themselves to a simple breakfast in bed. Occasionally, the boat rolled so deeply that they felt as though the deck would touch the water. Mrs. Brookfield made them coffee each morning, another indulgence from home. They spent the time lounging and reading belowdecks, but they soon recovered and made up for their days of fasting by eating lobster and roast grouse.

Although transatlantic journeys in first class were considered an opportunity to mingle respectably with single men, the S.S. *Lapland* was disappointing in that regard. Dorothy and Ros played shuffleboard with a doctor from Washington who took off his coat when the day was warm but fussily kept his gloves on. At a dance one night on deck, there was a "scarcity of swains," and even a boy of sixteen deserted them, which left only Arthur and the doctor. "There were a few clouds," Dorothy wrote, "behind which you could see the moon, and it would cast a beautiful light on the water, and then it would break through entirely. . . . It is too bad we lacked the necessary adjuncts for such a romantic setting, but even so, we stayed up until 11:30."

The passage was eight days, with little to distinguish among them: "walk, write, read, talk, play shuffleboard — eat, and then begin all over again." One morning Dorothy woke up to see the bath steward standing in the middle of their room, bellowing, " 'Bath, ladies!' with the most wearied look on his face, and goodness only knows how long he had been standing there. . . . He is the funniest little man, in absolutely skin-tight white clothes, and I wonder if he ever sits down."

From their deck chairs, they watched the whitecaps and the passing clouds, a lulling sight enlivened now and then by a breaching whale. Their best diversion was spying on a tall, dark-haired beauty who was traveling incognito. She sat alone not far from them and "affects the simple athletic style of dress," Dorothy wrote, "wearing a Panama plain suit, and rubber shoes." She was Miss Katherine Elkins of West Virginia, the daughter of a former senator and secretary of war, who had been carrying on a long-standing romance with Prince Luigi Amedeo, Duke of the Abruzzi. At the same time, William Hitt, the son of a former congressman from Illinois, was wooing her.

Newspapers in the United States and Europe had been breathlessly following her story for years; it included trysts in London and Lugano. A couple of months after the S.S. *Lapland* docked, Miss Elkins was reported to be in Vichy, where her mother was "taking the cure," and she remained in seclusion. The romance with the duke was finally broken off, at the insistence of the royal family, and she married Hitt in 1913. It was the culmination, the *New York Times* reported, "of a courtship the equal of which for romantic features it would be hard to find a parallel for in these matter-of-fact days outside of the covers of a novel."

As the boat drew close to Dover, it was joined by other steamers and flocks of seagulls. Dorothy and the Underwoods got up early to watch the docking and to see off the departing passengers. "The chalk cliffs were so very white," Dorothy wrote to her mother, "with the bright green fields coming to the very edge — and I loved the old fortresses. We weren't there long, but I saw my first comic opera Englishman — with pale blue spats and a monocle." After the boat pushed off again, she and Ros and Arthur spent the day running from one side of the deck to the other, trying not to miss anything. As they turned up the Scheldt River at Flushing, a picture-book village appeared, with bright-red gabled roofs. "All of Holland which we saw was just the same," Dorothy wrote, "so painfully neat and regular — and even the cows were spotless."

In Antwerp, she and Ros spent their first morning at the Royal Museum of Fine Arts, and Dorothy delivered her opinion about the collection to her mother: "I don't like Rubens' pictures — they are too spectacular, and his women are nothing short of beefy, but I liked the portraits, and I simply fell in love with the cunning little Dutch scenes from the little Dutch masters. But the old, historical scenes of Antwerp in the Middle Ages were killing, they were so out of proportion and no perspective, but they give a fine idea of the times."

The next day they woke up to a heavy rain but set out with Arthur for the zoological gardens and the Gothic Church of St. Jacques, tracing their way with their Baedeker. Tired and hungry after examining the cathedral, they decided to stop for a simple lunch. They went to the Hotel St. Antoine, where they ordered lobster, potatoes, and lettuce "and had a fine meal," Dorothy reported, "dining — as Papa said — not feeding." Then they were presented with the bill: seventeen francs (a reasonable seventy dollars a hundred years later). "We slunk away, feeling that we had been very gullible." As they made their way back to their hotel, Arthur kept pointing out that it cost more than their ten-course dinner the night before.

After touring Holland, they settled in for a long stay in the Dolomites, where the girls played tennis and hiked with Arthur and Mr. Underwood. In Cortina, near the Austrian border, Dorothy wrote a long, chatty letter to her sister Anna, exclaiming over a succession of Auburn weddings: "It does seem as though all my friends were getting married." She conveyed the beauty of the mountains and dwelled at length on the other guests at the hotel, mostly English and Italian, "with a few French & German scattered in." She could be a merciless observer and was quick to confirm national stereotypes: "The English people amuse me a great deal — for they are so like the books you read about them, that it is too good to be true. Every woman we have seen has her skirt sagging behind, and short in front. . . . They chirp up a lot at night, however, and are so much better looking that you can hardly believe they are the same people."

From Italy they went to Germany, then Switzerland, and one day Dorothy and Ros rode the funicular in Zermatt. They positioned themselves in the front, for the best view. Just before the car began to move, Dorothy said, "in stepped a perfectly enormous German." He had a big rucksack on his back and was wearing high hiking boots. The girls had on their own space-consuming attire, including their wide blue "merry widow" hats with tall feathers. "He pushed me over against Ros, and if the door hadn't been locked she would have fallen out."

Dorothy politely told him in German that the space was not really large enough for three of them, and asked if he would kindly move. He stared straight ahead, ignoring her. Rosamond, who spoke the language flawlessly, reiterated Dorothy's request, adding that it really was very crowded. This, too, was met with impervious silence. "We were good and mad," Dorothy said. She spitefully stepped on the man's foot, but he stood his ground. Tempted to poke him with one of her long hatpins, she concluded that it would have no effect, so they removed their hats and had "a most uncomfortable trip up that mountain."

In early September 1910, they arrived in Paris, where Ros's mother helped them get settled. Before her parents returned to Auburn, her father took them and Arthur to the Paris Opera to see twenty-year-old Nijinsky in *Scheherazade,* which was being performed that season by Sergei Diaghilev's Ballets Russes — perhaps the most influential ballet the company ever produced. Some of their friends had already been four times to see "the Russian dancers," as Dorothy referred to them. They were "the sensation of Paris." She liked the intricate toe dancing and Nijinsky's fantastic leaps, but she took particular notice of the exotic sets and costumes, designed by Léon Bakst. Nijinsky, clad in jewel-encrusted gold harem pants and a gold bra, played the Golden Slave, the lover of the Shah's favorite concubine, Zobeide. The sensuous Ida Rubinstein, who played Zobeide, wore her own harem pants, her torso and legs looped with pearls. In the middle of the ballet, the women bribe a eunuch to release the slaves, and stylized lovemaking ensues. It was a world away from Auburn's Burtis Opera House. "The whole thing was like a scene from the Arabian Nights," Dorothy wrote to Milly, only partly aware of what she was watching. Thinking back on it, she said that she and Ros were mystified when Mr. Underwood announced halfway through the ballet that he was taking them back to the hotel. They eventually overrode his concerns and stayed until the end. Even as an older woman, she was perplexed. "Something must have seemed indecent to him," she said, "but I can't imagine what it was."

Dorothy and Ros lived for a brief time in a dark, narrow house at 5 Avenue de la Bourdonnais, the finishing school a block from the Seine where they studied French. The walls of the drawing room were crowded with prints and paintings in ornate gold frames. Mme Rey, who ran the school, was "an aristocrat to her fingertips," Dorothy told her mother. She later described Madame as always wearing black dresses that had very high collars with little bones in them. The girls were more serious about their studies than they had been at Smith. Mme Rey had high expectations, and provided them with demanding teachers whom they described as the best in Paris. At the same time, they found "Madame" simple and kind, and she prepared delicious meals, especially on Sundays, when she served Parisian specialties like chestnut soufflé, which the girls considered "food for the gods."

The three other students, who were younger, initially thought she and Ros were "*eighteen* and were amazed when they found out how ancient we are — I know they think we have one foot in the grave," Dorothy wrote to her father. One of them, Nora, who was English, announced to them that all of the rich, vulgar American girls were marrying in to the English peerage for the titles, and that the men succumbed only because they needed the money to keep their estates going. Dorothy and Ros, irritated by her superciliousness — and by the truth of her charge — retorted in the best French they could muster. They had read E. M. Forster and Henry James, and they also must have thought of the true-life Miss Elkins, with her thwarted love for an Italian prince.

When they informed Mme Rey that they intended to explore the city by themselves, she threw up her hands, informing them that young ladies in France never stepped onto the sidewalk without a chaperone or maid. They explained that they had their parents' permission, and she gave in. They took *dictée,* art, and history in the morning, studied for a few hours, and then got to know the city, accompanied by *Walks in Old Paris.* They often went around town in *fiacres* — horse-drawn carriages that jostled for space with automobiles, buses, bicyclists, and pedestrians. The pungent smells of old Paris didn't bother them, but they never adjusted to the fleas in the straw at their feet; the bites lingered for weeks. "I know Cousin Josephine will take back her invitation when she sees me," Dorothy wrote. Her mother's cousin Josephine Beardsley had recently bought an estate in Cannes and had invited the girls to join Dorothy's parents there for a visit that winter. Dorothy described three large welts on her face, "which makes me look as though I had some evil disease. . . . After a taxi ride the other day, I came in with twenty-eight bites!"

One day the two American women were in a narrow, crowded street, and their *fiacre* stopped as a *cocher* in front of them backed up his horse, knocking theirs down. "We were perfectly terrified, but didn't dare get out, as you would surely get run over," Dorothy wrote to her brother Douglas, "and then our poor horse got up, but the drivers began fighting, and got purple with rage, and the other pulled out his whip, and started to beat our man, who whipped up the horse, and as we flew on, he hurled awful curses at the other man. He chased us for about three blocks, both of them screaming . . . and people rushed to doors and windows to see the excitement, while we, by that time, over our fright, were howling, it was so funny. Imagine such a thing in New York!"

Soon she and Ros were escorting Mme Rey around town. The erudite business-woman was uneasy on the modern streets of Paris. "She is so afraid of the crossings," Dorothy wrote to Milly. "She scuttles across the streets just like Mother, and when she gets in the middle, screams and almost has hysterics, and then runs back to the same side!" On a rainy day in November, Dorothy and Ros took her with them to Amiens Cathedral. They all admired the lofty lines, the stained-glass windows, and the light, even on a gloomy day. They took a tour, and as they were descending some narrow stairs, the guide stopped to point out the ceiling. Dorothy wrote, "As my head went back, my hat dropped off — in my hurry I had come away without any hat pins." On the roof, where they ventured out to examine the exterior from a different perspective, Madame, standing in a deep puddle with the rain pouring down, stopped the entire procession, to exclaim, *Ah, quelle belle simplicité!*

Dorothy and Ros went to the Rue de la Paix to see an exhibition of contemporary paintings. Matisse and Picasso by then were well-known friends and rivals. Years earlier, Gertrude Stein and Alice B. Toklas had introduced them at their salon; Stein's brothers, Leo and Michael, collected Matisse's work and helped to get him noticed. At the early exhibitions of Matisse, Derain, Braque, and Vlaminck — the key figures in the Fauve movement — one historian wrote, "viewers would give vent to the most powerful emotions, sometimes almost coming to blows. . . ." In 1910 Matisse was still working in hectic hues. Dorothy wrote home: "The contrast after the Louvre was too much . . . all the most startling colors, with queer and bizarre subjects — and the drawing was like that of a little child." Matisse, she declared, "thinks the only real art is the very simplest, with just two or three lines to express a figure." Decades later, she regretted her conventional aesthetic taste and her failure to buy a few inexpensive paintings.

They also toured the Conciergerie, the former royal palace, where prisoners were held before being led to the guillotine. "It was really an awful place, and some how seemed more terrible than the dungeons we saw in Germany," Dorothy wrote. "Poor Marie Antoinette lived in a tiny little cell, damp, and with practically no lights, and the contrast between that and Versailles seemed too awful — Madame told us all kinds of gruesome stories, and her husband's grandfather and great grandmother were guillotined from there."

On October 8, Rosamond's twenty-third birthday, she took Dorothy and several others to tea at the Pré Catelan, a new restaurant in the Bois de Boulogne. Dorothy ordered a birthday cake for the evening festivities at the school, and they played "Up Jenkins" and "Hide the Thimble" with the other students and Mme Rey's daughters, two unmarried women in their thirties, with as much zest as they had as ten-year-olds at the Underwoods' house.

Dorothy, a typical pampered student abroad, was grateful to her father for funding her trip and assured him that she was taking advantage of all that Paris had to offer. At the same time, she couldn't disguise her overwhelming desire to have a good time. She wrote to him, "You can't imagine how happy and contented I am here, and Ros and I just hop along the streets," before going on to describe their visit to the Palace of Fontainebleau. They were "much interested in Napoleon's apartments — his marvelous throne room and the place where he signed his abdication — and all his gorgeous suites. It made his whole story seem so real and recent to see all his furniture, just as it was — and even his hat was there."

When Madame Rey discussed Racine, Molière, and modern drama with her daughters, Dorothy admitted, she and Ros felt very ignorant. She pledged, "I am going to begin on 'Le Cid' immediately," and she asked, "Please write me about American politics. I am very much interested — *what* do you think of Roosevelt?"

A few months earlier, Theodore Roosevelt

— out of office and disaffected from the Republican Party for its lack of concern about "the plain people" and about the unchecked power of big business and party bosses — had given his "New Nationalism" speech in Osawatomie, Kansas. It was becoming the blueprint for his platform in the 1912 presidential election, when he would run as the head of his new Progressive Party against President William Howard Taft, Woodrow Wilson (by then governor of New Jersey), and the Socialist Eugene V. Debs. Roosevelt spoke about a square deal for the poor man, about the need for a strong federal government to regulate corporations, and about the world setting its face hopefully toward American democracy: "O my fellow citizens, each one of you carries on your shoulders not only the burden of doing well for the sake of your own country, but the burden of doing well and of seeing that this nation does well for the sake of mankind."

This inspirational rhetoric struck a chord with Dorothy, especially as an American living abroad. She was becoming vaguely aware of the civic responsibilities that came with adulthood. But, like any skillful correspondent, she wrote with her audience in mind. Her father heard about history, literature, and politics. Douglas, a popular, self-indulgent man-about-town, was the recipient of the most amusing gossip. When she was addressing her mother or her sisters, she focused on domestic matters, fashion, and excursions.

In the fall, she and Ros moved across the Parc du Champs de Mars to a sunny, one-room apartment with a private bathroom, at 6 Avenue du Général Détrie. They were pleased with their choice, but, she wrote to her mother, "imagine our rage on discovering that we aren't to have hot water! They still heat the water in the kitchen and bring it to you in tin pitchers." And she professed to be shocked by the movers, who "looked like pirates, with red sashes, and funny little tasseled caps — They just threw things into baskets and then dumped them over here — nothing done up, or labeled — You simply can't imagine the confusion and chaos which resulted."

Nevertheless, they were on their own at last, and they came to be amused at how little the modish Parisians cared about comfort. One night they went to a party along with "the two *demoiselles* Rey" and the other girls from the school. There was a log fire burning in the salon, but before long, Dorothy felt a chill creeping up her spine, and her teeth began to chatter. She knew it would be rude to put on her coat, but she finally went out to retrieve the fur. When she returned, her hostess laughed and said, "It is easy to see that you are American!"

In another letter to her mother, she described the penetrating cold as a prelude to a request for some acquisitions for her wardrobe. Ros was getting a dressy lavender suit made. Dorothy asked only for a good cloth dress and a formal gown that would be useful at home as well as in Paris, then added, "I want you to *answer this immediately,* as I don't wish to do any thing without consulting you." Despite her high regard for her mother, she found her frugality and her sporadic letters exasperating. Few of Dorothy's correspondents could keep up with her.

She wrote to Milly about the marvelous creations: "Dresses very scant, very short coats — and either hats which cover the whole head, like a skull cap — or perfectly enormous ones." Paris, she was not the first to point out, "is the most cosmopolitan city." Ros, who was almost as close to Milly as Dorothy was, wrote to her, too, in a tone of joking defensiveness: "I hope you won't think that it has been my influence which has corrupted Dot — she tells me you all think her letters are society 'journals,' but believe me, she has made lots of progress with her French, in spite of it."

During a rare quiet evening at Mme Rey's, they were reading their mail when the maid brought in a visiting card: three friends from Auburn had arrived. "We let out one wild yell, and ran into the salon, and fell on their necks," Dorothy wrote to her family, and "in a minute Madame appeared at the door, pale and trembling, for of course she thought some one was murdering us — not understanding the American expression of joy and surprise. Do you suppose when we are fifty — we will still scream like that?"

They had become friendly with the Howlands, two sisters and a brother they knew from home, whose aunt Emily was one of the country's leading abolitionists and suffragists. The brother, infatuated with Ros, showered them with books and flowers and French chocolates. She didn't reciprocate his affection, but they all went out companionably to expensive restaurants, the roller-skating rink, and the opera. On January 18, 1911, they went to see Isadora Duncan in her premiere performance of *Orpheus* at the Théâtre du Châtelet, with music from

Gluck's *Orfeo ed Euridice*. Duncan was already famous for her revolt against classical ballet and for her shocking private life. In 1909 she had run into Nijinsky in Venice. Reportedly, and perhaps in jest, she asked him to father her second child. Although she disliked the flamboyant sets of the Ballets Russes, she, too, had been dazzled by his 1910 performances in Paris. Several months later, the swashbuckling dilettante Paris Singer, an heir to the Singer sewing-machine fortune, fell instantly in love with her, and her second illegitimate baby was born in May 1910.

Dorothy thought Duncan's performance was one of the loveliest things she had ever seen. She wrote to Milly, "The stage was absolutely bare — hung in soft brown draperies — and she was accompanied by a very fine orchestra. . . . She just simply floated around the stage, which was so simple that it looked like ordinary walking." She thought, as others did, that Duncan "looked like the Winged Victory come to life — or a figure off a Greek coin — she danced entirely in bare feet, and it seemed perfectly natural, and quite different from the way the Russians did it. I never saw such an ovation . . . and such flowers!"

Before they left Paris in January 1911,

Dorothy and Ros splurged, setting themselves up with suits, everyday dresses, and several evening gowns each — which, they told each other, would be perfect for Auburn's formal events. This time Dorothy did not consult with her mother. One of her gowns was a closely fitted sleeveless blue satin with a very low neck and a long train; she had satin slippers dyed to match. Rosamond ordered a black velvet suit with a white fox collar and muff. "Oh, she was so beautiful in it," Dorothy told her grandchildren. "I felt I couldn't afford that, but I certainly enjoyed seeing her in it."

In their final month in Europe, they made the long-anticipated trip to Cannes to stay with Dorothy's rich relation, Josephine Beardsley Brown. Her parents already had arrived, and her father met them at the station. "I can tell you," Dorothy wrote to Carrie-Belle, "the sight of Papa was the best thing I have seen abroad."

Cousin Josephine, a lively, fun-loving cousin of Mrs. Woodruff, had grown up at Roselawn, an Italianate mansion on South Street in Auburn that backed onto Fort Hill Cemetery. When she was a baby, she was dropped by her nurse, which left her lame, and she walked with a cane. Josephine's father, William Beardsley, Dorothy said, had been "a perfect dragon," and he ruled his three daughters "with a rod of iron." Although he put out the word in Auburn that, upon marriage, each of them would be given a Victorian house, he disinherited Josephine's older sister Cora when she married someone he considered unworthy. Josephine didn't marry until her father died. She was forty-nine.

William Beardsley would have been even more enraged by Josephine's choice: Clement Brown was a tall, impressive-looking man with a Vandyke — but a mere clergyman, over a decade younger than she was, and "so poor," according to Dorothy, "that he lived in a boarding house where he had to stuff one of his windows with an old cloth."

Josephine and Clement showed Dorothy and Ros around their home, which they had bought only four months earlier. The main house was a palatial, half-timbered Queen Anne, flanked by sentries of towering palms. Off the Avenue du roi Albert, Villa Les Lotus had been built in 1883 by the duchess Albine de Persigny, wife of Louis Napoléon — ambassador to the court of Saint James. Josephine, in a tribute to her father's legacy, called her new home Roselawn. "It seemed like a dream," Dorothy wrote, to walk through the two-story entry hall, past the library and the billiard room with high, coffered ceilings, and to enter one of the grand salons and "find Mother and all the others — and a great crackling fire."

When she woke up the next morning, she looked out the window at the aquamarine Mediterranean glinting in the sun. The view from the breakfast room was even better, and she was torn between gazing at the sea and at "the all-absorbing choice of jams." The duchess had been an amateur botanist, and her plans for the gardens were influenced by a recent trip to Japan. She came back to Cannes with statuary and Japanese maples, along with various rare arboreal specimens. She also imported some wood and Japanese workers for the construction of her teahouse. She hired the French horticulturalist and landscape architect Édouard André to organize the nine-acre park. It had stretches of lawn interrupted by masses of junglelike palms and cacti, cedars, cypresses, magnolias, araucaria, fig trees, and eucalyptus.

The Browns employed twelve gardeners. "The mimosa trees are beyond adjectives," Dorothy wrote, "but imagine great trees of goldenrod, with the sun on it — against a deep blue sky! It was almost intoxicating after our dull Paris skies — and the air is so soft and delicious." The most remarkable flower bed contained dozens of varieties of flowers, all in various shades of red. When she got up the next day, the gardeners had changed the color scheme to all white. "Cousin Josephine," as she later put it, "said that when the weather got warm in the spring, along about the end of May, the gardeners would roll up the lawn — and throw it away, I suppose."

One day Ros and Dorothy went to Monte Carlo with the Woodruffs. It was a beautiful drive on the Corniche Road, winding high above the sea, through hill towns balanced on rocks, where all the houses were the same shade of gray, and then bright orange groves, which reminded Dorothy of a Maxfield Parrish picture. Far below the rocks was the jagged coastline, "with the blindingly white towns, standing out against the glorious sea." At Monte Carlo they went to the casino, which she and Ros found disappointing: "the people were such an ordinary uninteresting-looking lot — and the decorations were so tawdry."

Back at the villa, Josephine kept her company busy. "It has been as strenuous as Paris," Dorothy commented, "with so many engagements, and a mortal terror of being late to meals," which were served by footmen in striped waistcoats and short breeches. Every day they went out to drive in an open victoria with two men on the box and two horses done up in a dressy harness. "I never lived in such luxury and magnificence, and I can tell you — after a winter with a French family — I am ready to appreciate it."

After their stay with the Browns, the Woodruffs and Ros went to Barcelona, where it was cold and rainy. Although the girls were excited to see their first "aeroplane" meet, they were tired of sightseeing, and Dorothy told Milly that they were desolate: "We didn't see how we were going to put in the day." Walking down the street with Mr. Woodruff, huddled under their umbrellas, they were approached by a portly man with a gray beard. He stepped up to her father and said, "You must be an American." They chatted with him briefly, and then stopped in at a bank. When they came out, he was waiting for them on the sidewalk. He introduced himself as Mr. Stuart, "once from New York." He told them he had lived in Barcelona for twenty-one years, "being driven over by domestic trouble!"

He invited them to his house, saying he

had a few things that might interest them. "Papa said yes, so we puddled along behind," Dorothy said, surprised by the unlikely encounter and by Mr. Woodruff's courtesy to a peculiar stranger. Ros, who had withdrawn a significant amount of cash, whispered to Dorothy that she was sure he was going to rob them, as in stories they'd seen in the *Herald* about naive "Yankees." He led them to Rambla de Catalunya in the Eixample, the best part of town, "and the minute we got inside, our eyes flew open," Dorothy wrote. "It was like a very rich Oriental palace — and it was the last touch when his servant put a red fez on his head."

The house was a maze of rooms overflowing with priceless works of art: "You never saw so many pictures in a private house — and such wonderful ones!" This time Dorothy admired the Rubens, along with the silk rugs on the walls and the Persian carpets on the floor. One room, "The Lounge of the Queen Regent," had thirteen Goya tapestries, commissioned by the royal family.

Mr. Stuart, who was seventy-one, turned out to be William Whitewright Stuart, a graduate of Princeton and the son of a New York banker. He was a member of the Barcelona stock exchange but didn't consider himself a businessman. He described himself as a painter and a mountaineer. When Dorothy's father said they didn't want to take up too much of his time, he assured them his only engagements for the day were his piano and reciting lessons. He liked to preside over salons and dinners to which he invited artists and dancers and the nobility of various countries. Often he entertained his guests by playing the piano and singing operettas in Spanish and Italian; one night he recited from *Hamlet.* "It was a very weird experience," Dorothy concluded, but it made the sodden trip to Spain worth taking.

Then their year of travel, highbrow culture, and unlikely encounters was over. They were twenty-three years old and going home.

7
FERRY'S SCHEME

Ferry Carpenter and Nugget on Walnut Street, 1909

In 1912, when Ferry Carpenter set up
Hayden's first law practice, the town was a
modestly thriving outpost of four hundred
people or so, with three hotels; a Congregational church; a weekly newspaper, the *Routt*

County Republican; two livery stables; three blacksmith shops; Emrich's barbershop; two banks; two drugstores; two movie theaters; a surveyor's office; two general-merchandise stores; Ernest Wagner's saddle shop; and the Edison School, a two-story clapboard building with a big bell tower. The bell was rung not only to summon students but also to call parishioners to church and to issue fire alarms. John V. Solandt served as the doctor, veterinarian, and coroner. One of the two bathtubs in town was at the Hayden Inn; the other was at Emrich's, where the cowboys lined up on Saturdays for occasional baths.

Hayden didn't really need a lawyer, but Ferry didn't want to disappoint his father. Besides, he believed that everyone should have an official job to subsidize what he really wanted to do — in his case, ranching. He rented a narrow lean-to on Walnut Street, abutting the Yampa Valley Bank. Ferry asked his Elkhead neighbor, a carpenter named Al Galloway, to put up a wall in back so he could have a bedroom in Hayden during the winter, when the commute to Oak Point was impossible. Responding to Ferry's dual duties as lawyer and rancher, Galloway said, "I see, you're going to bleed 'em up here, and breed 'em back there." In the summer, Ferry rode to town each day — an extremely hilly round trip of twenty miles — on a Dayton bicycle he'd bought in Cambridge.

He didn't have many clients at first, and his income averaged about $125 a month, over half of it from his fees as the town's notary public. He spent many hours at the office talking to farmers, who liked to loaf and gossip in front of his stove while down the street their wives bartered eggs and cream for groceries. Influenced by the civic-spirited principles of Woodrow Wilson and by the work of the early settlers, Ferry became a prodigious community organizer. Among other activities, he joined the board of directors of the First National Bank of Hayden, and he persuaded the town board to replace the picturesque communal pump in the center of town with a proper water and sewage system.

The cattle business also took years to get fully established. In 1911 Ferry and Jack White owned ninety-three head of purebred Hereford cattle, which they raised and sold to other cattlemen, rather than running range cattle. They took their cue from the experience of the Colorado gold rush, knowing that it was usually not the miners who became wealthy but the merchants who sold them supplies and equipment.

The profession required some imaginative improvisations. In one of the early years, a big red shorthorn bull kept escaping from a homestead nearby and visiting their white-face heifers. Ferry and Jack made a couple of barbed-wire quirts. "We ran him home," Ferry told an appreciative group of stockmen in 1967, "and by golly he beat us back again." He had become a gifted storyteller, playing to his audiences, sometimes shamelessly. "We had to do something, and you'll realize what it was. . . . We stretched him out, and then began to dispute which one would hold the knife. . . ." He went on to describe Jack's mother as a lady who was fond of nice things; he said she had sent Jack some hardware for his cabin, including "a couple of glass doorknobs — which he got — and which the trespassing shorthorn bull went away with swinging."

Although Oak Point was about as far from the world of eastern privilege and power as Ferry could have gotten, he continued to cultivate some of its best-known exemplars. At Harvard Law School, he had sought out Frederick Jackson Turner, a faculty member who sometimes invited him to his house on Sunday for tea or a meal. Carpenter admired Turner deeply but questioned some of his more retrograde views. In his Frontier Thesis, Turner had decreed that the West was "the meeting point between savagery and civilization." And Ferry mentioned in a letter to Henry Bragdon, the Wilson biographer, that one evening in Cambridge, Turner rebuked his daughter, who had tried to contradict one of them. "Women's minds," Turner remarked, "are like the Platte River — a mile wide and a foot deep."

In Hayden, Ferry sporadically corresponded with Turner, writing entertainingly about his law cases, the coming of the Moffat Road, his progress in the cattle business, and the violent wars between cattlemen and sheep men over grazing rights. The battles had been fought throughout the West since the 1870s. Most of the ranchers in Routt County raised cattle, and they deplored sheep, which overgrazed, gnawing the grass down to the dirt, and polluted the streams where the cattlemen watered their herds. As Ferry put it, "The Sheep. Always we live in fear & hatred of them. In Wyoming on our north & Utah on our West they reign supreme & look across the line with covetous eyes on our green grass."

In October 1913, writing from Oak Point, Ferry asked Turner to recommend some new histories and biographies: "You see I'm away from the land of books, but I haven't lost my taste for them." He then described his job. One of his clients was a homesteader who was fighting the government to retain rights to the coal on his land. The case unfolded over three days and an evening in the town hall, the settlers cheering Ferry on. He wrote, "a crowd set out to tar & feather the Gov. Attorney who was representing the Interior Dep't — I still think it was the good looking lady stenographer whom he brot in who saved his hide." During the District Court's spring term, he represented a horse thief, whom he convinced to plead guilty. With his wife and baby in the court, the thief was sentenced to fourteen months to two years in the penitentiary, "much to the natives' disgust." Ferry's compassion, though, crept in between the lines. "I got to know the man very well & his Family & saw that his crime was only his futile effort to get even with some spiteful neighbors." In the previous term, he had prosecuted a right-of-way case against the railroad and had gotten his client a hundred dollars per acre for the three acres taken, plus a thousand dollars in damages. There was a note of pride from the twenty-seven-year-old attorney: "first time I ever faced a jury."

The Moffat Road was just about to reach Hayden, and Carpenter's clients had faced a "run of troubles." One man's irrigation ditch had been stopped up by the railroad, and he wanted an immediate injunction. The stage driver was demanding a redress after an automobile ran the mail coaches off the grade. The sawmill had shut down, and the company couldn't pay some of the men, so a lien had to be filed. "So it goes," he noted, "but always a little story out of real life & I like it."

The ranch was growing, and although his crops had been short that year and hay was expensive, he had managed to raise an impressive array of vegetables. He was ready for the winter, with a cellar full of two tons of potatoes, beets, and turnips; thirty-six quarts of rhubarb, twenty quarts of strawberry jam, and a little peach butter. He loaned his rifle to a neighbor, who had shot a buck, so he was sure of some jerked deer meat. He concluded his letter to Turner, "Well, guess I'd better roll in — I think of you all every now & again, taking a sup of tea in your parlour & I'd like mighty well to throw in with you, but seeing I can't you'd all better figure on going this way to the 1915 [Panama-California] Exposition & dropping off here on the Bear River & getting a first hand look at the way we try to knock the rough edges off these old Rocky Mountains & farm them."

Ferry was far from the guileless cowboy he liked people to think he was, a fact that didn't escape his neighbors. Respectful of his education and cleverness, they asked him to address an enduring challenge they all faced: the absence of eligible young women. In Elkhead, there was not a single one. It wasn't a community — just an agglomeration of isolated homesteaders. On Saturday nights, cowboys gathered at the cabin of Mr. and Mrs. George Murphy, an older couple who had been among the first pioneers in Elkhead. Mrs. Murphy, a plump, hospitable woman, cooked hearty meals for her company and talked longingly about building a schoolhouse, as other settlers had in their own locales, where children could get a good education and neighbors could gather for dances, picnics, church, and Christmas celebrations.

A solution occurred to Ferry that would solve both the cowboys' problems and Mrs. Murphy's: Elkhead was too far from Hayden for the homesteaders' children to go to school there. He realized that if Elkhead created its own district and school board, they could recruit new teachers every year or two — supplying the children with instruction, the residents with a community center, and the cowboys with a steady influx of prospective brides. What was more, the area contained valuable undeveloped anthracite coalfields, partly owned by what he called "unlimited eastern capital." When he and his neighbors organized, Carpenter said, "it was easy to vote a tax or bond issue or anything we wanted." Most of the homesteaders paid no taxes on their land, since they didn't have title to it yet — the costs were borne by a few Colorado landowners and the unknowing eastern capitalists.

As for the women they expected to attract, he once told a writer for the *Saturday Evening Post,* "We did not want strays. We had serious matrimonial intentions, and we decided that young, pretty schoolteachers would be the best bet of all." The *Republican* reported on August 5, 1910, that Carpenter had been out in the hills pressing the case for a separate district: "Come on school marms. Some nice-looking ranchmen up here. Now is your chance." The petition for the new district indicated that there were forty-four school-age children in Elkhead.

George Smith, who was then the county commissioner of schools as well as the owner of the *Republican,* called a meeting at the Murphys' house the following April, to form District 11. Twenty-five people attended, the paper reported, and "a bountiful dinner was provided by Mrs. Murphy." Smith presided over the election of board members. Because of the size of the district — 226 square miles — the group agreed to build two schoolhouses rather than one.

Those original schools in Elkhead — one on the Adair ranch and the other, the Dry Fork school, where Bull Gulch drained into Dry Fork Creek — were ill-equipped, drafty cabins, and they operated mostly in the summer months, whenever a teacher could be convinced to venture into the hills. Carpenter had something more ambitious in mind: a large, consolidated school that would provide a nine-month term and an education comparable to what urban children received at the best public schools. He was initiating a process in his neighborhood that was under way across the country: to raise and standardize the quality of teaching in rural areas, which was notoriously inferior to that of large, well-equipped urban schools. The state was aware of the dismal conditions in remote regions: education officials handed out postcards picturing six decrepit one-room schools, with the caption, "A National Disgrace."

For five years Carpenter, along with Paroda Fulton, the secretary of the Elkhead board, and their neighbors doggedly worked toward building one of the best schools in Routt County. Fulton had grown up in Mt. Ayre, Iowa, and gone to Drake University in Des Moines. She moved to Colorado in 1906 to teach school in Hayden and in the Little Snake River Valley near the town of Craig. Two years later, she married Charlie Fulton, who had been homesteading on Dry Fork since 1901. Until the arrival of Dorothy and Ros, and a teacher named Iva Rench from Muncie, Indiana, Paroda Fulton and Ferry Carpenter were the only college graduates in Elkhead.

On May 15, 1915, the *Republican* reported, after "much hot air and high flown oratory was indulged in, the district voted $5,000 in bonds to erect a fine central school house." Carpenter asked his sister Ruth to put out the word among her friends in New York, and according to his account, an advertisement was placed in a teachers' magazine, which described a superb school in the virgin hills. Promising generous pay, it said that no candidate would be considered without a recent photograph.

Like any good raconteur, Carpenter was

fond of embellishments, and one of his most popular stories was his roguish account of how Dorothy Woodruff and Rosamond Underwood came to be hired. As the applications for the jobs arrived, he said during a talk in Denver about his early experiences in Routt County, Jack White would call him on the one-wire telephone that was strung along the fence posts all the way down to Hayden, and report, " 'We got another one — it's a blonde,' and I'd say, 'Pin 'em up on the logs above the sink.' . . . Bye and bye it was halfway around the cabin with really flattering beautiful young ladies." The cowboys would drop by and study the photos, and when it came time to vote, they all had strong opinions. "So we decided we'd have a pure democracy," Carpenter said, "all the electors would decide."

When the cowboys couldn't reach an agreement, he pulled out a letter from two girls in Auburn, New York. "They went to Smith College and had traveled abroad and had many advantages that many of the local people hadn't had," he said. "But they didn't have one advantage, we later discovered — they didn't have a Colorado teacher's license." He laughed heartily, and the audience joined in. "We didn't think about that in those days." Nor did he worry that they had no experience as teachers, and "in fact had never done any work for pay."

He recalled that Charlotte Perry, the sister of his best friend, Bob, had graduated from Smith in 1911. He called Bob to "get a line on" the two women. Bob, a dapper thirty-one-year-old graduate of Columbia's engineering school, was the supervisor of the Moffat mine — owned by his father, Samuel M. Perry, a leading industrialist in Denver. The mine, forty-five miles southeast of Hayden, outside a town called Oak Creek, was named after Perry's friend and business partner, David Moffat, who built the railroad over the Continental Divide. Bob called Charlotte and immediately got back to Ferry. Bob was "excited when he called me," Carpenter said, his own voice rising and his drawl becoming more pronounced, "He said: '*Don't* overlook one of them! She was voted the best-looking girl in the junior class of Smith College! Don't let her get away from you!' "

Early on the morning after the teachers arrived, Ferry got a call from Bob, who was at the Hayden depot and wanted to know what the teachers looked like. Frustrated by his friend's inconclusive reply, Bob told Ferry he would meet him at the inn. When Ferry got there, he wrote in his autobiography, half a dozen men, including Bob, "were standing around admiring them. I could see by the glazed look on Bob's face as he stared at Rosamond that he was already smitten." Bob, knowing that Ferry often delivered letters and packages to his neighbors in Elkhead, took him aside and said, "Watch her mail. Let me know if some man is writing her." Carpenter omitted a key detail in his account: he, too, couldn't stop staring at Rosamond. As his son Ed recalled, "The question was, who's gonna win her, Ferry or Perry?"

8
DEPARTURE

Postcard of South Street in Auburn, New York, early 1900s

Soon after Dorothy and Ros returned from Europe, the appeals of bridge parties and automobiling began to wane, and in 1911 they went to stay in New York City for several months. They saw it as another adventure; their parents hoped that through connections in the city, they would encoun-

154

ter some men who might meet with their approval. At the Webster, a small hotel off Fifth Avenue on West Forty-fifth Street, they rented a suite with a sitting room, a large double bedroom, and a bath, for which their parents paid six dollars a day. Ros, who acquired admirers everywhere she went, was pursued by Charlie Hickocks, a lawyer for a shipping company. He had his own brownstone and frequently took her out, with Dorothy going along "as baggage." Although they were polite to him, privately they made fun of his odd looks and affectations, with Dorothy taking the lead. He had an unusually long neck topped by a very long, thin face. "We thought he was a regular 'Miss Nancy,' " she said. "He had his linen all embroidered with his initials and that kind of thing. Needless to say, Rosamond wasn't interested in him."

Back at home, they entertained guests at South and Fort streets, visited friends in other cities, and dallied with young men. For a few years Ros strung along another New Yorker, a lawyer named Billy, who expected to marry her, and whom she apparently saw as her default option if no one more exciting presented himself. The other men who pursued them were mostly studying at the Auburn Theological Seminary, which trained Presbyterian ministers. One of the most prestigious divinity schools in the country, it was headed by Allen Macy Dulles — the father of Secretary of State John Foster Dulles. Allen Dulles was a friend of Dorothy's parents, who considered the seminary a good source of suitors. Although her sister Carrie-Belle had married one of the seminarians several years earlier, Dorothy was scornful of the type. She wrote to Anna from Cortina about a guest in the hotel: "There is a queer looking youth with long, black greasy hair — and he looked just like the worst of the seminary students."

In their spare time, influenced by two generations of Auburn feminists and by their time at Smith, Dorothy and Ros supported Jane Addams's Hull House and advocated women's suffrage. They became members of the Cayuga County Political Equality Club, and in good weather, they stood on soapboxes in Owasco. In 1914 they organized a meeting at Suffrage Headquarters in the Woman's Union. Dorothy introduced the speaker, Mrs. Theodore M. Pomeroy of Buffalo, who talked about her work as a national officer of the club and explained why she was a suffragist. Mrs. Pomeroy described canvassing house-to-house and running meetings all over the city, so that women would be ready when their time came to vote. Thousands of women were attending, she said, immigrants included. In the future, "a mother who can instruct her sons in public questions will have more influence than another interested in a new hat. There is a psychological change in the world: in ages past women labored beside the men; then she came to be confined to house duties; now is the age of machinery, and woman's work has been taken away from her." She urged her audience to consider that when one thing goes out of your life, you must find another to replace it, and she reminded them that women had "especial interest in educational, health, and corrective departments of work." When tea was served, "Miss Underwood poured, assisted by Miss Woodruff."

By the spring of 1916, seven years out of college and not yet married, they began to think unenthusiastically about returning to New York City to pursue some kind of social work. They were "in this troubled state," as Dorothy put it, when an unusual opportunity presented itself. In April, Emily Callaway, the leading lady of the Jefferson Stock Company, was in town to rehearse for the summer season. Callaway, another Auburn girl, was a 1906 Wellesley graduate who had a letter of introduction to Rosamond from one of William Seward's grandsons. Ros's mother invited her to tea, and Ros and Emily began to talk about how difficult it was for women of their background to find absorbing and useful work.

Callaway mentioned that just that day, she had heard from a Wellesley friend, Ruth Carpenter Woodley, who had an adventuresome brother named Ferry Carpenter. She described his background and told Ros and Dorothy that he had worked with his neighbors for five years to build a consolidated schoolhouse in the Elkhead mountain range. Her brother was a man of vision, Ruth wrote to Emily, and he had asked her to look around New York for two young female college graduates who would consider teaching out there for a year or two.

Mrs. Underwood knew that Rosamond felt constricted in her life at home, and as Callaway spoke, she saw her daughter's animated response. She was not surprised to hear Ros say, "I'd like to try it myself, if my best friend and classmate from Smith, Dorothy Woodruff, would go with me." Ros rushed to the telephone to call Dorothy, asking her, "How would you like to go out to Colorado and teach school? You must come over immediately. We've got to talk about this!"

Within minutes Dorothy was at the door. On her brisk walk over, she had made her decision. They plied Callaway for more information and got Mrs. Woodley's address from her so they could write to express their interest. Nonetheless, Dorothy anticipated her family's alarm: "No young lady in our town," she later recalled, "had ever been hired by anybody."

A few years earlier, Ros had gone to a resort in Hot Springs, Arizona, to recover from a bronchial infection, and she had loved the informality and open spaces of the West. But neither woman knew much about the rigors of life in the Rockies. Their sense of the westward expansion came largely from Elinore Pruitt Stewart's *Letters of a Woman Homesteader,* serialized in the *Atlantic Monthly* several years earlier and then published as a book — now a classic of life on the frontier. They had been riveted by Stewart's account of living by her wits far from any urban center. Stewart wrote about a camping trip in December near her homestead in Burnt Fork, Wyoming: "Our improvised beds were the most comfortable things; I love the flicker of an open fire, the smell of the pines, the pure, sweet air, and I went to sleep thinking how blest I was to be able to enjoy the things I love most."

This, to Ros and Dorothy, was true romance. Stewart and her resourceful neighbor, Mrs. O'Shaughnessy, were roused by a long, haunting wail. Stewart thought it was the cry of a panther, but upon investigating, they found that it was a girl in a new loggers' encampment, in the throes of a difficult childbirth. The clearing consisted of two homes. Both husbands had been gone for two weeks, to collect their wages and some supplies. The women helped the girl deliver her baby, and when they realized that the families would have nothing for Christmas, they returned to Stewart's house and prepared a bundle of presents. For the children, they made paper birds, butterflies, and flowers; apples; and candies from fondant. For the new mother: oatmeal, butter, cream, and eggs, and a petticoat. They went back and decorated one of the empty cabins with pine boughs and a Christmas tree lit with candles. Everyone was enchanted. "We all got so much out of so little," Stewart wrote. "I will never again allow even the smallest thing to go to waste."

Their job applications submitted, Dorothy and Ros began to imagine themselves in a role much like Stewart's. Letters flew back and forth between them and Mrs. Woodley, who wrote that the train ride from Denver to Hayden was the most scenic trip in the country, and she described the beautiful hills of "Elkhead country," with the tallest of the Rockies visible in the distance. She downplayed the hardships and stretched the truth, assuring them that "from August till Dec. the weather will be glorious, cold nights and mornings but fine in the daytime. From Dec. till April the snow will be heavy and the weather cold. Everyone skis or snow-shoes and go on [bobsleds] when the roads are open. . . . If you are delicate, don't undertake it, but a girl of ordinary strength who likes out-door life and doesn't mind a few discomforts will get along beautifully."

The teachers, she noted, must be able to teach domestic science — "adapted to rural life, with canning etc. and some practical manual training for boys would be a help. Home Decoration would be a wonderful thing and really anything is acceptable that would enrich their lives." The domestic-science movement was led by middle-class women who had no maids or kitchen help, who believed that bringing modern methods of cleaning and cooking into the home would lead not only to greater freedom for them but also to curing the social scourges of alcoholism, disease, and even poverty. Mrs. Woodley said she had "refrained from enthusing," because she wanted the girls to know the conditions they would be confronting, but added that if they "would like to catch a glimpse of one of the last of our fast disappearing frontiers, I'd urge you to try it."

As for safety, she said that she spent much of her time in Elkhead, and there was little danger, "except what is always present when one lives in a primitive way. I mean you might be thrown from your horse, or you might let a log of wood fall on your foot etc.," but she added that these were nothing compared to "the liability of being run down by an auto" or driving one. Ruth advised them not to promise their parents that no harm could come to them. They should instead say that they would "live a life considerably freer of dangers than in Auburn, and a much more rugged, healthy one." In mid-June, Dorothy and Ros learned that two of their top competitors for the job had dropped out, "owing to parental objections."

Another of Ferry Carpenter's recruiters was Miriam Heermans, an old friend of Ruth's from Evanston and Wellesley, who in 1912, at Carpenter and Ruth's urging, had taught at one of the first schoolhouses in Elkhead for five months; Ruth stayed with Miriam on the Adair ranch, where the school was located. Miriam wrote to Ros and Dorothy on June 11, saying that she thought the jobs were probably theirs as long as their parents weren't adamantly opposed. Dorothy mailed Heermans's note to Ros, who was out of town for a few days, writing on the bottom of the letter: "Sounds like business — doesn't it! . . . I am awfully excited — I think I'd better acknowledge this — and hope I won't put my foot in. I shall say I think our parents can be managed."

Carpenter replied to Miriam on June 15, saying that he might be willing to take a chance on "those Auburn girls," but he wanted to know, "Will they take the grief that goes with such a job and have they the pep to shed it off and go right on like nothing happened? What education have they? Let me hear from you and tell them to write direct to me at once." He added that if she had "any doubt about their having the necessary gimp in them to handle this job why let them drop right now."

Miss Heermans indiscreetly sent Carpenter's note to Dorothy, saying, "He is really not as illiterate as this sounds but has

163

merely fallen into the Elkhead dialect!"

Dorothy wrote a long letter to Carpenter, earnestly describing their education, their travels, and their social work before admitting, "You see this may not offer much specialized training for the Elkhead work — but we shall do as much as possible before we leave — we are very anxious to try this position & will do our best to fill the requirements. You may be sure that we would expect to stick it out — whatever our experiences might be." Indicating their seriousness of purpose, she asked whether the school was equipped with good blackboards, books, and maps of the world and the state of Colorado, and she said they would like to see any information he had about the subjects they would be teaching.

He sent a wire confirming their employment, but the following week, their preparations were abruptly halted. War with Mexico appeared imminent, after Pancho Villa and several hundred of his men attacked a U.S. Army garrison in Columbus, New Mexico. President Wilson ordered the mobilization of tens of thousands of National Guardsmen, one of whom was Ros's older brother, Kennard Underwood. He had just made second lieutenant in Company M, and the Underwoods did not want two of their children far from home in potentially dangerous circumstances. Dorothy and Ros reluctantly sent a telegram to Carpenter saying that, under the circumstances, they had to refuse the position.

Then Wilson changed his mind. Preoccupied with the escalating war in Europe and the increasing bitterness between the U.S. and Germany, he initiated a mediation commission to negotiate the terms for a withdrawal. For the second time, the girls were told they could go. The school year was to begin in early August, and worried that in the interim Carpenter might have chosen two other teachers, Dorothy sent him a telegram on July 5, saying they were available after all, if the jobs weren't taken. Two days later, she heard back: POSITIONS OPEN AND YOU MAY CONSIDER YOURSELVES HIRED WILL WRITE.

Ros typed a businesslike letter to Ferry, reiterating Dorothy's request for information about the state syllabus and what books and supplies the school had. In response to a question from Carpenter about their living situation in Elkhead, she said they would rather board with a family than stay in a cabin by themselves. He replied that the district furnished all books and supplies, and said the school had a piano and would soon have a phonograph and records, which would be moved from one of the summer schools some miles away. It was a big project, he explained, to consolidate several tiny schools into one for a community that was so widely spread out.

The Princeton and Harvard man tailored his correspondence to "Miss Underwood" and "Miss Woodruff" to appeal to their ideals about teaching and to their excitement about a clean, active life in the Rockies. He told them about three Elkhead pupils who had just been to his cabin for dinner "and wanted to know all about you — I truly envy you the chance to be with those kids, as everything to them is a seven day wonder." He recommended that they read John Dewey's *Schools of To-morrow,* adding that although the conditions in Elkhead were unlike those in the urban schools Dewey wrote about, his philosophy of education should nonetheless apply: "learning by doing," rather than by rote teaching and the rod.

Given Carpenter's expectations for the school, he was surprisingly unconcerned about the new teachers' lack of credentials. Dorothy and Ros didn't begin to think in practical terms until after they were hired. Then, Dorothy said, "It began to frighten us very much. We'd realized what we'd done. We knew not the slightest thing about teaching, absolutely nothing." Addressing their anxiety about domestic science, they made themselves dresses from foulard, a twill-weave silk, which, Rosamond said, "we thought were handsome."

Cayuga County's blue bloods were shocked by the news. SOCIETY GIRLS GO TO WILDS OF COLORADO, the *Syracuse Daily Journal* declared on July 24. "Forsaking their beautiful homes . . . for the life of a school teacher . . . the Misses Rosamond Underwood and Dorothy Woodruff, leading society girls, left for Hayden. The announcement of the departure for the lonely place in the heart of the Elkhart [*sic*] Mountains, 18 miles from a railroad station, surprised society when it became known today. Both have figured prominently in the many social events which have taken place in this city in the last few years."

The women agreed that Ros would teach the older children, grades six through twelve. Dorothy, who was unsure about her skills in Latin and mathematics, would take grades one through five. They hired a teacher in Auburn to help them review some basic mathematics, and went to Ithaca to consult a rustic-schools expert at Cornell

University. Dorothy also visited the school superintendent in Auburn, who referred her to a teacher named Miss LeMay, from whom she received instruction on what she could hope to accomplish in a large class with widely different ages and abilities. Miss LeMay supplied her with a stack of books, "so I felt I at least had something to put my teeth into when I arrived," Dorothy said.

As always, their wardrobes were a consuming issue, but their needs were different now. Ruth Woodley wrote a nine-page letter to Ros instructing her what to bring. She recommended a divided riding skirt with knickers underneath. It unbuttoned front and back while on horseback, and it became an ordinary skirt when buttoned back up upon dismounting. She warned against buying an English riding habit — coat and knickers — because it "shocks the sensibilities of the natives." Long woolen underwear, good heavy shoes, rubber overshoes, a slicker, and galoshes were essential. She said that she always wore last year's clothes — a simple shirtwaist or two of light flannel and a skirt and a serge dress, plus a couple of summer dresses. "You will find laundry quite a problem," she said. "The last few years I've done my own." A week later, she added a bathing suit and bedding to the list, mentioning that they couldn't expect the standard of cleanliness to which they were accustomed. They forgot to buy the long woolen underwear but otherwise did exactly as she advised, sending away to Abercrombie & Fitch in New York for tweed riding suits with divided skirts. They also packed their fur coats.

As their date of departure approached, Carpenter wrote to say that they would have to take the Routt County teachers' examinations, which consisted of questions in twelve subjects, though he did not specify which ones. They would take the tests in Steamboat Springs in August, soon after classes started. Ros anxiously asked him to send copies of tests from earlier years, so they could prepare. He wrote back offhandedly, "Don't let those exams worry you at all for they're easy."

In his final letter, he described his trip on horseback to the scattered cabins that comprised Elkhead. One of the places he visited was a spot that "we call Little Arkansas, where they live on porcupine and bear cabbage and the quakers [quaking aspen] are so thick you can hardly ride thru from one place to another." He said there would be about thirty "head" — referring to pupils, not cattle. Until then, Dorothy and Ros hadn't been fully struck by the audacity and strangeness of their undertaking.

9
HELL HILL

Gore Canyon, Moffat Road, between 1907 and 1913

In Denver on July 27, as Dorothy and Ros boarded the train at the Moffat Depot, a man lifted their suitcases onto a brass luggage rack in the parlor car. There were facing leather lounge chairs near the back, with little tables between. They sat down and tried to work, but the dozen other people on the journey across the Great Divide made no effort to conceal their curiosity about the two young women. Dorothy wrote to her family the next morning from the Hayden Inn, "We were soon all bosom friends." The rapidly changing landscape was rejuvenating after the monotonous plains of the previous days. They soon left behind the soot and crowds of Denver, and the rolling brown prairie gave way to green foothills. They passed some farms and homes, then wound toward a high, broad mesa — the start of the Front Range. The air was clean and cooler as the pine forests began to thicken. The sky was a brilliant azure rarely seen in the East.

The train snaked up along the wide ridges. Then, suddenly, they were surrounded by spires and ledges of stone and passed through the first of thirty-three tunnels that had been blasted through the hard rock. The tracks were toylike beside jagged sand-colored cliffs that rose abruptly on one side, close to the train window, and chasms that dropped away on the other. The first canyon, Coal Creek, was followed by South Boulder. When they walked out to the observation platform, they saw valleys occasionally open up and rapids churning against the rocks far below. Dorothy wrote, "The altitude didn't bother us a bit — and although there was some snow — they all said they never saw so little — due to this intense heat." The trip would not have been advisable for anyone with vertigo or claustrophobia or a lack of faith in the technological advances that had made possible the building of the railroad. The Devil's Slide Trestles, two in a row, were built directly into the side of the mountain. The canyon floor was over a thousand feet below. The switchbacks were so extreme in some spots that when the locomotive rounded a bend, the train virtually folded in two. Ros wrote, "we hung out of the window and off the observation platform — talked to everyone in the car and found many interesting people — got as many side lights on the country as possible." The Moffat Road, Dorothy commented, "seems to be something of a joke — with its one train and delays — but long before we arrived I thought it was the most gigantic accomplishment I ever saw. We went through and over sheer rock, high mountains, & superb canyons — and I can't imagine how they ever did it."

They weren't the only ones to be astonished at the achievement. As an early historian of Colorado wrote, the building of the line "attracted the attention of engineers and scientists throughout the world." David Moffat's railroad, like so much of what they were already experiencing, represented a triumph of will and perseverance over prudence. It was also widely seen as a lifeline to people fighting to survive in Routt County — the difference, over the long term, between penury and a decent living. Ros and Dorothy learned more from the other passengers and, subsequently, from Carpenter, about the extraordinary man behind the railroad.

David Moffat arrived in Denver from Omaha, Nebraska, at the age of twenty on March 17, 1860. He had entered into a partnership with a man who supplied him with three drivers, two wagons, and enough paper and books to open a stationery store on Larimer Street. Moffat intended to return home to New York after he had made $75,000, a small fortune at the time. Instead, he broadened his endeavors over the next four decades to include banking (he rose from cashier to president of the First National Bank of Denver); mining (he came to own more than a hundred mines); streetcars (he was treasurer of two companies); and railroads (he had interests in at least nine of them).

In 1867 Moffat, along with former territorial governor John Evans, and William Byers, the owner of the *Rocky Mountain News,* joined investors from the East to form the Denver Pacific Railway, the first railroad into the city. Denver had been bypassed by the first transcontinental railroad — a joint undertaking of the Union Pacific and the Central Pacific, completed in 1869, which had chosen the less risky northern route through Cheyenne, Wyoming. This caused Thomas Durant, the vice president of Union Pacific, to gleefully announce that Denver was "too dead to bury." He underestimated Coloradans' faith in their state's future. The Denver Pacific connected Denver to Cheyenne and the national rail system, and it brought the city back from its post–gold rush slump.

Moffat was described by a friend as "quiet, unpretentious, lovable, a man of patience and courtesy" who "never spoke ill of anyone." Lovable he may have been, but his drive and political connections matched those of his rapacious eastern counterparts, E. H. Harriman and Jay Gould, and later, Gould's son George. Moffat also knew more than they did about Colorado's varied terrain and hidden riches, and his greatest ambition was to build his own transcontinental railroad, which would cross the Continental Divide.

One of Moffat's key backers was Sam Perry, the father of Ferry Carpenter's friend Bob. Perry, a director of the Denver Tramway Company, owned several coal mines and a great deal of land and some other businesses in Routt County. A railroad over the Rockies and into the Yampa Valley, he and Moffat believed, would mean an end to the isolation of residents to the west of the Rockies: prosperity for the mine owners, ranchers, strawberry growers, and tourism entrepreneurs; and vastly more power and profits for whoever managed to build the line. It also meant that Harriman and Gould would be denied access to some of the most valuable and stunning land in the United States.

Moffat continued investing in railroads until, in June 1902, portly and bald at sixty-two years old, he announced his plan to create a standard-gauge "air line" — the shortest, straightest route possible — over the Rocky Mountains. There were already narrow-gauge railroads in the Rockies. But Moffat's was the first standard gauge: its eighty-pound steel rails would be four feet, eight and a half inches apart, rather than three feet, made for bigger engines that could haul heavy cargo. Moffat was by then one of the richest men in Colorado. After two months in New York, he told the *Times* that he had completed the financing of his railroad. He promised it would reduce the travel time between Denver and San Francisco by twenty-four hours.

He intended to build the Denver, Northwestern & Pacific Railway, dubbed the Moffat Road, north and northwest from Denver to Salt Lake City. His decision to connect the two cities, he disingenuously told the *Times,* was not "for the purpose of entering into a competitive field or for the purpose of making another road to the Pacific Coast." It was simply to form "a link in the railroad chain." Moffat's road would join the San Pedro, Los Angeles and Salt Lake Railroad in Salt Lake City, which would run from there to southern California and thus "become a transcontinental proposition." Incensed at this taunt, Harriman and Gould prevented Moffat from using Union Station in Denver as his terminus, but Moffat built his own depot several blocks west.

The Moffat Road is still the highest standard-gauge railroad ever built in North

America. Although Moffat was not easily discouraged, his years of experience did not prepare him for the expense and technical challenges of the undertaking. Gunpowder and twenty tons of TNT were used along the route to bore into the rock, but the longer tunnels also required the use of electric drills, air drills, and "up-right boiler" steam drills. At some locations, the granite was rotten and difficult to prop up with timber. Although teams of Chinese, Italian, and Scandinavian muckers shoveled dirt out of the tunnels and hauled it away in wheelbarrows and horse-drawn carts and wagons, there never seemed to be enough of them.

The railroad's chief locating engineer, based in Denver, was H. A. Sumner. His greatest quandary as he plotted the sinuous path — nothing like the straight air line Moffat had pledged — was how best to tackle the treacherous stretch that rose to the summit, Rollins Pass, at 11,600 feet, and down the west side to Idlewild (now Winter Park). The workers called it "Hell Hill" and referred to five particularly tight switchbacks on the east side as the "Giant's Ladder." Sumner said of his task, "The battle of Gettysburg was a Quaker meeting by comparison." Moffat regarded Hell Hill as a temporary branch line to be used for several years to shuttle workers and equipment as well as tourists, cattle, and coal, across the Divide, until he could raise the money needed to complete a six-mile tunnel through James Peak. On maps, the route looks like a line drawn by a palsied madman.

Sumner's teams worked from both sides of the mountain. One of the parties on the west side was led by an imperturbable engineer, a husband and father of five, named J. J. Argo, who kept a record of his men's progress. They worked through two winters, hauling their tents, camp stoves, food, and surveying equipment on sleds from one location to the next. Arctic temperatures, blizzards, and drifting snow were daily occurrences from September through June. The wind blew some places clear of snow, but at many cuts, it was as deep as two hundred feet. They dug themselves out with shovels. When they suffered from snow blindness, they rubbed slices of raw potatoes on their eyelids at night, and they tried to deflect the glare during the day by lining their eyes with charcoal.

At Gore Canyon, the men at the top rappelled down the cliff, drove steel pitons into the rock, and attached ropes, prompting

Sumner to refer to them as "Argo's Squirrels." The workers below chopped down trees and made sixteen-foot sections of logs, which they floated down the Grand River. These were lifted out and attached to the ropes at the lower end, creating footbridges that swayed in the heavy winds. The workers, clearing a path to lay down a roadbed for the train, stood on the bridges as they drilled holes for dynamite with handheld star drills. Argo wrote in his diary one June day, "Built foot bridges in afternoon along bluffs. Hoklas fell in river and narrowly escaped drowning."

Newspaper reports described a worker whose arm was amputated; another lost both eyes. One man died after a mule kicked him in the head. Rockslides were common, carrying away workers and filling tunnel portals. In the summer of 1905, the construction crews at the top of the Divide had to work furiously to get two miles of snowsheds built in order to protect the most exposed tracks before the heaviest snows and winds descended. The workers' quarters were flimsier shacks attached to the sheds.

Once the freight trains started running, they required four state-of-the-art Mallet locomotives, designed by a Swiss engineer, run in tandem with "hogs," the second-most powerful engines, to get them up the mountain. Even when paired with gigantic rotary snowplows, the locomotives were defeated by storms and avalanches, which occasionally sent cars hurtling off the side of the mountain. Remarkably, no passenger was ever killed on the Moffat Road, although many were stranded at the summit for days or even weeks, waiting for the blizzards to subside and unprotected sections of the tracks to be cleared. There was at least one birth at Rollins Pass during a delay. The expense of snow removal accounted for 40 percent or more of the railroad's operational costs. One man recalled getting stuck at the top as a child: "They brought some Chinese in to shovel the snow. It was impossible. The big [rotary] snowplow chewed up two or three of the Chinese. After that, they refused to go out and shovel, and I don't blame them."

As the tracks were being laid, there were reliable rumors that Harriman intended to buy the railroad or put it under the control of the Union Pacific. He established a dummy power company to acquire land around Kremmling, west of the Divide, and block the Moffat Road's right of way at Gore Canyon. In the spring of 1904, Harriman's "consulting engineers" convinced the

Interior Department to set aside twenty-eight sections of land to build a reservoir there. President Theodore Roosevelt loved the wild lands and game of northwestern Colorado, and he learned from a hunting companion who was also a mining executive that Harriman, along with Gould, was manipulating the Interior's Reclamation Service. Roosevelt, no fan of monopolies, recently had fallen out with Harriman. He summoned the competing parties to Washington and quickly resolved the matter in Moffat's favor.

Despite the scheming of his enemies and the technical and meteorological hazards, Moffat built his railroad over Rollins Pass down into Hot Sulphur Springs and Troublesome, Yampa and Oak Creek. By March 1911 Moffat had spent his fortune on it, and he returned to New York, hoping to raise enough money to bore the long tunnel through James Peak. Without it, the railroad would fail. It is unclear where Moffat secured a promise for the required funds, but he returned that night to the bar of the Hotel Belmont, where he celebrated loudly with some friends. Although Harriman was no longer alive, some of his company's spies reportedly informed the lenders that if they went through with the deal, they could no longer expect to do business with Union Pacific. The next morning, the promise of assistance was withdrawn. Moffat died that day, March 18, in his room at the hotel, from a heart attack. He was seventy-one years old and had spent, by some accounts, $14 million of his own (the equivalent a century later of $310 million) on the Moffat Road.

As the *Denver Republican* reported the day after his death, a new power had risen in Wall Street in the early days of the building of the line, which was destined to dominate the railroad system of the nation: "Harriman would not have been Harriman had he permitted a rival line, financed mainly by local capitalists, to pluck his plums."

Sam Perry and other investors took the Moffat Road into receivership, and its official name was changed to the Denver & Salt Lake Railroad Company, although no one called it that. The Moffat Road reached Steamboat Springs in 1909, and Hayden, four years later. The line stopped at Craig, the town west of Hayden. The 6.2-mile Moffat Tunnel was not completed for another sixteen years.

For Dorothy and Ros, traveling on a glorious summer day, the sights along the route were a welcome distraction from their worries about teaching. So were the other passengers. They got to know a woman named Mrs. Chambers, a graduate of Bryn Mawr and the wife of a mining engineer. Dorothy described her as "one of the finest types of woman — having been to college — yet she lives in a narrow canyon — works terribly hard — has [three] small children — and was reading *Woman and Labor!*" Dorothy was referring to Olive Schreiner's 1911 polemic on the evils of imperialism, war, and the subjugation of women. Schreiner, a South African political activist, was highly regarded among American feminists.

Dorothy and Ros didn't know much about how women outside their closed social circle chose to live. While they were having bacon-bat picnics by a stream outside Northampton, a thirty-seven-year-old doctor named Susan Anderson was living alone in a log cabin in Fraser, on the west side of the Divide. Her duties included tending to the injuries of lumbermen and workers on the Moffat Road, and serving as the coroner for those who didn't make it. When Dorothy and Ros were pouring tea for suffragists in Auburn, their counterparts in Colorado were going to the polls. Susan B. Anthony went twice to push the cause there in the

1870s, but it was local women's organizations that prevailed. In 1876 women were permitted to vote in school elections and, in a referendum in 1893, they won full suffrage. Although the territory of Wyoming had granted women the vote twenty-four years earlier, Colorado was the first state. Anthony was not entirely pleased that her western sisters had done it without her. New York, despite all of the work of the Cayuga County suffragists, didn't permit women full voting rights until 1917, three years before the Nineteenth Amendment was passed.

In Auburn, women who didn't marry, like Rosamond's "Auntie," took care of their parents as they became old and infirm. They were little more than glorified servants and often died in the houses where they were born. In 1904, when the Underwoods went to Greece and Egypt, nine-year-old Arthur was left at home with Auntie, who was, as Dorothy put it, "a relic certainly of a very bygone day." Auntie's life was not the future Dorothy and Ros had in mind for themselves. "She did her hair in a big roll at the back of her neck with a net on it," Dorothy said. "She had a sharp New England accent, and she very seldom came to the table. She lived in a little bedroom at the back of the second story hall, did the family mending, and lived her life mostly there alone." One year Auntie needed a new winter coat, and Mrs. Underwood went downtown to buy one for her. Auntie put on the coat and said, "Oh, Grace, this makes me look like an old woman!" At the time, Dorothy thought it was one of the funniest remarks she'd ever heard. She said, "I thought then she was about one hundred."

Mrs. Underwood's family album contains a photo labeled "Auntie's corner." It shows a room with a narrow, neatly made bed covered with a crocheted bedspread, a side table and shelf crowded with knickknacks and an ornate clock, and an upholstered rocking chair with an antimacassar draped limply over the top. Dorothy often thought about Auntie as she grew up, and although she knew she was well taken care of, she said, "I don't know if anybody ever thought there was any need for anybody like Auntie to have any pleasure." Dorothy feared — correctly, as it turned out — that her smart, unlovely sister Anna, who yearned to be an astronomer, would suffer a similar fate. Although Anna took over the best bedroom at 15 Fort Street and ran the household, she did not have a life of her own. In 1907, ten years after graduating from Smith, she wrote: "[W]hile I have not taken to myself a husband or any other regular occupation, I refuse to write myself down any sort of an idler. I do the social and philanthropic things that come up in a small city, often take care of our own large family, revel in my garden, and have had two superlatively glorious trips abroad. You see, I'm happy like the country whose annals are dull."

The train climbed noisily, the wheels clacking as they rode over the track joints, past lingering patches of snow, curving around the pristine circle of Yankee Doodle Lake before making the final ascent, passing through the Needle's Eye Tunnel, high above the tree line. They were about a third of the way from Denver to Hayden. As they approached Rollins Pass, the train entered the snowsheds. The rail stop town at the summit was called Corona, or "crown." As another traveler remembered his arrival on a summer day: "Corona seemed like a settlement belonging to another planet. Vicious mountain winds shook, rattled, and banged loose parts of the layout. Spring and summer thunderstorms originated right overhead at this high altitude."

A 1914 brochure printed by the railroad described this CREST OF THE MAIN RANGE OF THE MAJESTIC "ROCKIES" as "lovely stretches of verdure, bespangled with myriads of beautiful blossoms, alternating with great drifts of glistening snow." Soon the line would extend to Salt Lake, the brochure claimed, adding, "The vast agricultural empire being opened by the building of this railroad offers exceptional opportunities to those seeking a home in this new west."

The train stopped to let the passengers off for lunch and to see the view from Rollins Pass, advertised by the Moffat Road in a famous poster as the "Top O' the World." Dorothy remembered that there were snowbanks as they approached the peak, and that the train pulled into "a little kind of a shanty place, where we had sandwiches and coffee."

It was Corona's restaurant, which was inside the snowsheds, a hundred feet from the tracks. The acrid fumes from the locomotives sometimes caused trainmen and passengers to pass out. The prices on the menu were high because of the journey the food had to take. Dorothy and Ros walked outside for some fresh air, turning away from the unsightly water tower next to the tracks. They had unobstructed views of the distant mountains, which receded, range after range, in a purplish haze until they disappeared behind the clouds. Despite its rough beauty, the spot felt desolate even on a cloudless summer day. The silence was broken only by the songs of meadowlarks and the loud, piping sound of pikas. Aside from miniature bursts of potentilla and larkspur, the "crown" was covered with nothing but snow, parched grass, rocks and boulders, and rusty tin cans — remnants of the railroad workers' meals, some years earlier, on the top of the world.

The next day, down in Hayden, Ferry Carpenter gave Dorothy and Ros a hand as they clambered onto the seat of an old spring wagon. Their driver, named Guy, was an eighteen-year-old clerk from Wagner's saddle shop. He was dressed for the occasion in a bright red sweater. Their trunks, topped by yellow slickers and secured by new ropes, towered behind them in the wagon's box-bed. The horses were saddled and bridled and tied to the back of the wagon. Leaving Hayden on the clear day of July 28, 1916, they followed Long Gulch Road and headed toward the Harrison ranch, eighteen miles north. Crossing the Yampa River, they passed the spot where F. V. Hayden's crew had camped not quite fifty years earlier, as they surveyed the Yampa Valley and the Elkhead Mountains.

The valley fell back behind a series of steep canyons and wide mesas. From a distance, the hills had looked welcoming, with rounded slopes that bore little resemblance to the jagged mountains they had crossed on the train. But the trip proved to be more strenuous than expected, and their admiration for the Moffat Road increased. The jarring wagon ride was a throwback to a mode of travel used in the early days on the frontier. By comparison, the train was a model of comfort.

Dorothy wrote, "We wound in and out and up and down, going at a pace that put our hearts in our mouths, and we were sure the trunks were either going to career over on us or our horses." Later, she good-naturedly described the ride as the most uncomfortable in her life. Spring wagons were larger and heavier than buggies, and more utilitarian. There was no back to the wooden seat, and "I was so short that my feet were about a foot off the floorboard, just dangling all day." At one point she looked down and saw that the wagon road seemed to be in motion, too, and she thought she was dizzy from the ride. She said to Ros, "Do you see something moving on the ground?" Ros replied, "Why yes, the whole thing is moving." They leaned over and saw an army of field mice skittering across their path. Every time they came to a dry wash, Dorothy said, "a most forbidding-looking place filled with rocks and boulders, that boy would lash those horses and make them run down over those awful rocks."

The hills, which had been green not long before, were scorched, and even the hardy clumps of silvery-teal sagebrush looked brittle. Even so, some of the wildflowers — sego lilies, Indian paintbrush, wild carrot, parsnip, and pink wild hollyhock — were still blooming. Ros commented on the beauty and variety of flowers and said that the landscape reminded her of Castle Hot Springs, with the cactus left out. Calf Creek, now dry, threaded its way through the valleys.

After a few hours, Guy drove down into a cultivated valley, home to the vast Adair ranch. John Adair had arrived in Hayden on horseback from Athens, Tennessee, in 1882 at the age of nineteen. By 1916 he had made a remarkable success of his cattle business. The Adairs, who had several ranches, were no longer living there, and the couple taking care of the place served the travelers a full dinner of meat, vegetables, and pie. When the two women offered to pay for it, their hostess was taken aback and refused the gesture, although she told them that the only money she had left was a ten-dollar bill she had put in her Bible several years earlier. Not long afterward, Dorothy learned that in the rural West, any stranger who stopped by at mealtime was fed as a matter of course. They continued on their way, and by late afternoon the country had grown wilder. Patches of bare earth were visible between bunches of sagebrush, and there were few trees to be seen. They crossed Calf Creek and stopped where the road did, at the bottom of a high hill. On top of it was a newly built house.

The door opened, and their landlady, fifty-four-year-old Mary Harrison, childlike in her size and her eagerness, ran out to greet them. Dorothy and Ros stepped down from the wagon into long grass and sagebrush, lifted their skirts, and walked up to the house. It was "a square box, part log and part frame," Dorothy wrote to her father the next day, "with a little smoke stack sticking up. The steps consist of a soap box shakily resting on stones. It is the simplest, plainest exterior — all built by themselves."

Mrs. Harrison looked older than she was, "tiny and skinny and wrinkled, with her thin gray hair slicked back, and with the most astonishing set of false teeth." Mary and her husband, Uriah, who went by Frank, had arrived from Missouri in 1897, taking several trains and, for the final leg of the journey, a covered wagon. They had been among thousands of families drawn to Routt County by the United States government with the promise of free land. Another couple arrived in 1914 at Dry Fork, south of Calf Creek, and thought that the low log shacks there resembled a prairie-dog colony. Their granddaughter recalled, "Survival was tough," but "if you dug a well and found water, you could make it for awhile."

The Harrisons had taken advantage of the railroads' special "homeseeker" rates for cross-country boxcar trips. At a nominal fee, they filled up a few cars with their farm machines, milk cows and draft horses, along with their furniture and family, and transported the entire household. The government's offer seemed too good to be true, and it was. The Homestead Act of 1862, signed by President Lincoln, was drafted by easterners who knew little about the climate and dry lands of the West. People came from Kansas, Iowa, Minnesota, Nebraska, Oklahoma territory, Kentucky, and Michigan — and also from Sweden, Russia, Bulgaria, Greece, and other points east. They did exactly what Ferry Carpenter did, laying claim to 160 acres, or more if they had family members over the age of twenty-one. Most were unprepared for the severe, arid climate and the intractable farming conditions. Ultimately, over one and a half million homesteads were granted, a total of 420,000 square miles — 10 percent of the land in the United States.

In the early years after the Harrisons arrived, northwestern Colorado was untamed. Although the Utes were only a legend by then, some of the notorious cattle rustlers and train robbers were still at large. The Harrisons' first ranch, between Hayden and Craig, had been a headquarters for the vast Two Bar outfit, owned by Ora Haley, one of the West's biggest and most despised cattle barons. The stockmen allowed their cattle to overgraze, and fought homesteaders and small farmers and sheep men for the few water holes and the green pastures. Haley ran tens of thousands of cattle on land throughout the central Rockies.

The Harrisons avidly followed stories in the newspaper and among their neighbors about "Queen Ann" Bassett, a beautiful young rancher, educated at a boarding school in Boston, who had grown up in Browns Park, northwest of Hayden and

Craig. Bassett's father was friendly with Butch Cassidy, who liked to read in the Bassett library, and at the age of fifteen, Ann became Cassidy's lover; her sister, Josie, got involved with Cassidy's best friend, Elzy Lay. Ann took it upon herself to fight off the cattle barons' "devouring invasion," starting in 1901 with Ora Haley's herds. In two sensational trials, in 1911 and 1913, she was tried for stealing and butchering a heifer belonging to the Two Bar. In August 1913 she was acquitted in the Craig County courthouse. She boasted in an unpublished autobiography, "I did everything they ever accused me of, and a whole lot more." Cowboys shot off their guns in celebration, the town band held a parade, and she treated everyone to a silent movie, which was punctuated by a slide proclaiming, HURRAH FOR VICTORY! An all-night dance followed, presided over by Queen Ann.

By 1915 the valley had quieted down, and the Harrisons were focused on their bottom line. Overextended with their creditors, they had no choice but to sell their ranch. When Dorothy and Ros arrived in Upper Elkhead, Frank and Mary were still finishing their new home. Making a living in the mountains was an even riskier proposition than in the valley. Contrary to Ruth Woodley's assurances about the climate, Elkhead was covered by snow for six months of the year. From December through March, temperatures sometimes dropped to 40 below, and springtime was no easier, with its ice, snowmelt, and heavy, wet adobe clay, known as gumbo, which clung to boots, stained clothes, and made the few roads and paths all but impassable. In late summer, creeks and streams dried up.

Nevertheless, the Harrisons shared with other Elkhead homesteaders the unshakable belief that the mountains were suited to farming and raising cattle. With the three youngest of their seven children at home — Ruth (twenty-two years old), Frank Jr. (twenty), and Lewis (fourteen) — they had built their house on a rocky ridge, away from the productive lands where the cattle grazed. There were no trees to offer shade in the summer or a windscreen in winter.

The women from Auburn were relieved when they went inside and saw that the house was relatively comfortable. Dorothy tried to reassure herself, along with her parents, writing that "there is just one layer of rough, unfinished board between us and outdoors, but I presume they will fix it before snow." The inside walls weren't up yet, just partitions made of blankets and rugs. "This lends intimacy to an unimagined degree and you know it — every time any one turns over in bed, and it is especially sociable when the wind blows."

Meals were eaten at one end of the large kitchen. The living room was outfitted with hardwood floors, pretty rag rugs, a couple of chairs, a folding bed, and a phonograph. "It's divided from Mr. and Mrs. Harrison's room by the best blankets," Dorothy wrote, "an artistic shade of gray." Their own room was reached by a set of "rather shaky and ladder-like" stairs. She and Ros shared an iron bed by the window, covered with a large featherbed and patchwork quilts. The other furnishings were a bureau, a wash-stand, and a table. Dorothy was touched by the care Mrs. Harrison had taken on their behalf: "pretty embroidered covers on everything, her best towels and such nice bedding, real sheets and pillowcases with lace edging!"

Guy insisted on helping to get their trunks upstairs, and they were soon settled, propping up a few family photos on the bureau. Aside from their books, there wasn't much unpacking to do, since the trunks held most of their clothes. Ros pointed out that if one of them fell out of bed, she would roll right down the stairs.

■ ■ ■ ■

PART THREE:
WORKING GIRLS

■ ■ ■ ■

Dorothy on her commute

10
TURNIPS AND TEARS

Dorothy and her students, 1917

Ros and Dorothy were surprised to find the Harrisons sophisticated and well educated. Dorothy declared, "It is an entirely new type to me, for we never see such keen, receptive wide-awake intelligent people living such hard lives." Mrs. Harrison had "a twinkle in her kindly blue eyes . . . and the most delicious keen humor." Mr. Harrison was big and "slow of speech and action with the softest voice and drawl. . . . Ruth is short and as fat as a pigeon, with shiny red cheeks and the merriest eyes and laugh — and *very* deaf." Lewis, the youngest, was "a perfect darling — *so* well-behaved and polite — and a regular little man — the way he works." She added, "They are evidently pretty well-to-do for the region and are even hoping for a bathroom someday!"

They described their surroundings as clearly as they could. "You simply can't conceive of the *newness* of this country," Dorothy wrote. "Here we are — a tiny cabin perched on a hillside covered with sage looking off in all directions . . . with here and there a creek lined with willows. We are on Calf Creek but it is dry now. We have been having several thunder showers which were terribly needed as the country was drying up and they only live by irrigation. The storms are wonderful, booming among the mountains and no one minds getting wet for it dries right off and the sun is soon out. Even the road, merely the surface turned over, which goes by the house, is new, and if anyone goes by, we all turn out to see them." Similarly, Ros commented, "The roads are not well defined, and it is easy to get confused, with miles of hills and valleys all about you and very few signs of habitation."

After breakfast on their first full day, Lewis saddled their horses and showed them to the schoolhouse, riding on his horse, Old Eagle. They had asked him to be their guide each day, for which they paid him, Ros said, "the princely sum of $2.00 a week." They wore their khaki riding suits, and Dorothy was comfortable on Nugget. Ros told her father that her horse was "not well known in these parts," but that "Mr. C." had obtained him, so she was sure he would be fine. She named him Gourmand because he stopped so often to graze. Mr. Harrison called him Ol' Gorman.

They rode down the hill from the Harrisons' and followed the bed of Calf Creek, bordered by fresh green cottonwoods, before veering east and passing through an alfalfa field that was still shimmering with dew. As they came to the top of a wide draw, they could look down and see the ranch buildings and hay fields of the Adair place. The scale of the ranch struck them even more than it had when they had stopped there with Guy. The horses ambled slowly up and down the steep hills, swinging their hindquarters for balance as they descended, twitching their ears and swatting the flies with their tails. Ros commented that their "steeds" knew they were green, and they "couldn't get any speed out of them at all — not having spurs or a whip." As they followed a narrow, winding path through the brush, Dorothy wrote, "it is a strange sight, like a topographical map — roll after roll of rounded bare hills with little water, creases marking them — and no sign of a human being or habitation." The snowcapped mountains in the distance were purple and blue, their colors darkening with the movement of the clouds. "It took us an hour and a half so you can see what their idea of two miles is!"

The first sight of the building in the distance elicited a burst of eloquence from Ros. "The schoolhouse stands high on a mountain or hill between the two districts called 'Little Arkansas' and 'Calf Creek.' It is the Parthenon of Elkhead! You can see it for miles around and it looked so near that we were amazed to discover the real distance." Dorothy wrote, "They didn't have time to finish the road, so the last 200 yards you climb straight up through rocks and sage to the school. It is *perfectly beautiful* and a monument to the courage and ambition of these wonderful people."

The school was constructed of gray-green mountain stones from nearby sedimentary rimrock. Put under crushing heat and pressure beneath the earth hundreds of millions of years earlier, the stone was streaked, as if, one Routt County resident said, by the paintbrushes of God. The formation extended at intervals over a hundred miles across Colorado and Wyoming. Residents referred to the building as the Rimrock School, or the Rock School.

They tied up their horses and went inside. The carpenter still had some work and cleaning up to finish. The desks — wrought-iron bases with wooden tops — had not yet been put in place or the books unpacked. But as Dorothy and Ros walked from the vestibule into the airy main room, they confirmed the accuracy of Carpenter's claim about the school's physical merits.

The floor was oak, and the walls were whitewashed and decorated with a ribbon of pale green painted stencil. The room, thirty by fifty feet, had high ceilings and enormous windows. There were long blackboards on either side. In the center was a folding wooden door, which would be closed during the school day to separate the classrooms, and thrown open for community events — weddings, elections, dances, and Sunday school, which was attended by adults along with the children, since there was no church in Elkhead. "The pride of the building," Ros wrote, "is the piano, (called by everyone in these parts — pie-anno.) The man who hauled it up there from Hayden, says he'll never haul it down. It took him 17 hours to get it there — and he got $5.00 for doing it!" The room was sunny and looked out onto valleys and mountains all the way to Utah and Wyoming.

Lewis showed them the basement, pointing out where the coal furnace would go. In another room, a complicated wooden contraption hung from the beams — the gymnasium equipment. A third room held a cookstove and benches for the classes in domestic science. "Mr. C. told us Friday," Ros wrote, "that we could have anything we wanted in the way of books and equipment. He is so fine and broadminded about things — and ready to co-operate in any way. The people in this country are all perfectly devoted to him, and he certainly has been a real missionary in this place, without being one in name or manner at all."

Five years earlier, after the Elkhead residents voted for the construction of the school, financing had to be obtained, and the few big ranchers in the area agreed to pay the taxes needed to support the project. So did the absentee owners of the anthracite coal deposits east of Dry Fork. Anthracite coal, which is extremely hard and burns cleaner, longer, and hotter than bituminous coal, was so close to the surface that it was exposed in some places, a glistening black. The owner of the largest tract was Sam Perry. As the coal in Pennsylvania was mined out, the owners believed that the anthracite in Elkhead would command a very profitable market. The entire field was estimated to be eight square miles, with deposits worth over $50 million.

Ferry anticipated that the population would soon double or triple, and said, "You didn't want to build a little wooden shack there." The Adair school and the Dry Fork school, slipshod affairs, would close, although a school for several primary students, known as Mountain View, was built in the far southern end of the district. In the Elkhead School, Ferry explained, "All the windows were made big, and all the light came in over the child's shoulders and no light came in on his face. . . . I had read up on it and I knew the light would come that way."

The homesteaders helped with the construction, clearing ground and hauling rocks, and they built a barn in back for the horses. Along with the coal furnace, the electric lights, and the domestic-science room, the school had a projector with educational slides donated by the Ford Motor Company. It even had a telephone. The final critical component was the teachers, and on August 4, 1916, the *Republican* reported that the two schoolteachers "come very highly recommended" and that "Elkhead people count on a splendid school this term."

The community was proud of its big new school. One of Ros's ninth-graders, Leila Ferguson, had come west with her family from Medicine Lodge, Kansas, with a few chickens and turkeys in crates and some equipment for the household, including a Singer sewing machine. Leila said that as a young girl, she had been taught by her mother, "and she wasn't much of a teacher. She had no patience." In 1910 the Fergusons were strong advocates of the new district, and Leila attended the Dry Fork school before Elkhead was built. "We had brand-new desks," she told Ferry's granddaughter Belle sixty-three years later. "I'll never forget seeing them uncrate those desks and knowing one was going to be mine. I wouldn't have put a mark on it, a scratch on it, for anything. I just loved every minute of school."

Everyone knew how difficult it would be for the children to get to school in bad weather; the site had been chosen with equal access in mind. A civil engineer created a survey indicating where each family lived and the number of school-age children, drew a series of concentric circles that indicated each mile mark, and then located a spot in the center. None of the students would have over a three-mile trip each way. "That consolidated point," Carpenter said, "was on top of a hill with not even a road to it." It also happened to have the finest views in Elkhead.

On Sunday morning, two days after their arrival, Rosamond wrote: "Dearest papa: *You* are just getting ready for St. Peter's. I have thought of you and mother so much, while Dotty and I have been sitting in the sun drying our heads, after washing them in the most wonderful soft sulphur water (which has to be carried about 1/4 mile from a spring!)." On Sunday mornings in Auburn, coachmen readied the carriages as the church bells began ringing around town.

The middle class and the poor walked to their neighborhood churches. Catholics had separate congregations for German, Italian, Polish, Russian Orthodox, and Ukrainian immigrants. At the Harrisons', Ros described the tranquil beauty of the mountains, the little creek, the sagebrush, the wildflowers, and "the cultivated spots" where "grain of all sorts flourishes."

Later, they accompanied the family in "the so-called spring wagon" to Sunday school at the schoolhouse — Mr. and Mrs. Harrison on the seat, and Ruth, Lewis, Ros, and Dorothy spread about in the back. It was the social event of the week, and virtually everyone turned out. Dorothy wrote to Milly, "Our beautiful new school seems so out of place, perched on that lonely mountain side and the people seem even more so." It was the teachers' first introduction to the neighbors. The men wore sombreros and overalls and spurs; the women were "nice & intelligent-looking — a lot of shy girls and a perfect swarm of small boys who were introduced to me en masse — as being *my* pupils." One little boy, whose family somehow had not been counted in the survey, told her that he would be riding eight miles each day.

Miss Iva Rench, an officious young woman

from Muncie, was teaching at Mountain View and had been conducting Sunday-school services at Elkhead. Her lessons consisted of "Pauline doctrines of the stiffest kind," Ros commented. She was not one of the more popular people in Elkhead. Nevertheless, she conducted an impressive Sunday-school sermon on Paul's missionary journey which Dorothy and Ros sat through in fear that she would ask them questions. "She is expecting to turn the [Sunday school] over to us, which is appalling," Dorothy wrote, "but I suppose we can do it."

On the first day of school, Tuesday, August 1, the new teachers got up at five-thirty and had a quick sponge bath. They ate breakfast with the Harrisons, and Lewis met them at the door at seven-fifteen with their horses. Ferry had exchanged Nugget for Rogan, a huge, awful-looking beast, Dorothy thought, with the stolid manner of a dray horse and a broad back that made for a more uncomfortable ride. When she mounted, she needed a boost from Lewis or Frank Jr., who, at the age of twenty, was still called "Boy" at home. The four Harrisons saw them off, laughing at the sight of the teachers futilely kicking their horses' sides as they tried to keep up with Lewis. As the family advised, they soon started wearing spurs, which reduced the ride by almost fifteen minutes.

A few students had arrived before the teachers, who barely had time to change out of their riding skirts and boots before the others began to appear. Dorothy had ten boys between grades one and five, and one little girl, age six, who was joined a few months later by a second. The boys, in bare feet, wore cutoff overalls and ragged shirts. The teachers were captivated: "Without any exception, they are the cutest-looking children I ever saw," Dorothy wrote, "every one freckled as they can be — hair cut very short and the most snappy eyes!" Ros said that the children's faces were all "burned to a crisp," and "I have so far only two boys — one of them Lewis Harrison . . . ! Others will come later, when they're not needed for the haying. I have six girls, five of them in the ninth grade!"

The children and their parents couldn't have imagined how nervous Miss Woodruff and Miss Underwood were. Ros confessed, "Dot and I are scared to death for fear we'll make a slip at school — the country side might be in a terrible to-do in consequence." They weren't yet fully aware of the awe with which college-educated teachers in such far-flung areas were regarded. They spoke perfect English and other languages, too. They valued education for its own sake, not simply as a way to escape the hardships of life at home. Most astonishingly, these two young women from New York seemed genuinely excited by the opportunity of teaching the children.

In the morning, the two classes met for opening exercises. Ros played "My Country 'Tis of Thee" on the piano and learned that few of the children knew even the first verse. She also had to teach them the Pledge of Allegiance. "Dotty does the speechifying," Ros wrote, "and reads the Psalms. She does it with all the composure of an experienced hand too!"

Dorothy attributed whatever success she had to her preparatory work with Miss LeMay in Auburn. It "has meant everything to me, for I have a definite system and could go right at it. The children love it and are going to do very well, I hope." She asked all of her students to come up to the front and sit on a long bench where they recited their lessons, "and they simply convulse me," she wrote, "as they sit there swinging those bare legs. . . ." She worked hard at arranging the best sequence of lessons, and in the early weeks, she changed it every day. Ros took a photograph of Dorothy in front of her class. She looks small in the large room, standing behind her high desk, but reasonably in command, the blackboard covered with her day's lesson and Ray's birthday announced in the corner. An American flag is pinned on the wall to her right, and the children are attentive, except for two boys whose faces are blurred as they turn to see what their friends are up to.

She listed her students for Milly: Ray and Roy Hayes ("Ray is the biggest boy and not all there"); Rudolph, Jesse, and Oliver Morsbach ("my cutest ones, *all* look exactly alike, talk every minute"); Tommy and Minnie Jones, two of ten children ("Tommy can't say an 's' and is an imp," Minnie "is very shy and demure — dressed so prettily in little checked ginghams with sunbonnet to match"); Jimmy and Robin Robinson ("very demure & good"); and Richard Ferguson, Leila's brother ("very bright & good").

Ros taught algebra, Latin, ancient history, history of the U.S., geography, and English. She wrote, "As soon as we get things going there will be other things — like sewing (a'hem!) and domestic science (a'hem! a'hem!!) that we'll have to have occasionally!" She found that although the students could read adequately and were hungry for work in English, they were not well grounded in mathematics. Recalling the help she'd gotten from her father as a child, she mentioned one kind of question that she'd never been able to solve, let alone explain: "I shall sigh for Papa on those Arith. problems!! His letter and the enclosures on 'Lost Motion' were so welcome. We laughed heartily over the latter." Dorothy was even more fearful of the subject. "We had perfectly terrible problems," she later said about her experiences in seventh and eighth grade. "You remember those old things about men digging a ditch and rowing against the current upstream, and oh, the percentages and everything."

Before too long, Rosamond was sounding more self-assured, telling her parents that both she and Dotty were getting their work systematized, and that the children were beginning to take hold. Her algebra and Latin came back to her, and she particularly liked teaching the ninth grade. "I'm very good on English and composition — but I hope to improve." The adults who came to Sunday school were astounded by their postcard albums of the tour of Europe — pictures of the Eiffel Tower and the Gothic churches and turreted lakeside resorts of Austria, Germany, and Italy. Thinking back to the way things were done in Auburn, Ros said they hoped to give some "Travel Talks" in the winter.

Ros told Dorothy that she looked 100 percent better than she had in Auburn, and Dorothy said, "I never felt so full of health and good spirits." Even waking up at dawn was a pleasure. She wrote to Milly, "It is perfectly amazing to me the way in which I have changed my hours, and you would hardly believe it if you could see me getting up a little before six, actually cheerful and animated! Eight-thirty is very apt to see us tucked under an astonishing patch-work quilt and sighing with joy as we hit our feather beds."

The school day, with a break for lunch at noon, ended at three-thirty. The teachers packed their meals in cut-plug tobacco tins, and Mrs. Harrison always added a piece of cake or pie. They generally stayed after school until six or seven P.M., working on the next day's lessons. One night the first week, they were caught in a storm on their ride home. Without any warning, the skies opened up and drenched the dry hills with a heavy rain. They put on their yellow ponchos, which they kept tied to their saddles, and stayed relatively dry. There were also occasional electric storms, which Ros described as "marvelous, lightning plays all about you, but it doesn't always follow that you have thunder and rain. — I presume the distances are responsible." When the lightning got close, the static electricity made their loose hairs stand on end, a signal to seek shelter.

As they arrived at the Harrisons' each evening, the family rushed out to greet them "like returning prodigals," as Dorothy put it. "We have the most sincere affection for them all, and our meals are always hilarious, we so mutually amuse each other — and such suppers!" Attentive as always to the pleasure of eating well, she wrote, "Hot fried chicken, big fresh peas cooked in cream and other vegetables, hot bread, cocoa or milk, and endless jams and pickles and some delicious dessert! The table groans with food." It didn't seem to occur to her that the seven-dollar weekly rent that she and Ros paid made much of this possible. Mr. H., as they referred to him, "asks such a sweet blessing." After supper, on clear nights, she and Ros went outside to admire the sunsets and the stars that appeared on all sides as darkness fell: "they are thick down to the mountain-tops —

great glowing eyes."

Frank Jr., who had dropped out of school after the eighth grade, refused their pleas to join Rosamond's class. He would have been older than any of the other students, and he later described himself as "too wild, I guess." He admired the teachers as "good sports from start to finish," though he was puzzled by their reaction to the lonely place where they had landed. "They were highly enthused over the whole deal. They couldn't take it in fast enough." They told him, he said, that they didn't think they could have done it "without Mother Harrison taking them in and making them a home. Well, turned around the other way, we didn't know what Mother could have done without them. They were quite a little comfort to Mother. It was kind of raw, the country was at that time. They were the highlight. They kind of broke the monotony for awhile, when those folks came and inhabited the schoolhouse."

Mrs. Harrison, Dorothy said, "evidently can't make out *why* we are teaching if we don't have to." Work was her life, not an aspiration. She asked them one evening, "You girls aren't here for the money you can make, are you?" and warned that it would be expensive for them to feed their horses in the winter. Ros told her parents, "She has been perfectly lovely to us — but she has fired questions at us, until she knows our life histories, and it's not her fault that she doesn't know our fathers' incomes! She evidently feels that we are different from the ordinary schoolmarms — and she is so concerned about us — and our comfort."

Galvanized by Mrs. Harrison's energy and fortitude and unfailing good humor, they tried to satisfy her curiosity about the books they read and what they taught at school. They were also grateful for her kindness as they ineptly tackled basic household chores. Dorothy described how they had set out to launder their silk shirts the first week, walking to the sulfur spring for water, then heating it on the stove. "We spent *all* of yesterday P.M. doing them," Dorothy wrote, "and she went into hysterics at our efforts. . . . *How* are we going to teach domestic science?" Mrs. Harrison took the contents of their laundry bags into the kitchen, and when they got home, they found everything washed and ironed on their bed. She told them, "You girls aren't used to doing this sort of thing, and I am." She charged them a dollar extra each week for doing their wash.

The teachers found their work strenuous but rewarding: preparing for classes, attending to the children's diverse academic needs, and seeing that everyone was paying attention and behaving. Dorothy said: "The most thrilling and satisfactory time in my day, is the time devoted to storytelling. . . . They make a mad scramble to pick up all loose papers, put their desks in order — and then fold their hands and sit at attention! When I stand there and look down at those eager little faces — I forget how naughty they are, and I try to thrill and please them as I never tried before." On Fridays, "I tell them about current events if I know any, and then two children from each room recite, they hang onto their suspenders & dig a grimy toe into the floor & just agonize through it."

Ferry was pleased with the "schoolmarms," as he teasingly called them. He wrote to Ros's mother, telling her that the young ladies were winning their way into the hearts of all the people in Elkhead. "Mrs. Harrison told me she couldn't say which one she liked best because she thought them both perfect. They have taken hold of the work with enthusiasm and as circumstances arise, their resourcefulness will be called into play, but there is no question about their making a success of the work and in all probability one which will be of big and lasting value to our whole county and state, and being blest with a good sense of humor they will enjoy everything as they go along."

They always welcomed his visits to the school. For one thing, he was their mail carrier to and from Hayden, although occasionally an absentminded one. "At last," Ros wrote, "the letters we wrote you three weeks ago to-day turned up in Mr. Carpenter's coat pocket I believe. At any rate, he told us Friday that he had found 'em and started them along." He ran a civics class, read Tennyson to the children, led the Boy Scout troop, and once the domestic-science class was under way, he helped out in the basement kitchen. He knew considerably more about cooking than Dorothy and Ros did, and one day, the *Republican* reported, he "gave a demonstration in corn bread making, old bachelor style. The corn bread was fine."

Dorothy was charmed but exasperated by the boys. At noon, they grabbed their tin pails, gobbled down their lunches, and chased woodchucks and squirrels until they were called back inside, or until someone got hurt. One morning she broke up three fights, and she spent many lunchtimes and recesses doctoring cuts with medical plasters and emollients from a kit provided by Ros's aunt Nellie. Virtually every day, she pulled out splinters and tended to cracked feet. "A trip to the 'First Aid' box is a panacea for all ills," she said. "My boys . . . say such funny things — but they are regular imps of Satan, too." Slow Ray "is a fine butt for all their teasing, they are such heartless little demons, & then he flies at them and the result is a pitched battle. When I say anything, he hurls himself on the ground and bursts into tears, which was disconcerting at first but I am learning to manage him. The day simply flies."

In class, Rudolph Morsbach, age ten, corrected Dorothy when she told the children that London was the biggest city in the world: "No, *Mam,* my father says New York is!" Dorothy responded, " 'Would you care to teach the class, Rudolph?' He wilted for a moment, then a happy look crossed his face and he said, 'Well, it *might* have been Kansas City!' " Dorothy was reading from the Book of Genesis about Joseph one morning when Rudolph the irrepressible, as Dorothy called him, volunteered: "Miss Woodruff, Papa told us about that & we have a book about it — at home, Miss

Woodruff, which you hain't never saw, Miss Woodruff." She replied sternly, "Never mind now, Rudolph," as the rest of the class giggled, but, she noted, "you might as well try to stop the north wind." He also informed her that Mr. Carpenter was the president of the United States. The boys ignored her warnings about the dangers of throwing rocks until she bribed them with the promise of a gift of rubber balls — a real inducement, since their own were made of string. One day Dorothy reported, "Rudolph cracked Tommy over the head with a board & nearly killed him."

Ros, with her far more sedate class, mostly girls, soon wrote to her mother that school was going nicely, "although my whole program was upset by the appearance of a new ungraded pupil; — they drop in all the time. The fights among the small boys continue to cause much excitement — they keep Dotty on the jump." She thanked her mother for sending a collection of Hans Christian Andersen fairy tales, saying that Dotty had been longing for stories to read to her students. There was always a need for more books. Carpenter wrote to Harrick's book store in Denver, identifying himself as the treasurer of rural School District No. 11, Routt County. He asked whether he could set up an account and immediately procure three copies of *Rip Van Winkle* and six copies of *Ivanhoe,* adding that he would like a 30 percent discount.

While Ros juggled her academic subjects, Dorothy confronted the matter of corporal punishment. The Harrisons' oldest daughter, Marjorie, who had taught at the Little Bear School, about fifteen miles north of her parents' ranch, visited the two classes one day and gave some advice to the novices. For one thing, she thought that Dorothy needed to exert stronger control over the boys. Dorothy was not convinced: "How *could* I spank those children? I have already reduced three to tears by 'after-school reproofs' and I think that is better than beatings."

A few weeks later, she was beginning to get a slightly surer handle on the situation. She wrote to her father: "Yesterday at recess Ray . . . now my devoted ally, came rushing in to tell me that 'Jimmy was getting the floor bloody something awful!' " Dorothy tore out, and "there was Jimmy having a nose bleed while the rest of the boys stood around in cold, unsympathetic silence." She asked what had happened, and Jimmy sobbed, "Rudolph punched my face," to which Rudolph replied, "Yes, ma'am, and

I'll do it again if he don't let me alone!"

Dorothy ordered Rudolph to get a pail of water and scrub up the bloody remains of the fray. He said the winter snow would take it off, but Dorothy stood over him until it was done. "You see how hardened I have become and I am as cool now as a regular nurse." She added: "The minute it is over, [they] are the best of friends. But I am determined to stop this fighting if I can. I had a visit from an irate mother the other day whose son's face resembled an ancient tomato when he got home, but I don't see what I can do about it after they leave school."

Over time, her attitude evolved even further. At the end of September, she wrote that her week had been very hard, "for the children were *so* bad — I wielded the ruler with great effect on green-eyed Roy yesterday & he is such a coward that I hope he will be scared into being good for some time. . . . They all lie with skill, & I can't find out who is the guilty one." Once when she had her back turned as she was mending a chart, her adhesive plaster disappeared from the table. They all swore they hadn't seen it. The next day Rudolph met her outside with the plaster in his hand, saying he had found it behind the barn. Dorothy told them that no one could have recess until the guilty one confessed. After a long silence, Jimmy's six-year-old brother, Robin Robinson, spoke up: "I did it." Dorothy let the others go and "tried to talk to him seriously but his great brown eyes fairly danced & he has a thatch of light hair which stands on end — & he is *so* irresistible in his rags & dirt!" When she asked why he hadn't told her before, he replied, "I didn't think I did it until today!" On October 26 she reported that the week had included only two whippings.

Dorothy affectionately described twelve-year-old Tommy Jones as "my despair." He "looks like an angel and is the worst of the lot. He can't say an 's' and when I try to get him to say it, he just hides his face and won't say a word. He doesn't know *anything,* just never having tried, and his spelling is a work of art." One Saturday in August, Tommy appeared at the Harrison ranch, "clutching a turnip as big as a cabbage in one hand, a squash under one arm, and a bunch of poppies squeezed in his hot little hand!" Mrs. Harrison asked him to stay for their midday dinner, and afterward he climbed up behind Dorothy on Rogan, and she and Ros took him home.

The Joneses lived in a tiny log cabin about

a mile and a half northeast of the Harrisons. It was beautifully situated in a clump of "quakers," with a thriving vegetable and flower garden. The cabin was divided into two rooms. The living room contained a sewing machine, one homemade chair, a long wooden box with a quilt over it (the family's supply closet), and an antiquated phonograph — a present from an uncle, the teachers were told. The logs were pasted over with newspapers, and the floor was bare. "The place was neat as wax," Ros wrote, "but pitifully empty." The Joneses had encountered rough times in Michigan and "came out here with *nothing,*" Dorothy said, "and after 6 years they practically have no furniture at all."

Soon after their move to Elkhead, the entire family had come down with amoebic dysentery, and four-year-old Herbie didn't survive. As Carpenter recalled, he and Mrs. Murphy, the able pioneer, had gone up to help. Sending the two oldest boys outside with water for the men digging the grave, Mrs. Murphy took a kettle of potatoes off the stove, threw the contents outside, and filled it with fresh water and some rice that she had brought with her. As the water boiled, she took out an old black underskirt and tore it into strips. She had the older girls use it to line the inside of the coffin, and fashioned two miniature pillows to cushion each side of Herbie's head. In the absence of a clergyman, Carpenter presided over the service with his Bible, and he remembered the quavering voices singing the hymn "Nearer My God to Thee."

When Dorothy and Ros arrived at the cabin, Tommy's parents had just gotten back from the school, where his mother had played the piano, and Herbert, the custodian, did some masonry. Ros wrote to her father that Mrs. Jones had played for seven hours — "practicing all her old pieces and had been blissfully happy at touching a piano again." The Joneses insisted that the teachers stay for supper. "I never saw a finer spirit of hospitality," Dorothy said.

The two parents, the children, and their guests couldn't all sit down at once. The kitchen consisted of a tiny stove, a rough-hewn table with two benches, and two chairs that had lost their backs. The table was covered with an oilcloth, a few china plates, tin cooking dishes, and a silver pitcher — a "relic of former prosperity!" The Joneses had no cows, and, Ros wrote, "they gave us their best for supper — poor things — they make flour and water do in place of the cream sauce Mrs. H. always cooks her vegetables in. I have three of the girls in my room — and they're so nice and well-behaved." Dorothy, who had sweet Minnie and rambunctious Tommy in her class, noted that Mrs. Jones kissed them goodbye and said such nice things about them that they almost cried.

On the way back to the Harrisons', Dorothy and Ros stopped at the Hayeses' house. One of the teachers' duties was to pay calls on the children's parents, to get a better sense of the "conditions" at home. It was a less happy visit. "Mrs. Hayes is a gaunt, silent woman with the sadness of ages in her face," Dorothy wrote. "She told us all the details of losing a little girl last spring. Ray and Roy hung on the door & were too shy to come in. Ray was a strange picture in overalls which had one leg torn off above his knee while the other dangled around his ankle," but, she added, "He has become my strong ally and doesn't give me any real trouble except for occasional wild bursts of tears. I tell you there is nothing monotonous about my days."

11
THE MAD LADIES OF STRAWBERRY PARK

Dancers at the Main Lodge, 1920s

When Dorothy and Ros had difficulty with their classes, they reminded themselves how much progress they had already made. In the early weeks after their arrival, they had spent every spare moment cramming for the state exams, knowing that if they didn't pass, Elkhead would be stranded without teachers, and they would return to Auburn in disgrace.

School was closed on Wednesday, August 14, for three days, and at seven A.M., they started on their forty-eight-mile journey to Steamboat Springs. They tied their bags and bundles to leather thongs attached to their saddles, hanging their sport suits separately, so they wouldn't wrinkle. Lewis rode behind Ros, and they stopped a few miles east of the Harrisons' at the Fredericksons' house. A couple of Swedish descent who had arrived from Nebraska in 1909, the Fredericksons lived on a ridge above Elkhead Creek in a cheerful log cabin with ruffled curtains and geraniums at the windows. They called it Sunny Shelf Farm.

The Fredericksons had come for dinner at the Harrisons' recently, and Ros described the two children as "fat as butter." She said, "I wish you could have seen those Swedish children 'stoke' the food. We had this for a menu — delicious cold ham — fried potatoes — peas — Lima beans — beet greens — beets — radishes — pickled peaches — gooseberry jam — pickles — lemon pie — milk — bread and butter and last but not least stewed tomatoes. Every one of the vegetables came from the H's garden and never have I tasted better." The two children, five and seven, "made away with all the various dishes set before them; but the tomatoes made the biggest hit. They passed their saucers again and again and the little boy sat and ate on long after we had all finished. Then his mother remarked later that he had grown so thin!"

The steep hillsides behind the Frederickson house provided good pastureland, and they were able to grow alfalfa and grains, but they soon found, like other Elkhead homesteaders, that 160 acres were not enough to provide for their family. Arthur Frederickson stacked hay each summer on the Adair ranch and mined coal for his neighbors in the winter at nearby wagon mines, small enterprises run by one or two men. Loads were hauled out by horses and sold by the wagon rather than by the ton. Others found additional sources of income by logging or by trapping animals and selling the hides.

When the teachers dismounted, Ros realized that her suit skirt had come untied and slipped off. She asked Lewis to look out for it on his way back, and told her family, "Think of my losing my suit skirt off my saddle and sailing about Steamboat in that dreadful khaki skirt for four days!" Mrs. Frederickson, a strong, husky woman, had agreed to take them the rest of the way to

Hayden. She drove an immense pair of horses hitched to a lumber wagon. Dorothy and Ros rolled around in back with the two plump Frederickson children and Miss Rench, who boarded with the family that year. She, too, was taking the exams. "We crossed 12 streams and went through 15 gates!" Dorothy wrote. "You can't conceive of anything like it, and we even *took down* a barbed-wire fence!" When they reached Hayden four and a half hours later, they had lunch at the inn and studied all afternoon. Ferry arrived at 6:45 to escort them to the depot.

The train ride took them through the valley to Steamboat Springs. The tracks followed the rushing Yampa River into a landscape of cultivated fields, a few large ranches with hundreds of grazing cattle, unbroken miles of shaggy fifty-foot cottonwoods, and, as they approached town, ponderosa pines and firs. The smooth-skinned aspens, with their pale green fluttering leaves, looked impossibly delicate by comparison. After dingy little Hayden, Steamboat Springs felt like a city — a town of about twelve hundred people centered on the generously scaled main street, Lincoln Avenue, and surrounded by mountains on all sides. "The air fairly sparkles, just like

Cortina," Dorothy wrote. "It is surely as beautiful as any watering place over there."

The setting may have resembled parts of the Old World, but the atmosphere was unmistakably American West, and Dorothy and Ros were no longer twenty-two-year-olds on a prolonged holiday. F. M. Light & Sons billed itself as "the pioneer clothing store of Northwestern Colorado." Men shopped there for cowboy boots, overalls, suits, and hats. One of its maxims was "A customer is not a cold statistic . . . he is a flesh-and-blood human being with feelings and emotions like our own, and with biases and prejudices." A & G Wither Mercantile offered everything from toothpicks to barbed wire. After their quarters at the Harrisons', the Steamboat Cabin Hotel felt sumptuous, with its gabled roof, contrasting wood trim, wraparound porch, and a room that looked out onto the river and the mountains. Dorothy noted afterward, "the nervous strain of the exams was *awful* for everyone makes so much of them here and you realize you are a public official. . . . They weren't as bad as they might have been, by any means, but *so* silly, and taking ten [actually, twelve] exams in two days is not a pleasure trip!"

The tests, taken by a few dozen women

and overseen by Emma Peck, who was the Colorado county schools superintendent from 1896–98 and again from 1912–20, were given in the district courthouse. Dorothy and Ros noticed that there was a one-eyed man kicking back in the corner, and they agreed that he must be one of the "spotters" they had been told would be in attendance, but later, they found out that he was a janitor. The subjects were arithmetic, reading, penmanship, physiology, orthography, history, school law, grammar, theory and practice (of teaching), geography, civil government, and natural science. Some of the questions were more idiosyncratic than they had expected, including "Describe the changes that take place in 'egg on toast' during the process of digestion," "Explain methods of bidding on and letting road work by contract," and "Give a physiological reason for not boxing children's ears." Ros wrote, "I presume we got through but not with very fine results, I fear. . . . I fell down on Colorado law and civil government."

On Thursday, after their first six-hour ordeal, they treated themselves to the hot sulfur baths down the street. They had not had an "all-over" since their night at the Brown Palace three weeks earlier. Ros loved the public swimming pool but found the stench of the water dreadful. In 1923 the town's founding father, James Crawford, described how he had been fascinated by "the very nest of springs" when he came upon them fifty years earlier, and how the sulfur "continues to the present time to attract the attention of the olfactories." The spring near the future site of the Moffat depot sounded then "exactly like a steamboat laboring upstream." That evening they got to know Mrs. Peck. She was three years older than Mrs. Harrison and about the same size. The state seemed to be full of invincible tiny women who never complained — a source of inspiration, particularly to Dorothy.

Mrs. Peck, formerly Emma Hull, first taught school at the age of sixteen in Clear Creek County, thirty-five miles west of Denver. Some of her students were older than she was. She liked to tell a story about a hulking seventeen-year-old who went home after the first day and told his mother that his teacher was "a little girl who isn't any bigger than a half pint." Three years later, Hull married Harry B. Peck, and in October 1883 they moved with their first two children to Hayden.

Dorothy described Mrs. Peck as "thoroughly delightful — and *such* stories as she told us! Originally her territory was as big as the state of Mass. . . . and she drove 1,200 miles her first year! She had four little children at the time she was teaching, took them all to school all day and kept house and did regular ranch work, too!" A reporter made the same observation a century later: "While she washed dishes, or mixed bread, or churned, she heard one child say his multiplication tables and upbraided another for never seeming to be able to learn the principal exports of Germany." Soon she was asked to teach at a new school in Craig, and when she heard she would have sixty-two pupils, she demanded that the board add another teacher for the older ones. It was the first "graded" school in the county. Like other frontier women, in addition to her work in the house and on the ranch, she took on wider duties as called for, delivering babies and closing the eyes of the dead.

The teachers finished the last exam on Friday afternoon, and that night Ferry turned up in Steamboat Springs and took them out for a celebratory steak dinner. He was on his way to Salt Lake City for his monthlong civilian military training at Fort Douglas. Although President Wilson was campaigning for his second term with the slogan "He Kept Us Out of War," the armed forces were preparing for possible American involvement in the European conflict. Carpenter had invited Bob Perry's sister Charlotte to join them. Charlotte had been two years behind them at Smith; Ros and Dorothy remembered her as an active participant in drama. She was tall and thin, with springy red hair and blue eyes. As one friend described her, she "moved like a bullet shot out of a machine gun." Charlotte, along with her own close friend from Smith, Portia Mansfield, had recently started the Rocky Mountain Dancing Club, later renamed the Perry-Mansfield Performing Arts Camp, hidden away in a corner of Strawberry Park, a few miles outside Steamboat Springs. The first of its kind in the country — more of a school, except in its rustic setup — it offered young women serious training in dance and theater. Charlotte insisted that they go see it and spend the night there.

The teachers readily agreed, curious about Charlotte and Portia and their ambitious undertaking. Ferry accompanied them on their two-mile walk through Steamboat Springs, along Soda Creek, and onto a narrow trail into the woods. Dorothy and Ros discussed school matters with him, aware that in his absence, they would be managing the school on their own.

Hiking along a trail of pine needles, they found themselves in a landscape that was completely unlike Elkhead — a densely forested hillside of fir trees and aspens that overlooked a green meadow and the close backdrop of the snowy Rockies. At the top of the steep bank above the creek, they passed six white canvas tents, their wooden floors built on a foundation of tree stumps. Partway down the hill, they came upon a clearing and the main lodge. It consisted of a dance studio, screened on three sides, and a big living room, its log walls stained dark, Elizabethan-style, and a stone fireplace at the far end. Hung on display were the skins of bears, coyotes, and wild cats — shot by Bob and Charlotte's older sister, Marjorie.

Charlotte, who was more artistic in her tastes, had always been uninhibited in her undertakings, pursuing her interest in theater despite her parents' misgivings. Once, when her father was in New York raising money for the Moffat Road, and she was taking part in a performance of *Robin Hood* at Miss Wolcott's School in Denver, she ripped the green felt off her father's billiard table for costumes. He had an explosive temper, but it didn't intimidate her. Her mother, Lottie, had expected her to be a Denver debutante. When she told her parents that she and Portia intended to start a dance camp, Sam Perry scoffed at the idea, but Lottie, more indulgent and open-minded than her husband, convinced him to let her try. He warned Charlotte that he would disinherit her if the camp failed.

They set out to make a go of things. Bob found a piece of land for them in Strawberry Park, and Charlotte and Portia spent two years in Chicago, living in Hull House, where they made enough money to buy the property. Charlotte gave Bible lessons and taught basketball, while Portia taught dance. In addition, Charlotte studied and taught drama and art, and Portia taught classes at the Hotel del Prado in classical, athletic, Russian, interpretive, eurythmic, toe, and social dancing. They also went to the Lewis Institute, where they convinced some Irish coffin-makers to show them how to make furniture that could be disassembled and screwed back together. They built a few large tables and a chair for the main cabin at the camp, then took them apart and put them on the train to Colorado.

There was an abandoned homestead on the property that served as Charlotte and

Portia's home — and soon as the camp's music room. They took blue theater curtains and hung them on rods held in place at either end by Y-shaped tree branches. Bob Perry loaned them half a dozen carpenters and an ill-tempered mule from the Moffat mine to help build the main lodge and the tents for campers. The two women worked alongside the men throughout the construction. They also cooked for them, and Charlotte had to tearfully consult with Bob when the workers threatened to quit, complaining that they couldn't eat the meals. Portia recalled, "He told us to soak the potatoes in grease, over-cook the meat, boil the coffee, and serve them soggy pie. We tried this formula, and they loved every bite."

The two made a good team. Portia, the self-confident, dreamy daughter of a Chicago lawyer, had rippling masses of auburn hair to her waist. Her father died soon after he saw her off to Northampton, and as a dance teacher, she largely supported herself, her sister, and her mother. At Smith, she had convinced the physical-education teacher, Senda Berenson — the sister of the art critic Bernard Berenson — to start a class in ballet. Berenson focused on classical technique while Portia experimented with an improvisational style inspired by

Isadora Duncan, whose work wasn't yet widely known.

In 1910, after graduation, Portia moved to Omaha. She had heard that the city had a vibrant cultural life, and she had no trouble getting work. She knew early on that, much as she loved to dance, her real gift was as a teacher. In Omaha, she saw Anna Pavlova, a former member of the Imperial Russian Ballet and the Ballets Russes, in *The Dying Swan,* a performance that she said changed her life. She was also strongly influenced by Sergei Diaghilev, whose "Russian dancers" had so impressed Dorothy and Ros in Paris. Like Diaghilev, Portia borrowed from many art forms — painting, drama, ballet, costume, and lighting — but she encouraged her students to move as naturally as possible.

As the camp got under way, Charlotte worked as chief set designer, costume-maker, and general manager. Portia was the choreographer. They enrolled fifteen students the first summer, including a girl from New York City whose parents, Francois and Mary Tonetti, were prominent sculptors and friends of Isadora Duncan. Alexandra Tonetti, who was thirteen that summer, recollected that Portia was "a sort of Greenwich Village artist," and Charlotte, rawboned and businesslike. "She grew straight and had never been twisted. Very Western." They made a profit of five hundred dollars after the first season and soon established a winter studio in New York and a summer traveling dance company. Sam Perry, no longer contemptuous about the venture, attended some of the performances and loaned them horses from his stable in Denver. Marjorie Perry led the students' afternoon and weekend trail rides. In coming years, the camp became nationally known for its superb teachers and choreographers and its experimental approach to the arts.

For the first decade, the camp was lit only with candles and kerosene. The hand pump drew water from the spring at the bottom of the hundred-foot cliff. The students made lanterns out of recycled peanut-oil cans, which they pierced in decorative patterns. A chandelier was created from a cast-off wagon wheel and hung from the ceiling. There were Indian rugs on the floors and flowers in an array of Indian baskets. Ros wrote to her parents about the living room, "really it is one of the loveliest and most artistic rooms I have ever seen." Dorothy and Ros could scarcely believe what Charlotte and Portia had accomplished in such a short time. Ros described the camp as "a dream come true, and these two girls saved every penny for it from their earnings as dancing teachers."

Many neighbors in Steamboat Springs, though, were shocked by the stories of barefoot young women in diaphanous dresses dancing on the lawn to the accompaniment of strange music. In the eyes of local ranchers, whose notion of dance was a good hoedown, the activities at the camp were sinful. They wouldn't allow their wives and daughters past the front gate, telling them that the two madwomen were in league with the devil. Milk and butter deliveries were left in the creek, to be picked up later in the morning.

Ros and Dorothy spent the next day at the camp, watching the students rehearse. "They dance in filmy costumes of chiffon — Greek style — and all colors," Ros wrote. "It was a fascinating sight — such a contrast between the Rocky mountain setting and the return to Rome and Greece." At noon, Bob drove up from Oak Creek, bearing freshly shot grouse. They spent the afternoon together and had a picnic with him at camp. "This Bob Perry," Dorothy wrote, "is very attractive and saved our lives by offering to bring us home by machine." Ros, for her part, was beginning to take more than a friendly interest in Bob, with his fine features, athletic prowess, and generosity.

They left the camp at eight-thirty on Saturday night, drove back to Steamboat Springs, where they picked up their belongings at the hotel, and continued on to Hayden, a three-hour drive. Several days earlier, when they had registered at the Hayden Inn, the proprietor announced to Dorothy and Ros, "You schoolmarms want to marry some rich ranchers & settle out here." Dorothy was sure they scandalized him when they showed up close to midnight with the most desirable bachelor in the county.

Bob called for them at five the next morning, and they stole out in the dark. It turned out to be a beautiful late-summer day, and his little Dodge somehow conquered the steep grades to Elkhead. Dorothy wrote, "We came sailing over the new road; when it looked impossible, we would get out, figure out the one way, and plow on." To the Harrisons' amazement, they got to within a mile of the house, the first time an automobile had ever made it that far. Bob carried their suitcases, they took their bundles, and they reached the house by seven A.M.

After a hasty glass of milk, he hurried back to meet his father at the mine in Oak Hills. "Imagine being escorted home 60 miles!" Dorothy wrote. "It has been *some* trip I can assure you — each night in a different bed and every hour crammed full! We were so glad to get home and had a most enthusiastic welcome from the Harrisons who were bursting with pride over a new Sears Roebuck stove & a new brass bed in our room!" What was more, Lewis had found Ros's lost skirt, caught in some sagebrush, when he had returned with their horses on Wednesday.

They soon received their teacher's certificates, signed by Emma H. Peck. Dorothy's average was 90 5/12, and Ros's, 90 5/6. Dorothy wrote to her father, "It is a great satisfaction for of course everyone will know it and they will have much more confidence in us now." Ros, noting the uncanny similarity in their scores, said, "Mother Dear, . . . Well, Dotty and I are overcome at these magnificent grades. . . . I think Mrs. Peck must have been perjuring her soul, to give them to us."

12
DEBUT

Dorothy and Ferry at Oak Point, 1916

Every August, Ferry Carpenter held a birthday party for himself at Oak Point, transforming his quiet bachelor's cabin into a boisterous all-night dance that drew more than a hundred guests, from many miles

247

away. That year he saw the occasion as a "kind of coming out party" for the teachers. On the evening of the party, Dorothy and Ros stayed at school until seven-fifteen, and then had an hour's ride to Oak Point, watching the sun set and the moon rise over the mountains. When they arrived, the party was well under way. Out front was a big bonfire of logs and brush, topped with an old washtub of coffee. The furniture had been moved outside to make room for the dancing.

"I wish you could have seen that picture," Ros wrote to her family. "The low ceilings — the log walls — dimly lighted by kerosene lamps — the musicians huddled over their fiddles, playing the strangest music, and the oddly dressed couples whirling through the steps of the square dances which are the popular thing here. . . . One dark complexioned cow puncher leaned against the door jamb calling the figures." They played quadrilles, waltzes, and two-steps, and she and Dorothy had more partners than they could count. "Bob Perry (whose sister I knew slightly at Smith) was there and so nice to us. He whisked us through the quadrille in great shape." Still, she added, "Mr. C.," for the first time dressed up in a white shirt and tie, "was a better dancer than Mr. P."

Ros was aware that, even in that peculiar locale, she was acting the part of a traditional debutante. Ferry's party was far more diverting than the balls at the Owasco Country Club, but she couldn't take seriously most of the men who presented themselves to her. One bachelor, a pig farmer named Roy Lambkin, asked her to be his company at supper. Lambkin had helped Carpenter break up his land and plant crops in his early years as a homesteader. "I had to lay down the law to him later," she wrote, "and assure him that schoolmarms hadn't a moment to themselves — Sundays were our busiest days!" She didn't add that the afternoons were reserved, after church, for Bob and Ferry.

Twenty-four-year-old Everette Adair, the son of the wealthy rancher John Adair, was especially persistent. The object of frequent jokes between Ros and Dorothy about his flamboyant style of dress and his flashy rings, he showed up at the house a few weeks later, leading two horses. When they consulted with Mrs. Harrison about the propriety of going riding with him, he poked his head inside and answered for her: "They will be just as safe as tho they were in the arms of Jesus." Still, as Dorothy put it after the party, the real "belle of the ball" was Carpenter's newly installed bathroom. Ferry wrote more graphically, "Everywhere guests rushed up to me and said: 'Happy Birthday! Show me the flush toilet!'"

At midnight, Mrs. Murphy served a supper of sandwiches, cake, and ice cream outside. Afterward, fueled by food and coffee, the dancers picked up the pace, and the fiddlers started a double quick. "How I wish you could have seen us madly dancing around those two small low-ceilinged rooms!" Dorothy wrote to her father. Ferry, in a letter to his parents, said that it was the fastest music he had ever "stepped to," but his partner was Annie Elmer, the prize hay pitcher of Morgan Bottom — the productive flat land just north of the Yampa River — and they had no trouble keeping up. "Round and round we tore — it was fine with the floor all to ourselves — an occasional whoop or yell of encouragement as 'Stay with 'em Tex' or 'Go to it Ferry,' & soon we all had our coats off & the sweat a rolling off of us — well there were no quitters & after nearly an hour the musicians gave it up & slowed down to a last step & quit amid much shouting & clapping."

By daybreak, the babies were asleep in their mothers' arms; most of the older children were piled upstairs in the loft on some bedding Ferry had strewn about. But Tommy Jones was still wide awake at five A.M. He told Ros, " 'Ere were 'ifteen auto 'ere 'at night!" She commented, "He can't talk any other way but he's cute as he can be." At six-thirty, the musicians played "Home Sweet Home," and people began getting into their rigs and autos. The two women rode wearily home and slept until noon.

Dorothy wrote to her father that it was "a never-to-be-forgotten experience," an impression Ros confirmed over sixty years later, when she said that as they rode back to the Harrisons', she realized it was "the first time in my life that I'd seen the sun set, moon rise, the moon set, and the sun rise all in one night."

At the time of the party, they had been in Elkhead under a month, and they reveled in their new social life. Carpenter and Perry were engaged in a serious but gentlemanly rivalry over Ros. Bob, despite his reserved temperament, was making his intentions clear. Ferry was less overt. He knew that Bob, with his collegiate good looks and promising career prospects with the Moffat Coal Company, was the more likely suitor.

His own future in the cattle business was uncertain. Still, he may have hoped that he could win Ros with his quick mind and appealing personality. In any case, the competition didn't interfere with the two men's friendship. If anything, it brought them closer together.

Virtually every Sunday until the worst of the winter weather, Bob made the forty-five-mile trip from Oak Creek to Hayden. It was another ten miles on horseback to Oak Point, then he and Ferry rode the final five miles together to the Harrison ranch. Bob's daughter-in-law, Ruth Perry, said, "It is remarkable that there was any courtship at all, given the distance." Bob's father, Sam, was known for his relentless work ethic, and "he was not one to give anyone much time off." Frank Harrison, Jr., observed the suitors at dinner each week with lively interest. Looking back on those months as an older man, he described Ferry and Bob as "young fellows with tail feathers blooming."

At the time, Frank Jr. was also trying to impress the women, as was virtually every other unmarried man in the vicinity. The county fair in Hayden, held at the end of the summer, attracted residents from all over Routt County, and the town and the fairgoers dressed for the occasion. The streets were ablaze with "Old Gory," as one of Dorothy's schoolchildren called the American flag. The students all had haircuts and looked "positively stylish." Everette Adair was wearing a bright red satin shirt and sash, a tan plush sombrero, high-heeled boots with jangling spurs, and his flashing rings. Frank whispered to Dorothy in awe-struck tones, "That shirt put him back seven and a half." Lefty Flynn, a strapping former Yale fullback from Greenwich, Connecticut, who had come west with the dream of becoming a cowboy, had bought the Harrisons' first ranch and "was the second best in the costume line — he had on a leather waistcoat embroidered in highly colored beads, front and back, & leather sleeves! Lefty had proved that Colorado isn't always dry — & was having a time." Although the state had banned alcohol in January 1916, four years before national prohibition, liquor flowed freely in Oak Creek and was not hard to come by in outlying towns.

The teachers picked up some packages at the post office, including one from Bob, which contained bunches of sweet peas for the women to wear that day. Then Frank escorted them to the fairgrounds, paid their entrance fee, offered to buy them pink lemonade, and secured good grandstand seats for the competitions. "I never saw such instinctive courtesy as these people have," Dorothy said, not considering that — nine years younger than they were — he might have amorous hopes of his own.

Dorothy and Ros watched the bucking horses, the ladies' race, and a relay race in which saddles were changed "in the twinkling of an eye." The festive mood darkened when a horse swerved and crashed through a fence, rolling down a bank. The rider escaped with a few broken bones, but the horse had to be put down. Frank accompanied the women to lunch at the Hayden Inn, and later, they ran into Isadore Bolten, a Jewish émigré from White Russia — Elkhead's most unusual bachelor. Carpenter had told them about Bolten's near mythic journey to the American frontier. His mother had died when he was a little boy, and he had learned the cobbling trade from an uncle. In his late teens, he wandered through Europe, stopping in libraries to read whatever he could find about the American West. He traveled to New York by steerage and borrowed some money from a cousin to get to Chicago, where he worked at Marshall Field's, then opened a cobbler shop. At night he learned English at Hull House, eventually finding his way to Elkhead, determined to become a rancher. Bolten told the schoolteachers in his thick accent, "I looked and looked for you young ladies to take you to dinner!" Ros wrote, "We were overcome by our popularity!"

Actually, she and Dorothy were accustomed to being admired and pampered, and they were baffled by occasional flare-ups of resentment. Iva Rench — a talented music and art teacher — was almost palpably hostile. She had been hired to teach at the tiny Mountain View School, not at grand Elkhead; it never occurred to Dorothy and Ros to wonder why or to think about how that might aggravate her. "Miss Rench descended on us one day," Dorothy wrote, accompanied by her class of four. "She seems to be awfully jealous of us, for some unknown reason — and like lots of good people, is very irritating. She didn't say *one* nice thing about the school or give us a friendly word." Then she added, "However, she helped me tremendously with suggestions and I was too grateful to be mad, as Ros was."

When Dorothy had to visit the dentist in Hayden, he charged her only a dollar — half price. Ros speculated it was because he took pity on her as an impoverished schoolteacher. Dorothy bantered with the dentist,

255

saying that he would never get rich at those rates. This companionable exchange infuriated the next patient: "I suppose she thought he would make it up on her," Dorothy commented.

Dorothy and Ros still didn't know about Ferry's ingenious matchmaking scheme. He, however, had discovered a secret of Dorothy's. Soon after the teachers' arrival, he noticed that she was receiving frequent letters from Grand Rapids, Michigan. He correctly surmised, before Dorothy's parents did, that — somehow, somewhere, between her departure from Auburn and her arrival in Hayden — she had been spoken for.

Six months before her trip to Colorado, Dorothy had met a twenty-nine-year-old banker, Lemuel Hillman, in Grand Rapids, where she and Ros were visiting childhood friends Betty and Monroe Hubbard. Hillman had roomed with Hubbard at Colgate, and he was a guest at a dinner the Hubbards threw for their houseguests. Hillman looked the part of a banker of that era, serious and trustworthy, with his short hair parted on the side and combed back from his brow, a pair of pince-nez often perched on his nose. His father ran a rubber business in New York City, and after graduation Lemuel worked at the United States Rubber Company in Philadelphia, intending one day to take over his father's plant. However, his mother, whom he adored, died suddenly, and his father remarried within the year. He and his stepmother did not get along. In 1911 Hubbard asked him to join a bond business he and some other friends were starting in Grand Rapids. Hillman needed no convincing to make the move. When Dorothy met him, he had just entered an investment-banking firm called Howe, Snow, Corrigan & Bertles.

She found him more entertaining than expected. He shared her intense curiosity about other people, and her sense of humor. She spent the evening talking to him in the parlor, and the next day he took her out to lunch and showed her his new office. They saw each other every day that week.

After Dorothy returned to Auburn, Hillman wrote to say that he had work to do in New York City and that he would like to stop and see her. Her family approved of him, and he visited again on the way back. They took a walk in Fort Hill Cemetery, where she showed him the monument to Chief Logan and her other favorite spots. When they sat down to rest on a bench overlooking the Woodruffs' house and garden, he asked her to marry him. Flustered, she said that she had given Rosamond her word about the trip to Colorado and that she couldn't possibly think of marriage just then. "He didn't like that very well," she recounted in later years. Disappointed but resolute, he wrote to her every day. When he learned that she and Ros would be spending the night in Chicago on their way to Denver, he insisted on meeting her there.

Dorothy agreed to have lunch with him. In a letter to her mother, she described the place he had chosen — the Blackstone Hotel, a luxurious establishment in the theater district — as "the most attractive hotel I have ever been in, outside of Paris." The air "was artificially cooled by refrigeration, and it was simply blissful" on that 90-degree day. Hillman ardently pressed his case, but Dorothy was concerned that people at tables nearby would overhear him. He impatiently paid the check and hailed a taxi. They followed Lake Shore Drive out of the city, and when they reached a long stretch of beach, he asked the driver to pull to the side. They got out to take a walk, and she finally said yes. "I realized," she said, "that I really was very much in love with him and he was the man I wanted to spend the rest of my life with."

He took her back to Mr. Underwood's house, but she wouldn't let him return that evening, saying that she didn't want to tell even Ros just yet. They agreed to marry as soon as she returned from Colorado. Further testing his self-restraint, she asked him not to disclose their news to anyone. She was especially determined to keep it from her parents, who were likely to demand that she return at once.

That night, buffeted by the heat, her excitement, and a loud thunderstorm, she couldn't sleep, but by the next morning she had recovered her equilibrium. She mentioned to her mother her lunch with Lem, adding that afterward they motored through the parks and along the lake. "It was so funny," she wrote, "to see crowds of people nonchalantly walking along hot city pavements in sketchy bathing suits."

Ros gleaned the truth on the train ride to Denver, when Dorothy absentmindedly said she had left her hairbrush in Grand Rapids. She reminded Dotty that they hadn't been anywhere near Grand Rapids, and wanted to know every detail about the proposal. Hillman ended up confiding in a motherly high school principal named Miss Daniels, with whom he was boarding. Dorothy had met her during her visit to the Hubbards and at the end of August, Miss Daniels wrote her a congratulatory letter, to which Dorothy responded: "It was a great comfort to hear from you — the first to know of our happiness" (Ros didn't count), "and it was so good of you to write me — It is all so new and unexpected — it all seems like a dream — and of course it seems much more so as I haven't yet written my family." She admitted that "Colorado would never have had charms for me if I had dreamed this would happen — but as long as I am here — I am finding it a fascinating life." And, she said wistfully: "I don't dare think how far off May is — won't you write to me some time, again?"

Ros, witnessing her friend's happiness about her engagement and her longing for Lem, inadvertently began to disclose her own state of mind. "What do you think?" she wrote to her aunt Helen the first week in October. " 'Hand and heart' marriages which mean getting your life-mate thru an agency are quite usual out here. I heard about one yesterday, the father of 2 pupils, and I simply gasped." Absorbed in a letter home on a nastily inclement day, she went on to offer some advice to her Aunt Helen, who wanted to buy a dog. Ros thought she should get an Airedale. She said a Scotch terrier would be too much trouble, and told her that Airedales "are so faithful and loyal, they'd stick to you and you can feed them anything." She had learned about them from Bob Perry, who owned two.

As if on cue, Mrs. Harrison called upstairs, "Yonder comes two fellahs on horseback." Perry and Carpenter were soaked and spattered with mud. "A regular hurricane at noon" had kept the women from Sunday school but hadn't deterred the men from their weekly visit. They spent the afternoon inside, sitting in the "best" room, as Ros put it, "the stove red hot and the folding bed serving as sofa, — five Harrisons and the four of us."

She made an affectionate observation about Ferry's choice of clothes: "You wouldn't dream any man could look as Mr. Carpenter did. Dot and I nearly expire over his costumes, — blue overalls, blue cotton shirt open at the neck and old rubber boots. Mr. Perry on the contrary wears a very nice-looking riding top and tends towards the immaculate." In that regard, he took after his father, Sam, whom a friend remembered as always "shaved and barbered to a hair," and dressed "like an English guardsman in mufti." Dorothy described Ferry as "the best 'raconteur' I ever heard. . . . He is so picturesque not only in appearance but his vivid cowboy slang and such wonderful insight into human nature. It really is a treat to have him as a friend."

Because of the lack of privacy at the Harrisons', Dorothy and Ros saved their intimate conversations for their horseback rides to and from school. Lem wrote long letters to Dorothy virtually every day; she had finally found a more copious correspondent than she. Her days were so full, she was able to reply only on Saturdays, and his letters were so long, she later said, that she read them as they jogged along to school. As Lewis rode ahead, she read some parts out loud to Ros, and they discussed the comparative merits of Ros's two suitors: Carpenter, the funny, intellectual risk-taker; and Perry, good-looking, steady, gallant — and well dressed.

That Sunday at the Harrisons', the men talked about the closely fought presidential race, in which Woodrow Wilson was running for a second term against Supreme Court Justice Charles Evans Hughes. Although the war was being fought from France to Russia, and the Allies needed help, Wilson pledged to remain neutral. Hughes continued to advocate greater readiness even after Wilson got a preparedness bill through Congress, and he criticized Wilson for his handling of the Mexican civil war. Teddy Roosevelt had dissolved the Progressive Party and endorsed Hughes. Bob was a firm Hughes man. Ferry was a Republican, but he remained a devout believer in Wilson, considering him surpassed only by Abraham Lincoln among American presidents. As he subsequently wrote, "Wilson's life *sunk* into the lives of many people who were fortunate enough to know or to hear or to read him. This to an unusual degree." Both passionately held forth, Dorothy swayed by Carpenter's arguments and Ros siding with Perry.

Everyone around the two women tailored conversations to their genteel sensibilities and did their best to keep them entertained. Dorothy and Ros never tired of the company of Carpenter and Perry, or of the Harrisons, who followed Bob's courtship of Ros with acuity. Mrs. Harrison ate some candy that Dorothy produced and laughed nervously at the lively political debate. "As for Mr. H.," Ros wrote, "he literally disappeared from view every now and then behind the sofa-cushions when he was too full of mirth.

It was an eventful afternoon for this house-hold as callers are almost an unknown quan-tity!"

Around that time, Mr. and Mrs. Harrison took them on a camping trip to California Park, a huge tract of public land laced with trout streams and pine forests in the moun-tains ten miles northwest of the house. On one Friday morning, as Dorothy and Ros went to school, the two Harrisons left to make camp, the horses loaded with supplies. Frank Jr., Lewis, and Ruth stayed behind to do the daily chores.

The teachers and children were distracted all day by the sight of dozens of cowpunch-ers rounding up cattle nearby, tearing around the schoolhouse and down the hill at breakneck speed. Dorothy wrote that it was a wonderful sight — "magnificent big creatures," galloping from one side to the other. "Sometimes we see hundreds of them in a long straight line silhouetted against the sky."

After school, one cowboy, a "dashing specimen," rode up to help them pack their horses: bedding, clothes, toothbrushes, and Ros's Kodak. They stared at his Mexican saddle, just sent to him, he told them, by a friend who had been in a fight with the "greasers." There was a hole through the back where the friend had killed a man. The saddle was stained with blood.

As they set out to meet the Harrisons, they were joined, Dorothy said, by a series of stunning-looking men in high, tooled boots with wicked spurs, chaps over their blue jeans, and sombreros. The men asked where they were going, "in the most frank curiosity — then told us to hurry," dubious about them riding such a long distance in unfamiliar territory, especially after dark. One man pressed matches on them in case they needed to build a campfire. Ros and Dorothy continued by themselves, exclaiming over the quakers, which were in their full autumn glory. "The sunset light on those sheets of gold with here & there a great black pine or a mass of red oak was the most superb riot of color I have ever seen," Dorothy wrote. As it got later, "the light would come in long shafts, just touching the tops, and it was positively ethereal."

Frank Jr., recalling how the teachers loved the fall in Elkhead, later said, "You know, after the frost had hit this country, we never thought anything about those quakers, they always turned yellow as soon as they frosted. They really marveled over the beauty of the country. You know, all we could see was the same old quakers." Ros and Dorothy climbed a narrow canyon bordering the Elk-head River, and there were tremendous bare cliffs on one side "which looked wrinkled with age, like 'The Ring' scenery and all we needed was 'Siegfried'!" Mrs. Harrison had tied rags to the trees for them to follow.

The horses began to flag, and as it got dark, the girls lost their sense of direction. They were reconciling themselves to a night in the brush when they heard a faint answer to their calls. Soon they were sitting around the campfire, wolfing down a supper of bacon, biscuits, and coffee. Mr. Harrison had made their beds — several layers of blankets with their slickers on top. They took off their shoes and crawled inside. In the morning, they looked out of their bedrolls at Mrs. Harrison making breakfast, "a little bit of a thin thing," wearing an old cap of Lewis's and his mackinaw, Ruth's divided skirt, and a gingham apron.

They packed up and rode off, stopping to fish at a spot called the Pot Holes, a series of boggy canyons where all of the streams drained and formed gravelly pools. Afterward, they took a shortcut home, a narrow cattle trail straight up Agner Mountain. Mr. Harrison had to chop down branches with his ax to make space for their wide loads. Ros, fully acclimated by then, described the ride as a "real corker" but said, "I'd ride one of these horses up a telegraph pole now and think nothing of it." Mrs. Harrison, though, did not like riding, and she screamed most of the way. Ros soothed her by talking about the trip her mother had taken down the Grand Canyon, telling her that " 'constant prayer' pulled her thru alive." Unconvinced, Mrs. Harrison got down and walked, and "Mr. H. guided his five lady passengers back to the home port, sans mishap."

■ ■ ■ ■

PART FOUR:
RECKONINGS

■ ■ ■ ■

"Hero No. 1"

13

THE CREAM OF ROUTT COUNTY

Oak Hills, 1915

The teachers worked Monday through Friday, and except for their morning duties at Sunday school and their preparations for the following week's classes, they were free on the weekends. Sometimes Bob managed to get to Elkhead on Saturday, to take the teachers on excursions without Ferry. They went with him on one "all day jaunt" to his future anthracite coal mine in Elkhead. "Mother dear," Ros wrote on September 2, "I am sitting under a pine tree with the most beautiful blue sky above — and a veritable grove of pines and quaking aspens about me. . . . We are having the best kind of a time. We rode all morning — now [Mr. P.] is interviewing the man who is in charge of the land while we sit and laze, until we eat our picnic lunch. The horses are grazing away nearby — and I wish you could see the whole scene — the little tent down between two hillsides covered with ferns and trees. We appreciate trees, after our sage brush."

As they were luxuriating, Bob's horse got loose, and when they noticed it was gone, they leaped up and began a frantic search, futilely calling and whistling. Perry got onto Dorothy's horse, Pep. She had traded in Rogan, offering a bonus, which the buyer refused. Pep was a small sorrel, and Bob galloped off, finally catching his horse halfway back to the Harrisons'.

The following weekend, he invited them to his house in Oak Hills, telling them he'd give them a tour of the Moffat mine. They would be joined by his sister Charlotte and Portia Mansfield, and by two young women from Lexington, Kentucky, who were coming for a visit. Dorothy and Ferry had discovered that each had a friend there: Anne Holloway, whom Dorothy knew from Smith; and Dot Embry, a Vassar graduate, whom Ferry had met when he was in law school. He had been sporadically wooing Dot for a few years, but without any apparent ardor.

On their way to pick up Dot and Anne at the Oak Creek depot, they drove to Bob's other property — a homestead in Twenty Mile Park, between Hayden and Oak Creek. It was set in a meadow of oat and wheat fields. Dorothy commented, "It is wonderful to see them break up sagebrush & change virgin land — into a fertile farm land." Bob's tiny shack was surrounded by "very high mountains all around which looked dark & cavernous as if they were peopled by gnomes, and I expected to see giants & ogres." After Bob spent some time talking to his overseer, they got back into the Dodge and "tore up, down, & around those mountains at a perilous pace and just reached Oak Creek as the train pulled in." Faced with three pairs of women, two of which contained "Dorothys," Bob simplified matters by calling Dot and Anne "The Kentuckys," and the teachers "The Auburns." Ros described the weekend as a lopsided house party, "the ratio being 6 ladies to 1 gentleman."

Bob's low-slung frame house in Oak Hills, its back porch strewn with saddle blankets and other paraphernalia, was even more comfortable and up-to-date than Ferry's cabin. It had electric lights, steam heat, a bathtub, and hot running water. Unwanted wildlife, though, shared it with him. Dorothy and Ros had learned from Marjorie Perry that during one of her recent visits, a pack rat had made off with one of her stockings, and she had to go home without it. Dorothy commented: "They are as big as cats, *on dit*, & called pack rats because they 'pack off' everything — that is cowboy slang for 'carrying away.' " The women slept in three double beds in the living room. They were chary of using Bob's blankets until he assured them that the previous guests had washed them. "Mr. Perry," Dorothy wrote, stayed on "the piazza, talking to us all the time."

The house stood on a bluff, overlooking an unsightly hamlet consisting of miners' boardinghouses, company stores, blacksmith shops, repair shops, an electric generator plant, and several shacks. The mines were in a narrow gulch with steep slopes covered by gnarled scrub oak. The main line of the railroad ran through the gulch, with several switch tracks leading to and from the tipple.

In 1916 workdays for the miners depended on the availability of railroad cars and market orders, and the mine usually closed down in the spring, reopening in September or October, when the weather got cold and demand for coal picked up. When the mines were working, steam hissed from numerous machines, whistles blew signals, and bells announced moving equipment. As cars were loaded, the racket was magnified by the sounds of the tipple shakers and coal falling into place. Coal smoke belched from the generator plants, locomotives, and steam-powered equipment. The burning slag pile emitted a stinking smoke of its own, and the air was filled with hot cinders that occasionally flew into workers' eyes. On a quiet Saturday afternoon, with the mines shut, Ros was able to focus on the "real grass terrace with lovely flower garden, whence came the sweet peas" for the county fair. Her determination to see the best of Oak Hills was the most overt indication so far that she was coming to reciprocate Bob Perry's feelings. Still, she added: "Oak Creek and Oak Hills are merely mining towns and very rough, — not at all like Hayden."

Ros was right. The culture of Oak Creek and the company town of Oak Hills, built for the miners and providing everything from housing and mess halls to doctors, bore no resemblance to the folksy atmosphere of Hayden or the bustle of Steamboat Springs. She and Dorothy, though, weren't privy to some of the more sordid characteristics of coal towns. Oak Creek — started by a disreputable operator named Sam Bell, who had been the sheriff and run the brothels in Cripple Creek — was built "to meet the needs of the men who dug the coal from the bowels of the earth and brought it to the surface for loading and shipping," wrote Paul Bonnifield, a former miner and local historian. "These miners were a special breed and they needed a town suited to their style." In addition to an Episcopalian church, respectable homes, and a log school outside town, Oak Creek had bars, gambling parlors, and brothels — or, as the church ladies later alluded to them over tea, "sporting houses."

The residents were German, Italian, Croatian, Slovenian, Czech, Greek, Turkish, Japanese, and African-American. The immigrant and African-American men, who had made their way west after the Civil War, worked in the mines. Their wives washed dishes, cleaned houses and commercial buildings, and in the summer picked lettuce and spinach on ranches in nearby Yampa. The immigrants formed their own clubs and gathered at one of the pool halls or gambling parlors after work. Italians (the most recent arrivals) and African-Americans lived in a neighborhood called Hickory Flats, near the tipple of the Pinnacle mine, owned by the Victor American Fuel Company. Hickory Flats consisted of dilapidated shacks coated with coal cinders and one-room cribs where prostitutes conducted business. It was known for stabbings and shootings, and the town marshal refused to go there after dark.

At times violent clashes arose. The local newspaper, the *Oak Creek Times,* gave matter-of-fact accounts of some incidents that occurred around the time Ros and Dorothy went to Colorado. "Man Beats Aged Miner: Murderous Foreigner Crunches Head of American"; "Mexican Meets Death by Severe Blow in Abdomen"; "Harry Gray . . . A Rope Rider, in Moment of Fear Plunges Sharp Instrument Through Heart of Routt County Boy." Women, alone during work hours at their homesteads in the countryside or their houses in town, were easy prey. In June 1917 a young woman was attacked by a Greek friend of her Italian husband. When her husband returned unexpectedly and came upon the friend pressing his wife against the kitchen table, one hand over her mouth, the other tearing off her clothes, he blew the man's brains out.

It was all part of the West's growing pains. Notwithstanding the Panic of 1893, brought on by excessive speculation in railroads, American industries and homes were voracious consumers of coal, and Sam Perry and David Moffat, who personified the symbiosis between mining and railroads, were determined to deliver it to them. In 1902 Moffat's railway company was organized with the financial backing of Perry; the future senators Charles J. Hughes, Jr., and Lawrence C. Phipps; and several other Colorado tycoons. The deal included the acquisition of twenty-seven hundred acres in Routt County, in an area known to be rich in bituminous coal. Perry convinced Moffat to route the railroad through Oak Creek. In return, he named his mining venture the Moffat Coal Company, although locals referred to it as the Perry mine.

Sam Perry had grown up on a farm in Nebraska and moved to Chicago, where he worked for a jeweler on Lake Street in the business district. The store burned down in the Great Chicago Fire of 1871, and Sam saved many of the goods. He married the boss's daughter, Lottie Matson, a delicate girl who suffered from severe asthma. Sam and Lottie spent their honeymoon in Georgetown, Colorado, one of the silver mining towns that had been established during the gold rush. A few years later, they settled in Denver, believing that the dry air would improve Lottie's health. Sam became one of the directors, then the president, of the Denver Tramway Company, which built the suburban line. He also began investing in gold and silver mines near Breckenridge and Dillon, and in the coalfields of Routt County.

By 1908 the Moffat Road had made it over the Divide and into Oak Creek. Sam Perry and his business associates also bought a flat, open property not far away that they called Phippsburg, after Sam rejected "Perryville." The area around Oak Creek was too narrow and steep for the railroad yards, roundhouse, and car and engine shops, so they were built in Phippsburg instead. Many believed that Oak Creek and Phippsburg were destined to be the two largest towns in Routt County. In 1908 the "townlet" of Oak Creek had fifty people;

four years later, it was bigger than Steamboat Springs — 1,033 registered voters, compared to 954. By then five other mining companies had set themselves up in the vicinity of Oak Hills.

On business trips from Denver, Perry and Moffat stayed in Moffat's personal railcar, the *Marcia,* named after his daughter. It had an interior of cherry mahogany, oak, brass, silk, and stained glass. The floor was carpeted, and the wallpaper was embossed velvet. After an evening meal in the dining car, they walked onto the observation platform to see how the work was progressing. A sign was erected on the road heading south by the mine: COAL: THE CREAM OF ROUTT COUNTY. Local promoters referred to coal as "black gold." The company eventually printed an advertisement featuring a photograph of a wooden coal car loaded with blocks of coal the size of boulders and three adorable children sitting on top, holding smaller pieces in their hands.

As in other mining towns, relations between owners and workers were tense. In addition to the physical demands, the double shifts, and the perils of the work, miners had virtually no control over their lives. From 1908 until 1912, Perry's men took a special train from Phippsburg to Oak

Hills every day and paid for their own transportation. Things got a little easier when they were moved into a cluster of cabins at Oak Hills called "the Circle." The housing, supplied with electricity, was better than many others had. But miners were paid in scrip, counterfeit money printed by the company. It was good only at the expensive company store, or through the black market in town, where each mine had its own contacts. Workers for the Moffat mine took their scrip to a contact in Oak Creek, and sold it at a loss of fifty percent, or sometimes much more. The man might give a drunk miner only a dollar for scrip worth five dollars. The store or bar owner was reimbursed by the mine's pay clerk, who took his cut of the profit. The blacksmiths who repaired miners' picks, shovels, and drills routinely cheated them. In order to have more productive working areas or a better mining "buddy," some men paid their coworkers to switch places with them in the mine. That, too, caused resentment.

Accidents were an inevitable part of the job. Explosions in the mines could be caused by gas, smoke, or even coal dust. Men were injured or killed by falling rocks from the roof, especially in areas of shale or fossil remains. If the props were not properly set, the roof caved in. This happened most often near the mine face, where the mountain was rearranging itself — "taking weight" — as the coal was removed. Inexperienced workers smoked cigarettes as they carried powder, caps, and fuses. Efforts were made to institute safer procedures. The Moffat Coal Company hired experienced shot-firers to place the explosives, but it passed along the cost to the miners by charging higher prices. Although the company was known to be "one of the most careful and considerate" in the state, of the half-dozen explosions in Oak Hills, the worst was a dust blowout years later at the Perry mine. The dust caught fire, and flames ignited the coal, causing a chain reaction that resulted in a massive ball of fire. "When the wind and fire came out of the mine portal, it threw cars, rails, and the tipple clear across the draw in an arch of fire and destruction," a Colorado inspection report noted. Five men were killed. Afterward, a list of new safety precautions was added, including, "No lights, matches, cigars, cigarettes or pipes allowed in mine."

In 1910, when the miners in a coalfield in Boulder County went on strike, so did the men in Routt County. In Oak Hills, workers demanded scales to weigh the coal, the right to live where they wanted, and to be free from the costs incurred by the shot-firers. The strike was quickly put down, but the United Mine Workers continued to organize, and the unrest throughout Colorado never really ended. Three years later, in September 1913, local miners joined a statewide walkout that started to the south near Trinidad and culminated in the infamous Ludlow Massacre. Twenty people were killed there, including eleven children, when the National Guard opened fire. Miners retaliated with increasing force around the state.

That fall, the Moffat Coal Company erected guard towers with spotlights and machine guns around its mines, and in November, the companies in Oak Hills reopened with nonunion men. Bob Perry was in charge at the Moffat mine, with his father's close oversight, and an organization of mine owners hired the Baldwin-Felts detective agency to provide security. Baldwin was notorious for its brutal strike-breaking tactics, including an armor-plated car, deployed at Ludlow, that had a swiveling Gatling gun mounted in the back.

In Oak Hills, for a short time, the striking workers fought back more or less with impunity. When a mob of miners and their wives marched to the Pinnacle mine to object to new guards installed at the tipple, the man in charge of security was stoned and clubbed, and the sheriff escorted him to the train to Denver. A few weeks before Christmas, some miners' wives, who were shopping for presents, were denied credit at Bell Mercantile. They hauled the owner outside the store and beat him up. One night, when strikers fought scabs in the bars and on the streets, women and children were sheltered in the bank basement. The state militia was finally summoned.

The United Mine Workers had promised a strike fund for the workers, but it never materialized in Oak Hills, and the situation grew desperate that winter. Some workers left the area; others chose to return to the mines rather than starve. On March 20, 1914, two miners walking by the railroad tracks were shot to death by two nonunion men. One of those arrested for the murders was released on bond and worked as a rope rider at the Moffat mine. Not long afterward, as Paul Bonnifield put it, "a string of cars broke loose and 'accidentally' killed him." In April, President Wilson sent federal troops to Colorado, and the 12th U.S. Cavalry arrived in Oak Creek. The strikers were defeated.

■ ■ ■ ■

On Saturday morning, Bob took Dorothy and Ros through the Moffat mine. The other women elected to stay home, but the teachers, who understood that he had a complex and demanding job, were interested to learn more about his work. He had wanted to be a doctor, but Sam needed him to help run the coal company. Bob knew that his years at Columbia, his comfortable cabin, his good clothes, his Dodge, and the gifts he liked to bestow upon the teachers would not have been possible without Sam's perspicacity and hardheadedness. The only son, he never seriously thought about defying his father.

Bob was good at his job, and although he was firmly anti-union, he often listened to the complaints of one of his young employees on this volatile subject, explaining, "First we have to think about production." The success of the Moffat mine, the most modern in Colorado, was critical. If it shut down, so would the others in the Yampa coalfields. Moreover, the Moffat Road depended on the regular transport of coal. If the railroad was abandoned, most of the businesses in northwestern Colorado would close, settlement would stop, and towns would die.

Bob showed Ros and Dorothy how the coal was mined. They passed the shower rooms, the mess hall, and the mine office where he worked and where the miners stopped each morning to take their numbered metal chips from a board on the wall. They put their chips on a hook fastened to their lunch buckets, or to the front of their leather belts. Not far from the mine portal was the powder room, where explosives were kept. It was a concrete-lined hole dug into the mountain and hung with black powder pellets. Secured with a steel door, the room was built far enough away that if there was a fire or gas or dust explosion in the mine, it wouldn't reach the powder supply.

The mine had three pits. At its main entrance, an electric hoisting plant ran the cable system for the mine cars, although mules were still used to take the coal to the main haulage way. As the women walked into the narrow entrance, the tunnel dropped steeply. Bob told them that there were fifteen miles of tunnels connected to "rooms" under the hills. Three hundred miners worked there, in helmets that resembled hard leather baseball caps, with a carbide lamp burning on the bill. They also wore long underwear, to keep warm and to prevent coal dust from settling on the unexposed parts of their bodies.

Miners considered it bad luck for women to go into mines, but Bob brushed aside the superstition. Dorothy and Ros, in their own helmets, noticed the eerie shadows that the lamplight made on the tunnel walls. "We saw all the different processes, stumbled along in those dark, wet chasms with our flickering lights," Ros wrote, "and marveled at the thought of it all. I never appreciated 'coal' before." A fan forced the stale air out of the ventilation shafts, but as they descended, it became increasingly claustrophobic. Coal dust hung in the air, and there was a musty smell of standing water. The roof was reinforced with six-foot wooden props, which creaked under the weight of the mountain. The tracks made by rats were visible in the dust.

Each day the men went to work with their pickaxes and shovels. If there were pools of water, they pumped it out. Miners, two to each room, loaded the loose coal into the cars, then hung a chip on the cars they had filled. The rope rider pulled them to the surface, where the check-weighman measured them and recorded the weight and car numbers. The chips were then returned to the board, and the weighman transported the cars to the tipple. There were some details that Bob left out of his account. The miners always checked their tonnage and counted the number of chips to be sure that all of their cars had been weighed. On the trip to the weighman, the rope rider occasionally "lost" or changed a number. Men were paid by the ton, but if any ordinary rock — called bone — found its way into a car, the miner wasn't paid for that load. If a man didn't return at the end of the day or was found dead in the mine, he was identified by his numbered chip.

At the end of their shift, workers cut out a space underneath the coal. The goal was to avoid "shooting on the solid," which crushed the coal into slack; they wanted valuable lump and nut coal. Then they drilled holes for the explosives and placed the charges. Only the shot-firer remained, to be sure the charges were tamped in and the fuse was the right length. Mine explosions were caused by a shot "blowing out" or going off at the wrong time. The shot-firer lit the powder and "shot the coal down," breaking it up into chunks to be loaded into cars the next day.

As the women walked back to the surface

of the earth, Ros was struck by the enormity of the enterprise — a feeling reinforced that afternoon when they gamely accompanied Bob four miles, behind two mules in a steady rain, to Phippsburg, where the roundhouse and other engine and car-repair buildings had just been finished. Sam Perry had spent heavily on the improvements, and it was an impressive sight — no better way, Bob must have felt, to show the woman he loved the role the Perrys were playing in the future of the West. Dorothy, though, was shaken by her experience in the mine. She wrote afterward, "I am glad to have done it, for I never need to go through another. I was scared & didn't like it."

It poured throughout Saturday — an equinoctial event, Perry told them. The women all slept late both mornings, while their imperturbable host started the fire and made breakfast. His housekeeper was sick, so Charlotte and Portia, who were used to cooking for large groups at camp, took over the other meals. Dorothy and Ros helped with the dishes. The food was magnificent, they said: grouse for breakfast, and for dinner, duck and ice cream.

Before they left on Sunday, it stopped raining, and Ros took a picture of Bob leaning casually against the back-porch rail with one of his Airedales. The downpour had turned the rough roads into a slurry of mud. Perry put chains on the tires, and they started home — six women squeezed into his little car. Dorothy was glad that for once she and Ros hadn't overpacked; they had just put a change of clothes into their knitting bags. The chains didn't make much difference, and after skidding in the mud for several miles, they returned to the Oak Creek depot and took the train. Charlotte and Portia got off at Steamboat Springs, while the others continued on to Hayden. The Harrisons had invited Dot and Anne to stay with them for the rest of their visit.

Dorothy and Ros were worried about how they would get to school, and everyone got up early on Monday morning. Bob had assured them that he would borrow an automobile, but as it turned out, everyone in Hayden who owned one had gone to a funeral some forty miles away. The storm had blown down the telephone wire, so they couldn't call the school and let the students know they would be late. While Bob worked on the transportation dilemma, they visited Mrs. Peck and observed a class at the Hayden School.

At noon, Bob returned in a seven-passenger Marmon — an unusual sight in Hayden, with its whitewall tires, long, gleaming black nose, and two gentlemen in the front seat. The Marmon's owner, a sheep man from Wyoming, insisted that he was going to Elkhead anyway, and said he gladly would take them. The other man was Ferry's ranching partner, Jack White, whose bristly hair stood straight up from his head. With his rugged good looks, gruff courtesy, and bone-crushing handshake, he appeared to have stepped out of a dime-store Western. Bob, reassured, took the train back to Oak Creek. "We were all piled into the tonneau," Ros said, "and had a most wonderful ride out."

Along the way, the sheep man kept turning around and firing compliments at the women, as they prayed he would make the difficult turns. When they spotted a coyote, the man jammed on the brakes and pulled out a rifle. White took his six-shooter from his hip pocket. Both fired and missed. Dorothy, falling into her prescribed role, wrote: "Imagine being in a beautiful machine & having two men shooting from the running board!" The men soon stirred up a flock of sage grouse, also known as cocks of the plains, "& we were fairly trembling with excitement as they loaded up. Mr. White killed two beauties & then showed us the gory process of cleaning them. They gallantly presented them to us and we made a triumphant entrance, much to Mrs. Harrison's excitement." By then it was mid-afternoon. The teachers swore to each other that they wouldn't miss another day of school all year, a vow they kept.

14
"Unarmed and Defenseless"

Bob Perry and Mascot at his cabin in Oak Hills, 1916

Ros was turning thirty on October 8, and Bob and Ferry had promised to take them to a scenic place south of Hayden called Williams Fork. They were looking forward to a busy weekend, starting with a teachers' conference in Hayden on Saturday and ending with the excursion on Sunday with their friends. On Friday, though, Ferry telephoned them at the schoolhouse to say that he had heard from Dr. Cole, the aptly named company doctor at Oak Hills, that Bob wasn't well. The birthday outing would have to be postponed. Claiming that he knew nothing more about it, he said he guessed there wasn't much the matter.

When the two women woke up the next morning to another deluge, they changed their minds about riding to Hayden, although they knew that Mrs. Peck would be disappointed not to see them at the conference. Ros wrote a get-well note to Bob.

Dear Mr. Perry:
We surely were sorry to hear via Mr. Carpenter and Dr. Cole that you're not feeling up to the work. I hope it's nothing serious. . . .
This is just to convey to you our sympathy and the hope that whatever is the matter — it won't last long.
The Auburns

Dorothy scrawled a hearty P.S. at the bottom of the page:

Cheer up! We'll have that birthday party yet — all the merrier for being postponed. What's in a date?

In the afternoon, they rode to a neighboring ranch to make a phone call for Mrs. Harrison. They were told that Carpenter had left suddenly for Oak Creek, and they suspected there was some trouble at the mine, but they weren't overly concerned. On Monday evening, however, as they were riding home from school, Everette Adair hailed them, and as he rode up, he asked breathlessly if they had heard the news about Bob Perry.

The previous Wednesday, October 4, as Bob was getting ready for bed, he had stepped outside his cabin in his undershirt and trousers. Two men suddenly appeared from around the corner, their faces masked with blue handkerchiefs. One pressed a rifle against his stomach; the other put a revolver to his head. Speaking in heavy accents, they said, "Don't scare, don't scare, we want money," and told him they were going to take him into the mountains. Bob protested that he wasn't dressed to go anywhere on such a cold night and told them the money was in the house.

They forced him inside, allowing him to get dressed. The taller man took Bob's wallet from the table; it contained two five-dollar bills and some change. The man's companion — broad-shouldered and barrel-chested with light brown eyes — demanded tobacco and helped himself to a Colt .32 and a holster in the cabinet. He also picked up a watch, but when Bob ordered him to put it back, the tall man grabbed it and threw it on the table. They stepped into the kitchen and packed some food to take with them.

The kidnappers bound his arms to his sides and led him outside at gunpoint, warning him not to holler. Soon the men were arguing with each other in a foreign language. Bob surmised that they were disagreeing about which route to take from the cabin. They led him away, making slow progress through the back country above the mines, avoiding the trails in the creek bottoms where they might be seen and were more likely to leave tracks. After an hour or two they paused to rest in an aspen grove, where a crude shelter had been built out of boughs, and the remains of a campfire were evident.

The short, stocky man handed his rifle to his companion and took down another rifle they had tied to a tree. He then stepped to one side and made some hand signals, apparently to another confederate higher up in the brush. The tall man, who was dressed in brown overalls, a brown coat, and a gray mackinaw, tied Bob's arms behind him and held the rest of the length of rope. They resumed their circuitous journey, stopping for the night at the top of a ridge outside Oak Creek. They built a fire, bound his feet, and tied the long end of the rope to a high tree branch. Bob attempted to loosen his bonds and was warned that if he tried again, they would kill him. The kidnappers alternated keeping watch.

The mine whistles awoke them at seven A.M. The tall man, who was younger and had a better command of English, told him that they had been hired by someone in Oak Creek to kill him, but what they really wanted was money. They ordered him to write to his father in Denver and demand that he bring them $15,000 (the equivalent a century later of about $300,000); then they would release him. If he refused, they would shoot him.

After haggling with his captors about whether his father must deliver the money alone and whether the horse should be white or red or red *and* white, they agreed that Perry Sr. could ride a white horse and that he could be accompanied by Bob's milk man, Ed Griffin, who would ride the red horse the captors had seen him on before. Evidently, they were familiar with Oak Creek. They gave Bob a pencil and paper, and he wrote two copies of the ransom note, one addressed to his father's Denver office and the other to his parents' house on Grant Street. As they ordered, he wrote that the police were not to be notified, and that if a posse appeared, they would kill him before the rescuers got anywhere near him. Figuring the men could not read English, Bob added a few details of his own:

Thursday, 7:00 a.m.

Dear Pop,
   . . . [T]hey are very definite as to what will happen to me if they do not get the money. They speak a foreign language which I cannot understand. It seems to me that they are "touched." Anything you will do is O.K. to me. If anything should happen to me, give my love to them all. For I have done all that I can . . . They say if you send the money you can come on a white horse, and that you may bring another man with you —

Ed Griffin on Lazarus. You are to walk the hills straight west regardless of the roads, or, as they say, "as the sun hideth," and they will stop you some time during the day. They tell me we are to start walking tomorrow. BOB

When he had finished, he was given a grubby little book of one-cent stamps. Bob put two on each letter, wrote "Special Delivery" on the envelopes, and informed the men that the letters would cost more — ten cents each. They asked whether they would have to sign anything for the postmaster, and Bob told them just to buy the extra stamps and drop the letters into the box. The tall man went off to Oak Creek with the letters but soon came back with another demand. Bob duly added: "P.S. They just return to say that it must be gold."

The man reappeared about four hours later in different clothes: a brown suit, a dark flannel shirt, an overcoat, and new shoes. He changed his shirt again and pulled on his overalls over the trousers, then his mackinaw. He also brought back a sack containing several loaves of bread, a pound of butter, twelve cans of Tuxedo tobacco, a ham, and four pears. He took three cans of tobacco for himself and gave nine cans to the stocky man — a chain-smoker in a black slouch hat who puffed on his pipe through his handkerchief. The kerchief slipped down while he slept, and Bob took note of his features: a broad, flat nose and a heavy mustache, with hair that seemed to grow across his face rather than down. His hands were large and red with stubby fingers, and his right thumbnail was bruised. Bob had little appetite, but he managed to eat some bread and butter. He asked one of them to fetch him some water from Little Trout Creek, near where they were camped. When he complained of being cold, the tall man loaned him his overcoat.

On Thursday evening, after dark, Bob and his captors set out again, and the stocky man became furious when he saw that the ropes binding Bob's arms had become loose. The captors spoke urgently to each other, and the tall one again threatened him, telling him that if they found the rope loosened again, they would kill him. Besides, he said, "There are about thirty of us around here, and you could never make a getaway." Bob doubted their talk about a group of co-conspirators but not their willingness to shoot him.

At daybreak on Friday, after walking through a light drizzle, they stopped in a deep gulch called Little Middle Creek, where the men told him they would stay until the ransom was delivered. Cold and damp, Bob asked them to build a fire. They hesitated, thinking the smoke might be seen, but finally consented and made breakfast, frying some of the ham and tearing off pieces of bread. Bob lay down by the fire to rest, but the long end of the rope had been fastened so high on a tree branch that it tugged uncomfortably. The stocky man untied it, which provoked further words with his companion.

Sometime before eleven A.M., Bob dozed off. When he woke up, both kidnappers were asleep. Under the taller man's jacket, he could see the edge of the holster holding his own automatic; his rifle was on the ground at the foot of a tree about six feet away. Although his upper arms were bound, he managed to work free his feet and his forearms. Bob leaned over and tried to grab the gun, but it was just beyond reach. Instead, he jumped over the tall man and seized the rifle from his companion.

The kidnapper woke up and grabbed the rifle back with both hands, but Bob shoved it against his chest and then awkwardly wrested it from him. Bob backed up to the tree where the second rifle was lying. He angled the stocky man's rifle at them both, telling them to run or he would kill them. As the tall man reached for the automatic and started toward him, the stocky man came at him from the other side. Bob repeated his command, but the tall man ignored him, and Bob fired, hitting him in the chest. The man reeled and fell but got up again, standing unsteadily.

Bob took both rifles and ran in the opposite direction. He stopped briefly about three-quarters of a mile from the gulch and managed to work his arms free. He soon reached the Ben Male ranch, where he called Oak Creek and reached his father, who had just arrived.

Sam Perry had been about to set out with Ed Griffin to deliver the money to the kidnappers. In the hours since he had received the ransom note late Thursday night, he had called Ferry Carpenter to convey the terrible news, obtained the gold with the help of a Denver banker he knew, and chartered a train to Oak Creek. Now, vastly relieved, Sam set out to meet Bob at the ranch, accompanied by Marjorie, four detectives from the Denver police force, and Dr. Cole, a family friend. Ferry, too, had headed for Oak Creek to join one of the posses being organized to capture the renegades.

Sam doted on Marjorie, his firstborn, treating her like a son. Every year she accompanied him on a weeks-long hunting expedition. As one newspaper account described her, "Wearing a heavy flannel shirt and chaps, like a cowboy of the plains, she has ridden through the wildest regions of the state, shooting deer and bear and even an occasional mountain lion." One year she returned with a bear cub she named Perrywinkle and kept in her parents' backyard in Denver. (As an older woman, when her two favorite dogs died, she skinned them and used their pelts as rugs.)

The *Denver Post,* always alert to the exploits of the Perry family, reported that Marjorie, the "Denver society girl and experienced bear hunter, is leading one of the posses that is hunting thru the mountains of Routt county for the surviving one of the two Greeks who kidnapped her brother. . . . [S]he knows the ground to be traversed as well as any of the men and better than most of them. The young woman is heavily armed." Bob Perry told the *Post* in an interview on October 8, "I think they were amateurs in the brigand business, but they were thoroly in earnest about what they were doing, and I guess I was lucky to get away with a whole skin."

Once Bob had time to eat and rest, he led his group through the hills to the spot where he had shot the kidnapper. The newspapers didn't hold back. "Oak Creek," the *Rocky Mountain News* reported, was "a scene of the wildest excitement, the streets teeming with aroused Americans." At around eight P.M. on Friday, they found the tall man lying on his side in Little Middle Creek Gulch. The moon was shining under a light cloud, and they could see a revolver on the ground next to his hand. His clothing was in disarray, and there were two bullet holes, one through the chest and another through his right temple.

On Sunday morning, the coroner of Routt County impaneled a jury of six and held an inquest at Oak Creek. The dead man was identified as George Katsegahnis, a Greek miner who had worked briefly for Perry in the mine. Ferry served as Bob's lawyer, and after various witnesses had been called, it was determined that the bullet through the temple was the one that had killed Katsegahnis, and that his partner was Jim Karagounis, who worked with him in the mine. The matter of who fired the fatal shot was not resolved, but "County authorities," the

Oak Creek Times reported on October 9, "have accepted the explanation that George Katsegohnis [*sic*] the younger and brainier of the two kidnappers, who was injured by young Perry when the latter was forced to shoot in making his escape, killed himself." The owner of the Oak Creek Cemetery refused to allow him to be buried there, arguing, as an item in the *Oak Creek Times* put it, "We, as a people, do not want this class of citizens, dead or alive, in our midst."

The Greeks in Oak Hills were fearful about retaliatory attacks. One man wrote a long letter to Perry on October 11, telling him that none of the other Greek miners was complicit in the crime, and that if they had a chance to capture the kidnapper, they would kill him. He said that some of his friends at the Moffat mine had quit already and went on, "I presume you know it, that the town is against to me, and not having any protection of yours, is no use for me to stay here at all, anyway I ain't forgetting your past favors. . . ." The next day the *Oak Creek Times* reported the "wholesale arrest of local Greeks . . . on slender clues or no grounds at all, but later they were released."

A wanted poster went up in the nearby towns, with a detailed description of the fugitive based on information provided by

Bob: "Nationality Greek, age 40 to 50 years, height 5 ft. 7 in. weight 170 lbs., complexion dark, eyes peculiar, had heavy moustache, nose broad and flat, right thumb nail with spot from bruise. Was bareheaded when last seen: grey brown check shirt, eight hob nails in sole of each shoe." The poster offered a thousand-dollar reward for information leading to the arrest of the suspect, half to be paid by Sam Perry, the other half by the Routt County commissioners.

On Sunday morning, two sisters named Leota and Loretta Crosswhite, who owned a confectionery store in Steamboat Springs, were taking a walk to the springs and spotted a man by the railroad tracks fitting the description of the fugitive. They hurried back to town to tell the deputy sheriff. Karagounis surrendered without resistance and readily admitted his part in the kidnapping. He denied killing his partner, saying that the man was too badly wounded to move and that he had been forced to leave him in the creek bed. The reward was split between the Crosswhite sisters.

Bob Perry, accompanied by Ferry Carpenter, went to the jail in Steamboat Springs on Monday to identify Karagounis. "The Greek greeted Bob with a smile," Carpenter wrote in his autobiography. "In turn, Bob shook hands with him and called him Jim." On January 12, 1917, James Karagounis was tried in the district court in Steamboat Springs — the building where Dorothy and Ros had taken their teachers' examinations the previous August. He was convicted of kidnapping and "assault with deadly weapons with a confederate." He was sentenced to life plus six and a half years in the state penitentiary. Two years later, he was knifed to death by another inmate.

On Friday, October 13, Ros began a prosaic letter to her mother about exercises they had conducted at the school to celebrate Columbus Day. The children had performed a play, songs, and recitations before an audience of mothers and babies. Ros and Dorothy had made costumes out of some of Mrs. Harrison's old tablecloths and a few wisps of cheesecloth, and the children made paper crowns and ruffs. Ros joked about her growing ease at the piano, pounding out the pieces after a week or two of practice — "even Papa wouldn't recognize my touch!"

"Now I have a long story to tell," she began in a seamless segue. She wrote how Everette Adair had inquired about Bob Perry, either with poorly concealed spite or an unfortunate choice of tense: "You girls knew him, didn't you?" She noted exultantly, "We both felt at that — that he'd been killed and was no more. He had *almost* been killed — but had a marvelous escape. It's the most extraordinary tale in the century, and in this country I didn't know such things happened." She said she would send the newspaper accounts, "that you may read a thriller!"

Indeed, newspapers around the country carried the story, with descriptions of Perry's athleticism and college credentials, his father's prominence in the Denver business world, maps of the route Bob took with his captors, illustrations of him shooting Katsegahnis, and copies of his "Dear Pop" ransom letter. Reporters added their own flourishes: "Unarmed and defenseless, dressed only in his pajamas," the *Denver Post* initially reported, Perry "was completely at the mercy of his assailants who with knives and guns threatened him continually, and frequently beat him when he failed to obey promptly the commands given him." On October 8, after an interview with Bob, the *Post* declared in its headline on October 8, "I HATED TO SHOOT KIDNAPER" SAYS PERRY. SON OF MINE MAGNATE TELLS VIVID STORY OF DEATH BATTLE WITH POLITE PAIR OF BRIGANDS.

The *Los Angeles Morning Tribune* published the story on its front page.

Back in Elkhead, Ros informed her mother, "Everyone seems to feel that Mr. Perry is perfectly safe now. The Greeks are scared to death of him, and he's very well liked at the mine. These men were notably 'no good.' . . . Don't think that kidnapping is customary out here or worry! It's as unusual here as in Auburn."

On an October Sunday afternoon a few weeks later, just as Ros and Dorothy had given up on seeing their friends, the two men showed up to take them on a long ride. Bob brought with him from the Oak Hills company store two mackinaws (brown for Ros, green for Dorothy) and some heavy woolen gloves they had asked for. Ferry, lacking presents and a story of courageous struggle with two desperadoes, fussed over the women's failure to bring woolen underwear for the winter.

Dorothy wrote of "Mr. Perry," he "looks thinner & worn; and of course it was thrilling to hear his account of the kidnapping." He showed them the Luger he now carried in his coat pocket, and demonstrated its accuracy on their ride home by shooting a porcupine. At his family's insistence, he had hired a bodyguard, but he asked the man to stay at Ferry's cabin while they visited the teachers, and Dorothy noticed that he didn't seem remotely concerned about his safety.

In Rosamond's Elkhead photo album, under a picture of Bob posing on horseback in white shirt, jacket, necktie, and fedora, loosely holding his rifle, she wrote "Hero No. 1." Pasted next to him is "Hero No. 2" — a candid shot of Ferry on skis, caught with his head thrown back in a moment of unrestrained laughter. She wrote underneath, "A very good likeness."

Ros was discreet about her deepening affection for Bob, but Ferry knew that he had lost the competition.

15
"THE DARK DAYS ARE VERY FEW"

Ros taking a picture of Bob on Thanksgiving

On an unseasonably warm Saturday at the end of October, the teachers got up at six, took their cold sponge baths, cleaned their room, mended some clothes, washed Ros's hair, and worked on their lessons. They had made most of the home visits already, but they had a few left in the farthest hills. That afternoon, they rode up into Little Arkansas, the area of heavy aspens Carpenter had described in his letter to them before they left Auburn. It turned out that people there really did eat bear cabbage and porcupine. Dorothy commented, "I *don't* see how these people make a living — with just a tiny log cabin in a clearing — & a potato patch! Think of living in the country & not having a cow or chickens — everyone is 'pulling Taters' now and burying them for the winter."

One place about two and a half miles north of the schoolhouse was particularly forlorn, a tiny cabin on the peak of a mountain, surrounded by aspens. It was the home of a family of "poor whites" from Kentucky who had five children, three of whom had joined Dorothy's class. "I was positively terrified by the mother's appearance," she wrote. "She is tall & gaunt with a wisp of bright red hair — and 2 horrible tusks of teeth." The cabin was "dreadfully dirty . . . and for furniture she had a stove, three double beds and two stools — for seven people! I felt *so* sorry for the poor creature." Attempting to start a conversation, Dorothy asked her if she liked the country. The woman replied, " 'Naw — 'pears like me & Chris don't care about nothin' any more!' What can life mean, but mere existence to people like that? The children are neat & clean at school & no wonder they love it."

Now the students' frayed clothes were less picturesque than they had seemed in August. Tommy Jones wore a torn shirt, a ragged coat, and a duster around his neck. Six-year-old Robin Robinson was bare-legged in cutoff overalls and practically disappeared inside Jimmy's coat, which was in shreds and so big on him that his hands dangled inside the sleeves. Their mother, a cultured woman from France whose family disowned her when she married a cowboy, had died during childbirth, when Robin was three. Nine-year-old Jesse Morsbach, who informed Dorothy that the biblical Abraham came from Kansas, wept because his shoes, which he tied together with string, constantly flapped open and tripped him; he started wearing old rubber boots instead. Even children from some of the relatively well-off families were in rags, because the "freight" hadn't come — their annual shipments from Sears Roebuck.

With no warning one afternoon, the temperature dropped and a snowstorm descended. Few of the children had worn coats to school, and they set off for home at a dead run. The teachers were moved by the students' attempts to cope, and by their good cheer in the face of such adversity. Jesse's brother Rudolph, Dorothy wrote to her father, "said he always ate radishes to keep him warm!" She asked her sisters for help, suggesting that they collect some old scarves, sweaters, and coats for the children: "They are hard working, self respecting people — very proud, but I am sure we could manage to give them some clothing." Dr. D. L. Whittaker, the new doctor in Hayden, came up to examine the students and found several cases of enlarged tonsils and poor eyesight, among them Lewis Harrison, who needed glasses. Lewis was also told that he would have to go to Denver to have his adenoids removed. Tommy Jones had an ulcer inside his right nostril, causing nosebleeds.

The Woodruffs and the Underwoods had come to think of Dorothy and Ros as missionaries, and they responded to their daughters' pleas for help. Dorothy's father took her letters to his office and had his secretary type them up. Grace Underwood, using Ros's typewriter, transcribed the letters herself. Copies were distributed to friends and family in Auburn. The two families, and the city's congregations, went to work. In late fall, Ros's mother spoke at a monthly meeting of the King's Daughters of the First Baptist Church, a group of wealthy young women intent upon improving the lives of the poor. Their motto was: "Look up, not down; look forward, not back; look out, not in; lend a hand." Mrs. Underwood passed around pictures that Ros had sent of the children and the schoolhouse.

Soon boxes and barrels began appearing in Hayden; they were taken to Elkhead whenever someone had a wagon available. Dorothy and Ros put clothing donations in the supply closet and distributed them when the need arose. Early one afternoon, a box of clothes from Ros's aunt Nellie was delivered just before a blizzard struck. Ros tore open the box and clapped a sweater and shawl and her own green coat on three of the girls who had come to school in cotton dresses.

One box from the Woodruffs was full of sneakers and rubber overshoes. Ros told the boys that if they made goals for a basketball court and laid out the field, she would donate the ball, and she and Miss Woodruff would coach — a generous if improbable thought, probably inspired by the basketball lessons Charlotte Perry had given to children at Hull House in Chicago.

Grace Underwood sent books from her daughter's childhood library, and as Ros unpacked *Things Will Take a Turn, Each and All,* and a Dickens storybook, she thought about how happy she was to see them being used by the children rather than stored in an attic box. She and Dorothy started a library of their own, and the students loved borrowing books. Louisa May Alcott was a favorite. Ros had to tactfully dissuade Mrs. Underwood from sending any more *Spirit of Missions* from the Episcopal Church, telling her, "They like spicier reading here in Routt Co!!" Zane Grey was popular among the adults.

The teachers were also recipients of the cross-country literary exchange. When Ferry was through with his magazines, he passed them along to the teachers: the educational reviews, the *Yale Review,* the *Unpopular Review,* and the *Christian Science Monitor.* Ros asked her mother if she could send along copies of the *Atlantic* and the Sunday *New*

York Times as well.

Two days of blustery October wind and rain shook the house and blew in their bedroom window. The third morning they woke up to a blinding snowstorm. Waving aside the Harrisons' advice to stay home, they rode to school, leaning into the wind as they tried to make out Lewis on Old Eagle ahead of them. Ferry, assuming they wouldn't be able to get there and planning to substitute for the day, arrived just as they did. Fourteen children were already inside, and they had a fire going in the furnace. Robin Robinson's father mined the anthracite coal on the hillside and hauled it to the Rock School. It burned so hot that the grates lasted only six weeks. The children lined up their shoes, caked with mud, in front of the furnace to dry them out. Even the horses had trouble extracting their hooves, and the teachers couldn't see how the children had made their way on foot. Ferry spent the day doing odd jobs around the building, observing the classes, and chatting with the students. The teachers ate their lunch indoors with the students, as they always did on stormy days. Dorothy told Anna, "The din would make your hair stand on end. We laugh about it, for we are just like those oblivious mothers who don't

317

hear their children." That night the snow stopped falling, and Ros noted, "a heavenly crescent moon and one of the real western sunsets makes me hopeful for tomorrow."

Like the sudden shifts to clear skies, the students' responsiveness in class compensated for the most trying moments. Dorothy found that it wasn't hard to distract them from their discomfort. Drawn as the children were to tales at sea, she told them in current-events class about the destruction of the *Memphis,* an armored navy cruiser that had been struck by a seaquake a few months earlier in the Dominican Republic. The boat was wrenched from her anchorage, tossed above the waves, then repeatedly slammed into the harbor bottom. Three sailors were washed overboard, seven were killed when some steam pipes burst, and thirty drowned after their lifeboats capsized in the gigantic waves. Robin, unable to contain himself, shouted, "We have a *crick* by *our* house!"

Dorothy wrote, "The nicest part about it all is the way they love school, and their rapt attention is really thrilling," and, in another letter, the children "fairly eat up work, and I rack my brains to keep them busy." She told them a story at the end of every day and made up a long series about a little boy who was traveling around the world on a spectacular boat — the best way she had found to teach geography. When she held up her postcards from Antwerp, Zermatt, and Paris, there was a stampede to the front of the room as everyone jostled for a closer look. Ros told her mother, "My Ancient History class gets the collection of Greek p.c.'s and views of Corinth today."

They all loved an excuse for a school party, and spent weeks preparing for Halloween, laying in a supply, as Ros put it, of peanuts, apples, and other provisions, along with more galoshes and heavy stockings. Ferry bought decorations in town, and the teachers arranged for a ghost in the closet, apple-bobbing, and pin the tail on the donkey. The children made a decorative border of witches and pumpkins on the blackboard while Dorothy and Ros set the tables in the basement. They had some trouble with their popcorn balls. "We wasted a can of molasses," Ros wrote, "and got into a terrible mess, before we finally 'swam out'! By 6 o'clock we had about 60 good balls, and they vanished like snow under the noon day sun."

Report cards were issued to the children each month on two-sided preprinted index cards, with a signature line for the parents.

Dorothy prepared them for her fourteen students, hesitating over the choice of grades: A (admirable; 95–110), E (excellent; 85–95), F (fair; 75–85), P (poor; 60–75), and M (very poor; below 60). The report cards stated: "Any Grade lower than FAIR will not be honored by promotion." She wrote, "I felt so *mean*," adding that it still felt odd to her to be in a position of such authority. Nevertheless, she doesn't seem to have given any of the children a P or an M, even slow Ray. And, she went on, "Our 'warrant' is now due and I don't suppose any one ever felt prouder than we will of that *earned* money!"

School was closed for Election Day, November 7. About seventy-five men and women cast their ballots there, while back home in suffrage country, only men were going to the polls. Ros had written earlier about the primary, a ritual that she imagined taking place at public buildings across the country. "Just here I'd like to remark that it is a beautiful sight to see happy family parties hand in hand casting their ballots in a fine clean school room — no smoking — no profanity!!!"

It was a close election. Wilson had stuck to his promise of nonintervention, while

Charles Evans Hughes continued to attack his stand, and argued that Wilson's support for progressive labor laws was inimical to industry. Ros wrote to her brother George and his wife, "It has seemed so queer to be so far away from any political excitement. I hear you and Ken [the second lieutenant] are quite the leaders in the Hughes Alliance, George. We have been so crazy to hear the returns." Around noon on November 9, Ferry telephoned the school to say that so far Wilson had won three more states than Hughes; the California results were yet to come in. "What an election it has been!" Ros commented. Wilson "is idolized out here and it is astonishing to hear how he's considered. Hughes' strength is not in the west!"

The following Sunday, Ferry and Bob arrived at the Harrisons' with sacks of mail and buffalo meat (rare even in that part of the country), duck, celery, and an issue of the *Breeder's Gazette.* Carpenter told them that some buffalo had been shipped in recently for breeding, and that one bull had rampaged and had to be shot. They ate it for dinner, and it joined the list of exotic meats they had sampled — deer, bear, elk, and rabbit. Lewis recently had trapped a muskrat, and the Harrisons laughed when

Ros asked if they were going to eat it, too. There was great excitement when Frank Jr. went up Agner and returned with a buck slung over the back of his horse. He came in at suppertime waving a bloody liver, which, Dorothy said, "was the signal for much rejoicing — it is a welcome change to us all, and the fact that it is against the law only makes it taste better." There were very few deer and elk at the time, and the homesteaders, often desperate for food, ignored the injunction against hunting out of season.

Dorothy and Ros longed for a newspaper with more information about the election results. Ferry told them what he knew. As expected, Wilson appeared to have carried most states in the West, but he had eked out a victory in the Northeast and the Midwest. Ferry also seized the occasion to talk about Wilson's years at Princeton and his extraordinary intellect. He said that the president was a long-suffering idealist, working for the good of the country despite his personal distaste for public life. Ros, in keeping with her family's Republican sympathies, wrote, "We've been so excited waiting to hear the presidential returns. I can't *bear* to have W.W. reelected and I guess he surely has been now." The margin of victory was slim.

If California had gone for Hughes, Wilson would have lost the election. Echoing Ferry, not Ros, Dorothy told her family, "It is *real* utopian democracy out here — & so interestingly in conflict with all our inherited prejudices."

Everette Adair, oblivious to the teachers' disparagement, began to accompany them home from school. One fall evening he presented them with a box of candy, "clear from Hayden!" as he put it, causing Dorothy to remark to her audience at home, "He is such a ridiculous, vain, picturesque boy!" Another day, as they were heading back to the Harrisons', Everette rode up to them and suggested they stop to take a look at Shorty Huguenin's cabin. Huguenin, whose French parents had emigrated to Colorado in 1877, was married with two daughters and ran a restaurant and an ice business in Hayden. He was building a homestead near the school, and Ferry had arranged with him for Dorothy and Ros to live there in the worst of the winter months, when the two-and-a-half-mile commute would be too difficult.

The women were beginning to vaguely anticipate the difficulties. It was only the first week of November, and their horses went crashing through the ice in Calf Creek every morning. When they got up one day, it was 10 degrees. Still, by noon it was hot, and the air was so clear it almost vibrated. They had deep snow for a few days, followed by a day when the temperature rose from 20 to 95 degrees. In mid-November, during a rare week of good weather, the snow melted off the south side of the hills, giving the women a new view as they rode to school: one side naked and brown, the other clad in snow. It was hard to imagine that the winter would be quite as bad as everyone predicted.

Coming upon Shorty's cabin, Everette laughed and said, "Your winter residence looks like a hog pen, only it isn't large enough to be a comfortable hog pen!" For once they found his comments apt. The work had only just started, and Ros wrote to her mother, "It is the funniest looking affair you can imagine. So far, merely logs laid on top of each other — just like a corn crib with no signs of doors or windows."

Since the lumber wasn't even sawed yet, they decided they would stay at the Harrisons' for a while longer. Dorothy admitted, "I couldn't bear [the prospect of living there], if it weren't for the convenience of having it so near the school." Ros dismissed her mother's worry about blizzards; she was sure the horses would find their way home. Striking a colloquial note, she added, "Also, if it ever storms too bad, we have our packing trunks with *all our bedding* in it, in the supply closet at school, and supper enough in the Domestic Science larder to last us through."

Even before Thanksgiving, they were beginning to plan for Christmas, since their presents for the Harrisons and the children would have to be bought in Auburn. Dorothy had trouble deciding what to give Mrs. Harrison, who wouldn't have any use for extravagant gifts. Trying to get her mother to imagine their landlady's limited horizons, Dorothy wrote, "She hasn't been farther than the school house since last February — I think perhaps one of those spool baskets nicely fitted out would please her, a bright colored one. I think she would like something different to look at." Mr. Harrison was boarding up the kitchen, "daubing" with cement and sawdust, fortifying the house against the winter blasts. Soon Dorothy and Ros gave up on the idea of staying in Shorty's cabin and were relieved by their decision. They loved the morning and early-evening rides and knew that they couldn't oversee their own comfort the way

Mrs. Harrison did.

The children cut willow sticks for poles and started skiing to school on the curved slats from old barrel staves, which they propped up against the stone building before they went inside. Seeing the students' meager midday meals, some of which consisted of nothing but cold fried potatoes, Ros and Dorothy began cooking soup on the basement stove. Robin Robinson later remembered getting snowed in during November and running out of "grub." His father and a neighbor skied to Hayden to bring back some food but got delayed by a storm and didn't return for three days. "That school lunch at noon was about the greatest thing in our lives," he said. "We had nothing at home to eat but boiled wheat."

On sunny days at recess, the students liked to ski down the hill and across a pond. The teachers, who had never been on skis, took part enthusiastically. Dorothy wrote, "I went down a fine long hill today and it took me 35 minutes to come up! All the little boys went by me with gleeful smiles . . . while 'teacher' puffed & panted up the hill — they walk up on skis but I can't do that & had to plow through snow up to my knees." The boys cheered when the women got to the foot of the hill without falling.

Ros noted, "The sun is certainly a joy — the dark days are very few. The little boys' hands are at last emerging white and clean. The dirt of ages is being worn off by the winter snows!" The girls in her class were inclined to stay inside at lunch hour, reading from Aunt Helen's gift to the school — the "High School Series," a selection described by its publisher as "clean, wholesome stories that will be of great interest to all girls of high school age" — but Ros pried them from their seats and shooed them outside.

Dorothy's children continued to elicit contradictory impulses in her. One afternoon, noticing that Jimmy Robinson was shivering, she took him into the supply closet and gave him a sweater. A few minutes later, she had to usher in Tommy Jones to punish him for disobedience. He began to weep, saying, "You give Jimmy a sweater and *me* a whipping!" Dorothy wrote to her mother, "Wouldn't that have melted a stone? He is literally in rags so I gave him one, too, & he was soon wreathed in smiles with tears pouring down his cheeks. I know you think I am a brute but you ought to be with me for a day — I'll bet you'd think you were in a lunatic asylum." Then, with the querulousness that occasionally still surfaced when she was feeling overlooked, she said, "You never mention school and I wonder if you ever think of me at the noon hour — eating sandwiches, while you consume salads & soufflés."

None of her letters disclose her engagement, but she must have sent a telegram in late October, since her father wrote to express his approval. In his even, sloping handwriting on Auburn Button Works letterhead, he began:

My dear Dot
We had a very good visit from Lem and he confirmed the impression his former visits made — I like him very much indeed, and I am entirely satisfied that he will make you just the husband I could wish for you; he has high ideals, coupled with good business sense & I think sound judgement. Money is not the first thing with him, but I am confident you will never come to want if he has his health. . . .

The two families were sometimes incredulous that the "girls" could be as contented as they said they were. Dorothy responded to Anna, who had asked what it was like to be so far away from her fiancé: "You want to know about my *real* feelings but they vary! I could, of course, be very easily homesick but I won't let myself and I know I *must* stay." She wrote confusedly, "You have all been so lovely about Lem . . . of course, it is terribly hard not to see him for so long but on the other hand, I am very happy, and the weeks go by very quickly. Of course, I get discouraged when things go badly at school and when I don't get mail for a long time but you know Ros and I have to cheer each other on. It never lasts long, and I am so absolutely well that I am always blatantly cheerful & happy." And, she pointed out, they had a surrogate family: "The Harrisons are too good to be true, & I love them all."

They were ready for the Thanksgiving holiday. After school that Wednesday, they rode with Lewis to Oak Point, and Lewis returned home with their horses. Ferry had two big horses hitched to a sleigh, and a new moon lit their way to town. Dorothy wrote that she had an odd feeling, "flying into Hayden in that funny little home-made sleigh — as if I were really about a hundred years in the past — going to a Thanksgiving party. . . . [Y]ou can't know what a glorious feeling we have on these precious vacations!"

Ros was even more elated. Bob had just asked her to marry him. As Dorothy later recalled, "Having become engaged myself, I could see that romance was sprouting very heavily with Bob and Ros." Ferry could not have missed the signs either, and he must have stifled his disappointment over dinner with the teachers at the Hayden Inn, and afterward, at his office, where they sat around the stove talking about politics, education, religion, and the Boy Scouts. He was the troop leader in Hayden, and two boys appeared, asking to take the examination. That night Dorothy and Ros shared a lumpy bed at the inn and took the seven-fifteen train with Ferry to Oak Creek, where they were enthusiastically greeted by the Perry family and other guests: Bob, his parents, Charlotte and Marjorie and Portia Mansfield, by then all good friends of theirs; and a cousin, Mrs. Holbrook, from Milwaukee.

It was a momentous introduction to Sam and Lottie. Bob had just told his parents the news, but Ros hadn't yet informed Mr. and Mrs. Underwood. Instead, she wrote, "They are a lovely family, very devoted and full of fun. . . . Mrs. P. is quite frail, but very sweet and bright." Almost identically, Dorothy commented, "Mrs. Perry is a most cordial, enthusiastic person, sweet as she can be," but added, "Mr. Perry is a stern old war horse without much to say." The attractive Mrs. Holbrook was "a woman about forty whom they nearly killed off in their athletic zeal."

Sam Perry had organized Thursday's activities. Driving a sleigh pulled by four mules and loaded with seven pairs of skis, he took the entire entourage, except his wife, to the top of a mountain, where the teachers had their first skiing lessons. They returned to the house in time to lie down for a few minutes before dressing for dinner at four. "My *gown* for the occasion was my last year's blue serge, but it was quite all right," Ros wrote. Mrs. Perry had arranged the seating with place cards. Ferry, as Ros referred to him at last, dropping the formality of "Mr. Carpenter," had brought sweet peas for a centerpiece, and Mrs. Holbrook had created a framed silhouette for everyone: Dorothy's was a figure on skis, and Bob's, a man bound in rope. The eating "assumed real proportions as an occupation," Dorothy wrote. They devoured everything that Bob's housekeeper put before them: duck, grouse, fruitcake — and fresh vegetables and fruit of all kinds, a particular treat out of season. After dinner they played a card game called Racing Devil, and danced to the Victrola. Dorothy, oppressed by the steam heat, opened the door a crack to let some fresh air into the room.

Soon after Thanksgiving, Ros wrote to her parents, starting the letter with the command: "Please read this together." Mrs. Underwood complied, putting the letter in her desk drawer. She wasn't able to retrieve it until half past ten that night, when she and her husband returned from a dinner in town. Mr. Underwood, awed by her self-control, admitted that he never would have been able to wait. They sat down to read it by the lamp in the living room, then read it two more times before sending Ros a deliberately cryptic telegram: WE ARE ALL WELL AND HAPPY AFTER RECEIVING YOUR LETTER. Ros, like Dorothy, had asked that her engagement be kept secret until they returned to Auburn and could make the announcement themselves. Her father wrote on December 13, "I hope you & Dorothy understood our telegram & that no one else did. How I wish we could see you both!" Ros had told her parents that Mr. Shaw, who ran the telegraph office in Hayden, liked to gossip about their telegrams. Ros's mother wrote that it would be hard not to share the good news, "but you can trust us dear."

She didn't hesitate, though, to tell the family, summoning to 72 South Street all of the Auburn relatives. They peppered her with questions over lunch. Was it about Arthur? Was he engaged? Fired from his job? Or was it Ros? She said only that she had a letter from Arthur that she wanted to get their advice about. Aunt Helen was late to arrive, but finally, Mrs. Underwood ushered them into the music room, where she read Arthur's letter. It was so banal that they knew the real news was from Ros. Mrs. Underwood requested silence until she had read the letter all the way through. As she came to the end, she broke down in tears.

Then everyone started talking at once. George Jr., who had been pacing up and down the room, came to a stop before his mother and whispered, "I think it's wonderful." Aunt Helen rushed home to write to Ros, recalling the anxious weeks before she left for Colorado: "To think — you . . . set your face westward little thinking your Fate was there!" She also congratulated her on her high standards. "I could dance for joy that you never were weak enough to be coaxed, harried, cajoled, pushed . . . or fooled into taking the near right thing! As I march through them . . . — Harold-Dudley-Charlie-Douglas-Billy, Theologues & the Lord knows who — they all are found lacking, they did not move *you* — the inner soul of you. I am all for Bob — already — you love him — *das* [*ist*] *genug.* But when did you begin to be interested in him — when he was in danger?"

George Jr., following the same line of thought, wrote, "I know he is a *real man,*" underscoring the last words three times. He asked her to tell Bob that he was mighty glad to have him for a brother, and added, "Won't this old town sit up and take notice when the good news is told?" Mrs. Underwood told her, "It is an awfully comforting feeling to know that if anything happened to us, you would have someone to lean on, & fill your life with the best that life affords." Her father wrote, "It was a pity you could not have been here to see your bombshell explode. You would have enjoyed it."

The jubilation at the Underwood house indicated both how much the family had come to appreciate Ros's experience in Elkhead and how relieved her parents were that, contrary to all expectations, she had found a fiancé whom even the most strait-laced matrons of Auburn could admire.

Ros's mother then asked the Woodruffs to come for Sunday supper. There was an air of excitement when everyone sat down at the dining room table, and Mrs. Underwood said, "Let's take hold of hands circling the table and congratulate each other." Carrie Woodruff — acting more like her daughter than like herself — burst out: "Is Rosamond engaged?" and Grace replied, "Yes she is, to Bob Perry." Carrie said that she knew it was either Mr. Perry or Mr. Carpenter, but she couldn't have guessed which one. Carrie could wholeheartedly share the Underwoods' joy, calling to mind Dorothy's upstanding banker, and she must have pitied Grace for being unable to meet her future son-in-law for another five months.

In her own letter to Ros, Mrs. Woodruff revealed a warmer side than Dorothy was inclined to grant her, and more resilience. Despite her reservations about the Elkhead adventure, she had come to recognize that it was inevitable and — implicitly, at least — how it had begun to change them all.

Dearest Rosamond,
    What thrills of pleasure and excitement you have given Mr. Woodruff and me! . . . My dear children I do congratulate you — from the bottom of my heart.

Everything that you and Dorothy have written about Mr. Perry and Mr. Carpenter have proved their kindness, thoughtfulness, and devotion. . . . It is lovely to think of you as being so happy, and I realize fully that after this year neither you nor Dorothy would have been truly contented doing the same things which kept you busy before you went away. As I think of you and Dorothy growing up together, it certainly is extraordinary that your interests and occupations have always been identical. It is an unusual friendship which will I am sure never diminish — O how lovely it is that you both have this new bond of affection!

16
THREE-WIRE WINTER

Lewis Harrison breaking trail, 1917

In early December, Dorothy wrote to Anna that they had ridden to school that day in a blizzard. She admitted, "the wind & snow just cut — I can tell you." The following week, Mrs. Harrison, uncharacteristically, was close to despair. Her husband and

Frank Jr. were at another ranch trying to thrash, Dorothy wrote, "with an antique thrashing machine which Mr. H. *would* buy — against her better judgment." A thrashing machine, which separated the grain from the chaff and the straw, was set up at a central location so that ranchers nearby could use it. The grain had to be dry, or mold would grow in the sacks. The fact that they were still at it in December indicated the difficulties they'd had with the machine and their desperation to save what grain they could. Although a new one had been ordered, no one knew when it would arrive. "Farm life can be really tragic," Dorothy observed, "so much of it is uncertain and I pity the women!"

Mrs. Harrison's practical nature was a contrast to Mr. Harrison's aspirational one. He foresaw a future in which their pastures would be full of healthy cattle and their apple orchard would bear fruit for the market as well as the family. However, the winter descended with unexpected velocity. The Harrisons had no sheds for most of the livestock, not enough feed, and they were running out of coal, which meant long trips for Frank Jr. over unbroken roads to the nearest wagon mine. "You can't imagine how hard every thing is out here — to just keep alive," Dorothy wrote. "Boy goes very often after coal — an all day trip or maybe two — with four horses, and he is lucky to bring home a sled half full." The cattle milled around the house at night, seeking warmth and looking balefully in the windows.

Mrs. Harrison commended her two boarders for their hardiness. She had joined in the correspondence to and from Auburn, and she wrote to Carrie on December 6:

My Dear Mrs. Woodruff —
. . . I want to thank you for lending us these nice girls of yours for this winter. I know it must have been hard to give them up, but we surely do appreciate having them. I feel like it was a big undertaking and took a lot of courage — but they are not lacking in that. They seem to enjoy everything — this morning I was helping Miss Woodruff to get started & it was blowing and snowing. I said, "it is pretty bad — I wish you had started 1/2 hour ago as tis getting worse." She said, "Oh I like the sound" and they get on their horses & ride off as if they were perfectly at home on them. Of course they write you about their work & everything they do but I

just wanted to tell you how very much we think of them & how nice & sweet they are *all* the time. I try to do all I can for them to make it comfortable but it is not hard to do things for girls that are so appreciative as they are.

Sincerely yours,
Mrs. Harrison

The storms continued almost without letup through December. With snow covering the top of the barbed-wire fences, it was already what they called "a three-wire winter." At night, despite Mr. Harrison's daubing, it snowed through the chinks in the logs upstairs onto Dorothy and Ros's bed, and many mornings they woke up under a coverlet of snow. Mrs. Harrison came up the ladder at five A.M., thumped on the floor, and called out, "Girls, time to get up." She left them a pail of boiling water, which they poured into their pitcher, to break up the ice on top. They took turns being the first out of bed — rushing to the washstand, hastily scrubbing themselves under their nightdresses — and then put on their riding breeches, skirts, silk blouses, and sweaters. Downstairs they warmed their feet on the rim around the stove and laced up their boots while Mrs. Harrison prepared breakfast: salt pork with cream sauce, cereal with cream, biscuits and jam, and coffee. Afterward they dashed upstairs, made the bed, picked up their books and papers, and returned to the kitchen to make sandwiches for lunch and put on their outer garments.

They wore heavy tights and bloomers and pulled oversize German socks over their shoes and galoshes. These outfits were topped by their fur coats and woolen scarves. Ros wrote to Aunt Helen, "We can hardly heave ourselves into the saddle, but once there, we sit warm as toast, and the riding in the snow is most exhilarating." They always rode with snowshoes hung over their saddles. Dorothy said, "I thought if we fell off and I fell down in deep snow I might be suffocated."

The children had none of this insulation. "They just have to stand it, so they do," Ros said. Dorothy's pupils often arrived in tears, and she rubbed snow on their hands and feet, thinking that it was a quick way to warm them up. The older ones later wrote in their yearbook, "In the morning there were always at least a dozen small boys holding a crying concert around the furnace. But when noon came, who thought of such a thing as frosted feet and fingers?"

As the snow got deeper, Lewis Harrison

marked the path to school with willow whips, and he broke the trail each morning after a fresh snowfall — a small boy on a large white horse, up to its withers in snow, plunging through a vast rolling white hillside. On December 10, a several-day blizzard blew in, and at dawn on the thirteenth Dorothy and Ros saw a dozen cattle huddled around the henhouse with the snow up to their bellies and about six inches piled on their heads and backs. Dorothy commented, "This snow is very thrilling and beautiful from the inside looking out, but we *now* have the working girls' point of view!" She described her ride that day to her sister Herm, "It snowed so hard that we could only see a few feet in front of us — & it was like looking into white cloth. I kept my eyes shut most of the time — for one thing there is no danger of us running into anything! We looked like arctic explorers this morning, and all I could think of was a desert of snow." Ros took her boots out of the stirrups and trailed them in the powder on either side of the narrow path.

There were only fifteen children at school that day. The three Mitchell boys, who had joined Dorothy's class — Claude (twelve), Richard (eleven), and Joseph (nine) — walked three miles from home in snow that was almost up to their necks in some spots. Others arrived on horseback, some riding behind their fathers, who sat around the basement furnace all day, relishing the unaccustomed time off and a chance to relax in the warmth with their neighbors. The storm ended just before school let out, but then the wind began to blow, creating sweeping drifts with nothing to stop them for fifty miles.

The two groups of students began the Christmas season by preparing a box of presents for the Children's Hospital in Denver. Dorothy wrote, "It would make you cry to see what the children have brought from their treasures! A squirrel hide, piece of porcupine hide, dried oak leaves, and an old Christmas card!" They helped the students make raffia napkin rings and place-mats for their parents; the teachers had to explain what the napkin rings were for. Dorothy tried to teach the boys how to cross-stitch, "and it was *awful*! It was *'Miss Wood-rough —'* every other second — with sticky needles to thread — and I shudder to think of the results for 'Mama.' " Ferry gave the teachers a can of powdered milk that they used to make cocoa. Although Dorothy thought it was revolting, she told the boys it was fine, and they smacked their lips over it.

One morning the students told the teachers when they arrived that a pack rat had run into the supply closet. The closet was also the teachers' changing room, and Dorothy — determined to save face before her students, and to spend the day in dry clothes — braced herself to go in. As she started to pull on the brown skirt she wore for class, she saw that it was in shreds. "Wasn't that a shame — & I a poor teacher?" she commented. Her petticoat was still serviceable, "although lacking in a vital place," and since it was the only cotton one she had left, she asked her mother to send another. With the children's help, they set traps for the rat, which had also eaten the tops of all of their plants except the paperwhite narcissus, which was in full, fragrant bloom.

They took advantage of a lull between storms to spend a Friday night with Paroda Fulton, the secretary of the school board; her husband, Charlie; and their four boys. As they rode over the hills, it was very cold but clear. On such afternoons, the farthest mountains were deep blue and appeared so near, Dorothy wrote, that you felt as if you could walk to them. "This immense expanse of snow reflects the color of the sky — until it is really bluer than any Impressionist pictures I have ever seen." When the sun slipped behind the mountains, it shed a rosy glow all around them. Then a full moon rose. The snow was marked only by the hieroglyphs of small animals: foxes, coyotes, mice, and varying hares, which turned white in the winter.

In the social hierarchy of Elkhead, Mrs. Fulton was a "personage," as Dorothy described her. Only two years older than the two teachers, she had a reputation for being "exclusive," with her education and teaching background, her formal manner, and her executive abilities. She was credited, along with Ferry Carpenter, with setting high standards for education in Elkhead. Even before her own children were of school age, Paroda had served on the school board and advised the inexperienced teachers who showed up to teach at the early one-room schools. The books in her house included Dickens and Shakespeare, and she often made loans to Ros from her library for use in the classroom.

Her two guests watched as she got supper, talking to them and moving around the tiny kitchen with her baby perched on her hip. "She is one of those calm, poised people whom I always admire," Dorothy said. They discussed plans for the school Christmas party and agreed that Paroda would serve as the general manager. The program — play, recitations, carols — would start at about three-thirty, followed by the lighting of the tree, distribution of the children's stockings, supper, and a dance.

Soon after their visit, another blizzard struck, and Dorothy began to yearn for Auburn: "I shall think of you so much [on Christmas] day & wish with all my heart that I could fly home. Don't think I am homesick for I am too busy but you *do* want me to miss you all, don't you? . . . Just think — next year Lem and I will be coming home for Christmas. . . . No 'visiting' about it, you understand, but coming home!" She and Ros called the girl in the Hayden post office and begged her to try and get the mail out to Elkhead. The girl intercepted a man who worked on the Adair ranch, and he took it up the mountain to them. The sack was full of letters and packages, and the Harrisons talked about it for days. Dorothy's aunt Mollie sent a box of ornaments for the tree, packed so carefully that none had broken.

With Paroda Fulton organizing most of the party's events, the teachers had to worry only about the decorating of the room and the children's presents and exercises. The barrels containing the gifts, held up by the Moffat Road, which had taken to three-day-a-week service, were delivered to the school just in time. Even the teachers were awed by the contents: clothes and Christmas stockings for every child. The stockings, sent by the King's Daughters in Auburn, were stuffed with candy, soap, baseballs, caps, mittens, and purses containing coins. Dorothy wrote, "Everything was so new & such a quantity — we were simply speechless & I don't see how we can thank them."

On the Saturday before Christmas, Dorothy and Ros went to school to clean the room and wait for the tree, which some Elkhead volunteers brought in at four. Three children helped decorate it with candles and ornaments from home and popcorn and straw chains made by the students. They built a stage for the play and hung the piano with colored paper streamers and red bells, which stretched across the room to the stage. As the teachers were working, they looked out and saw their friend Isadore Bolten laboring straight up the hill on his skis, carrying a mail pouch. Dorothy and Ros agreed that it must have weighed fifty pounds.

Isadore, a member of the school board, had endeared himself to them by taking an active interest in their work, and they were awed by his extraordinary personal story. After leaving Chicago, he had worked on farms in Wisconsin and South Dakota, and then he read in the *Denver Post*'s supplement, the *Great Divide,* about the glories of the Western Slope. He walked to Elkhead from Steamboat Springs and supported himself at first by working at the Adair ranch. When he was looking for land to make his claim, he came upon Ferry and Jack White repairing a fence, and Ferry directed him to "rimrock country." He built his cabin with a steeply pitched roof, like the houses in Russia, so the snow would slide off more easily. As a homesteader, he wasn't looked kindly upon. Ranchers didn't like the influx of new settlers and all the fences that were closing off the open land. They were particularly unwelcoming, he felt, because he was Jewish.

He didn't mind making certain changes to ensure that he was accepted by his neighbors. He convinced Ferry to help him get his name legally changed from Israel Boloten, and he became a Mason. Admiring Ferry's library and envying his status in Hayden and Elkhead, Bolten persuaded him to give him lessons in the law. Ferry later said, "I swear he was about the brightest law student with whom I ever talked." Ferry bought some cobblers' tools for the school so that Isadore could give the boys a weekly class in shoemaking.

That evening Bolten stayed at the school until Dorothy and Ros finished, and he strongly advised them not to go home in the dark. The wind had been blowing hard all day, and the trail would be covered. The women knew the Harrisons would worry about them, but decided he was right, and after assuring him they would spend the night there, he skied home.

The basement was warm, with its furnace and stove, and they cooked a meal of cream-of-tomato soup and fried potatoes. Still unsure of themselves in the kitchen, they painstakingly followed the recipes in *The Boston Cooking-School Cook Book* (the first edition of *Fannie Farmer*). They were pleased with their impromptu supper, and they melted snow in a pot to wash the dishes, as Mrs. Harrison sometimes did. Otherwise, she simply stepped outside and snapped off a long icicle from the roof.

They were just about to take their bedding from the supply trunk when they heard a whoop outside. It was Frank Jr. and a hired man sent over by Mrs. Harrison. The women felt like two naughty children, sorry about the worry they had caused. The sky had cleared, and aided by the snow's reflected light, they could see quite well in the dark. Dorothy described the trip home, "four of us single file — just riding along in that whiteness. . . . 'Boy' was ahead of me — so long & graceful, riding bareback & singing weird cowboy melodies."

The Harrisons and the teachers opened their presents on Christmas Eve. Dorothy wrote of Mrs. Harrison, "I don't suppose she ever saw so many things, although they were few compared with our usual number." Dorothy and Ros gave her a lamp for the kitchen and the sewing basket Mrs. Woodruff had prepared. Mrs. Harrison gave them each a waterproof bag to hold their papers and carry on their saddles; their string bags weren't much use in the winter, no matter what method they devised to protect them from the snow. Ros's mother sent Mrs. Harrison an apron, a dress, a set of handkerchiefs, and some mincemeat and preserves; and Dorothy, some books for school and a pair of angora gloves. The teachers gave Lewis a leather scabbard for his gun, "which delighted his soul," Dorothy said, and Frank

Jr. an electric torch.

Ros received a scarf from a family friend, and Dorothy, a yellow hand-knit sweater from her aunt Mollie. Ros was happiest with some photographs from home taken at Aunt Helen's house on Thanksgiving Day. "I just had to hold back the tears — when I opened that, and saw you all sitting there!" Dorothy had the same reaction to a photograph her mother sent of herself: "I nearly burst into tears — it is so *beautiful* . . . and I look and look at it. . . . The light on your hair is marvelous, and your dress is so lovely. I am *so* proud of my mother!" And there was a box from Lem. Exhibiting a sure sense of his fiancée's tastes, he had wrapped the presents with beautiful paper and gold cord: a black umbrella handle inlaid with gold, an "exquisite" set of Thoreau, a Russian novel, a box of candy, and, she added, "I guess I won't tell you the other," referring to a negligee, presumably, or some other romantic offering.

Ros did not say whether she had bought something personal for Bob, but she and Dorothy had planned well ahead for identical gifts for him and Ferry. A month earlier Dorothy had asked Lem to buy two cast-iron boot scrapers, made to resemble dachshunds, she had seen at a store in Grand

Rapids the previous winter. Together they weighed ninety pounds. Lem sent them by express mail, and Dorothy wrote that they "nearly caused a riot in Hayden." Mr. Shaw — who had said to Ferry that summer, when the teachers had to temporarily call off their teaching plans, "Get out you handkerchief, Ferry! The girls have turned you down" — told Ferry that the cost for shipping the heavy package was $4.80. He was particularly impressed that Lem had prepaid, commenting, "He must think a lot of that girl!" Ferry and Bob gave Dorothy and Ros two wolf hides they had admired in town that fall, which they were having made into rugs.

Late on Christmas afternoon, in the midst of yet another blizzard, families began arriving at the school on big sleds, wagons, and horses. Dorothy wrote, "My heart just ached for those poor people as they came in — covered with snow, and half frozen — many of them having been on the road for hours — some of them . . . never got there at all." Ros added, "I cannot describe to you the scene! . . . Old and young — in all sorts of costumes, most of them having endured what they call out here much 'grief' to arrive at all, gathered together to celebrate the big day in the year, and forget the hardships of winter."

The children were treated to their first Santa Claus: Shorty Huguenin in full costume, who burst in, shaking off the snow. Shrieks filled the room as the stockings were distributed and their contents examined. Ros told her family that "the children were wild with joy." The year before, there had been no gifts, and a little boy had asked Dorothy the previous week why not, since children in stories always got presents. Dorothy found Oliver Morsbach, Rudolph's seven-year-old brother, behind the piano "in a trance of joy — over a doll's tea set, probably intended for a girl & mixed by mistake — but he just *loved* it!" The play was followed by pieces prepared by Dorothy's children, then by some Christmas carols. The seven youngest children sang "Holy Night" in high, quavering voices. Ros was pleased with it all but said, "Babies wailed through the performances, and then proceeded to be sick! — not that I wondered." She fed them the favored antacid of the day, aromatic spirits of ammonia — a blend of ammonia, ammonium carbonate in alcohol, and distilled water perfumed with lavender, lemon, and nutmeg oils — "not knowing what else to do."

Large quantities of food were spread out

on the tables downstairs. The pianist didn't get there, but a fiddler did his best ("it was pretty bad," Ros said), and the dancing — Virginia reels, folk dances, and quadrilles — began at eight. "You would have laughed to have seen Dotty and me," Ros wrote, "being put thru the paces of the square dances, with two of the rustic swains! . . . I think it's stupid that we don't dance them any more." Dorothy commented, "You do a queer kind of jig step . . . and then solemnly 'promenade' around the room, arm in arm, and then you are dumped with no ceremony whatever — the quadrilles are fascinating & I love to do them — they have so much dash & everyone enters into it with such spirit."

She evoked it all for her family: "It was such a queer assemblage way out here, on top of a mountain, in a storm. Some of the men kept on their hats — most of them smoked. Some were dressed up, even to a collar, but suspenders were the predominant feature. Tired, gaunt-looking women trying to keep children off the floor or put crying babies to sleep & one after another, the little children would topple off to sleep, & were rolled up and tucked away from underfoot." Even so, there seemed to be babies everywhere — under tables, on benches, desks, piles of clothing — until "you didn't dare sit down without investigating." All of this "in our beautiful modern building, handsomely decorated! I wonder if there is anything so fine, and so remote, in the country."

At midnight Ros and Dorothy, heedlessly defying the tradition of the all-night party, slipped out and set off for home. It was still snowing, and about a mile from the Harrison ranch, Pep stumbled and fell in the deep snow. The women were frightened, recalling stories they had been told about people losing their bearings in winter storms. But they followed the instructions they had been given for this kind of emergency, removing the snowshoes from their saddles and leaning over to drop them onto the snow. Dismounting in the winter was always difficult because of their layers of clothing, and this time they had to strap on their snowshoes in the deep powder. Pep lunged and flailed as he tried to get up, and they were a poor match for the 1,000-pound horse. They finally coaxed him back onto his feet and to the trail.

When they reached the ranch, they chopped through the ice in the buckets by the barn to water the horses, unsaddled them, and stumbled into the house. Dorothy said, "I know there's a bottle of whiskey here because I saw Old Man Harrison have some one night." In Auburn, they never would have thought of consuming hard liquor, but they hunted until they found the bottle, and each took a large swig. Dorothy noticed that the whiskey gave them "a good furnace inside," and they climbed the stairs and fell into bed with their boots on. The next morning, the family returned. One of them commented, "You had quite a time last night, didn't you?" It was all written in the snow.

A few days later, they left for a New Year's party at Bob's cabin in Oak Hills. Covered by masses of wraps and blankets, they rode to Hayden in a sled full of straw pulled by Frank Jr. on his horse, reading novels, eating Christmas candy, and clutching hot-water bottles. The train was supposed to leave Hayden at seven-fifteen, but when they got there, they learned that it wasn't expected even to depart Denver for twenty-four hours. Used to the delays, Dorothy filled some of the time writing letters. She told Herm that "the place is full of men — such a funny lot . . . and they all vied in entertaining the school moms — as they all call us — such hair-raising stories of people lost in the snow — frozen to death, & then old settlers' stories of Indians, etc. How you would have loved it all."

Milly, who was planning a long stay with them in February, was next. Dorothy blithely described the worst months of the year in Elkhead, telling her she could ride one of Mr. Harrison's horses, learn to ski, join them at school, and "see the neighborhood." Her visit, Dorothy said, would be a godsend, making the winter pass quickly and bringing the joy of being with her again. "Of course, we have a fierce amount of snow," she continued, "but . . . the cold is dry & not bad at all . . . It is a glorious day — and 22 degrees below! Do you think you will mind?"

When Dorothy and Ros finally left for Oak Creek, they settled in for the beautiful ride along the river. The towering cottonwoods looked like another species in the winter, their dark branches coated in feathery white depth hoar. The cattle stood out sharply against the snow. As they passed through Steamboat Springs, the train made a sickening, grinding noise when the engineer jammed on the emergency brake and the rail crumpled underneath them. The car rocked and pitched alarmingly before coming to a slow, screeching halt.

Dorothy continued her letter to Herm —

in pencil, on the back of a Barkalow Bros. dining car conductor's report. "We can't say a word, we are so glad to be alive, but I imagine we will stay here *all* day. They have sent for a wrecking train & we still hope to make Oak Creek tonight. Do you suppose I shall still have nerve enough to urge Milly to brave this railroad?" In derailments on the Moffat Road, train cars sometimes tumbled off mountainsides and into rivers. The railroad was diligent about getting the cars and debris from the wrecks back to the rail shops, so it could salvage as much as possible, but the deepest canyons of the Rockies were the resting place, here and there, for rusting train carcasses.

They were aggravated by yet another delay. "We had to possess our souls in patience while they sent out an S.O.S. to Phippsburg," Ros wrote to her father, so they were pleased when the conductor showed them "the whole works," including the inside of the locomotive cab. They had their picture taken in front of the train. The seventeen-foot engine dwarfed the two women, Ros in her fur coat, holding her clutch; Dorothy in wool and a porkpie hat, her hands thrust deep in her pockets. At two P.M., a wrecking train and crew arrived from Phippsburg. Bob and Marjorie were on board, with a fitted lunch box containing turkey sandwiches, cookies, and milk. Departing again eight and a half hours later, they arrived at Oak Creek at eleven-thirty P.M. They didn't have much time or energy for the holiday party, "having been 15 hours on the way from Hayden."

The next morning, they got a ride home in the caboose of a thirty-five-car freight train to Mt. Harris, a coal town near Hayden. It was poorly lit, and in place of seats, it contained two cots: "The bumps are not to be taken standing," Ros commented. Bob had arranged for a sleigh to meet them at Mt. Harris, and they had a snug moonlit ride to the Hayden Inn. Ros wrote, "Our holiday is over and to-morrow we go back to work and shall be very busy getting new plans for the next month. The corner has been turned now — 1917 is here and the time will fly till we are back home again."

Dorothy thanked her mother for allowing Milly to make the long trip to see them, saying that she had been walking on air ever since she got the final confirmation. "You may be sure that I shall even take more care of Milly than I would of myself." And she wrote to Anna, "You probably think it would be like a trip to Siberia but I think she could have a good time." She called

Ferry to tell him the news, and he laughed, telling her that Mr. Shaw had just seen him on the street and informed him, "Well, Mildred's coming!" And then Ferry said, "I've got a little greeting for you from Lem!" She didn't mind. "It really isn't as much pure nerve as it sounds but more Western interest in everyone's affairs."

She began to look at the Harrisons through Milly's eyes: the milling cattle, the clucking chickens, the house draped once a week with drying underwear. Milly was to get one of the boys' rooms. It had only a bed in it, but Dorothy hoped that with the featherbed, Milly wouldn't feel the need for anything else; she would, though, have to get up in the cold and the dark, as they did. "I know she will be horrified at our clothes & I hope *she* will have something pretty," she wrote to her mother. "Just think of all the things I want to ask & talk over!" She ended with an apology for the brownish tinge to her script: "This ink freezes every night — hence its color." And she told her mother, "I sent Herm the Hayden paper, which I thought might amuse you. Please save it and my pictures. I might want them someday."

In the depths of the worst winter in anyone's

360

memory, outings were restricted, and Dorothy's cabin fever became apparent. On some weekends, even Bob and Ferry failed to make it. "I doubt if we have any of the diversions which we have been so lucky about. We just plain have to *stay*," she wrote to Anna. Lewis amused himself by shooting his .22 out the window to make a coyote stop howling. Ferry managed to take the Boy Scouts for a "snowshoe hike" one clear Saturday, and they spent the night at his cabin. Some fathers, inspired by their sons' resoling accomplishments, started giving carpentry lessons to the older boys. Mr. Harrison ventured into Hayden to buy nails: "Imagine taking a 2 day trip for *nails*!"

They were lucky not to be snowbound on the day of Milly's arrival. Lewis escorted Dorothy and Ros to Oak Point, and Ferry took them by sleigh into Hayden. The road was in a bad state, and the three friends, invigorated by the outing and the prospect of welcoming another Auburn girl to Elkhead, carelessly invited the third traveling mishap within two weeks. Describing Ferry as "rather a casual driver," Dorothy wrote to Anna that in the midst of a particularly entertaining story, the sleigh tipped over and she found herself flying through the air with her enormous overshoes shooting past her face. She landed neatly on her feet, like an acrobat, some fifteen feet below the road in a ditch, buried up to her waist in powder. Ros and Ferry were facedown in a drift, along with their possessions. Ferry brushed himself off, helped Ros back into the sleigh, and then made his way down to rescue Dorothy. "Well, we bundled back & started off — *only* to tip over again! This time there was no bridge & it was merely a little snow down your neck."

Milly, Dorothy said, made a complete conquest of the Harrisons and the schoolchildren. Apparently encouraged by her admiration of their managerial skills in the classroom, Ros wrote, "I have to pinch myself at times to realize that it is really I who am teaching. It's such an education as I never hoped to receive." Every Friday after recess, the teachers opened up the doors between the classrooms, and Milly taught the children folk dances, accompanied by the Victrola. On Valentine's Day, Dorothy had a bad cold, and Milly insisted on substituting for her. She wrote to Anna that she had her hands full with seventeen students, and Ros said, "She had a time she won't soon forget. She seemed to get a good deal of entertainment out of it, 'tho, and survived." Milly oversaw the younger children as they worked on their valentines, commenting, "they really showed quite a lot of ingenuity," and after school, helped Ros prepare for the evening dance.

The teachers had become adept at organizing community-wide parties. Ros had started a group of Camp Fire Girls, the sister organization to the Boy Scouts, and the girls fixed up a small room in a corner of the basement, equipped with a sofa and "boarded off by the big boys," as Milly put it, "where all of the babies are to be stowed for the night." Ros's girls also decorated the classroom and made fourteen cakes and towers of sandwiches. There were no more jokes about bumbling in the kitchen; Ros approached it all with the efficiency of a restaurateur. Everyone was in good spirits, and the evening was sparklingly clear. The fiddler arrived on skis, with his fiddle over his shoulder. Ros's girls served the supper, charging five cents each for a cup of coffee, a sandwich, and a piece of cake. Ros reported that they cleared over twenty dollars, enough to pay for the costumes for the play, an ice-cream freezer for the community, and a nest egg for the Camp Fire treasury. It was the first time the families didn't provide the food, and the decorations were skillfully executed. "The home-made or rather school-made effusions were hailed with more enthusiasm and delight than Zepp's best," Ros wrote, referring to a stationery store in Auburn. The "tiniest scholars" hopped around on the dance floor, having been "demoralized" by Milly's dance lessons. "Even the poor little blinking babies had a better time than at Christmas."

In the last week of February, Dorothy and Milly and Ros went to Winter Carnival in Steamboat Springs. They had been hearing about the event for months. Marjorie Perry, along with her other outdoor activities, was a skiing enthusiast. Several years earlier, she had become friendly with Carl Howelson, a thirty-four-year-old champion skier from Norway. He had lived in Denver, where he worked as a stonemason, but he went every winter to the Hot Sulphur Springs Carnival. Marjorie met him there, and persuaded him to visit Steamboat Springs. In 1913 he moved to Strawberry Park. He introduced the sport of ski jumping to the town and organized cross-country skiing races. These events turned into the carnival, the annual weekend highlight of the winter season in Routt County.

Still, Dorothy was concerned about the final weeks of school. It was nearly April, when the students would be needed to help with the farm work, and the melting snow and mud would hinder their efforts to get there. "We will have to work *hard* to get backward children up to par — and get ready for closing day," she wrote. Ferry had told them that they would need to present some sort of exhibition of the students' work, but he was vague about the specifics, so Dorothy asked Anna to visit Miss LeMay, who had helped her prepare for her classes, hoping she would have some suggestions. They also conferred with Paroda Fulton. She helped them work out their calendar, their final lesson plans, and the closing ceremonies. State law required that they teach twenty days every month, and they calculated that if they added a few Saturdays, they could finish their classes on April 12. They then visited the school in Hayden, to "match up" their work with that of the teachers there and to see what they were planning for the end of the year. Ros wrote, "We're counting the weeks now . . . six from today will be Easter Sunday and it will come before we know it."

Caught up in their work and unable to get their letters to town, Dorothy and Ros stopped writing home. The two last letters they sent from Elkhead were dated late February 1917. On March 3, Milly sent a telegram to her parents from Steamboat Springs: TWO SPLENDID DAYS, WONDERFUL SKIING, GIRLS LEFT THIS AFTERNOON ON A FREIGHT FOR HAYDEN. I SHALL STAY HERE WITH MARJORIE TILL TUESDAY THEN TAKE THE TRAIN FOR DENVER WITH HER. . . .

Early springtime in Elkhead, beginning in mid-March, had its own excitements and drawbacks. At night the snow froze solid — a treacherous surface to navigate. In the morning, Calf Creek ran swiftly under a fragile layer of ice; by the afternoon it was a brown torrent, rushing higher and faster each day. Spring at the Harrisons' came sooner than it did up at the schoolhouse, where patches of mud over a layer of ice were, as the locals put it, "slick as snot," causing Pep and Gourmand to skid and stumble.

The glimmers of the approaching season made the children restless, and so did the extra work the teachers gave them in preparation for their exams. Everyone looked forward to the end of the school day. As Dorothy and Ros rode home, Lewis helped them spot returning blackbirds and robins, killdeer investigating the wet patches of the meadows, and butterflies flitting low across the snow. When Lewis unsaddled their horses and stood in one place too long, he sank almost to his knees in mud that had the consistency of thick chocolate pudding. His boots made a rude slurping sound as he extricated them.

By the last day of school, the aspens were beginning to leaf out, and sage buttercups and bluebells and stretches of brilliant green grass were eclipsing the snow. The closing exercises took place on Thursday evening, April 12. Parents left home twelve hours in advance. "In spite of the fact that it was impossible to get a horse over the roads on account of the melting snow," the *Routt County Republican* reported, "about 30 parents and residents walked upon the crust early in the morning and were on hand for the exercises." Dorothy's students, dressed up as characters from Mother Goose, delivered monologues, and Ros's acted in a farce. The teachers played an unexpected role in the proceedings: Ferry presented each of them with a gold medallion — a gift from the Elkhead Board of Education. On one side was a simple etching of the stone building, and on the other, their names with an inscription: "For bravery in attendance, loyalty in work, as teacher 1916–17."

The *Republican* reported, "The attendance and the work at the school throughout the long and exceptionally severe winter have shown that a winter school is feasible for the rural districts of any county." After the ceremony and before the dance, the adults gathered for a "war meeting." Two weeks earlier, President Wilson had declared in the House of Representatives that "the world must be made safe for democracy." After learning of the Germans' intention to begin unrestricted submarine warfare, he deferred his plea for a just and secure peace: "It is a fearful thing to lead this great peaceful people into war, into the most terrible and disastrous of all wars, civilization itself seeming to be in the balance. But the right is more precious than peace. . . ." The assembly in Elkhead uniformly pledged their support for the war.

17
COMMENCEMENT

"At the Great Divide on our trip to Ferry's homestead," 1923

On Saturday, April 14, Mr. Harrison and Frank Jr. loaded the teachers' trunks onto wagons with runners attached, and Dorothy and Ros left for Hayden. From there they took the train back to Denver, where they were joined by their parents. Finally, Grace and George Underwood had an opportunity to meet Bob and the senior Perrys. The next morning, Ros woke her mother early, climbing into bed with her in one of the Perry guest rooms to show her the gold medallion. Sam and Lottie had a dinner party that night, attended by family friends, where they announced Bob's engagement to Rosamond. Ferry had come, too, from Oak Point. Grace Underwood recorded in her diary, "All so happy. Our new son is lovely."

The following week, the Underwoods and Woodruffs left for Chicago, and Grace noted: "Soldiers guarding all bridges as we cross over Mississippi." Platt Underwood, Ros's uncle, was at the station to meet them, along with Lemuel Hillman. Dorothy had anticipated the reunion with her fiancé with some trepidation, having spent far more time and in much closer quarters with Ferry and Bob than she had with him, but as soon as she saw him, she said, "he looked very natural and very good to me." He was fit after his training in the Naval Reserve, and unabashedly delighted to see her.

Years later, though, it was the departure

from Elkhead that Ros and Dorothy recalled most vividly. Ros said of that day, "I lost my heart to the west right then and there." In truth, she had lost it many months earlier, perhaps as early as the July morning in Hayden when they rode in the spring wagon from Hayden to Elkhead for the first time. So had Dorothy, who recalled, "I fell in love with that beautiful country. We didn't know whether or not we wanted to make this a career, and it was decided for both of us. If we hadn't married, we would probably have continued." Although they didn't question the social convention dictating that finding a good husband meant forfeiting a profession, they regretted that they would be sacrificing some of the intimacy of their friendship. For the first time, the two friends were preparing for lives apart. Ros and Bob would start off in his house in Oak Hills, with the promise of Denver in their future. Dorothy would move to Grand Rapids. In some ways, they were likely more apprehensive about this departure than they were as they set off together for Colorado. Ros told her grandchildren that the year in Elkhead was the best in her life. It was clear that Dorothy felt the same way.

They were together until their wedding days. Back in Auburn, caught up in parties and planning, they nevertheless found time to assemble matching photograph albums, embossed in gold lettering on the front with their names and COLORADO 1916–1917. In one of the last shots that Ros took in Elkhead, Dorothy crouches by the henhouse in the sun-hardened mud. Surrounded by chickens, wearing a graying apron of Mrs. Harrison's over her dress, she is burning the contents of the cardboard box they used as their scrap basket. Looking up at Ros, she smiles broadly. The lower eaves of the main house are hung with three-foot icicles, sharp as rapiers.

At four P.M., on April 28, the Underwoods stepped into their carriage to ride the short distance to the Woodruff house. Dorothy's mother was hosting a formal tea for fifty guests to mark the two engagements. Dorothy and Ros were dressed in white, and Ros wore a corsage of sweetheart roses and pink sweet peas, a gift from Bob, who had not yet come east for the wedding. The *Auburn Citizen* described the party as "one of the most attractive of the afternoon functions ever held in this city."

The two women were inundated with letters, telegrams, and spring bouquets. Meanwhile, across the street at Aunt Helen's house, a package arrived that Ros and Bob had planned months earlier — the first offspring of their alliance. Helen had not yet gotten her new dog, and as Grace wrote in her diary, "The Airedale pup named 'Coal' with collar marked R. M. Perry, Oak Creek, Colo.," showed up at about the same time that Helen arrived from New York. "The pair took to each other at once, and are great cronies."

Rosamond married Robert Perry at St. Peter's Episcopal Church in Auburn on June 30. Four days later, Dorothy married Lemuel Hillman at her parents' house on Fort Street. Ros was the matron of honor and Milly the maid of honor.

Both Ros and Dorothy made return visits to Elkhead as soon as they could. In May 1920 Ros traveled alone from Oak Creek for the high school graduation of five seniors, her former students: Leila Ferguson, Ina Hayes, Ezra Smith, Helen Jones, and their intrepid guide, Lewis Harrison. She and Bob already had two small children of their own, and it was the first time that she had left them overnight. Preparing for the weekend, she ripped up a four-year-old black suit skirt, shortened it, and pressed it. She hurried to pack, took a late train to Hayden, and arrived at three A.M. Despite the hour, Ferry met her at the depot. The boxcar had been replaced with a solid two-story brick station.

The next day he took her on a tour of two new projects on whose boards he served: the Solandt Memorial Hospital, named after Hayden's first doctor/veterinarian/coroner; and the building site for the consolidated Hayden Union High School. The Elkhead School's first graduating class was also its last. After that, the school district was incorporated into Hayden's, and although the younger children stayed on at Elkhead, the high school students boarded in town during the school year. The tiny mountain community couldn't offer the range of classes and facilities that would be available in Hayden. Carpenter didn't dwell on the diminishing fortunes of Elkhead, and he got Ros to see it his way. "Both buildings are going to be perfectly splendid," she wrote to her mother. "Think what it will mean to the poor people around the country to get medical & surgical care of the proper kind. The school is going to have everything down to a swimming pool." It was the first such pool, Ferry told her, in Routt County.

That afternoon he dropped her off with his ranching partner, Jack White, and Jack's wife, Ann. Ros found Ann White, a onetime society girl from Evanston, Illinois, a fascinating amalgam of East and West. Before her marriage, Ann had staked her own homestead claim outside Steamboat Springs. "She is very attractive — and her clothes are right up to date — *Vogue* is her constant companion — in spite of which she does *all* her own work — including washing, ironing — making butter — caring for the 2 boys 4 & 2 — running a car — and caring for her house which is quite large for these parts." The Whites had an enclosed porch, with a window seat doubling as a toy chest. Inside were two toolboxes with real saws, hammers, and screwdrivers. A trapeze hung from the ceiling, and the little boys rode horseback around the property without parental supervision.

Late Saturday morning, the women rode to Oak Point for a quick lunch with Ferry before continuing on to the school. It had rained hard all night, but as they headed out and the air began to clear, Ros had a rush of euphoria: "The hills stretched out in front of us — and Bears Ears loomed up." As the trail reached the main road to the schoolhouse, they saw a diminutive figure on horseback heading up the hill. It was Mrs. Harrison, carrying a huge sack of dishes for the banquet. Ros wrote, "She nearly fell off her horse — she was so glad to see us." Mrs. Harrison told Ros that she had been taking care of two grandchildren for three months, and she was so determined to enjoy the ceremonies that she had asked Mr. Harrison to stay home with them. And so "poor 'Pa H.' missed seeing Lewis graduate."

The boys came running out of the schoolhouse — Dorothy's former students, grown larger. They had recently received a telegram from her, and clamored for information about what she was doing. Ros told them that Miss Woodruff, now Mrs. Hillman, was living in Michigan with her two-year-old son and her husband, who worked in a bank. The women went to the teacherage to change their clothes; Ros's "girls" were waiting there for her and gave her an ecstatic welcome. Eunice Pleasant, the soft-cheeked but tough-minded teacher of the older students, was living there that year. The commodious stone cottage, completed the year after Dorothy and Ros left, was built out of the same rimrock as the schoolhouse. It contained a kitchen, a living room, and a library downstairs, and two bedrooms upstairs. It too had generous windows with clear views into Utah and Wyoming. When Eunice took the job, she wrote to her sister-in-law, "I think the chief joy in the whole situation will be having a home of my own."

Eunice had met Ferry Carpenter at a dance in Hayden when she was visiting her brother, a musician in an orchestra in nearby Craig that was playing that night. She was young and single, spoke fluent German and some Greek, and had been teaching school since she was fifteen — paying her way through Kansas University over six years by alternating semesters of teaching and attending classes. Ferry had served in the war as a lieutenant, training recruits in Arkansas and Texas, and he was still single, but his marital scheme for Elkhead had an impressive record of success. In addition to Ros's marriage to Bob Perry, the two subsequent teachers at Elkhead, from Massachusetts, married local men.

Ferry asked Eunice to dance and started right in with his Elkhead sales patter. Afterward, Eunice wrote that she was impressed with what she heard of the enterprising community, the winter sports, and the dances at the school, which were famous for miles around. "This place is as much a community center as a school," she explained. "I have met all kinds of school boards, and been asked all kinds of questions, but this is the first time a school board member ever asked me whether I danced, with the idea that my being fond of dancing is in my favor."

Her letters were full of praise for Ferry. "I would never have gotten through had Mr. Carpenter not assisted me in various little ways. . . . He's all business — and kind friendliness — and immune to other sentiment." His advice about keeping house was both practical and singular. Suggesting that she make oatmeal cookies, which would "keep forever," he told her he filled a jar as big as a barrel to get him through the winter. "He discoursed on the merits of a dish-mop, and gave me a lecture yesterday on wearing sufficient warm clothing when riding." He often showed up at her house with gifts: a mixing bowl, a mousetrap, and, one cold day, two sticks of butter in his pockets. It was Ferry's style of courtship, and it worked. Two months after the graduation, he and Eunice were engaged.

When Ros stepped into the school again, she was overcome. There were dozens of bouquets of the class flower, dog's-tooth violet, on the windowsills and around the room. Miss Rench was the primary-school teacher that year at Elkhead, and she lived in her own cabin nearby. The walls of her classroom were covered with the children's work, which was far more elaborate than anything Dorothy had overseen: woven rugs, baskets, clay modeling; bas-relief maps of the schoolyard, the school district, and the county; calendars; and paintings.

Ros asked her mother to send the letter on to Dorothy, and addressed part of it to her friend: "Dotty, Miss Rench's exhibit was simply marvelous. I told Ferry my one regret was you weren't there — but I feared her exhibit would make you sick! I congratulated her & she said with that saucy look 'Oh — just the material outcome of a little work'! I wanted to hit her."

At seven P.M., Eunice hosted a banquet for forty at the cottage: the graduating class and their parents, the school board, and selected guests. Dinner was served by three of the other younger girls, who carried out their duties flawlessly. The three banquet tables were set with wildflowers, and each place contained a gold-tasseled program made from blue construction paper by two of the graduating students. Ros observed that "everything was very correct." Eunice described "Mrs. Perry" as one of the most charming people she had ever met — "just the best type of all-round college girl."

The dinner included a full roster of speakers, with Lewis Harrison as a representative of his class. Quiet, steady Lewis was in agony at the thought of public speaking, but Ros reported to her mother that he gave the best talk of anyone. Afterward, they all walked down the hill for the graduating exercises at the school, where the rest of the parents and siblings had gathered. Professor George Reynolds, a Shakespearean and biblical scholar who headed the English Department at the University of Colorado at Boulder, gave the main address. He told the audience that he had been to a great many rural schools in numerous western states, and none compared to Elkhead. Ros said, "He was simply carried away with all he experienced & saw," and he told her that "the combination of these Eastern College girls working with these Westerners had produced these most interesting results!"

Carpenter presented the diplomas to each of the graduates, and a community dance followed. Ros noticed with the sympathy of a young mother that their friend Paroda — who now had five sons — looked sad and tired for the first time. Ros, too, was a little worn, as Mrs. Harrison wrote in her own letter to Mrs. Underwood after the event. "She looked her own sweet self — but she really is thin. She said her clothes just hung on her." Bob was still having difficulty with union and safety issues at the mine, and Oak Hills was not the kind of place they would have chosen for their early years of marriage. Sam Perry had been staying with them at a guest "bungalow" that Bob had built next to their house, and Mrs. Harrison pointed out that having "Grandpa P. there so long must have been the most trying — & he being sick part of the time." Ros had some gray hairs already, "but don't you worry about that — for she is just as pretty as ever — & every one was so glad to see her."

Despite Ferry's pending engagement to Eunice, that night he chose Ros for the first dance. She danced until three A.M., and said that she never again expected to go anywhere in her life where she would be the popular belle she was in Elkhead. "Think of an ex school marm and mother having such a good time!"

During the summer of 1923, Dorothy and Lem left their two children at home with the housekeeper and went to Elkhead. In 1921 Ros and Bob had moved from Oak Hills to Denver, where Bob ran his father's office, and they had their third child. On the trip from Denver to Hayden, the two couples drove up to Rollins Pass. Dorothy, her hair cropped short, wore trousers tucked into tall leather boots and a long pocketed cardigan buttoned up the front. Lem wore knickers, kneesocks, a tailored shirt, and a necktie. In a picture taken by Ros, he leans protectively over his wife.

Dorothy and Ferry were curious about each other's spouses, and before visiting the schoolhouse, she and Lem went to Oak Point. She was impressed with Eunice's intelligence, but — fiercely proud of her closest friends — felt that Eunice paled a little next to Ferry, with his quirky dynamism. Outside, she took a picture of him, bending over to grip the hand of his toddler, Ed, as they ambled through the garden. An American flag on a twenty-five-foot pole fluttered behind them near the cabin.

When Dorothy and Lem were visiting, Ferry invited some friends to join them, and the party turned into a series of hazing rituals for Lem. As Dorothy recalled, the men stood around waiting for an opportunity to ridicule "this dude from the East." His New York accent was a particular source of amusement. "They just loved it, and they'd crowd around and listen to him talk." They found out that he had never been on a horse, and Dorothy was afraid he would disgrace himself. "I needn't have worried," she said, laughing. "He got on and . . . the horse went tearing around and he just handled him beautifully." Then the men said they wanted to go shooting. Unaware of Lem's training in the Michigan National Guard, they assumed he had never held a .22. He was handed a rifle, and when a flock of sage grouse rose into the sky, he brought down every bird.

Epilogue

Jimmy Robinson and Jesse Morsbach (right) in front of the school, 1916

Today two of the three year-round residents of Elkhead, Cal and Penny Howe, live in a comfortable log house and run a ranch on the old Harrison property. Nailed above their fireplace are several weathered cottonwood boards they scavenged from the ruins. Except for the stone foundations of the homestead and two apple trees — the survivors of an orchard planted by Mr. Harrison and Frank Jr. — the boards are all that is left. Hayden, now a bedroom community for Steamboat Springs, is a town of about sixteen hundred, its businesses struggling to hang on. Ferry's old law office, sagging with age, is uninhabited. In 1978 his cabin was struck by lightning and burned to the ground, but his grandson Reed Zars, an environmental lawyer who lives in Laramie, Wyoming, rebuilt it, assisted by friends and family members.

On a warm day in February 2009, I went to see Oak Point, along with Rebecca Wattles, the fifty-three-year-old granddaughter of Paroda Fulton. Paroda moved with her family to Hayden in 1922, and they built a ranch on the Yampa River. The property, now owned by Rebecca and her brother, contains the homestead built in 1881 by William Walker, one of the first settlers to arrive after the Utes departed. Rebecca's father renovated the cabin, and her son and his family live there now.

Rebecca and I followed the winding county road through the hills to where the snowplow stopped. We got out of her truck and put on our skis. There were no houses in sight — just barbed-wire fences pushed at odd angles by winter storms, and sagebrush and scrub oak poking through the snow. The day was cloudless and the snow so dazzling that I wondered if Ros and Dorothy had survived the winter without sunglasses. It took me a moment to register a tall, angular man in his fifties wearing a red T-shirt and baseball cap, approaching on skis in a swift diagonal stride. As he got closer and greeted us with an open smile, weathered face, blue eyes, and western drawl, I almost called out, "Ferry!" Reed said that when he looked at old photos of his grandfather next to photos of himself, he had trouble telling them apart.

The ascent to the cabin was steeper than Reed had let on. When we reached the top, we saw nothing but hills and mountains in every direction. A century after Ferry chose the spot for his homestead, the view was virtually unchanged. Reed had replaced his grandfather's fireplace of river stones with a woodstove, installing solar panels on the roof and a wind turbine behind the cabin. As we walked up the steps, he showed me a long rusted cast-iron boot scraper in the shape of a dachshund — Dorothy's Christmas present to Ferry in 1916. Rising out of its back was a narrow bar that looked capable of removing even the thickest wads of gumbo. "By all rights, this is yours — if you can lift it."

Reed told me that Ferry had dissolved his partnership with Jack White in 1926 and leased the Dawson Ranch near Hayden, where he had first worked as an eighteen-year-old. Two decades later, he bought the property — ranch house, barns and other outbuildings, and almost twenty-five hundred acres by the Yampa River. He hung a white sign at the end of the driveway by Route 40 with its new name, the Carpenter Ranch.

For a time it seemed that the railroad would be the boon that everyone in the valley had expected. When the 6.2-mile Moffat Tunnel through James Peak was completed in 1928, trains shuttled between Denver and the Western Slope without the costly delays and catastrophic accidents caused by the original route over Hell Hill. Cattle arriving in Denver from Routt County were identifiable by the soot on their noses, acquired when the train went through the tunnel. The homesteaders were paid well during the Great War for their grain and beef. But afterward, as the demand for ranch products dropped and the Depression set in, they were unable to repay their loans. There was no market even for Ferry's "growthy" Herefords, painstakingly bred for their large size and the quality and quantity of their meat, and he almost lost his ranch.

"Something had to give," Lewis Harrison wrote in 1977 in an unpublished memoir. "Marginal operations were the first to go." In the end, only about 40 percent of homesteaders nationwide were able to "prove up" on their claims. The Harrisons confronted "washed out reservoirs, uncompleted ditches, over-estimated land yields, and declining equipment quality." Mr. Harrison, suffering more acutely from stomach ailments that had plagued him all his life, sold the ranch, and he and Mrs. Harrison moved to Oak Creek, where several of their children lived. Lewis noted that at the time, "income in that thriving community was much more promising." Frank Jr. worked at the Moffat mine, and occasionally, so did his father, who also started a dairy and raised some chickens. Mr. and Mrs. Harrison had just enough money to get by.

Ferry's ranch made a comeback, and he went on to become the district attorney for Routt, Moffat, and Grand Counties. Although he was a firm Republican, in 1934 he was appointed by FDR's interior secretary, Harold Ickes, to be the first director of the Division of Grazing — now the Bureau of Land Management. He implemented the Taylor Grazing Act, which addressed the crisis caused by unregulated overgrazing on public lands in the West, and entailed putting an end to the sheep and cattle wars — still being fought at gunpoint. He cajoled the two parties into finally speaking to each other, and without consulting Ickes — a proud advocate of big government — he created local advisory boards, made up of state and regional members of the stockmen's industry, to regulate land use. Infuriated by this act of insubordination, Ickes tried to fire him. But Roosevelt was impressed, writing to Ickes, "In less than fifteen months after the law was enacted, the cattle and sheep men have buried their differences and combined in a joint effort to abolish unfair range practices and to conserve natural resources," and when Senator Taylor appealed to the president, FDR reinstated Carpenter. Ickes subsequently secured his resignation, and Ferry returned to the ranch. He became one of the most storied cattlemen in Colorado.

Another was Isadore Bolten, the Elkhead School's cobbling teacher, who raised sheep as well as cattle, because sheep provided two crops: wool in the spring and lambs in the fall. Before the Grazing Act, it was a practice that bordered on suicide. One year a group of cowboys rode into the area where Isadore's sheep were grazing, set fire to one of his wagons, and slaughtered much of his herd. Still, he persevered. He was an even cannier rancher than Ferry was, and he, too, belatedly found a well-educated bride. Nine years after Dorothy and Ros left Elkhead, Isadore married a librarian from Rawlins, Wyoming, where he wintered his sheep and spent his evenings at the public library. He bought the Harrison, Adair, and other ranches, and eventually acquired twenty-five thousand acres, described as one of the largest singly owned tracts of land in northern Colorado. He told someone who was curious about his life, "There was nothing for me in Russia — absolutely nothing. I had the whole world to move about in, but some kind destiny pulled me toward America. It is remarkable that there was a place in this distressed world where a penniless alien, knowing not a word of the language, could work out a place for himself." He died a millionaire in 1951, at the age of sixty-six. The remains of his homestead can still be seen south of the Elkhead

School, leaning into the earth. Part of his pitched roof rests against one log wall.

On February 20, 1930, Dorothy and Lem walked to a dinner party in the new suburb of East Grand Rapids. He recently had been promoted to president of the Old Kent Corporation. They were on a narrow lane when a car veered toward them. Lem pushed Dorothy out of the way, but he was struck and killed. He was forty-three years old. The bank's monthly bulletin commended his benevolence, wit, and now quaint-sounding banking practices: "He was a keen student of the securities market. He never gave his consent to the purchase or sale of a bond in which he did not honestly believe."

The country was mired in the Depression, and suddenly Dorothy was a single mother with four children between four and twelve years old. Lem's scrupulousness as a banker did not yield enough in the way of savings to fully support the family. Nor did she inherit any money from the Woodruff family business. Her brother Douglas, who was running Auburn Button Works, had turned the factory into one of the earliest manufacturers of plastics in the country. He considered President Roosevelt a traitor to his class and Dorothy was incredulous when he refused all government contracts. As competition increased, the business failed. Other early businesses also went under, and like many post-industrial cities, Auburn suffered a century-long decline.

Dorothy prepared for her future by taking courses in typing and shorthand. She became friendly with other working women, establishing a club for them called the Hillman Guild. By 1932, at a salary of twenty-five dollars a week, she was running the Grand Rapids chapter of the Red Cross. When the Grand River overflowed after heavy rains, she went down to help the Ottawa Indians, who had nothing to eat but raccoons. Ferry, despite his problems at the ranch, visited her several times in Grand Rapids, bringing phonograph records of his favorite cowboy songs for her children.

She wrote a terse entry in the spring of 1934 for her twenty-fifth Smith reunion book: "At present trying to run a full-time job and bring up four children." Her daughter Caroline told me that she didn't know how her mother would have coped if she hadn't worked in Elkhead and seen how the women there managed their lives. "That year in Colorado became part of who she was," Caroline said. "She took life by the throat and dealt with it."

Ros's comments in the reunion book were far happier. She wrote chattily about her years with Dorothy in Auburn ("Those . . . years, were, as I look back upon them, like the Biblical ones — delightful ones of plenty!"), Europe, and Elkhead; her married life in Oak Hills and Denver, and her young family's summers at their cabin in Strawberry Park. But several weeks later, Bob began suffering from fatigue and black-outs. Dr. Cole, the Moffat mine doctor and family friend, diagnosed a brain tumor. Bob and Ros went to the Mayo Brothers' Hospital for the operation. Although it was successful, he came down with pneumonia, an illness that was often fatal in the days before antibiotics. He died in Rochester, Minnesota, on July 27, 1934, at the age of fifty.

Not long afterward, the mines in Oak Creek began to run out of coal, and in the 1940s, one after another closed. The town now has about eight hundred residents, some small businesses, and the Tracks and Trails Museum in the old Town Hall building. There are few cars or people on Main Street, and in Oak Hills up the road, all that remains of the Moffat Coal Company are the concrete foundations of a hoist, the heavy arches that supported a tipple, a flattened area by the creek where the company town stood, a water tower, some holes in the hillsides — the old entrances to the mine — and some piles of burned-off red slag. The anthracite coal deposits in Elkhead, for which Sam and Bob Perry had such hopes, turned out to be of poor quality and not worth mining. Oak Creek's depot, a former headquarters for the Moffat Road, was sold in 1967 for thirty-five dollars. It is now a vacant lot.

When Dorothy and Ros were in their late sixties, Ros took her on a trip to the Caribbean. It was 1955, and Ferry's wife, Eunice, had died from heart failure the year before. Ros had important news for her friend: Ferry had asked her to marry him. It was four decades since he had lured the Auburn women to Elkhead. Ferry's children, like Dorothy, were delighted. His younger son, Willis, a lawyer in Denver, told me, "Dad was worried about how the news would affect us, but we all said, 'Yes, of course.' " Ros knew that Ferry would not leave the ranch, so she moved from her big Tudor house in Denver. If she had any trouble adapting to ranch life, she didn't say so. In the summer of 1960, her great-nephew arrived from Auburn for a visit. She took him up to Oak Point, and as they were walking around, Ros told him that rattlesnakes lived in the vicinity. She advised him to buy a new pair of blue jeans at F. M. Light & Sons. As long as the jeans were unwashed, she said, they would be thick enough to protect his legs from the fangs of any rattler.

All fifteen of Carpenter's grandchildren, who were too young to know Eunice, grew up thinking of Ros as their grandmother. One of them, Belle Zars, told me that sometimes when she was staying at the ranch as a girl, she would come downstairs in the morning and see Ferry waltzing with Ros to the kitchen radio.

In August 1973 I met Aunt Ros and Uncle Ferry. I spent my eighteenth summer working on a ranch in Carbondale for Rosamond's granddaughter Roz, who had three children. At the end of my stay, we went to the Carpenter Ranch. Ros had become a good cook, and with the help of her housekeeper, she served an old-fashioned luncheon on the sunny back porch. It was hard to see in the gracious elderly woman the beautiful young adventurer my grandmother had so often spoken about.

Afterward, Ferry said that he had something to show me. He put on his cowboy hat, and we climbed into his battered pickup truck. He drove through Hayden and across the river, and we began a long, jarring ride into the hills. At eighty-seven, he was still witty and voluble, concentrating more on his stories than on his driving. The homesteaders, Ferry told me, had long since moved on, their cabins mostly dismantled and the lumber carted off to be used elsewhere.

We pulled up on a high, rocky ridge covered with withered beige grass, scrub oak, and wildflowers, just behind the Elkhead School. It had been boarded up and padlocked in 1938, after its windows were broken and it was ransacked. The basement furnace and stove were carted off, along with the two slate chalkboards and most of the children's desks. A no-trespassing sign was posted. Ferry identified the mountains that surrounded us: Bears Ears, Pilot Knob, Agner, the Flat Tops. We sat on the steps and had our picture taken by a ranch hand who had come with us. Ferry said with satisfaction, "That's three generations, sitting right here." When I was back at college in the East, he sent me a letter on his official stationery: CARPENTER HEREFORDS, WEIGH-A-HEAD — SINCE 1909. He wrote,

"Sure wish you could be here this Saturday when we sell our bull calves. . . . Ros joins me in sending love & hoping you come visit again. Ferry." He enclosed a photograph of one of his prize bulls, 2,455-pound Biggie.

Ros died the following February. She had written a letter to Ferry, asking him to send some gifts from the money she left to him. The first recipient was Dorothy Hillman, her "great friend," as she invariably referred to her, of eighty-three years. She also had requested that the Elkhead School be pictured on the front of the memorial booklet. The service was held on a cold day in the white-frame Congregational Church of Hayden. The windows were covered with yellowing paper that was designed to resemble stained glass, and the old organ was jammed into the right-front corner. It was drafty inside, but the pews were closely packed with friends and relatives from Auburn, Denver, the ranch, Hayden — and some students from Rosamond's class of 1917. Those who couldn't squeeze into the church were seated in the parish house, rigged with a public address system. Dorothy, who was sick, was unable to make the trip.

At a time when only 10 to 15 percent of students in the country who started high school ended up graduating, four of Ros's students had gone on to college and others to professional school. Leila Ferguson, who had so cherished her first school desk, became an award-winning teacher in Colorado. She said of Dorothy and Ros six decades later, "They really and truly had the interests of the children at heart. . . . What they didn't know about teaching methods, they made up in zeal." Ezra Smith was a teacher in Michigan. Helen and Florence Jones — two of Tommy Jones's sisters — were registered nurses. Lewis Harrison went to Colorado State University and got his master of science in forestry at Iowa State University. His education was subsidized by a fund established jointly by Ferry Carpenter and Ros's mother. In 1957 Lewis became the chief forester for the state of Missouri.

Several of Ros and Dorothy's former pupils spoke at the memorial. Lewis talked about Miss Underwood and Miss Woodruff, "who came riding into our lives in a spring wagon late one afternoon." He said, "Little did I realize at the time the important and lasting influence it was going to have, not only on me, but on most youths and many adults of the Elkhead community." Robin Robinson, by then a sixty-four-year-old

Hayden businessman and chairman of the Solandt Memorial Hospital, said, "I'll never forget the first morning when Lewis Harrison and the two new teachers rode up to the school. . . . I don't believe there ever was a community that was affected more by two people than we were by those two girls."

During my visits to Hayden and Elkhead in February 2009, I had wanted to ride from the old Harrison place up to the schoolhouse, but there were no horses and no one to break trail. Instead, Rebecca Wattles and a friend from the Hayden Heritage Center had arranged for us to make the climb by snowmobile. Sam Barnes, the public works director of Hayden and another grandchild of Elkhead homesteaders, provided three Arctic Cats and was our guide for the day. Rebecca took a steep turn too quickly, tipping over in the deep powder, as Ferry had with Dorothy and Ros in his sleigh. Sam — a tall man of few words and a generous girth — stopped and helped her to set things right. We made a noisy arrival, snow flying out on either side of the machines. When the engines were shut off, the silence felt like a reproach.

It was another brilliant, balmy day. Sam unlocked the door and threw open the shutters. Sunlight slanted in, revealing the outlines of where the blackboards used to hang. Sometimes the school is rented out to hunters, and there were half a dozen bunk beds in the middle of the room, along with an open kitchen and a bathroom by the back wall. The huge windows had been replaced with smaller ones. Otherwise, the room looked much as it had when Lewis first showed it to Dorothy and Ros. It wasn't hard to imagine Miss Woodruff trying to keep order on her side of the room while Miss Underwood walked around examining the older students' work on her side. The basement was in some disarray. There was a gaping dirt hole where the furnace had been ripped out of the concrete floor, and no sign of the domestic-science room. The folding wooden door that had separated the two classrooms was lying on its side; half a dozen wrought-iron bases of the children's desks hung from the rafters. So did an ungainly wooden exercise apparatus — all that was left of whatever had constituted the gymnasium.

The school was a source of inspiration, though, until it closed. One evening in the summer of 1935, Charlotte Perry and Portia Mansfield, who had been running their performing-arts camp for twenty years, drove up from Strawberry Park with their new dance teacher, thirty-year-old Agnes de Mille. She had asked them if they knew where she could see her first square dance. The camp directors had a knack for attracting uncommonly talented young dancers, choreographers, and actors — among them Merce Cunningham and John Cage, who arrived together and in 1944 created their second major collaboration there, a play-dance called *Four Walls.* It starred Cunningham and Julie Harris. In the late 1920s, over three summers, Ferry Carpenter had taken his young nephew Richard Pleasant to the girls' camp. Pleasant lived in Maybell, a town of twenty-five people in far western Colorado, and Ferry thought that Portia and Charlotte could impart some culture to him. Pleasant went on to found American Ballet Theatre, with Lucia Chase, in 1940. Later, a boys' camp was added at Perry-Mansfield, and Dustin Hoffman studied acting under Charlotte.

At the schoolhouse that night, women stood on one side of the room and men on the other. As Portia described the scene, a group of "ancient and bearded" fiddlers were playing, and de Mille watched as the cowboys, in Levi's and boots, whirled the women about in their full-skirted dresses.

Portia asked the fiddlers to play "Turkey in the Straw," and when they struck up the tune, she urged "Aggie" to do a solo. De Mille jumped out to the open floor and began to dance, startling the cowboys, who called out, "That's it, girlie! You get 'em! Go to it!" As the music ended, a long line of dancers grabbed de Mille by the hand and "cracked the whip," sending her out the open doors of the schoolhouse into the sagebrush.

Seven years later, her ballet *Rodeo,* accompanied by Aaron Copland's exultant score, was performed for the first time in New York, by the Ballet Russe de Monte Carlo, with de Mille as the lead dancer. She received twenty-two curtain calls, and Rodgers and Hammerstein asked her to choreograph *Oklahoma!* De Mille told Portia, recalling her visit to Elkhead, "I think *Rodeo* began that night."

I walked outside and stood on the stoop where I'd had my picture taken with Ferry in 1973. The rough hills, softened by layers of snow, wandered off toward Utah and Wyoming. The people who built this school on top of an unpopulated mountain were aroused by the same vision of America's future that drove Ferdinand V. Hayden, David Moffat, and Sam Perry. That dream also sparked Charlotte and Portia and Dorothy and Rosamond, and the students they taught. Frederick Jackson Turner once urged Ferry to write down the details of his daily life on the frontier. He replied that he was too busy. But others recorded as much as they could, with pencil stubs in a derailed train car and in ink thinned by the cold. When Ros first glimpsed the school, she exclaimed, "It is the Parthenon of Elkhead!" Six-year-old Robin saw a churning ocean in the "crick" outside his father's log cabin. The graduates of 1920 described gazing out from the school at the seemingly limitless miles of blue and purple mountains. They felt, they said, as if they were standing on top of the world.

ACKNOWLEDGEMENTS

This book was a collaborative undertaking. I reconstructed the events described here with the unflagging help of dozens of people, many of whom shared intimate details about their parents', grandparents', and great-grandparents' lives. My thanks go first, wholeheartedly, to my mother, Hermione Hillman Wickenden, and my aunt, Caroline Hillman Backlund, to whom *Nothing Daunted* is dedicated. Both retired librarians, they saved Woodruff and Beardsley letters, photographs, and memorabilia going back to the mid-1800s. Without them, I could not have told the story.

I am very grateful to my contemporaries, and to their surviving parents, in the Underwood, Perry, Carpenter, and Cosel families. When I contacted Rosamond's granddaughter Roz Turnbull, in Carbondale, Colorado, for the first time in dozens of years, she instantly called her ninety-year-old mother, Ruth Perry, to enlist her help. Several months later, we all met up in Steamboat Springs. There and in subsequent e-mails, letters, and family papers, they conveyed what they knew about Ros's year in Elkhead, and about the lives of the Perrys: Sam and Lottie, Charlotte and Marjorie, and Bob and Rosamond.

Ferry Carpenter's granddaughter Belle Zars, who lives in Austin, Texas, and is writing a book about the Elkhead community, generously supplied me with interviews she had conducted in 1973 with Ferry and the children of several homesteaders, and with copies of the letters Eunice Pleasant wrote from Elkhead to her sister-in-law, Gertrude Pleasant. She sent me Ros's photo album and provided invaluable personal contacts. She helped me find Iva Rench's and Isadore Bolten's homesteads, and reminded me of the cast-iron dachshund boot scrapers that Dorothy and Ros gave to Ferry and Bob for Christmas in 1916. Belle's brother Reed Zars entered into my project with enthusiasm, showing me Oak Point in February 2009 and the two successive summers. He and his daughter Cordelia joined Rebecca Wattles and me in July 2009, when we explored Elkhead on Rebecca's horses, Titian and Troy (Reed and Cordy went on mountain bikes).

Mary Pat Dunn, the former curator of the Hayden Heritage Center, was a warm, dedicated guide to the center's collection. She and Rebecca, who is president of the board of directors, organized my other Elkhead excursion that year: on skis and snowmobiles. Sam Barnes, the public-works director of Hayden, provided the snowmobiles and the key to the schoolhouse. The owner of the school, Mary Borg, came along. She teaches at the University of Northern Colorado in Greeley and became a resource on the school's history and on the Meeker rebellion. Her family secured a historic designation for the building in January 2008. Penny and Cal Howe, who live on the property once owned by the Harrison family, have given me lunch, tours of their ranch, descriptions of old threshing equipment and the seasons and wildlife of Elkhead, stories about Lewis's and Frank Jr.'s visits to the place where they grew up, and an understanding of how deeply the early settlers were attached to their land.

Ros's son Kennard Perry — who lives in the Tudor house that Ros and Bob built on the outskirts of Denver — and Ken's daughter, Barbara, talked to me about Ros, Sam, and Bob, the Moffat Coal Company, and the exploits of Marjorie Perry. I found Lewis Harrison's daughter, Jane Harrison Telder, in Grand Rapids, Michigan, and her son, Richard, in Atlanta, Georgia; they rounded out the life story of Lewis, the undersize fourteen-year-old boy who guided the teachers to and from school each day.

Two of Rosamond's grandsons, Peter Cosel and his brother Rob, met me in Norwalk, Connecticut, in the fall of 2009 and let me root through their family's boxes of papers until I found Ros's letters from Elkhead, her mother's diaries, and the legal envelope full of newspaper clips about Bob's kidnapping.

Timothy Jones, the grandson of another pioneering Colorado schoolteacher, Leah Mae Mahaney, sent me her unpublished autobiography about her experience teaching in Kremmling, Colorado, in 1916, at the age of nineteen.

Professional and amateur historians, from Auburn to Oak Creek, assisted me with resourcefulness and verve:

AUBURN AND OWASCO LAKE
For over a year, Sheila Tucker, the Cayuga County historian, worked with me to track down Auburn characters, events, photographs, and genealogies, and she read

Chapter Two for accuracy. Peter Wisbey, the former executive director of the Seward House Museum, and Jennifer Haines, the education director, conveyed little-known facts about the Sewards and early Auburn history; Barbara Woodruff and Erik and Sheila Osborne were generous hosts at their cottages on the lake. Barbara and Jean Marshall (Ros's niece by marriage) took a group of us to dinner at the Owasco Country Club. Erik loaned me family papers and gave me glimpses into his remarkable ancestry. David Connelly, who is writing a book about the prison reformer Thomas Mott Osborne, Erik's grandfather, tipped me off to Osborne's friendship with FDR. He, too, read the Auburn chapter. Devens Osborne and Betsey Osborne, Leland Underwood Kruger Coalson, Richard L. Coalson, and Chuck Underwood Kruger helped me sort out five generations of their families, and supplied scrapbooks and personal histories.

Eileen McHugh, executive director of the Cayuga Museum of History and Art, pointed me to sources on the Woodruffs and Beardsleys and the Auburn state prison. Joanne O'Connor, an insatiable Auburn history buff, and her brother, Peter, own the summer house on Owasco Lake that once belonged to Rosamond's parents. Peter showed me around one summer afternoon; Joanne sent a steady supply of newspaper clips and books. Joe O'Hearn, who publishes "O'Hearn's Histories" of Auburn, a monthly online newsletter, unearthed obscure information about various secondary characters. My friend Mike Connor, who grew up in Auburn, read the chapter and cheered me on in the project.

PARIS, CANNES, AND BARCELONA

Friends at the *New Yorker* helped in various ways: Peter Schjeldahl, with the Fauve movement and the relationships among Gertrude Stein, Picasso, and Matisse; Paul Goldberger, with the architecture of Les Lotus in Cannes; and Jon Lee Anderson, with old Barcelona.

Marianne Billaud, Marie Hélène Cainaud, and Marie Brunel, of Ville de Cannes, Archives Municipales, sent photographs and histories of Villa Les Lotus; Christopher Glazek helped with French translation and Nicholas Backlund with Paris and Cannes research; Janet Skeslien Charles looked into the location of Mme Rey's school; Jean Strouse put me in touch with David Smith, who contacted Sandra Ribas in Barcelona, who uncovered the identity of the mysterious art collector Mr. Stuart, whose name was mentioned (and misspelled) by my grandmother in one of her letters.

DENVER, THE MOFFAT ROAD, AND STEAMBOAT SPRINGS

Debra Faulkner, the historian of the Brown Palace Hotel, told me about the hotel's early days and showed me the guest ledger signed by Ros on July 26, 1916. Moya Hanson, a curator at the Colorado Historical Society, was an excellent guide to Denver's past.

Dave Naples, president of the Moffat Railroad Museum project and the Grand County Model Railroad Club, was an amiable companion on this part of my journey. He read and made adjustments to the "Hell Hill" chapter, and supplied me with details about the size of the locomotives and the setup of the parlor cars. He showed me the site of his future museum in Granby and took me around Fraser, where Dr. Susan Anderson practiced at the turn of the twentieth century; her examination table and the contents of her doctor's bag are in a room upstairs at the Cozens Ranch & Stage Stop Museum.

One of my happiest early discoveries was Ros's oral history at Tread of Pioneers Museum. When I put the CD in the computer and heard her inflections and turns of phrase as an elderly woman describing her year in Elkhead, I felt as if I were listening again to my grandmother. I have since spent many hours in the museum, assisted by curator Katie Peck Adams and executive director Candice Lombardo. Daniel Tyler and Betty Henshaw were solicitous hosts, as were Renny Daly and Jain Himot — proving my grandmother's point about the hospitality of Westerners. Holly Williams, who has maintained a decades-long relationship with the Perry-Mansfield Camp, led me further into its remarkable history. The former executive director, June Lindenmayer, provided contacts and context. Karolynn Lestrud, the camp historian, sent early photographs. T. Ray Faulkner, a retired professor of dance who worked as the assistant to Portia and Charlotte from 1957–65 and as a volunteer from 1969–2008, was a delightful source of personal recollections about them and the early days of modern dance.

OAK CREEK, HAYDEN, AND ELKHEAD

Mike Yurich, a full-time volunteer at Tracks and Trails Museum (part of the Historical Society of Oak Creek and Phippsburg), assisted by Laurie Elendu, was one of my guides to the town. Mike, inspired by a homesteader who spoke to his fifth-grade class, has spent some sixty-five years collecting photos, old-timers' stories, newspaper articles, and miners' equipment. Ferry Carpenter was the commencement speaker his senior year, and, Mike told me, "that clinched the interest." He spent several afternoons talking to me about Oak Creek's colorful past. Paul Bonnifield, a former coal miner and conductor on the Denver and Rio Grande, taught me about the geology and the coal-mining history of Routt County as we toured Oak Hills and Phippsburg, where he grew up in a shack built by the Moffat Road. In a series of evocative e-mails, he also enabled me to see and feel what it was like to be inside a mine and in Oak Hills when the coal companies were in operation.

No one was more scrupulous about her area of expertise than the late Jan Leslie, who served for many years as Hayden's unofficial historian. Much of what I learned about Hayden came from her, in e-mails and packages of clippings and photos. Betsy Blakeslee, the manager of the Carpenter Ranch, gave me the run of Ferry's library — an excellent way to gauge the breadth of his mind and interests. There are shelves of volumes on Woodrow Wilson and Abraham

Lincoln, around the corner from a section on cattle breeding and one on poetry. As Betsy and I skied around what is now the property of the Nature Conservancy, she explained the conservation and educational work the group does, along with the ranching. Laurel Watson, the curator at the Hayden Heritage Center, helped with final questions about the town; Tammy Delaney and Heather Stirling discussed what they knew about Isadore Bolten; Bain and Christine White gave me a tour of the former Hayden Inn, now their house, which they are meticulously restoring; Bette Rathe, at the University of Northern Colorado, gave guidance about Colorado students' final exams.

LIBRARIES

I would like to thank Nanci A. Young, the college archivist at Smith College Archives, and Amy Hague, the curator of manuscripts at the Sophia Smith Collection, for their patience with numerous requests. At Princeton University Library: Christine A. Lutz, assistant university archivist for public services, Seeley G. Mudd Manuscript Library. At the Denver Public Library, Western History/Genealogy Department: Ellen Zazzarino, senior archivist/ librarian, and Bruce

Hanson, researcher. At the Huntington Library: Peter Blodgett, H. Russell Smith Foundation curator of Western historical manuscripts, and Katrina Denman, library assistant for Western history.

A number of people were key to the creation of this book, which began as an article in the *New Yorker*. It was David Remnick, with whom I have worked for sixteen years, who prodded me to start writing again for the magazine. His lucid prose and ferocious work ethic are a perpetual source of inspiration. Emily Eakin was my editor on the piece; her astute suggestions continued to influence me throughout the project. Others with multitudinous skills who saw the article through: Henry Finder, Daniel Zalewski, Mary Hawthorne, Ann Goldstein, Lila Byock (who masterfully fact-checked both the piece and the book), Virginia Cannon, Hendrik Hertzberg, Pamela McCarthy, Elisabeth Biondi, Caroline Mailhot, Jessie Wender, and Mengfan Wu. Outside the magazine, the first person I heard from was my incomparable agent, Amanda Urban, who e-mailed at six-thirty on Easter morning, after reading the article, urging me to write a book. Ron Bernstein soon followed with his own notes of encouragement.

I am indebted to friends and family who read and improved the book. Connie Bruck saw the possibilities in the final story before I even started writing, read it more than once, and goaded me at every step. Katherine Boo did a superb edit from Mumbai even as she was finishing her own book. David Rompf, Roger Rosenblatt, Daniel Tyler, Betty Henshaw, Hermione Wickenden, Cynthia Snyder, and Lauren Collins were my first generous readers. Nicholas Trautwein and David Grann read parts of the book and were trusted consultants; David Greenberg, an associate professor of history at Rutgers University, kindly read all of it for accuracy.

Thomas Mallon helped me to look at letters in a new way. Alexa Cassanos, Ann Hulbert, Claudia Roth Pierpont, Anne Garrels, Constance Casey, Lawrence Wright, Kip Hawley, David and Peter Wickenden, and Norma Weiser had sound suggestions. Andrea Thompson, Chloe Fox, Betsy Morais, and Natalie Shutler helped me track down stray facts, and Chloe proofread the galleys. Maria Alkiewicz Penberthy told me about her great-grandmother Jane Kelly, the 1888 Smith graduate who went on to become a doctor; Maria handed over her own archival materials from the Sophia Smith Collection.

At Scribner, I would like to thank the entire team that produced this book. My inspirational editor, Nan Graham, read it several times and had unerring guidance on everything from where to begin to the shape of the epilogue. Susan Moldow has been the shrewd, attentive publisher every writer longs for. Others who lent their vision and skills include Rex Bonomelli, Carla Jones, Beth Thomas, Kate Lloyd, Brian Belfiglio, Roz Lippel, Kara Watson, Paul Whitlatch, and Dan Cuddy.

Nothing Daunted is, in part, about the strength of family ties. In my case, these include not only the industrialists and matriarchs of the nineteenth and twentieth centuries but also my father, Dan Wickenden, the writer and editor who inspired my career. My daughters, Sarah and Rebecca, have the radiant spirit and good humor of their great-grandmother, and her blunt honesty. They indulged my perpetually preoccupied state and pulled me away from the computer when I had been there too long. Becca sat down one day and assembled a draft of the bibliography. Over the years, my husband, Ben, has taught me a lot about reporting, and he helped with some of the investigative challenges posed by this project. He offered steady counsel from start to finish. For his integrity and devotion, I am indebted to him every day.

NOTES

Much of *Nothing Daunted* is based on approximately one hundred letters written by Dorothy Woodruff and Rosamond Underwood, starting in 1897 and ending in 1973. Dorothy wrote forty letters home from Europe in 1910–11, which became the foundation of Chapter 6. From July 1916 to February 1917, together they sent fifty long letters to their families from Elkhead. I was extraordinarily lucky to have two such engaging and trustworthy correspondents.

Virtually all quotations from Dorothy's letters are from the Dorothy Woodruff Hillman Papers, Sophia Smith Collection, Smith College, Northampton, Massachusetts. Quotations from Rosamond's letters, from Grace Underwood's papers and diary, and from Ruth Carpenter Woodley's and Miriam Heermans's letters are courtesy of the Perry and Cosel families. Quotations from Lewis Harrison's unpublished memoir about his parents, Uriah and Mary Harrison, are thanks to Lewis's daughter, Jane Harrison Telder, and his great-niece, Linda Harrison Williamson. I have retained their spelling, punctuation, and peculiarities of style.

I drew as well from Dorothy's oral histories about her years growing up in Auburn and her nine months in Elkhead. Both were taped and transcribed in Weston, Connecticut, in the early 1980s by my mother. The transcripts are in the Sophia Smith Collection. On May 15, 1973, Rosamond's friend Eleanor Bliss interviewed her at the Carpenter Ranch about her experience in Elkhead. That oral history is in the collection of the Tread of Pioneers Museum in Steamboat Springs.

Bob Perry's kidnapping was reported in papers across the country and in the *Routt County Sentinel,* the *Routt County Republican,* the *Oak Creek Times,* the *Rocky Mountain News,* the *Yampa Leader,* the *Denver Times,* and the *Denver Post.* Most of Colorado's early newspapers are available online, at the Colorado Historic Newspapers Collection.

Ferry Carpenter's papers are scattered. His family and mine have some of his letters. Tapes and CDs of his talks and reminiscences are in the Denver Public Library's Western History collection; the Colorado Historical Society in Denver; and the Tread of Pioneers Museum. Ferry's letters to Henry Bragdon, one of Woodrow Wilson's biographers, and notes about Ferry's recollections of Woodrow Wilson (which he used when writing his autobiography, *Confessions of a Maverick*) are in the Princeton University Library. The Huntington Library, which contains the papers of Frederick Jackson Turner, has three letters that Ferry wrote to Turner between 1913 and 1926.

Chapter 1: Overland Journey

One chronicler observed, "Prick South Street at one end": Chamberlain, 28.

They also reread the letter: July 18, 1916.

there were few signs of life: Greeley, "The American Desert," in *An Overland Journey,* June 2, 1859.

Ros signed the register: Guest Register # 78, July 26, 1916.

On a day: Hunt, 24.

Modeled after the Campanile: Interview with Debra Faulkner, historian, Brown Palace Hotel, July 20, 2009.

In his first day's edition: Rocky Mountain News, April 23, 1859.

"the new El Dorado": Barney, 17.

Denver City became an indispensable: Imagine a Great City: Denver at 150, exhibition, November 22, 2008–Winter 2010, Colorado Historical Society, Denver, CO.

he reported on June 20, "we have tidings": "Gold in the Rocky Mountains," in *An Overland Journey.*

A month earlier, a man from Illinois, Daniel Blue: Blue was saved by an Arapaho who carried him to his lodge, fed him, and took him to the nearest stagecoach stop. The story was also reported by Henry Villard, "To the Pike's Peak Country in 1859 and Cannibalism on the Smoky Hill Route," *Cincinnati Daily Commercial,* May 17, 1879, in Grinstead and Fogelberg, 9–11. Libeus Barney provided a fuller account, with some particularly lurid flourishes, 24–25.

One entrepreneur with grandiose ideas: William J. Baker, "Brown's Bluff," *Empire Magazine,* December 28, 1958; "The Palace Henry Brown Built," *Rocky Mountain News,* April 22, 1984.

The project took four years and cost $2 million: Hunt, 34.

the Brown Palace already had been sandblasted: Interview with Faulkner, July 20, 2009.

an 1880 tourists' guide called it "an unknown land." Denver society referred to it as "the wild country": Duane A. Smith, "A Land Unto Itself: The Western Slope," in Grinstead and Fogelberg, 135–46.

Chapter 2: The Girls from Auburn

And she never cooked a meal in her life: Recollections of Mildred Woodruff, wife of Dorothy's brother Douglas. Undated.

The Beardsley family and its connections: "They Prospered with the Abundance," account by the Auburn Fortnightly Club, seventy-fifth year, 1957, 24.

The many uses for cornstarch: Ayers, 139; *Oswego Daily Times,* September 29, 1876; Monroe, 183–85.

At family gatherings, he produced jingles and poems he had written: "A Reminiscence of My Father, George Underwood," by Rosamond U. Carpenter, in Ruth Brown's "The Abundant Life," 11.

Dorothy's great-uncle Nelson Beardsley later became a partner of Seward's: "Major Beardsley," *Auburn Weekly Bulletin,* January 26, 1900; Obituary: Nelson Beardsley, *Oswego Daily Palladium,* January 15, 1894.

One of her aunts, Mary Woodruff, was a good friend of Seward's daughter Fanny: Jennifer Haines, e-mail, January 18, 2011.

stunned by the crime: Goodwin discusses the trial and its effect on Seward's national political reputation, 85–87.

Seward was out of town, and Frances wrote to him with the news: Letter from Frances to William Seward, August 21, 1847, William Henry Seward Papers, Department of Rare Books and Special Collections, University of Rochester.

but when Seward returned from Washington, his once disapproving neighbors referred to him: "They Prospered with the Abundance," 10.

One of Ros's nieces: Sheila Tucker, e-mail, April 21, 2010.

Presidents Johnson and Grant and General Custer: Peter Wisbey, e-mail, September 7, 2010.

One summer, Dorothy's extended family rented Willow Point: Amy Dunning Underwood (1883–1960), who was married to Rosamond's brother George Jr., wrote: "The Hermon Woodruffs and Will Beardsley had it one summer. . . . Every Sunday morning we would meet and have an informal prayer meeting, as I remember, Mr. Woodruff usually conducted." From an undated account, "Lake Life Flourished," courtesy Leland Coalson.

whom an Auburn neighbor referred to as "a

very dangerous woman": Penney and Livingston, 110.

Eliza was a tall, regal woman whose glorious black eyes: Stanton, *Eighty Years and More,* 435.

For two decades Eliza was the president: David W. Connelly, "WEIU Helped Women Cope in Harsh World," *Auburn Citizen,* March 2, 2009.

In 1911, when FDR was a twenty-nine-year-old state senator: David W. Connelly, e-mail, October 18, 2010.

Auburn's rapid growth from a quiet village: Auburn and Its Prison: Both Sides of the Wall, booklet for exhibition at the Cayuga Museum of History and Art, Summer 2003.

Anyone who broke the rule of silence was flogged with the "cat": Storke, 155.

In 1831 Alexis de Tocqueville and Gustave de Beaumont visited the prison on behalf of the French government and reported: ". . . when the day is finished, and the prisoners have returned to their cells, the silence within these vast walls, which contain so many prisoners, is that of death" (Tocqueville and Beaumont, 32). Elam Lynds, who helped devise the system and carried a bullwhip, told them, "A prison director, especially if he's an innovator, needs to be given absolute and assured authority. . . . I consider punishment by the whip as the most effective and also the most humane. . . ." (Damrosch, 57).

When he got out, he and a former prisoner: Frederik R-L Osborne, Introduction, *Within Prison Walls,* 2; Chamberlain, 261; Rose Field, "The Personality and the Work of Thomas Mott Osborne," review of *There Is No Truce* in the *New York Times,* March 31, 1935.

Today, the Osborne Association runs treatment, educational, and vocational services in New York prisons; they also help ex-offenders find jobs and adjust to life after their release. Frederik Osborne, Thomas Mott Osborne's grandson, is its president.

Her earliest memory, she told her grandchildren: "Assassin Czolgosz Is Executed at Auburn," *New York Times,* October 29, 1901. According to the *Times,* Czolgosz was buried in the prison cemetery, but a groundskeeper at Fort Hill Cemetery swore to Sheila Tucker, the Cayuga County historian, that he knew the gravesite.

reflecting the romantic Victorian view, called Logan "the best specimen": Henry Howe,

Historical Collections of Ohio, Volume 1,
Cincinnati: Published by the State of
Ohio, 960.
*"that masterpiece of oratory which ranks along
with the memorable speech of President Lincoln at Gettysburg":* Monroe, 9.

Chapter 3: "A Funny, Scraggly Place"

*"one of that peculiar and persevering
class" . . . The* News *declared: Rocky
Mountain News,* December 30, 1874, and
June 15, 1875.
A thin, obsessive scholar: Foster, 246–52.
*"very desirable that its resources be made
known":* Hayden to Columus Delano,
Washington, D.C., January 27, 1873, L.S.,
Hayden Survey, R.G. 57, National Ar-
chives. Quoted in Goetzmann, 516.
*He gave lectures in Washington and New
York:* "Western Scenery: Interesting Facts
Concerning Our National Parks," *New
York Times,* April 16, 1874.
*William Blackmore, a British investor in Ameri-
can ventures:* Foster, 229.
*The most serious trouble between the settlers
and the Utes:* For a lucid account of the
influence of the Hayden *Atlas,* Milk Creek,
the mining camps, and the White River
Agency, see Sprague, *Colorado,* 78–100.
" 'The gun no good' ": Lou Smart's letter, a

vivid first-person description of her family's dealings with the Utes, was written from Hot Sulphur Springs on November 2, 1879, and published in *History of Hayden & West Routt County*, 2–7.

"My idea is that, unless removed": Young, 34.

A log school and a store were built on the homestead of Sam and Mary Reid: Leslie, *Anthracite, Barbee, and Tosh*, 34; Leslie, *Images of America: Hayden*, 9–23.

A man named Ezekiel Shelton: Robert S. Temple, in *History of Hayden & West Routt County*, 282.

Chapter 4: "Refined, Intelligent Gentlewomen"

Seventy-five of Dorothy and Ros's classmates: Annual Report of the President for 1905/1906, Smith College Archives.

One graduate wrote: Elizabeth Spader Clark, *Class Book, Smith College, Nineteen Hundred and Nine*, 169.

Addams had longed to go to Smith: Knight, 20–21.

"influence in reforming the evils of society": "Last Will and Testament of Miss Sophia Smith, Late of Hatfield, Mass." Smith College Archives.

President L. Clark Seelye wrote: "Smith College," Official Circular, No. 3, 1877, Smith

College Archives.

"refined, intelligent gentlewomen": from "In Memory of Rosamond Underwood Carpenter."

However, since most of them had "neither the call nor the competence": William Allen Neilson, 7.

After a week at Wood's Hole in the summer of 1902: Jane Kelly, "1880 Class Letters," Sophia Smith Collection, Smith College.

Smith's entrance examinations, which included: "Specifications of the Requirements for Admission," *Catalogue of Smith College, Forty-Third Year, 1916–1917.* Smith College Archives.

Delta Sigma, which was, one of its founding members emphasized: "Early Days of Delta Sigma Invitation House," Esther M. Wyman, Class of 1911, January 1958, Sophia Smith Collection, Smith College.

Students were allowed to invite gentlemen: Nanci Young, college archivist of Smith College Archives, e-mail, December 14, 2009.

"It was a fine opportunity . . . [Y]ou will not become the useless members": Springfield Republican, June 14, 1909.

At the chapel exercises, President Seeyle spoke of the first Smith class: Springfield Republican, June 15, 1909.

Chapter 5: Unfenced

When he arrived at Princeton and read the "Freshman Bible": Carpenter, *Confessions,* 33.

Farrington sounded like the name of an English resort town: Ibid., 1.

In November 1904 he gave a speech in New York: Startt, 46; Bragdon, 337–38.

He officially introduced it to the Board of Trustees: Bragdon, "The Quad Fight Plan," 312–36.

The prospect of not getting into a club: Confessions, 38.

Wilson told Ferry, "Some of the wealthy New York and Pennsylvania people": Ibid., 40.

"To the country at large, his dispute with the Princeton clubs was analogous": Bragdon, 330.

telling his acolyte: "At those great state institutions": letter from Carpenter to Bragdon, November 30, 1967. After Bragdon's book was published, Carpenter sent him detailed responses to chapters as he read them. These letters are part of the Woodrow Wilson Collection, 1837–1986, Box 62, Folder 17, Department of Rare Books and Special Collections, Seeley G. Mudd Manuscript Library; Princeton University.

"When you go out into the world and have to make your own living": E. S. W. Kerr inter-

view with Ferry Carpenter, June 6, 1967, Woodrow Wilson Collection, Princeton University.

Aristocracy, he informed a despondent Ferry Carpenter: Confessions, 41.

Wilson had gotten to know Frederick Jackson Turner: Bragdon, 194, 233, 236; E. David Cronon, "Woodrow Wilson, Frederick Jackson Turner, and the State Historical Society of Wisconsin," *The Wisconsin Magazine of History,* vol. 71, no. 4 (Summer 1988), 296–300.

"They wore big black hats": Confessions, 4–15.

During a raid on Paint Creek: The journalist was Hatton W. Sumners. "Charles Goodnight visits John B. Dawson on Dawson's Ranch," 1911, in Wilson, 28–29.

As one of Dawson's granddaughters described it: Wilson, 122.

The alfalfa was so high . . . "cure anything from gripes": Farrington Carpenter, oral history, OH 42, Colorado Historical Society.

In the Princeton library: Confessions, 20.

As Carpenter recalled, Dawson "could read but he couldn't write": OH 42.

Carpenter said he felt as if he had stumbled on a gold mine: Confessions, 45–46.

Carpenter asked his father for a loan: Ibid., 50.

The last thing Ferry wanted to do: OH 51, Denver Public Library.

which he proposed to do: Confessions, 45.

He described the improvements he had made upon his first claim: Department of the Interior, United States Land Office, Farrington R. Carpenter applications for homesteads, August 10, 1907, and August 14, 1914. Homestead Certificate, Department of the Interior, United States Land Office, Glenwood Springs, CO, March 20, 1920.

It was as thrilling to him as the American Revolution: Confessions, 45, 46.

Chapter 6: The Grand Tour

Their parents held afternoon card parties: "They Prospered with the Abundance," 1957.

Seward, though, was a loyal patron of Delmonico's: Thomas, 93, 191.

The incomprehensible instructions: Ranhofer, 1007.

Miss Elkins was reported to be in Vichy: "Miss Elkins Not in Paris," *New York Times,* August 28, 1910; "Miss Elkins Bride of W. F. R. Hitt," *New York Times,* October 28, 1913.

they went to see Isadora Duncan . . . baby was born: Kurth, 248–69.

The main house was a palatial, half-timbered Queen Anne: Gayraud, 48.

an amateur botanist: Cunisset-Carnot, 304.

One room, "The Lounge of the Queen Regent": La Vanguardia, May 14, 1910.

He was a member of the Barcelona stock exchange: "W. W. Stuart Dies in Spain," New York Times, April 1, 1914.

Often he entertained his guests: La Vanguardia, April 23, 1911, and January 24, 1905.

Chapter 7: Ferry's Scheme

In 1912, when Ferry Carpenter set up: Confessions, 57.

The bell was rung: Leslie, Images of America: Hayden, 25.

Galloway said, "I see you're going to": Confessions, 58.

He didn't have many clients: Ibid., 65.

The cattle business also took years: According to Ferry's son Ed Carpenter, Ferry and Jack ended the first year with a loss of $477.88. Ferry's father continued to subsidize them until 1914, when they had 225 head and made a profit of $2,150. America's First Grazier, 47.

"We ran him home," Ferry told an appreciative

group: Speech at Colorado State University, accepting the Stockman of the Year Award, February 1967; Tread of Pioneers Museum.

one evening in Cambridge, Turner rebuked his daughter: Letter from Farrington R. Carpenter to Henry Bragdon, December 11, 1967, Woodrow Wilson Collection, Princeton University.

Carpenter assured Bragdon that by then Wilson no longer shared Turner's view of women. Carey Thomas, the second president of Bryn Mawr College and a well-known suffragist, had hired Wilson to teach history there in 1884. Carpenter wrote that Thomas had "knocked out of [Wilson's] head his theretofore belief that all women's minds were incapable of matching men's intellectual structures." But Bragdon says that at the time, Wilson believed that women lost their femininity when they chose to work with men. Wilson wrote to a friend at Bryn Mawr, "I find that teaching women relaxes my mental muscle."

As Ferry put it, "The Sheep. Always we live in fear & hatred of them": Letter to Frederick Jackson Turner, October 6, 1922. TU Box 31A (20), Frederick Jackson Turner Papers, Henry E. Huntington Library and

Art Gallery, San Marino, CA.

In October 1913, writing from Oak Point: October 13, 1913, TU Box 20A (3), Ibid.

A district attorney in Steamboat Springs instructed Ferry to take on the jurors one by one, as you would if you were shooting ducks. The DA said that he'd know when they were convinced: "When a man gets interested in something he is listening to, his neck begins to stretch as you grip his attention. When his Adam's apple comes out so far that it finally chins itself on his collar, you know you have him." Women — not yet allowed to be jurors in Colorado — would be more difficult. "They are always so conscious of how their back hair may be looking that they never allow their necks to stretch and therefore can't be totally swayed by oratory." *Confessions,* 71–72.

"Well, guess I'd better roll in — I think of you all every now & again": Letter to Turner, October 13, 1913, Frederick Jackson Turner Papers, Huntington Library.

"We did not want strays": Beverly Smith, "America's Most Unusual Storyteller," *Saturday Evening Post,* April 12, 1952.

Twenty-five people attended, the paper reported: "Elkhead District Formed," *Routt County Republican,* April 21, 1911.

education officials handed out postcards: Zimmerman, 81, citing *Country School Legacy: Humanities on the Frontier* (Silt, CO): Country School Legacy, 1981, 46.

Fulton had grown up: Rebecca Fulton Wattles, in *History of Hayden & West Routt County,* 186.

he said during a talk in Denver about his early experiences: "The Adventures of a Tenderfoot," January 9, 1964, Denver Public Library.

Early on the morning after the teachers arrived: Confessions, 81–84.

As his son Ed recalled: America's First Grazier, 54–55.

Jack White was married in 1915, and I suspect that he played an unacknowledged role in Carpenter's scheme. A few years earlier, either during a trip home or at a dance in Steamboat Springs (accounts vary), Jack had met a fearless society girl from Evanston — Ann Ehrat. The daughter of a wealthy importer, she had left for Colorado in 1908 and homesteaded on Cow Creek, south of Steamboat Springs, with her brother, William. Jack's success at wooing Ann could well have spurred Ferry's notion to recruit more women like her to Elkhead.

Chapter 8: Departure

Postcard of South Street: The gates in the left foreground are the entrance to the former Beardsley Roselawn estate.

Dorothy introduced the speaker, Mrs. Theodore M. Pomeroy: "For Which Mrs. Pomeroy Was Prepared Because She Was 'Born a Suffragist,' " *Auburn Citizen,* June 8, 1914.

She was not surprised to hear Ros say: Grace Kennard Underwood, explanation of how Rosamond and Dorothy came to be hired at Elkhead School, and their early weeks, undated and unfinished.

Stewart wrote about a camping trip in December: Elinore Pruitt Stewart, 198.

"We all got so much out of so little": Ibid., 211.

The domestic-science movement was led: Shapiro, 3–10.

War with Mexico appeared imminent: Cooper, 319–21.

He had just made second lieutenant: "Kennard Underwood a Second Lieutenant," *Auburn Advertiser-Journal,* June 10, 1916.

Chapter 9: Hell Hill

"seems to be something of a joke": There were actually several passenger trains each day by 1916, weather permitting.

As an early historian of Colorado wrote: Stone, 50.

This caused Thomas Durant, the vice president of Union Pacific, to gleefully announce: Boner, 10.

Moffat was described by a friend as: Stone, 51.

He promised it would reduce the travel time: "New Line West of Denver: David H. Moffat Completes Its Financing Arrangements," *New York Times,* June 22, 1902.

The Moffat Road is still the highest standard-gauge railroad ever built in North America: The section on the building of the Moffat Road is reconstructed from accounts in Bollinger, Boner, and Black, and from information provided by Dave Naples.

The railroad's chief locating engineer: Bollinger, 33–42.

"The battle of Gettysburg was a Quaker meeting": Boner, 81.

Argo wrote in his diary one June day: Bollinger, 38.

Remarkably, no passenger was ever killed: Interview with Dave Naples, June 30, 2010.

There was at least one birth: Ibid.

"They brought some Chinese in to shovel the snow": Tom Ross, "Railroad Came to Steamboat 100 Years Ago," *Steamboat Pi-*

lot, January 16, 2008.

He established a dummy power company: Bollinger, 35–39, 42.

Although Harriman was no longer alive: Boner, 164–65.

Susan B. Anthony went twice to push the cause there: Stephen J. Leonard, "Bristling for Their Rights: Colorado's Women and the Mandate of 1893," in Grinstead and Fogelberg, 225–33.

"[W]hile I have not taken to myself a husband": Smith College, *Class of 1897 Reunion Book,* Smith College Archives.

As another traveler remembered: "My 1926 Trip to Corona," by William O. Gibson, in Griswold, 149.

described this CREST OF THE MAIN RANGE: Griswold, 31.

advertised by the Moffat Road in a famous poster as the "Top O' the World": Bollinger, back jacket.

John Adair had arrived in Hayden on horseback: Janet Adair Ozbun, in *History of Hayden & West Routt County,* 126.

Their granddaughter recalled, "Survival was tough": Audrey Galambos, e-mails, September 16–17, 2009. Galambos's grandparents were Earl and Vella Rice.

Ultimately, over one and a half million homesteads were granted: The National Parks

Service and the Homestead National Monument of America: http://www.nps.gov/home/historyculture/bynumbers.htm.

The Harrisons' first ranch, between Hayden and Craig, had been a headquarters: Lewis Harrison, "Sketch of the Life," 68; Jan Leslie, e-mail, February 12, 2010.

Ann took it upon herself to fight off the cattle barons' "devouring invasion": McClure, 97–106. As Jan Leslie put it in a January 20, 2010, e-mail, "It wasn't her perceived role as a rustler that made her a heroine when she was acquitted — this was the classic western movie plot that pitted the small rancher against the powerful cattle baron."

Nevertheless, the Harrisons shared with other Elkhead homesteaders: The *Routt County Republican* reported about Elkhead on May 31, 1912: "The land is unusually rich in the hills and valleys there and will produce wonderful crops. It is a wonder how that country is settling up."

Chapter 10: Turnips and Tears

the stone was streaked, as if, one Routt County resident said, by the paintbrushes of God: Paul Bonnifield, e-mail, July 7, 2010.

The entire field was estimated to be eight square miles: Ninth Biennial Report of the Inspector of Coal Mines, State of Colorado

1889–1900, 87–88.

"You didn't want to build a little wooden shack there": Ferry Carpenter, interview by Belle Zars, August 12, 1973.

"All the windows were made big, and all the light came in over the child's shoulders": Ibid.

One of Ros's ninth-graders, Leila Ferguson, had come west with her family: Richard Ferguson, in *History of Hayden & West Routt County,* 179.

"We had brand-new desks": Leila Ferguson Ault, interview by Zars, July 16, 1973.

"That consolidated point": Carpenter, interview by Zars.

He admired the teachers as "good sports from start to finish": Frank Harrison, Jr., interview by Zars, July 18, 1973.

"Mrs. Harrison told me she couldn't say which one she liked best": Letter dated August 29, 1916.

he "gave a demonstration in corn bread making": *Routt County Republican,* February 7, 1917.

In class, Rudolph Morsbach, age ten: Rudolph's classmates also were amused by his comments in class. The graduates of the class of 1920 wrote in their yearbook, "Rudolph was telling a story in English class, of an accident which happened to a couple of deer-hunters. He was getting along nicely with his story, until he came to the most important part — when he became mixed and said: 'After the man was shot, his partner built a fire, but, it was so cold that the wounded man froze to death. Then he got a pair of skis and went to find help!' "

He asked whether he could set up an account: Farrington R. Carpenter to Harrick's bookstore, October 26, 1916.

"and four-year-old Herbie didn't survive": "Death of Herbie Jones," *Routt County Republican,* August 19, 1910.

As Carpenter recalled, he and Mrs. Murphy: Confessions, 79–80.

Minnie's granddaughter Penny Turon told me that many decades later, the Jones family had a reunion in Elkhead on the schoolhouse steps. They went to the site of the old homestead, and looked for Herbie's gravesite, but it had disappeared under the grass.

Chapter 11: The Mad Ladies of Strawberry Park

A couple of Swedish descent who had arrived from Nebraska in 1909: Christy Fredrickson, in *History of Hayden & West Routt County,* 182.

One of its maxims was "A customer is not a cold statistic": Lockhart, 18.

A & G. Wither Mercantile offered everything: Dorothy Wither in "Everything Seemed to Center Around the Railroad," *Three Wire Winter,* 20th Issue, Spring 1985.

The town's founding father: James Crawford, "Steamboat Springs: The Promised Land," 1923 interview with Thomas F. Dawson, Colorado State Historical Society, in *Frontier Magazine,* April 2000.

Mrs. Peck, formerly Emma Hull, first taught school: "Some Notes on the Life of Emma Hull Peck and Her Work in Routt Co., As Told to an Inquiring Reporter," April 13 and 27, 1984; "Emma Peck Dies; Was Pioneer in Routt County: Did Much to Develop Schools in This Section," paper unknown, in Tread of Pioneers Museum. "Story of Routt County Schools Is the Story of Emma Peck," *Steamboat Pilot,* 1959.

She liked to tell a story: Ibid.

A reporter made the same observation a century later: Ibid.

As one friend described her: T. Ray Faulkner, letter, July 27, 2010.

The first performing-arts camp in the country: Tricia Henry, "Perry-Mansfield School of Dance and Theatre," *Dance Research: The*

Journal of the Society for Dance Research, vol. 8, no. 2 (Autumn 1990), 49-68.

When she told her parents that she and Portia: "A Divine Madness," 1979 documentary on the Perry-Mansfield Performing Arts School & Camp.

but Lottie, more indulgent and open-minded: Pam Wheaton, "Charlotte Perry — Grand Lady of Theatre," *Steamboat Pilot,* September 18, 1975.

Charlotte gave Bible lessons and taught basketball: Lucile Bogue, *Dancers on Horseback,* 42–43.

"He told us to soak the potatoes in grease, over-cook the meat": Portia Mansfield, "Charlotte Perry Honored," *Steamboat Pilot,* September 24, 1970.

In Omaha, she saw Anna Pavlova . . . in The Dying Swan: Bogue, *Dancers,* 30–31.

She was also strongly influenced by Sergei Diaghilev: Ibid., 39. Diaghilev hired the best choreographers, dancers, and composers in Europe. Stravinsky, Debussy, and Ravel wrote ballet scores for him; Picasso designed his sets. Portia went on to study dance in Paris and Milan as well as Chicago and New York, where she worked with Mikhail Mordkin.

Portia borrowed from many art forms: Ibid., 31, 34.

"She grew straight and had never been twisted": Ibid., 44.

In coming years, the camp became nationally known: Portia filmed some of the early dances. Her films are now part of the collection of the Perry-Mansfield Camp at the New York Public Library for the Performing Arts.

Chapter 12: Debut

Ferry wrote more graphically: Confessions, 84.

said that it was the fastest music he had ever "stepped to": August 16, 1916.

"young fellows with tail feathers blooming": Frank Harrison, Jr., interview by Zars, July 18, 1973.

Lefty had proved that Colorado: Flynn's bride didn't like ranch life; nor, it turned out, did he. He ended up in Hollywood, acting in and directing westerns, finding himself well suited to perpetuating a vision of the West that Americans wanted to believe in. He also, reportedly, became close to F. Scott Fitzgerald and his daughter Scotty, who visited him after he moved to South Carolina ("Maurice Flynn Heads for Hollywood . . . and back . . . and back," *Craig Daily Press,* May 10, 2008).

always "shaved and barbered to a hair":

"Tribute to Sam Perry Is Paid by Annie Laurie," *Denver Post,* July 29, 1929.

"Wilson's life sunk into the lives of many people who were fortunate enuf to know": Carpenter, letter to Henry Bragdon, November 29, 1967, Woodrow Wilson Collection, Princeton University.

"You know, after the frost had hit this country, we never thought anything about those quakers": Frank Harrison, Jr., interview by Zars.

Chapter 13: The Cream of Routt County

In 1916 workdays for the miners: Paul Bonnifield, e-mail, September 4, 2010.

was built "to meet the needs of the men who dug the coal": Bonnifield, "Oak Creek," 3.

"Man Beats Aged Miner": Oak Creek Times, September 30, 1915.

"Mexican Meets Death by Severe Blow in Abdomen": Ibid., April 20 1917.

"Harry Gray . . . A Rope Rider": Ibid., July 26, 1917.

In June 1917 a young woman was attacked: "Italian Resident Shoots Greek Who Attacks Wife," Ibid., June 22, 1917.

In 1902 Moffat's railway company: Black, 256.

four years later, it was bigger than Steamboat Springs: Oak Creek Times, October 13, 1912.

A sign was erected on the road heading south: Bonnifield, e-mail, June 28, 2010.

featuring a photograph of a wooden coal car loaded with blocks of coal the size of boulders: Photo courtesy of Kennard Perry, Ros's son.

But miners were paid in scrip: Bonnifield, e-mail, December 29, 2010.

as they carried powder, caps, and fuses: Interview with Bonnifield, Oak Hills, June 14, 2010.

Although the company was known to be "one of the most careful and considerate": "Five Killed in Explosion at Perry Mine Last Saturday," *Oak Creek Times,* February 19, 1921.

The Moffat Coal Company hired experienced shot-firers to place the explosives: Interview with Mike Yurich at Tracks and Trails Museum, Oak Creek, July 3, 2009.

"it threw cars, rails, and the tipple": Annual Report of the Colorado Coal Mine Inspection Department, 1921.

In 1910, when the miners in a coalfield: "A Strike Is on at the Perry Coal Mine," *Routt County Republican,* July 1, 1910.

Baldwin was notorious: Martelle, *Blood Passion,* 95.

In Oak Hills, for a short time: Bonnifield, "Oak Creek," 4–6.

"First we have to think about production": Earnest "Dude" Todd, interviewed by Bonnifield, April 6, 1978.

Todd worked for Bob Perry and subsequently served as the town manager of Oak Creek for eleven years. Bob helped him resolve disputes when he could. In an e-mail on June 24, 2010, Bonnifield wrote: "The town of Oak Creek was controlled by Andy Black, who ran the gambling, drinking, and prostitution. Earlier, Dude saw Andy shoot a man. Yet he successfully challenged Andy on many issues. The only way that Dude could have succeeded was with the unflinching support of someone out of sight. That person had to be Bob Perry. There is no other person with the power, the personal courage, or sense of fair play."

They passed the shower rooms, the mess hall, and the mine office: This description of the Oak Hills mines and the workers' jobs was derived from e-mails and interviews with Yurich and Bonnifield between July 2009 and December 2010.

Chapter 14: "Unarmed and Defenseless"

The previous Wednesday, October 4: The details of Bob's kidnapping were reconstructed from the records of the district court, Routt County, Colorado, filed November 24, 1916, January 3, 1917, and February 17, 1917, and from contemporaneous newspaper articles and letters.

"Wearing a heavy flannel shirt and chaps": Denver Post, October 8, 1916.

One year she returned: "Bear Cub Captured as Trophy of Hunt by Marjorie Perry." From Marjorie Perry's scrapbook, newspaper and date unknown.

(As an older woman, when her two favorite dogs died): Interview with Kennard Perry, June 10, 2010.

"Denver society girl and experienced bear hunter": "Miss Perry Heading Posse for Kidnaper" Denver Post, October 8, 1916.

as an item in the Oak Creek Times *put it:* "Does Not Want Bandit in Oak Creek Cemetery," October 10, 1916.

and went on, "I presume you know it, that the town is against to me": Letter from John Frangowlakis to R. M. Perry, Oak Creek, October 11, 1916.

The next day the Oak Creek Times *reported:* "One Kidnaper of Robt. M. Perry Dead and Others in Jail," October 12, 1916.

"The Greek greeted Bob with a smile": Confessions, 86.

knifed to death: Interview with Mike Yurich, July 3, 2009.

Chapter 15: "The Dark Days Are Very Few"

Dr. D. L. Whittaker, the new doctor in Hayden: Zars, e-mail, October 4, 2010.

Ros's mother spoke at a monthly meeting of the Kings Daughters: "Colorado Mountain School, Where Miss Underwood Teaches, Described," *Auburn Citizen,* December 1, 1916.

Robin Robinson's father mined the anthracite coal on the hillside: Interview with Bobbie Robinson, Robin's son, December 9, 2010.

the choice of grades: From an Elkhead report card of 1918–19; Zars, e-mail, October 4, 2010.

There were very few deer and elk at the time: Penny Howe, e-mail, November 6, 2010.

"That school lunch at noon was about the greatest thing in our lives": Bobbie [Robin] Robinson, "In Memory of Rosamond Underwood Carpenter."

Soon after Thanksgiving: Maddeningly, Ros or her mother must have removed the letter she sent about her engagement. Her collection of correspondence contains only her family's response to it, and an anguished letter from the New York lawyer Billy, who had hoped to marry her. He wrote that the news "sort of broke me up (to put it mildly)," and went on, "Now I

450

must lock up in my heart the thoughts of the past years which have been the happiest of my life, come what may, no one will ever be equal to them. . . ." These letters were neatly bundled and tied with a red ribbon.

Chapter 16: Three-Wire Winter

"In the morning there were always at least a dozen": Manahna, 1920.

After leaving Chicago: Herbert P. White, interview with Farrington Carpenter, July 11, 1970, Denver Public Library.

In derailments on the Moffat Road, train cars sometimes: Dave Naples, e-mail, July 18, 2010.

Several years earlier, she had become friendly with Carl Howelson: Jean Wren, "The Gypsy Life & Loves of Marjorie Perry," *Steamboat Magazine,* Winter/Spring 1991.

After learning of the Germans' intention: Cooper, 357–89.

Chapter 17: Commencement

"I fell in love with that beautiful country": Dorothy Woodruff Hillman, letter to Belle Zars, August 20, 1973.

"one of the most attractive": "Reception Given Former Auburn Girl in Denver," *Auburn Citizen,* October 10, 1917.

she wrote to her sister-in-law, "I think the chief joy in the whole situation": Letter from Eunice Pleasant to Gertrude Pleasant, August 27, 1919.

woven rugs, baskets, clay modeling: Routt County Republican, May 28, 1920.

and Mrs. Harrison pointed out: Letter to Mrs. Underwood, June 10, 1920.

Epilogue

A century after Ferry chose the spot for his homestead, the view was virtually unchanged: There was one difference. A plume of white smoke rose in the distance, from the coal-fired power plant in Hayden. The Hayden Station is across the street from the Carpenter Ranch. Much as J. B. Dawson made way for the Moffat Road train tracks in front of his door, Ferry sold the land to the power plant, then owned by Colorado-Ute Electrical Utility, in September 1962. "He felt it represented progress, in the classic frontier sense," Reed told me. In 1993, Reed was the lead attorney for the Sierra Club when it sued over air pollution violations at the plant in Hayden. In 1995, the court cited the plant for thousands of violations of the Clean Air Act. The EPA joined the action in 1996, and the owners of the plant settled, agreeing to major upgrades. The air in the valley is much cleaner now: emissions of sulfur dioxide from the plant have dropped by 85 percent, particulate matter by 70 percent, and nitrogen oxides by 50 percent.

He hung a white sign at the end of the driveway: The Carpenter Ranch was sold in 1996 to the Nature Conservancy, which runs it as a working ranch and a research and education center.

Cattle arriving in Denver from Routt County: Cows, Cattle, and Commerce: 100 Years of the Railroad in Steamboat Springs, Tread of Pioneers exhibition, June 8, 2007–May 9, 2008.

The homesteaders were paid well during the Great War: Zars, 74.

"Something had to give": Lewis Harrison, "Sketch of the Life," 73–75.

Roosevelt was impressed, writing to Ickes: Hubbard, "Butting Heads," 22–31.

Another was Isadore Bolten: Sylvia Beeler, "County Profile: Isadore Bolton, the West's Outstanding Stockman," first of a series in the *Daily Press,* January 23, 1974.

one of the largest singly owned tracts: Ibid., January 28, 1974; February 5, 1974; February 14, 1985.

"There was nothing for me in Russia": "Isa-

dore Bolten Dies of Heart Failure in Rawlins Home," *Rawlins Daily Times,* February 17, 1951; "Bolton died at 66 after an Horatio Alger Life," first of a series in the *Daily Press,* September 2, 1993.

Other early businesses also went under: Still, in recent years, the city has had a renaissance in some quarters. In 2009 the heavy-metal band Manowar rented space in the Button Works' early brick building on Logan Street. By the time I got there to look around, carpenters and electricians were at work turning the abandoned factory into condos.

Ros's comments in the reunion book: Smith College, *Class of 1909 Reunion Book,* June 1934, Smith College Archives.

Oak Creek's depot, a former headquarters for the Moffat Road: Mike Yurich e-mail, November 9, 2010.

In the summer of 1960, her great-nephew arrived from Auburn: Chuck Underwood Kruger, e-mail, July 17, 2009.

A no-trespassing sign was posted: Eunice Carpenter, "On Thinking It Over: The Passing of the Elkhead School," *Routt County Republican,* October 19, 1938.

"Ros joins me in sending love": In a letter to my mother three years later, in shakier handwriting, Ferry wrote about Dorothy,

"She & I have a bond that never gets weaker — I guess it's the joint venture we both partook of & whose echoes never died out.

"I've undertaken to write an autobiography — not just a series of happenings & events, but of what kind of ride you are in for, when you're willing & anxious to get into the battle & try to make it conform to your ideals even tho they may not be 100% right.

"Good bye, dear, as time rolls on we become more & more family. With love, Ferry."

her "great friend," as she invariably referred to her: Dorothy died five years later, on May 13, 1979. On her ninety-second birthday, her son Douglas thanked her for handing down a good set of genes. She replied, "Douglas, you are welcome. I only wish it could have been something a little more tangible!" (From Douglas Hillman's remarks at Dorothy's memorial service at St. Mark's Episcopal Church in Grand Rapids.)

The windows were covered with yellowing paper that was designed to resemble stained glass: Jan Leslie, e-mail, February 9, 2010.

At a time when only 10 to 15 percent of

students in the country: U.S. Commissioner of Education, Annual Report 1915, Washington, D.C.: 1915, quoted in Zars, 44.

"They really and truly had the interests of the children at heart": Ault interview by Zars.

Several of Ros and Dorothy's former pupils spoke: "In Memory of Rosamond Underwood Carpenter."

Ferry had arranged the service, and presided with his usual aplomb. He lived to the age of ninety-four, working on the ranch until the end. He died in his bed on December 12, 1980. His three children were there, and his son Ed swore that his last words were "Do you want to hear a story?"

drove up from Strawberry Park with their new dance teacher, thirty-year-old Agnes de Mille: Lucile Bogue interviewed Portia and Charlotte about the square dance, which Bogue describes as taking place at a country schoolhouse on a mountain behind Hayden. The school, undoubtedly, was Elkhead. I evoke the scene as Charlotte described it to Bogue, *Dancers,* 82–83. Charlotte later recalled that when she and Portia saw *Rodeo* performed in New York, "we thought we caught overtones of this joyous outburst." Ingrid Matson Wekerle, "Charlotte Perry, in Loving Memory, December 21, 1889–October 28, 1983," 8.

among them Merce Cunningham and John Cage: Silverman, 64.

Bogue writes that "Cage inserted nails and paper in the piano strings," shocking even Portia and Charlotte with his innovations. That year Cunningham, still relatively unknown, headed the dance department. Portia said, " 'The girls liked him, although his defiance against the normal basic rhythms of dance shook them up a good deal. He was a severe teacher.' " Bogue, *Dancers,* 105–6.

In the late 1920s, over three summers, Ferry Carpenter had taken his young nephew Richard Pleasant: By all accounts, Pleasant was a shy, awkward teenager. Carpenter had no use for him on the ranch, but encouraged him to spend time at the camp and helped him get into Princeton. Pleasant and Lucia Chase started American Ballet Theatre in 1940. Ibid., 126–27.

Ferry's son Willis told me that even though Ferry showed little interest in Pleasant around the ranch, Richard worshipped Ferry and left everything in his will to him. "Dad went to NYC," Willis wrote in an e-mail on July 6, 2010.

"Cleaned out Richard's apartment in one weekend, selling everything (including valuable art pieces) to a junk dealer for a pittance, and came home with only a huge load of Navajo blankets (the only items of 'value' in Dad's estimation). Dad took great pride in his efficiency as an executor!"

The graduates of 1920 described: They also wrote, in their foreword: "Manahna is an Indian word meaning 'The Years.' We have chosen it as the name for our book, because this is, not merely the history of our senior year, but the story of our school; of our hardships and our pleasures, our organizations and our classes — in fact, the history of our life during the four pleasant years that we have spent at Elk Head."

BIBLIOGRAPHY

Books

Abbott, Carl, Stephen J. Leonard, and David McComb. *Colorado: A History of the Centennial State.* Rev. ed. Boulder: Colorado Associated University Press, 1982.

Andrews, Thomas G. *Killing for Coal: America's Deadliest Labor War.* Cambridge, MA: Harvard University Press, 2008.

Athearn, Frederic J. *An Isolated Empire: A History of Northwest Colorado.* Colorado State Office, Bureau of Land Management, Denver, CO, 1976.

Ayers, Robert Curtis. *From Tavern to Temple: St. Peter's Church, Auburn, The First Hundred Years.* Scottsdale, AZ: Cloudbank Creations, 2005.

Barney, Libeus. *Letters of the Pike's Peak Gold Rush (or Early Day Letters from Auraria).* San Jose, CA: Talisman Press, 1959.

Black, Robert C., III. *Island in the Rockies:*

The Pioneer Era of Grand County, Colorado. Granby, CO: Country Printer, 1969.

Bogue, Allan G. *Frederick Jackson Turner: Strange Roads Going Down.* Norman, OK: University of Oklahoma Press, 1998.

Bogue, Lucile. *Dancers on Horseback: The Perry-Mansfield Story.* San Francisco, CA: Strawberry Hill Press, 1984.

Bollinger, Edward T. *Rails That Climb: A Narrative History of the Moffat Road.* Golden, CO: Colorado Railroad Museum, 1979.

Boner, Harold A. *The Giant's Ladder: David H. Moffat and His Railroad.* Milwaukee, WI: Kalmbach Publishing Co., 1962.

Borneman, Walter R. *Rival Rails: The Race to Build America's Greatest Transcontinental Railroad.* New York: Random House, 2010.

Bragdon, Henry Wilkinson. *Woodrow Wilson: The Academic Years.* Cambridge, MA: Belknap Press of Harvard University Press, 1967.

Brettell, Richard R. *Historic Denver: The Architects and the Architecture: 1858–1893.* Denver, CO: Historic Denver, 1973.

Brown, Margaret Duncan. *Shepherdess of Elk River Valley.* Denver, CO: Golden Bell Press, 1982.

Burroughs, John Rolfe. *Where the Old West*

Stayed Young. New York: William Morrow, 1962.

Carpenter, Edward F. *America's First Grazier: The Biography of Farrington R. Carpenter.* Fort Collins, CO: Vestige Press, 2004.

Carpenter, Farrington R. *Confessions of a Maverick: An Autobiography.* Denver, CO: State Historical Society of Colorado, 1984.

Chamberlain, Rudolph W. *There Is No Truce: A Life of Thomas Mott Osborne.* Freeport, NY: Books for Libraries Press, 1935.

Cooper, John Milton, Jr. *Woodrow Wilson: A Biography.* New York: Alfred A. Knopf, 2009.

Cornell, Virginia. *Doc Susie: The True Story of a Country Physician in the Colorado Rockies.* New York: Ivy Books, 1991.

Crum, Sally. *People of the Red Earth: American Indians of Colorado.* Santa Fe, NM: Ancient City Press, 1996.

Cunisset-Carnot, Paul. *La vie a la campagne,* P. Roger, 1911.

Damrosch, Leo. *Tocqueville's Discovery of America.* New York: Farrar, Straus and Giroux, 2010.

Dewey, John, and Evelyn Dewey. *Schools of To-morrow.* New York: E. P. Dutton, 1915.

Ellis, David H., and Catherine H. Ellis.

Steamboat Springs: Images of America. Charleston, SC: Arcadia Publishing, 2009.

Florman, Samuel C. *The Existential Pleasures of Engineering.* 2nd ed. New York: St. Martin's Griffin, 1994.

Foote, Mary Hallock. *A Victorian Gentlewoman in the Far West: The Reminiscences of Mary Hallock Foote.* San Marino, CA: Huntington Library, 1972.

Fossett, Frank. *Colorado: Its Gold and Silver Mines, Farms and Stock Ranges, Health and Pleasure Resorts; Tourist's Guide to the Rocky Mountains.* New York: C. G. Crawford, 1880.

Foster, Mike. *Strange Genius: The Life of Ferdinand Vandeveer Hayden.* Niwot, CO: Roberts Rinehart Publishers, 1994.

Gayraud, Didier. *Belles demeures en Riviera, 1835–1930.* Editions Gilletta–Nice Matin, 2005.

Gero, Anthony, ed. "Willowbrook, 1817–1960: A Part of Lost Owasco," in *Owascos Stories: A Glimpse into Owasco, New York's Past 1792–2005.* New York: Jacobs Press, 2005.

Goetzmann, William H. *Exploration and Empire: The Explorer and the Scientist in the Winning of the American West.* Austin: Texas State Historical Association, 2000.

Goodwin, Doris Kearns. *Team of Rivals: The Political Genius of Abraham Lincoln.* New York: Simon & Schuster, 2005.

Grace, Stephen. *It Happened in Denver: From the Pike's Peak Gold Rush to the Great Airport Gamble, Twenty-five Events That Shaped the History of Denver.* Guilford, CT: Twodot, 2007.

Greeley, Horace. *An Overland Journey from New York to San Francisco in the Summer of 1859.* New York: C. M. Saxton, Barker, 1860.

Grinstead, Steve, and Ben Fogelberg, eds. *Western Voices: 125 Years of Colorado Writing.* Colorado Historical Society. Golden, CO: Fulcrum Publishing, 2004.

Griswold, P. R. *Denver and Salt Lake Railroad, 1913–1926.* Denver, CO: Rocky Mountain Railroad Club, 1996.

Guy, William Augustus. *Principles of Forensic Medicine.* New York: Harper & Brothers, 1845.

Hall, Benjamin F. *The Trial of William Freeman for the Murder of John G. Van Nest.* Auburn, NY: Derby, Miller, 1848.

Hayden, F. V. *Annual Report of the United States Geological and Geographic Survey of the Territories, Embracing Colorado and Parts of Adjacent Territories; Being a Report of Progress of the Exploration for the Year 1874.* Washington, D.C.: Government Printing Office, 1876.

Hayden, F. V., *Geological and Geographical Atlas of Colorado and Portions of Adjacent Territory.* 1881.

Heilbrun, Carolyn G. *Writing a Woman's Life.* New York: Ballantine Books, 1988.

Herbst, Jurgen. *Women Pioneers of Public Education: How Culture Came to the Wild West.* New York: Palgrave Macmillan, 2008.

Hill, Alice Polk. *Colorado Pioneers in Picture and Story.* Denver, CO: Brock-Hafner Press, 1915.

Homans, Jennifer. *Apollo's Angels: A History of Ballet.* New York: Random House, 2010.

Horne, Alistair. *Seven Ages of Paris.* New York: Alfred A. Knopf, 2003.

Hubbard, George U. *Which End of a Buffalo Gets Up First?: True Tales of Early Colorado.* Denton, TX: AWOC.COM Publishing, 2005.

Hughes, Robert. *Barcelona.* New York: Vintage Books, 1993.

Hunt, Corinne. *The Brown Palace: Denver's Grande Dame.* Denver, CO: Archetype Press, 2003.

Jones, Peter Lloyd, and Stephanie E. Przbylek. *Around Auburn: Images of America.* Charleston, SC: Arcadia Publishing, 1995.

Kauffman, Polly Welts. *Women Teachers on the Frontier.* New Haven: Yale University Press, 1984.

Knight, Louise W. *Jane Addams: Spirit in Action.* New York: W. W. Norton, 2010.

Kurth, Peter. *Isadora: A Sensational Life.* Boston: Little, Brown, 2001.

The Leading Citizens of Cayuga County, New York. Boston: Biographical Review Publishing Company, 1894.

Leonard, Stephen J., and Thomas J. Noel. *Denver: Mining Camp to Metropolis.* Boulder: University Press of Colorado, 1991.

Leslie, Jan. *Anthracite, Barbee, and Tosh: The History of Routt County and Its Post Offices, 1875–1971.* Hayden, CO: Walnut Street Publishers, 2005.

Leslie, Jan, and the Hayden Heritage Center. *Images of America: Hayden.* Chicago: Arcadia Publishing, 2010.

Leslie, Jan. *Routt County Rural Schools: 1883–1960.* Steamboat Springs: Legacy Books and Resources, 1998.

Limerick, Patricia Nelson. *The Legacy of Conquest: The Unbroken Past of the American West.* New York: W. W. Norton, 1987.

Lockhart, Annabeth Light. *F. M. Light &*

Sons: One Vision, One Store, 100 Years, 1905–2005.

Mallon, Thomas. *Yours Ever: People and Their Letters*. New York: Pantheon Books, 2009.

Martelle, Scott. *Blood Passion: The Ludlow Massacre and Class War in the American West*. New Brunswick, NJ: Rutgers University Press, 2007.

McClure, Grace. *The Bassett Women*. Athens, OH: Ohio University Press/Swallow Press, 1985.

The Military Occupation of the Coal Strike Zone of Colorado by the Colorado National Guard, 1913–1914. Adjutant General's Office, House Committee on Mines and Mining. Denver, CO: Smith-Brooks Printing Company, 1914.

Miller, Irby H. *The Ozark Clan of Elkhead Creek: Memories of Early Life in Northwest Colorado*. Yellow Cat Flats, UT: Yellow Cat Publishing, 1989.

Monroe, Joel H. *Historical Records of a Hundred and Twenty Years: Auburn, New York*. Geneva, NY: Humphrey Printer, 1913.

Orcutt, William Dana. *Wallace Clement Sabine: A Study in Achievement*. Norwood, MA: Plimpton Press, 1933. (About Jane

Kelly's husband, a Harvard physics professor and crusader in the science of acoustics.)

Osborne, Thomas Mott. *Within Prison Walls.* 2nd ed. Rome, NY: Spruce Gulch Press, 1991.

Peavy, Linda, and Ursula Smith. *Pioneer Women: The Lives of Women on the Frontier.* New York: Smithmark Publishers, 1996.

Penney, Sherry H., and James D. Livingston. *A Very Dangerous Woman: Martha Wright and Women's Rights.* Amherst: University of Massachusetts Press, 2004.

Przybylek, Stephanie E. *Around Auburn: Images of America.* Vol. 2. Charleston, SC: Arcadia Publishing, 1998.

Putala, Claire White. *Reading and Writing Ourselves into Being: The Literacy of Certain Nineteenth-Century Young Women.* Greenwich, CT: Information Age Publishing, 2004.

Ranhofer, Charles R. *The Epicurean: A Complete Treatise of Analytical and Practical Studies on the Culinary Art.* New York: R. Ranhofer, 1908.

Rasenberger, Jim. *America 1908: The Dawn of Flight, the Race to the Pole, the Invention of the Model T and the Making of a Modern*

Nation. New York: Scribner, 2007.

Robb, Graham. *Parisians: An Adventure History of Paris.* New York: W. W. Norton, 2010.

Rosell, Lydia J. *Auburn's Fort Hill Cemetery: Images of America.* Charleston, SC: Arcadia Publishing, 2001.

Schivelbusch, Wolfgang. *The Railway Journey: The Industrialization of Time and Space in the 19th Century.* Berkeley: University of California Press, 1977.

Schreiner, Olive. *Woman and Labor.* New York: Frederick A. Stokes, 1911.

Seward, William H. *The Works of William H. Seward.* Vol. 1. Edited by George E. Baker. New York: Redfield, 1853.

Shapiro, Laura. *Perfection Salad: Women and Cooking at the Turn of the Century.* Berkeley: University of California Press, 1986.

Silverman, Kenneth. *Begin Again: A Biography of John Cage.* New York: Alfred A. Knopf, 2010.

Sprague, Marshal. *Colorado: A History.* New York: W. W. Norton, 1984.

_____. *The Great Gates: The Story of the Rocky Mountain Passes.* Lincoln: University of Nebraska Press, 1981.

Spring, Agnes Wright, ed. *A Bloomer Girl on*

Pike's Peak, 1858: Julia Archibald Holmes, First White Woman to Climb Pike's Peak. Denver, CO: Western History Department, Denver Public Library, 1949.

Stanko, Jim. *The Historical Guide to Routt County.* Routt County Board of County Commissioners, 1979.

Stanton, Elizabeth Cady. *Eighty Years and More: Reminiscences 1815–1897.* New York: T. Fisher Unwin, 1898.

Startt, James D. *Woodrow Wilson and the Press: Prelude to the Presidency.* New York: Macmillan, 2004.

Stewart, Elinore Pruitt. *Letters of a Woman Homesteader.* 1914. Reprint, New York: Houghton Mifflin, 1988.

Stone, Wilbur Fisk. *History of Colorado,* vol. II. Chicago: S. J. Clarke Publishing Co., 1918.

Storke, Elliot G. *History of Cayuga County.* Syracuse, NY: D. Mason, 1879.

Stratton, Joanna L. *Pioneer Women: Voices from the Kansas Frontier.* New York: Simon & Schuster, 1981.

Terry, Walter. *The Dance in America.* New York: Harper & Row, 1956.

Thomas, Lately. *Delmonico's: A Century of Splendor.* Boston: Houghton Mifflin, 1967.

Tocqueville, Alexis de, and Gustave de Beaumont. *On the Penitentiary System in the United States and Its Application in France.* Philadelphia: Carey, Lea & Blanchard, 1833.

Turner, Frederick Jackson. *Rereading Frederick Jackson Turner: "The Significance of the Frontier in American History" and Other Essays,* with commentary by John Mack Faragher. New Haven: Yale University Press, 1998.

Webb, Walter Prescott. *The Great Frontier.* Reno: University of Nevada Press, 1964.

Weir, L. W. "Routt County." In *Colorado Historical Encyclopedia.* Denver, CO: Colorado Historical Society, 1960.

West, Elliot. *The Contested Plains: Indians, Goldseekers, and the Rush to Colorado.* Lawrence: University Press of Kansas, 1998.

Wilson, Delphine Dawson. *John Barkley Dawson: Pioneer, Cattleman, Rancher,* 1997.

Wolle, Muriel Sibell. *Stampede to Timberline: The Ghost Towns and Mining Camps of Colorado.* Chicago: Sage Books, 1974.

Wolmar, Christian. *Blood, Iron, and Gold: How the Railroads Transformed the World.* New York: PublicAffairs, 2009.

Young, Richard K. *The Ute Indians of Colorado in the Twentieth Century.* Norman: University of Oklahoma Press, 1997.

Zimmerman, Jonathan. *Small Wonder: The Little Red Schoolhouse in History and Memory.* New Haven: Yale University Press, 2009.

Articles

"A Motion Picture Melodrama in Real Life." *Cleveland Plain Dealer,* March 9, 1917.

"Along Oak Creek." *Steamboat Pilot,* October 17, 1906.

"Assassin Czolgosz Is Executed at Auburn." *New York Times,* October 30, 1901.

"Big Doings at Oak Creek." *Routt County Sentinel,* December 6, 1907.

"Boston Capital in Moffat Road: Eastern Financiers Here to Decide Upon Investment." *Oak Creek Times,* March 7, 1912.

"Denver's Future to Be Bright." *Denver Field & Farm,* May 6, 1911.

"Embryo Townlets: Townsite Boomers at Work on Oak Creek." *Yampa Leader,* October 6, 1906.

"EXTRA! Kidnaper Is Slain." *Denver Express,* October 6, 1916.

"Gould & Harriman Parleying for Peace." *New York Times,* January 30, 1907.

"Hayden's Expedition — Movements of the Party." *Rocky Mountain News Weekly*, May 21, 1873.

"The Hayden Hunters." *Denver Daily Times*, June 7, 1875.

"Held for Ransom, Kills One Captor and Then Escapes." *Chicago Daily Tribune*, October 7, 1916.

"Historic Throop Martin Homestead on Owasco Lake Just a Century Old." *Auburn Citizen*, November 17, 1917.

"History of Auburn Correction Facility: The 'Best Prison in the World.'" New York State Department of Correctional Services, *DOCS Today*, April 1998.

"Ivy Day at Smith." *Boston Transcript*, June 14, 1909.

"Jury Disagreed in Queen Anne Trial." *Steamboat Pilot*, August 16, 1911.

"Kidnaped Heir Slays One Captor." *Los Angeles Morning Tribune*, October 7, 1916.

"Millionaires Join Moffat." *Steamboat Pilot*, January 15, 1908.

"Moffat County Court News." Squib about Ann Bernard's acquittal of cattle rustling. *Routt County Republican*, August 22, 1913.

"Moffat Holdings Are Transferred." *Steamboat Pilot*, June 21, 1911.

"Moffat Short Line." *Steamboat Pilot*, July 30, 1902.

"Opening of Union Annex Marks Climax of Splendid Effort of Auburn Women." *Auburn Citizen,* June 5, 1923.

"The Palace Henry Brown Built." *Rocky Mountain News,* April 22, 1984.

"Perry-Mansfield Camp for Girls Brings Many Summer Visitors to Routt County." *Steamboat Pilot,* May 29, 1930.

"Phippsburg." *Corona Telegraph* 8, no. 2 (March 2007).

"Progress on Oak Creek." *Steamboat Pilot,* February 13, 1907.

" 'Queen Anne' and Tom Yarberry Are Arraigned." *Steamboat Pilot,* August 9, 1911.

"Robert M. Perry to Wed New York Girl." *Oak Creek Times,* May 4, 1917.

"Samuel Perry Dies of Blood Clot on Brain." *Denver Post,* July 22, 1929.

"Scientists on the March." *Rocky Mountain News,* July 15, 1874.

"Splendid Plant at Perry Mine." *Yampa Leader,* July 4, 1908.

"Summary of the Work of the United States Geological Survey." *Rocky Mountain News,* November 29, 1874.

"Surviving the Ute Massacre." *New York Times,* October 29, 1879.

Baker, William J. "Brown's Bluff." *Empire Magazine,* December 28, 1958.

Curtis, Olga. Two-part series: "Farrington R. Carpenter: The Success Story of a 'Failure' " and " 'Yarnin' Champ of Yampa Valley." *Empire Magazine,* April 11 and April 18, 1965.

Dunham, David. "When the Outlaws Gathered for Thanksgiving." *Empire Magazine,* November 20, 1977.

Fleming, Roscoe. "A Word Picture of the New Director of Revenue." *Steamboat Pilot,* July 31, 1941.

Giannini, Bern. "Richard Pleasant, from Humble Beginnings a Yampa Valley Country Boy Conquered the World." *Steamboat Magazine,* Summer/Fall 1990.

Goff, Dick. "Ferry Carpenter, Cattleman-Citizen." *Ideal Beef Memo,* November 5, 1979.

Gower, Calvin W. "The Pike's Peak Gold Rush and the Smoky Hill Route, 1859–1860." *Kansas Historical Quarterly* 25, no. 2 (Summer 1959).

Hubbard, George H. "Butting Heads: Farrington Carpenter's Dramatic Role in the Taylor Grazing Act of 1934." *Colorado Heritage,* May/ June 2010.

Jowitt, Deborah. "Saving Perry-Mansfield." *Dance Magazine,* January 1992.

McCormick, Robert. "Capitol Cowboy." *Collier*'s, March 5, 1938.

McGraw, Pat. "Farrington Carpenter, Hayden Rancher, Storyteller, Dead at 94." *Denver Post,* December 16, 1980.

Paolucci, Christina. "Honoring Juilliard's Ties to America's Oldest Performing Arts Camp." *The Juilliard Journal Online* XIX, no. 7 (April 2004).

Perry, Robert M. "Perry Tells Jury Details of Kidnaping in Mountains." *Rocky Mountain News,* October 9, 1916.

Wilson, Woodrow. "What Is a College For?" *Scribner's Magazine,* November 1909.

Wren, Jean. "The Gypsy Life & Loves of Marjorie Perry." *Steamboat Magazine,* Winter/Spring 1991.

Oral Histories, Speeches, and Interviews

Carpenter, Farrington. "Memories of Isadore Bolton and Yampa Valley Pioneers." Interview by Herbert P. White, July 11, 1970. C MSS OH 52. Western History Collection, Denver Public Library.

_____. Interview by Vi Ward, May 21, 1959. Discussions of J. B. Dawson, David Moffat, Carpenter's homestead claim, and other subjects. OH 42. Colorado Historical Society.

_____. Oral History. Reminiscences of life in Hayden. June 29, 1977. C MSS OH132-6. Western History Collection,

Denver Public Library.

_____. Oral History. Memories of boyhood and youth in New Mexico, homesteading in Colorado, early law practice, sheep wars. January 9, 1964. C MSS OH51. Western History Collection, Denver Public Library.

_____. Interview by E. S. W. Kerr. "Quadrangle Plan," June 18, 1967. Woodrow Wilson Collection, 1837–1986, Box 62, Folder 17, Public Policy Papers, Department of Rare Books and Special Collections, Princeton University Library.

_____. "Historical Interview, Farrington R. Carpenter, Director, Grazing Service, Department of the Interior." Interview by Jerry A. O'Callaghan, Bureau of Land Management, about the Taylor Grazing Act, July 9, 1981.

_____. "The Adventures of a Tenderfoot, Reminiscences of Farrington Carpenter." Speech at the Denver Public Library, January 9, 1964. Cassette & NO.OH51. Western History Collection, Denver Public Library.

_____. Speech at Colorado State University, accepting the Stockman of the Year Award, February 1967. Tread of Pioneers Museum, Steamboat Springs, CO.

Carpenter, Rosamond Underwood. Interview by Eleanor Bliss about her year at Elkhead. Oral History Recordings. Disc 2, L 1457.2. Tread of Pioneers Museum.

Todd, Earnest. Interview by Paul Bonnifield about Bob Perry, for whom Todd worked as a bodyguard after Bob was kidnapped. April 6, 1978.

Unpublished Papers, Memoirs, and Pamphlets

Bonnifield, Paul. "Oak Creek: The Town with Character, Resolve, and Magnanimity," *Town Album: Photo History of Oak Creek, Colorado, 1907–*. Diamond Jubilee Special Booklet, June 1967.

Carpenter, Farrington. Letters to Frederick Jackson Turner: October 13, 1913; October 6, 1922; July 8, 1925. TU Box 31A (20). Henry E. Huntington Library and Art Gallery, San Marino, CA.

_____. Letters to Henry Bragdon: undated, and November 26, 29, 30, December 3, 11, 1967. Woodrow Wilson Collection, 1837–1986, Box 62, Folder 17, Department of Rare Books and Special Collections, Seeley G. Mudd Manuscript Library, Princeton University.

_____. "Woodrow Wilson As I Knew Him." October 4, 1973. Woodrow Wilson Collection, Princeton University.

"Commencement Dinner, ElkHead School." May 22, 1910.

"Commencement Exercises of Elk Head High School." May 22, 1910.

Harrison, Lewis. "Sketch of the Life of Uriah Franklin Harrison and Mary Virginia Jones Harrison of Northwest Colorado." 1977. Hayden Heritage Center, Hayden, CO.

Homestead Application No. 2442, Farrington R. Carpenter, Land Office at Hayden, Routt Co., CO, August 10, 1907; Homestead Entry Final Proof, Department of the Interior, U.S. Land Office, Glenwood Springs, CO, No. 01885, August 14, 1914; Homestead Certificate, Department of the Interior, U.S. Land Office, Glenwood Springs, CO, March 20, 1920.

"In Memory of Rosamond Underwood Carpenter: Story of a Pioneer Teacher in the Rocky Mountains." Memorial booklet for Rosamond's service, the Congregational United Church of Christ, Hayden, CO, February 7, 1974.

Mahaney, Leah Mae Carnine. *Memories: Autobiography, 1896–*.

Manahna. Elkhead School Yearbook, 1920.

"Map of the Elkhead School District," Routt County, CO. Prepared by P. C. Carson, civil engineer.

Neilson, William Allan. "Smith College: The First Seventy Years," Smith College Archives. Unpublished typescript.

"$1000 FOR KIDNAPPER." Poster announcing "reward for information leading to the arrest and conviction of the Greek who was a party to the kidnapping of Robert Perry." October 8, 1916.

Perry, Ruth Brown. "The Abundant Life." 2006.

————. "The Abundant Life, Book II." 2006.

————. "Moffat Coal Co. 1906–1940s." 2009.

"A Recollection of Martha Coffin Wright by her Daughter Eliza Wright Osborne." Osborne Family Papers. Syracuse University Libraries, Manuscripts Department.

Scales, Laura Lord; Margaret Townsend O'Brien; Elsie Baskin Adams; Mary Mensel. "White Lodge." Building Files Collection, Box 113, Folder 15. Smith College Archives.

Seelye, Rev. L. Clark. "The Need of a Collegiate Education for Woman." Paper presented for the American Institute of Instruction at North Adams, July 28, 1874.

Wekerle, Ingrid Matson. "Charlotte L.

Perry, In Loving Memory." December 21, 1889–October 28, 1983. Tread of Pioneers Museum.

Wilson, Woodrow. "Princeton in the Nation's Service," Inaugural Address as president of Princeton University, 1902.

Zars, Margarethe Belle. "A Study of a Western Rural School District: Elkhead 1900–1921." Thesis presented to the faculty of the Graduate School of Education of Harvard University, 1986.

Documentary

Aitken, Leonard. "A Divine Madness." Co-produced by Candice Carpenter, Oak Creek Films. Made possible by the Colorado Council on the Arts and Humanities, the National Endowment for the Arts, and Residents of Steamboat Springs, 1979.

MORE PHOTOS FROM DOROTHY WOODRUFF'S ALBUMS

Minnie Jones and Marie Huguenin

The teachers' room at the Harrison ranch

Charlie and Paroda Fulton with their children

Rosamond's class

Dorothy burning her trash by the henhouse

Isadore Bolten's cobbling class

On sunny days at recess, the boys liked to ski down the hill by the school

485

■ ■ ■ ■

A READING
GROUP GUIDE:
NOTHING DAUNTED

BY DOROTHY WICKENDEN

■ ■ ■ ■

QUESTIONS FOR DISCUSSION

1. In the prologue, Wickenden calls Ros and Dorothy's adventure "an alternative Western." What do you think she means by this? After finishing the book, do you agree? How does their story compare to your idea of the classic Western?

2. Dorothy and Ros, Wickenden writes, were "bothered by the idea of settling into a staid life of marriage and motherhood without having contributed anything to people who could benefit from the few talents and experiences they had to offer" (page 41). How does this statement influence your perspective of Ros and Dorothy? What did they eventually pass along to the students of Elkhead? What did they learn from their students and their families?

3. How are Ros and Dorothy different from each other? How are they similar?

4. Each section and chapter opens with a

photograph — from Dorothy as a twelve-year-old in Auburn to Bob Perry outside his cabin in Oak Hills. How did these pictures shape or enhance your reading of *Nothing Daunted*? How did they add to your understanding of the setting and time period?

5. Similarly, how did the inclusion of letters and notes enhance your reading? Was there one particular or memorable correspondence that stood out to you?

6. William H. Seward was known as a firebrand for representing the black defendant in a notorious murder case and for befriending abolitionist Harriet Tubman. What influence did Seward, Tubman, and other strong personalities in Auburn have on Dorothy and Ros?

7. How would you define Ros and Dorothy's teaching experience in one word? How did people react to their arrival in Elkhead? How did the girls' families react to their decision to leave the comforts of their homes in Auburn?

8. How would you describe Ferry Carpenter? Wickenden writes that he "believed that American democracy was born on the frontier" (page 100). What effect did the lawlessness and opportunities of the West have on Ferry's imagination and aspira-

tions? How did the frontier influence Ros and Dorothy?

9. Discuss the title of the book. Do you think it refers to the heroines' courage? What kind of education did Dorothy and Ros themselves receive in the West?

10. After Ros and Dorothy applied to be teachers, Ferry was told that one of the applicants "was voted the best-looking girl in the junior class of Smith College!" (page 152). What advantages — educational, social, physical — did Ros and Dorothy have over other applicants? What were their potential disadvantages?

11. Ros and Dorothy received nearly identical scores on their Colorado teachers' exams. Ros wrote to her mother: "I think Mrs. Peck must have been perjuring her soul, to give [those scores] to us" (page 246). What did she mean?

12. How did the structure of the narrative, with its flashbacks to the past and flashforwards to the current day, influence how you read *Nothing Daunted*?

13. Do you think anyone else could have written this story about Ros and Dorothy's time in Colorado? How would the story have been different if it was not written from the perspective of a family member?

ENHANCE YOUR BOOK CLUB

1. Wickenden writes that Dorothy "recorded an oral history, speaking with unerring precision about her childhood and about her time in Colorado. Retrieving the transcript of the tape, I was reminded of the breathtaking brevity of America's past" (page 12). Try recording a brief oral history of your own, perhaps about an important trip you took, a big event in your family, or some other significant milestone. Did you remember details from the story that you had forgotten by saying it aloud?

2. Find some old letters, postcards, diaries, or other artifacts of your family's past. After reading and taking notes on their contents, write a short narrative of an event from within — a trip, a wedding, or some other event. Be sure to include whatever details you can to give it real shape.

3. Prepare some recipes that have been passed down in your family. Perhaps, like the miners of Oak Creek, members of your family were immigrants, bringing recipes with them. Alternatively, look through a relative's cookbook for something you've had with them before. Bring the dish to your book club meeting and share the history of the dish.

A CONVERSATION BETWEEN DOROTHY WICKENDEN AND *NEW YORKER* EDITOR DAVID REMNICK AT McNALLY JACKSON BOOKS, NEW YORK CITY, JUNE 23, 2011

David Remnick: Dorothy and I started at the *New Yorker* at about the same time — I as a writer and Dorothy as executive editor. There is no one at the *New Yorker* who has helped transform the magazine more. Her gift for language, her gift for people, and her extraordinary sense of judgment and fairness have benefited everybody and everything that she's touched. So I'm doubly delighted that she decided to write this book.

Dorothy, what were you thinking? Most writers are writers, and most editors are editors. You opened a drawer, both spiritually and physically, and something happened. What made you decide to write when you opened this drawer and found the letters of your grandmother?

Dorothy Wickenden: My mother gave me the letters twenty years ago, and said,

495

"These are your grandmother's letters from Colorado." I knew the stories well because she had told them to me when I was little. I had wanted to read them one day, but I forgot about them because I was bringing up two children and had a busy job. I stuck them in the back of a drawer. Then one day, in the fall of 2008, I was laid up with a broken ankle for two weeks and I was sitting with my left foot propped up on my desk with a bag of ice over it. I thought, "Time to clean out some old files." I found a folder way in the back that said "Dorothy Woodruff Letters 1916–1917." I started reading the first letter, which my grandmother had written right after they arrived in the tiny frontier town of Hayden. It began, "My dearest family, can you believe I'm actually out here in Colorado?" It was very far away from where she had grown up in New York, and I was pulled in immediately. She wrote those letters when she was twenty-nine years old. Even though her voice was totally familiar to me, I was reading them as a middle-aged editor, and I knew from the first page that this was a great piece of writing and an amazing story. I sat down and I read them all. And later I came to David [Remnick] and said, "You know, I have this story about my grandmother. Do you think we can do something about it in the *New Yorker*?"

DR: How well did you know your grandmother? What was the familiarity you had from life rather than from found objects and letters?

DW: She died after I graduated from college. She was ninety-three. She lived in Grand Rapids, Michigan. I lived in Weston, Connecticut. She'd visit us a couple of times a year, and it was always a great event. She was tiny, four foot eleven, a little lady with white hair, but a complete powerhouse. She had an unbelievably dynamic character. Somewhat Victorian, but with a spirit of independence and can-do. She was always a wonderful storyteller, but I didn't realize quite how good she was until I read the letters.

DR: What did you see in the letters? What did they suggest in terms of a story? Finding letters in drawers is the way any number of novelists might begin their narrative.

DW: My grandmother and her friend Rosamond had grown up in a very wealthy industrial city in midstate New York. They were brought up as proper young ladies. They went to Smith College at a time when few girls had any kind of higher education. Afterward, they were expected to return to

Auburn to marry. They didn't want to do that.

DR: Why not?

DW: They were somewhat contemptuous of the young men they met. When I was in college, I went to visit her. "Dorothy, dear," she said, "do you have a beau?" That was the word she used. And I said, "No, I haven't really met anybody interesting yet." And she said, "Well, as you'll discover, most men are terribly stupid." My cousin was in the car, and she hastily added, "Oh, not your father. Not your uncle."

There was a very prestigious seminary in Auburn — the Auburn Theological Seminary — where a lot of the young women found their husbands. My grandmother and Ros just thought they were too effete and really not worth considering. So, they graduated from Smith, went back home, and did not marry. Then they convinced Rosamond's parents to take them to Europe for a year and they went on an extremely lavish trip.

DR: The Grand Tour.

DW: The Grand Tour.

DR: So, they were like Henry James characters.

DW: Totally like Henry James characters, and they did the whole thing, went to about six countries, ended up in Paris. In 1910. At the age of twenty-two or twenty-three. On their own because their parents had gone home. They had the time of their lives. They went to the opera every other night. They went to see Isadora Duncan dance when she was at the beginning of her career. They saw Nijinsky dance in *Scheherazade.* My grandmother wrote a letter home almost every day to someone in her family. She had six siblings. And she wrote different kinds of letters to each one, depending on what his or her interests were.

DR: All of these letters became available to you?

DW: Yes, later on, after I finished the *New Yorker* piece. I hadn't even known about the Europe letters.

DR: In Henry James, the woman of means goes east — Isabel Archer. All the great heroines — they go to Paris, they go to London. Your grandmother and Rosamond go west. How did that happen and why? That's your story — go west, young girl.

DW: That's the story. They got back after this unbelievably wonderful trip to Europe. And not surprisingly, they were bored by the constricting rituals of Auburn society. Ten-course luncheons, charity balls, bridge — for six long years.

DR: They didn't want to go to the big city?

DW: They did go to New York one year, where, once again, their parents expected them to meet somebody eligible. Ros was very beautiful — tall and willowy, with thick brown hair. Men kept falling in love with her.

DR: And she was not interested?

DW: There was one very persistent young man in New York. He was in shipping. But my grandmother made it clear that he was not up to Rosamond's standards. She described him as a "regular Miss Nancy," and said, "Needless to say, Rosamond wasn't interested."

So, they were in Auburn, bored out of their minds. They were feminists, and they were in the heart of suffrage country. The women who initiated the Seneca Falls Convention of 1848 lived in Auburn. Dorothy and Ros went out and stood on soapboxes — literally — and advocated women's rights. As my grandmother put it, "My parents thought this was absurd. We were in this troubled state of mind when an unusual opportunity presented itself."

Rosamond had tea with an acquaintance, a graduate of Wellesley, who'd just gotten back from visiting a friend whose brother ended up being the hero of my book: Ferry Carpenter. Ferry was a young lawyer and homesteader on the Western Slope of Colorado, which was still mostly unsettled. He and his neighbors had just built a beautiful stone schoolhouse in the mountains for the children of homesteaders, and he was looking for two cultivated young teachers from the East. Ferry went to Princeton and Harvard Law School, and Ros immediately perked up. She rushed to the telephone: "Dotty, we must talk about this. We've got to go out and teach school in Colorado." My grandmother, who lived around the corner, ran over. They instantly decided, yes, we're going to do this.

DR: But this is crazy. Colorado in those days is the other side of the moon!

DW: Yes, and they knew very little about the West. And they knew, as my grandmother admitted, absolutely nothing about teaching.

DR: In what spirit did they go there? To do good? For an adventure? In the spirit of Teach For America?

DW: It was the beginning of the Progressive Era. They were brought up with the sense that you should do good for others. And they also thought it sounded like a lark. They applied impulsively and, to their amazement, they got hired. Then, my grand-mother said, "We realized what we had done. We didn't know anything about teaching, and we began to be very frightened."

DR: At what point did they realize that Carpenter had a motive?

DW: This became the comic crux of the book. Ferry was a visionary. He really had an earnest desire to educate the children of these homesteaders. He had high ideals, which he conveyed in the letters he wrote to them. But he didn't tell them he had an ulterior motive. He lived up in Elkhead, which was a settlement of about twenty-five people. There were no single young women, and the cowboys were lonely and asking Ferry for help. So he decided to build this schoolhouse, and then use it as a lure for cultivated, pretty young women from the East. The idea was that a few teachers would come out every year or two, an ongoing source of marriageable women for all the young cowboys.

DR: You had to work with big themes about women, feminist history, expansion westward, otherness in America. Sometimes you read a family story and it's just itself.

DW: Sometimes when you're doing a research project like this, everything just falls into place. People began giving me things. My aunt and my mother were librarians, so they had kept all the photographs and letters. My grandmother had said that her grandfather lived next door to William Seward, Lincoln's secretary of state. When I went to Auburn, and to the Seward Museum, and I asked the executive director whether she remembered correctly. "Oh, yes!" he said. He pointed out the library window at the municipal parking lot. "Harmon Woodruff. He lived right there and his children played with Seward's children."

Auburn was a major stop on the Underground Railroad, and Seward hid slaves in his basement. Some of these big themes of American history had just preceded my grandmother's time. Dorothy and Rosamond learned their history through their relatives, who would tell stories about their neighbors. After the Civil War, Seward had helped Harriet Tubman buy a house down the street. When my grandmother was three or four, she'd see Tubman, an elderly woman, riding her bicycle up and down South Street, stopping to ask for food donations for her home for elderly African-Americans. I got the personal side and the bigger backdrop, and I tried to meld the two.

DR: You go from archive to letter drawer

to museum and, like a reporter, like a historian, you're building a base of information. And then you get to the writer part and it has to have an architecture.

DW: One of the great things about my job is that I work with some of the best writers in the world. I watch how great narratives are written. But I defied one of my own rules. I almost always tell writers who get tangled up in their narratives: Just tell it chronologically. If you try these fancy moves, they can be a disaster. So I wasn't sure about the flashbacks. The trick was how to do them, and do the bigger panorama of American history, without losing sight of my main characters.

DR: Your mother is very much alive. And, I presume she read this book. Was it revelatory to her? Did she know everything?

DW: She knew most of it because one of the things she did as a devoted daughter and librarian was transcribe every letter — which made my job much easier. She knew the stories anyway because her mother had told them to her over and over again when she was growing up. But she didn't know all the history of Auburn. She didn't know the early history of Denver. I spent part of one chapter on the building of the railroad that the heroines took over the Continental

Divide. The railroad was only three years old. It was a four-car train on a winding track that went all the way up and over the Continental Divide. My grandmother said in her letter, "This is a miracle of engineering. I don't know how they ever did it." And I thought, "I wonder how they did do it." I did some reading and research and I found an expert on the building of this railway. It was an incredible story. So I was telling the story of Dorothy and Ros on the train, and I stopped and had a little interlude on the history of the railroad, and then I came back to them when they got to the top of the mountain.

DR: How did it make you feel differently about America? It seems to me that this is a real American story and these two women both embody and bump into a lot of large American themes.

DW: I found the writing really liberating. You and I spend so much of our days thinking about all the horrors of the twenty-first century — the floods, and the tsunamis, global warming, and the wars. My grandmother's story was an escape to a simpler time. It was also a very idealistic time.

I also loved my characters and what they said about America. It was right before World War I. Most of these people had no experience of war. They hadn't experienced the Civil War. So these aristocrats from Auburn and these dirt-poor homesteaders all shared the idea that America was the greatest country in the world. They thought they were going to build something really extraordinary on, of all places, a remote mountaintop. They were going to build a school, which, to the homesteaders, symbolized America and moving beyond who they were and where they had come from.

The ending wasn't particularly happy, but the fourteen-year-old son of the homesteaders they lived with would go out every morning and break the trail for them. They could never have found their way to the schoolhouse on their own. It was three miles. I found his daughter and grandson. His grandson said, "My grandfather, Lewis, talked about your grandmother with such admiration. He always made me feel that education is the most important thing in your life." Lewis went to college on a scholarship funded by Ferry Carpenter and Rosamond's mother; he went to graduate school and became the chief forester for the state of Missouri. It's a great American success story. That year changed his life just as it changed my grandmother's life and Ros's life. Both women said that for all of the wonderful things that had been bestowed upon them, this was by far the best year of their lives.

ABOUT THE AUTHOR

Dorothy Wickenden and Ferry Carpenter, August 1973

Dorothy Wickenden has been the executive editor of the *New Yorker* since 1996. She also writes for the magazine and is the moderator of its weekly podcast *The Political Scene.* She is on the faculty of The Writers' Institute at CUNY's Graduate Center, where she teaches a course on narrative nonfiction. She lives with her husband and her two daughters in Westchester, New York.